WAGON 537 CHRISTIANIA

By the same author
Så sandt vi lever (Novel, 1989)
Chop Suey (Novel, 1994)
Velfærdets offerblod (Essay, 1995)
Mathias Kraft (Novel, 1997)
Venteværelse (Novel, 1999)
Stormpassager (Novel, 2003)
Ytringsfrihed (Essay, 2006)

Per Šmidl

WAGON 537 CHRISTIANIA

A novel

To Bonnie Mandoe without whose
insistence this book would not have been
and Andrew Miller who helped me
make it through the final phase.

A Nine Lives
Edition

SERVING HOUSE BOOKS

WAGON 537 CHRISTIANIA
© 2011 Per Šmidl

ISBN 978-0-9858495-7-3
Set in Palatino by Toptryk Grafisk Ap
Design by Peter Jørgensen, VizArt Profilizing.
Originally published by Fiction Works
Høstvej 4E - 288 Kgs. Lyngby, Denmark

A Nine Lives Edition
Published by Serving House Books
Copenhagen, Denmark, and Florham Park, NJ

www.servinghousebooks.com

First Serving House Books Edition 2013

"People who wish to live in a freer society are not tolerated."
Steen Eiler Rasmussen

"When you're headed for the border,
Lord, you're bound to cross the line."
Kris Kristofferson

"The life of these Indians is nothing but a continuous religious experience. The spirit of wonder, the recognition of life as power, as a mysterious, ubiquitous, concentrated form of nonmaterial energy, of something loose about the world and contained in a more or less condensed degree by every living object—this is the credo of the Pit River Indians."
Jaime de Angulo

PART ONE

Twenty-seven years old and I'd already had enough…

That just about sums it up. And Melanie was right when she told me it was absurd. She said it later the same day I woke to see her haloed by the sunlight that streamed through the open door of my wooden caravan-wagon.

I'd had more than enough. So much more in fact that

when the change came it was in the nick of time. Of course my guardian angel did it to me on purpose. That is the way such things work. I was to be kept in suspense until she knew for sure I would move into that four-wheeled wagon in Freetown Christiania, the one that was raised on blocks at the foot of the old ramparts in Copenhagen and became sort of an appendix to the Wagon Village in the district called the Dandelion.

Guardian angels are great psychologists. They know the importance of getting their clients to hit rock bottom and hit it hard. When I was properly squashed, the wagon was sent to wheel the change into my bloodstream. Squatted *Christiania* a stone's throw from the center of Denmark's capitol city provided the framework. All year round the air resounded with the hammerblows of people rebuilding their own lives out of scavenged materials; the sounds of the motley life going on around our circular fireplace smack in the middle of The Wagon Village; kids' screams in the twilight zone. There was the chaotic community spirit and the feeling of having been set free, that whole personal freedom-and-responsibility thing…

But to give you an idea of how it came about I have to go back a bit further to the time after my divorce when I was busy vegetating in the co-op apartment on the fringes of Østerbro. Peering through the dirty windows, I could see holes in the wide macadamized street below. The entire neighborhood was a redbrick waste. There was not a single tree in sight. Down on the corner from my place, a chocolate factory was filling the air with the sickeningly sweet smell of cocoa that we locals breathed when we woke up in the morning or returned from work or lugged our red and white plastic bags from the supermarket. Round the clock. Our years and decades artificially sweetened. It was enough to drive you nuts. Walking along the broken sidewalks, we avoided each other's eyes and tried to keep our balance between the five-storey masonry that towered all around us.

My little brother, who I had been very attached to in childhood, was worried about me. And it is not something I am making up either. He really and sincerely was. Having finished his engineering studies at the age of twenty-five, he was already so mature and responsible he had to share the wisdom of how to behave. It got on my nerves. He never missed a chance to lecture me, and it was not for the sake of my wellbeing either that I needed to pull myself together. No, it was to finish my studies without "unnecessary delay". A lot of sense that made! It used to bother the shit out of him that I did not seem to care much one way or the other if I ever got a steady job. The way he carried on, you would think it was a personal affront that I was in no hurry to get to where he dreamt of getting to. He just could not stand by and *look* at me waste my life. Or so he said. It really was a disgrace the way I refused to "save" myself.

But while my own brother kept pestering me with his nonsense Martin, my friend from Christiania, took real action. When the time was ripe, my guardian angel used Martin as agent. First Martin got us the two tickets for the Rolling Stones' concert in the Brøndby arena, and then, soon after that, he called my attention to the "gypsy" wagon that after he got busted Bankruptcy Benny had left up for grabs in Christiania.

It was about a quarter of an hour before the concert. I had gone to the men's toilet to piss. But even though I was fit to burst I could not. I don't know what was the matter with me. It had been like that for some time. I could not, for the life of me, piss in public. I was too goddamned nervous or tense or something. Anyway, there I was holding my cock when Martin (with his perfect sense of timing) walked in and stood next to me. For him, pissing was not a problem. Nothing was. He could sing Waltzing Mathilda and piss on the floor of the main train station if that is what he wanted. Problems was something you had if you were a loser. Martin tore his tool out, pissed and slung it up and down in what seemed to me a very nonchalant way. Packing it away again, he turned to me and said:

"Listen Bro, what's going on here? Why don't you get on with it?"

I shook my head and looked sadly at my cock. "It can't," I said. "It makes me nervous when there are other people around. And then, I can't."

Martin surveyed my—I'm sure—rather sorry figure. "But why don't you just come on then. The concert's about to start."

"Don't you think I know that," I said. "But I have to piss like hell. You go on ahead. I have my ticket. I'll find you."

And, sure enough. As soon as Martin was out the door I was pissing like an elephant. A minute later, I found him in his seat. It was ten minutes into Billy Preston's warm up set. Martin leaned over to me:

"Do you want to know a secret? I wouldn't be able to piss either, if I lived in that godforsaken apartment of yours. Man, I don't think I would even be able to breathe. It's got to be like living in your own coffin. There's central heating. Great! But there's no *air*. It's suicide made comfortable that's what it is. Death on the installment plan with amenities. How often do I have to tell you to come live with us on the reservation."

Martin was right. For as long as I had known him, he had tried to get me out of the clutches of conformity and out to Christiania on the other side of Copenhagen. In Christiania people had turned their back on consumer capitalism, manipulating medias and the patronizing Danish state bureaucracy. In the former military garrison that he nick-named "the reservation", you could do things that were unthinkable to the rest of the Danish population. I knew all the arguments. I had heard them all before. I totally agreed too, but I had never paid the kind of attention that I did now.

"HOW?" I shouted.

"How, how! It's just something you decide to do. Where there's a will, there's a way. We'll figure it out." Martin had shouted these words right into the back of a guy's head. Now, the guy turned around and looked at Martin sort of offended like. Of course Martin couldn't care less. He just glared at the fellow, grinned and kept shouting: "Where there's a will, there's a way. Verstehen *Sie*."

When he had finished shouting Martin shut up and in-stead concentrated on a hash pipe, which was being offered him by the guy in the next seat.

God only knows what got into me. I have never been much of a hash smoker, but when that pipe was handed to me, I took two huge tokes that sent me straight back to the toilets. I got sick so quickly I almost did not make it in time—to the *women's* toilet—before I started puking. Boy did I puke. I could not have puked more to save my life. Out came everything I had eaten during the last few weeks. Or so it seemed. Heaps of lumpy puke filled the bottom of the sink before my bleary eyes. Drenched in sweat, puke and drool on my chin, I heard Billy Preston end his set. The sound was faint and distant as if it had to pass through oceans of water to reach me. As if I were drowning. Christ almighty, I thought, now there's intermission.

The thought inflated my insides. Something like a bub-ble rose to my lips, and I let out a puffing sound like the fat and slow bubbles that rise to the surface of thick hot por-ridge.

"Yuck! Check out that guy barfing over there! God is *he* re-pulsive!"

That is the music I heard when the girls came through the door: "Isn't there anybody we can call to get him out of here!"

Dumb clucks. If they'd had any brains, they would appreciate that I was puking in the sink and not in the foyer where they'd slip in it and get my stinking puke all over them. How would they like that? What did they want me to do? I was wrung out, emptied, nauseated to my very soul.

But...the deeper you fall, the higher you may eventually soar.

Little by little, the girls disappeared. Little by little, I got better. Finally, I felt strong enough to risk returning to the concert hall. And when The Stones let it all out in "Satisfaction", for my part, I let out all my misery, shouting along: "I can't get no sa-tis-fac-tion, but I try, and I try, and I try-y-y-y!"

It wasn't until afterwards that I came back down. And then, what a nose dive *that* was! Waking the next day, I found myself alone in my centrally heated coffin in Østerbro with my x-wife's belongings stacked in a corner of the living room. Everything was just as I had left it. And me! Well, I was stuck right back with my longing for her, my nervous tension, existential doubt and the uncertainty about what to do with my life. At first, it gnawed like hunger at my insides. Then, it seemed to come from outside like a blade cutting into my flesh: Just twenty-seven fucking years old and already I'd had enough. Again, I felt like puking. But immobilized as I was and suffering like an idiot, I could not even do that anymore. At the concert, I had at least been able to empty my stinking guts. Shit.

Yet, in my soul, I was puking like hell, silently, antiseptically and without the slightest taste in my mouth. I don't know that I had ever felt this rotten before. I was so god-damn lost with no idea what was going to happen to me. If I wanted anything at all, it was for someone some friendly giant say to come in, hold his nose, pick me up and throw me out like some festering fish into the courtyard and there leave me with my feet sticking out of a trashbin as a warning to other people. I didn't give damn where, how and why just as long as it was done.

This is how it was with me before I moved into the wagon. I felt rotten through and through. Forgotten were the breathless thoughts of freedom I had hatched and cherished not so very long ago, every single decision and resolution. Paralyzed by grief, I kept on dragging my slimy trail across the parquet floors of that godforsaken apartment in godforsaken Østerbro.

Truth is: I would have made a magnificent lost cause, except for the fact that I was no cause at all. I mean I could not piss in public, nor could I say a word if there was anything even remotely resembling an audience around. And if I tried to do it anyway, I would stammer and perspire like hell. In my armpits, two wet splotches would appear to announce my impotence.

Being tongue-tied in public, however, is not nearly as painful as not being able to piss. The bladder that you have for words doesn't fill up the same way as the bladder you have for piss. Keeping one's mouth shut does not make one feel the call of nature. You may sweat a bit, but that's all. You don't feel like a public disgrace. As a matter of fact, if you're smart, you can turn it to your advantage. Sitting there, all clammed up, all you have to do is put on a slightly distant and supercilious expression. Peoples' low self-esteem will come to your assistance. It will whisper in their inner ears that the reason you're not saying anything is because you know *better* than them. The reason you're silent, is because you don't want to waste your words on such retards. It won't cross anybody's mind it's because you are too god-damn tense and miserable to speak. It's really pretty sad, if you ask me. I mean that people don't have more confidence in themselves.

I wouldn't talk so much about this if it were not for the fact that most people suffer more or less unconsciously from a disturbing sense of inferiority. Why else would they take things so goddamn seriously? If they liked themselves just a wee bit more they wouldn't move a finger except to bring joy. And they wouldn't give a shit about power, money, fame and conquest either. Behind the defensive front people put up, this lack of self-trust is what determines how they act and think and dream. What goals they set for themselves. If you want to exploit this, all you have to do is behave like you are Success personified. Be a good actor, and it doesn't matter how much of an idiot you are. People don't trust their own intuitions enough to doubt you. Prod their insecurity a bit, and they'll be puddy in your hands. They'll kiss your ass and throw their money at you. Before you know it, they may even be hanging medals on you.

This sort of thing is really very psychological and delicate. I mean all that about the inferiority complex that expresses itself as conceit and thirst for power, say. If you ask me, it just goes to show how sick things are: The complex people lug around with them and try so hard to conceal often is what motivates their worldly activity. And if to their anxiety, there happens to be added a certain amount of ambition, chances are the complex is successfully compensated for by accomplishment. The greater the complex, the greater the accomplishments it can lead to. Compensation will take place no matter what, which is why a gigantic inferiority complex can make a man president of a republic, but not another Beethoven. For a man to compose music

12

like Beethoven's, he needs to love life and creation. Compensating for the painful hollow inside is not the same as composing from a feeling of fullness, wonder and worship.

So what did it matter that I couldn't piss in public urinals? As if anyone would ever notice. Most people don't notice anything anyway unless it is shoved right before their noses, or if it so happens that they're preoccupied with that thing at the moment in question. If they discover anything or become aware of anything beyond their own immediate needs, it's only because they have been on the lookout for precisely that thing in advance, or because it was what they expected to see or have been paid to keep an eye out for. The objective is to neutralize the curiosity, so that it doesn't disturb them in their sleep. The means for doing this are the monstrous blinds they grow to shield their eyes and protect them from hostile elements. Just think if one day those things became visible to people at large? What a disappointment it would be! Instead of tearing the damn things off the wearers would probably have them pierced so that they could decorate them with rings and amulets and such things. But I'm forgetting what I wanted to say...

It was two years since I had started my so-called studies at The University of Copenhagen. What motivated these studies was not so much any genuine pursuit of knowledge, as it was the impression I had that getting an education, aside from being what society demanded of me, was also indispensable for experiencing happiness in this life. Education equaled happiness and *not* getting any education equaled unhappiness and failure. But, true or false, if something is accepted by almost everybody around you, it requires a self-confidence that borders on madness to reject it. So, no wonder I was under the influence of this propaganda. On a daily basis, I did my best to convince myself that getting a university degree was indeed traveling the road to my destiny. Finding the subjects meaningless and feeling bored I mesmerized myself into believing they were, in fact, very interesting. The interest I was showing in my studies is comparable I guess to the interest that prison inmates take in the license plates they make hour after hour, year after year.

Still, not even collective psychosis could hide the truth from me. Not forever anyway. All the while I sat at my table reading fat tomes about tribal kings in the West Africa of the eighteen hundreds telling myself that education was indispensable to the experience of happiness and to the earning of a living, I had a feeling that it was all a hoax: a hoax designed to conceal the real life I felt inside me and which I needed badly to understand and come to grips with then and there, in a Northwestern Europe that was nearing the end of the twentieth century.

Yet I went on suppressing this feeling, suspecting it to be false simply because it was mine…

When I think of how I swallowed the lies that were served me, the whole thing seems perverse. Like hundreds of thousands of other young people, I had fallen victim to a socially transmitted virus: something intended to make people refuse to take themselves seriously; something designed to make them reject all they truly feel and experience with their minds, bodies and souls. At a tremendous price, I, too, had acquiered the *a*dvanced *d*efense *s*yndrome ADS. This illness enables individuals to shoot down any original thought that shoots across the firmament of their minds when they are alone at night, and the bedside lamp has been turned off. Instead of trusting my own thoughts like true friends, I had been programmed to turn them into enemies that tempt me to see things the way they really were. I do not know how to put this exactly. It was as if I had come close to a fenced-in area, where signs informed the

14

intruder to turn back. One read: "STOP!" Another: "PRO-HIBITED AREA AHEAD!" And finally a bit further along the dirt road: "TRESPASSERS WILL BE SHOT WITHOUT WARNING!"

And me, what did I do? I did as I was told. I kept backing up and leaving. I didn't dare go on for fear I might get to know too much. The price of persisting seemed too great—too great, too mad and too lonely. I was unable to trust my gut feelings enough and turn a deaf ear to the din. Like almost all the people around me, I preferred to go on living in stress and running the treadmill of a false education. Rather than being my own lawgiver, I preferred to go on taking directions from others; rather than being still and thinking about the facts of life, I preferred to rush from one thing to the next, get all sorts of important tasks done, endlessly advancing to the next and the next and the next; rather than getting off the merry-go-round of madness, I preferred trading in today for a much hyped tomorrow which never comes. When the ice you're skating on is thin, safety lies in your speed. So I kept skating as fast as I could in an attempt not to disappoint the expectations of others.

Had it not been for Martin, I would probably have gone on skating and being nauseated and taking exams and getting jobs and pursuing goals other than my own; most likely, I would still be crucifying myself on the cross of falsehood. Like they had done to so many others, the frightening nature of the inexplicable and unbending forces would have hitched me to the spinning wheel of a workaday world.

It went on right up until I puked my insides out and came to a full stop in that apartment on outer Østerbro.

It was ten or eleven days after the Stones concert that Martin called me on the phone to tell me about a "gypsy" wagon in Christiania that was simply "dying" for me to move into it.

Once the decision had been made, I didn't think twice. Like a somnambulist, I purchased the wagon, moved it to the Dandelion, fixed it up and got rid of the apartment. My family was horrified. "You must be out of your mind." My father held his head between his hands and looked at me over the rim of his glasses. Then, he started shaking his head too like I'd just let him in on a plan to assassinate the prime minister: "Don't you know that those people out there are mentally ill," he groaned.

It may sound strange, but it was some time before I registered what I had done, and what had happened. It was not until later that the reality of the situation caught up with me.

I had lived in my wagon a week or two when one afternoon I woke from my dazed state and found myself standing beside my bicycle between some tall nettles out in an abandoned military garrison populated with squatters. I pinched my leg to make sure I was not dreaming. No. It seemed real enough. To make double sure, I unbuttoned my fly and emptied my bladder down to the last drop. And *that* was real too. There I was pissing with people walking by behind me. Without my noticing it, I'd gotten better.

Remembering, but still a bit dazed, I climbed the rampart and looked around me. In the moat below, I saw ducks, swans and coots swimming on the waters' shiny surface, which reflected the clouds in the sky. All that remained of the city I had left behind was a distant hum of traffic. I brushed the road dust off my pant legs and straightened up again. The wind that used to buzz in my head was now whispering high in the treetops instead. Inside me, everything seemed empty and quiet.

Could it be true? Had I really succeeded in ridding myself of my anxieties? In one giant leap! My heart, which of late had felt more like a lump in my throat, was beating softly in its rib cage. Yes, there was no denying it: I had come to. That was it. After participating in a false competition, I had come back to a place I had known as a child. The contrast to my former existence was manifest. Back then, before the leap, when, for example, I left my flat at—let us say—twenty minutes to ten on a Wednesday morning, because I had to be at a lecture at the University at a quarter past, well, then I could be damned sure that precisely ten minutes past ten, I would park my bicycle and, like a robot, glance at my wristwatch, get my bag of books off the rack and start lugging it towards the main entrance. I never met anybody I knew on the way, and if by some odd coincidence, I happened to meet someone, I didn't stop. And that would have been all right too—just greeting the odd someone as I rode by, I mean, without getting off and exchanging handshakes and words, it would have been fine as I say, if only I had been on my own way, if I'd had a sense of who and what I was and where I was going in this world. But that was exactly what I didn't have. For that matter I didn't have it in the wagon either. Or at least not in the beginning! Only there, it had become possible to find out about such things. The situation had become unlocked, and things were open in all directions. No longer was everything a given beforehand. I felt there was hope for me again.

It's one of those Wednesday mornings that life is full of. It's twenty minutes to ten. I am standing in the middle of my wagon. Perhaps it's only moments ago that I swung my legs out of the bed, and perhaps I haven't even put on clothes yet. I've dropped out of the university, and nothing is planned for the day, with the exception maybe of getting some breakfast, and also—if there is time—getting a shower in the new communal bathhouse. Aside from this very tentative program, the day is empty, just as empty as on that first Wednesday when the Lord still had his feet up after having created the world and was longing for his son to come, take possession of his creation and breathe some life into it.

But here I go again losing myself in the primal mists. For in reality, there I still am and still only in my birthday suit. Now what? Where to? And… what on Earth is that! What's going on? What's that Gasolin tune doing in my head? And do I really *have to* yell it out loud for all to hear:

> "There are many many dreams
> that have gone by the wayside.
> But it's not so very bad,
> I can still laugh and I'm laughing
> as I'm sittin' here alone
> in my little shed."

Yeah! That's all very well indeed old chap. You can still laugh. Good for you. But perhaps, now, it would be better to get a move on. Find your cleanest dirty shirt and go scrounge up some food.

There was no refrigerator in my wagon. If I wanted food, I had to venture out into the world to get it. That's all honky dory with me, I think to myself, and quite as it should be. But now, how does that Gasolin song begin?

> "The times we're living in are cold,
> everybody's freezing
> but we're not so very badly off
> in this here re-ser-va-tion."

On your marks, ready…GO!

From my wagon it's about a seven-minute walk to the grocery store in Langgade Street. I will get my two usual rolls, a bit of cheese and the quarter liter milk I need for my coffee, and maybe a bit of butter to go with the bread. My long hair a tangled mess after the night, flip-flops on my feet, hands in my pockets and the large checkered lumberjack shirt flapping in the wind, I'm on my way driven by hunger and restlessness. My stomach is grumbling. Rumbling and grumbling. It's that same old rumble in the jungle sensation telling me there's no getting to the damn store fast enough. But alas! To get there, I have to pass The Omelet, which is the name given to the oval lawn in front of the Dandelion's yellow "City Hall" building. The Omelet is encircled all around by great old cobblestones and flanked by low and very quaint pastel colored houses with red tiled roofs. And of course, wouldn't you know it, as soon as I get there, I run into Martin. The way he stands there, it's just like he has been waiting for me. Sitting with legs wide apart on his Petersen bicycle, he is shouting to some kids that are running around.

The moment I see him and he sees me, there's a great grumble in my rumble:

"Howdy-dah, di-dah!" Martin is looking at me with his typical big grin. First comes a sort of homegrown greeting and then those surgically penetrating eyes he always skewers me with. Say, have I by any chance heard of the "immaculate conception" that has "miraculously" occurred in Christiania last night? I say I have not, and I want to add something about a certain rumble in my grumble. But before I manage to get a word in, Martin has launched into the dramatic tale of a white Christiania girl, who a couple of nights ago, has given birth to…a pitch black boy. "Pitch black!" Martin repeats the words emphatically and sinks his eyes a notch deeper into mine. However, he goes on, there is a hitch.

"Sure. Of course, there is. There always is. A hitch in the

pitcher."

Martin pretends not to hear. There is only one hitch, he says again: The girl's boyfriend of the last four years is as white as she is. Hmm! Well, this cat sure was in for the surprise of his life, when the midwife produced a black baby from his girlfriend. What the hell was THAT! A case of black magic, or what?

According to Martin the poor fellow was so shocked, it took him a long time to collect himself enough to think the situation through logically. But eventually, he had hit on the question of how it had happened. And this is the interesting part. For although christianites are a notoriously superstitious bunch, there was—after all—a limit. It was hard *even for them*, Martin says, to believe that the white boyfriend was the father—and that there were recorded cases of such happenings in the genealogical history of the Danes in general.

Anyway, it soon surfaced that the mother had met a black guy at the carnival last year. Apparently, she had been very drunk. But, no! When confronted with this fact, she just kept on denying everything. She had met him sure, but she had not done *that* with him! No Way!

Throughout the entire pregnancy she had kept a tight lip about it. And at the same time, of course, her anxiety about what might appear at the end of the tunnel had nearly driven her out of her mind. Would the child be white or black?

My belly is growling and the suspense of the story is making my head spin. My feet are restless.

It could have gone either way, Martin says. The last twenty-four hours before conception had been pretty hectic. Right from the word 'go' there had been full on activity and the sperm cells—white as well as black—had shot out at top speed, each of them just dying to reach the egg first. This egg, which was fit to burst from sheer readiness, was dangling in the ovary, temptingly, tauntingly, cheering the combatants on from its elevated position. It had been a very exciting race. For even though the white bozoes had a head start of about six to eight hours on the black bozoes, in the end, the white bozoes were overtaken at the finishing line.

But what did *we* know after all? Martin adds and puts on a sort of mystified expression. People talked so much, and one should not believe everything they said.

Not until about twenty long minutes later am I able to continue on my way towards breakfast. Forty meters. That's as far as I get. Right outside the gate, on the broad patch of broken asphalt in front of the district of the Dandelion, at the confluence of Langgade Street and Dyssebrogade Street, I run into Roland the Sideburn, who is mobilizing people to help his little sister put a new floor in her room up in the "Chariot of the Sun" building. When I happen along, he has already stopped two others. He's telling everybody that they will get all the breakfast they can eat if they join in. The more we are the merrier, he says, and the sooner we will be done with it. It somehow appeals to me. The floor bit, I mean. We humans need floors to stand on. Solid ones. So why not let go and float along, play it by ear and trust the stream to carry me wherever it is I am destined to go. Suppose it's the finger of fate that in the person of Roland the Sideburn has been dispatched on this Wednesday to intercept me? Roland, by the way, happens to be a nice guy who never hesitates to pitch in when someone needs a helping hand. As far as the little sister with the long blond hair is concerned, I would not mind getting to know her better. Not that she's super beautiful or anything like that, but when she looks at you, her eyes are strong with that streak of vulnerability, which I find so irresistible in women. Who can tell what such a floor-job might lead to? I mean, once a girl has her floor laid down, she'll probably be in need of

21

some plumbing too. She or one of her girlfriends.

I go along. An hour later I have had breakfast and find myself on my way to a houseboat in the South Harbor for some keys. The guy isn't in but is expected back in an hour or two. To kill time, I hang out with some friendly hippies sitting around a wooden rowboat with flowers planted in it. I'm not back with the keys until four o'clock, and at five, the floorgang calls it a day and sets off for the Moonfisher Bar to see what is brewing. A band is setting up in the corner. Between ten and eleven that evening, I find myself slightly drunk and talking up a brunette with a small golden cross in her necklace. She says she is living in The Pig Sty, and…

To make a long story short, I leave home starved and with a rumble in my gizzard. It is a perfectly ordinary Wednesday morning, and I don't get back to my wagon until two nights and two days later, completely worn out, grimy, stinking of sweat and no less starved than when I set out. The only difference, aside from the grime, is that now the store is closed, and I will have to go on a foraging expedition to the communal wagon in search of something to eat. With a bit of luck, I might find a crust of bread with hair on it behind the stove. And it will be better than nothing. A crust of bread is all I'm asking for. I'm not picky anymore. At that hour and in the condition I am in, almost anything will do.

But now reader, it's time to reveal something to you: the good old Earth has circled the sun thirty times since the day I shook the dust from my pants in Christiania and looked around me. The man telling the story is no longer the impulsive and impatient young desperado that he was when he lived it. Today, the pace is somewhat slower, and I need to stop, think things over and try to understand. To satisfy this need will take about ten pages. You are welcome to skip these if that sort of thing bores you, or if you just can't wait to hear what happened to the young man. Or... you can hang in there. It is up to you.

First of all, this is what was not supposed to happen: I was not supposed to be sitting here writing again. The reason I settled on this island was because I wanted to break this old habit that has kept me busy for so many years. I figured that if I removed myself and turned my back on European civilization, if I surrounded myself with a section of humanity that doesn't give a fuck about belles-lettres and "literature" —well, then I would be freed of it all.

Still, there's also something else involved, namely the hunch that I have already said if not all of what I have to say, then at least most of it. If ever I took up the pen again, there would only be leftovers to record. This, then, is what has been left over. So be it. If wringing my guts to get at the last drops of juice is what I must do, well, then that's what I will do. Come to think of it, this move away from a civilization in the throes of senseless consumerism and prostration before the altar of money and technology is in continuation of the move I have told you about in the previous pages. You might say that in this way, I have stayed true to the loves and antipathies of my youth, proving them to be more than passing whims. It seems I am to remain out of step with my world and times, always busy removing the same splinter from my soul. Things may have changed, but not a whole lot is new under the sun. Like me! I'm still standing at the same old crossroads, feeling the same old urge to tell myself a bit more of the story. The man I was yesterday is challenging the man I am today to a duel. And I have accepted. After all, he's the guy I descend from. What we are dealing with here, then, is more than leftovers. It's showdown on main-street.

It was after the break with Amiel's mother (a break that all but knocked me cold) that I arrived on this far away island. Here, I gradually found new strength and courage. Disappointed as I was, I was also happy to have escaped foolish and deluded Europe and to breathe again in a sunny spot on the globe. Soon, I felt open, mellow and insouciant again. I was congratulating myself daily on my good fortune. Now, I'm no longer so sure. It's not that anything bad has happened, but, of late, I have sometimes felt an inexplicable gloom. Inexplicable I say, and unpardonable too, since I have the responsibility for five-year-old Amiel, whose mother was an English actress in Prague that—when the kid was two-and-a-half—left for London with the theatre ensemble and disappeared. Later, there was a sloppy letter written on paper torn from a note pad. In it, she explained how she had been unable to stand the sight of me. She did not say much, but even so, she didn't forget to mention that, in her eyes, I was a fool for all my pride, and a failure. How she had been able to endure life with me for so long was beyond her. She had not known to what extent she was fed up with me until she met the love of her life. When something like that happened to someone, she went on in her large longhand scrawl, when someone met the love of his or her life etc. etc. Needless to say she would come for Amiel. Of course, she would. Only it could not be "right now," since "right now," she was not even sure where exactly she would be living in London. Perhaps in two or three months. In any case, the life she was leading at the moment was not for kids. She hoped that I could understand "at least that much"…

I sure could.

Responsibility and treason was all that was left. Most of it is gone, but I remember how one early afternoon back in

Prague I was sitting on the bed with my head in my hands watching the boy at play. He was placing wooden blocks one on top of another making towers. I was feeling precisely as abandoned as I was. Nothing happened, and there was absolutely nothing remarkable about the moment. Still, for some reason, it's this moment and not another that has remained with me. Later that day—as we were walking on the wide and newly restored sidewalk along Stefanikova Street in the direction of Plzenska and Novy Angel shoppingmall—I had what amounted to a vision. My eyes watered, my heart pounded and my breathing was laboured. I didn't dare look at the boy. It had all become too much. Here we were the two of us, both abandoned. His tiny hand so warm in mine told me that he knew I would always be there for him. Yes, and that we would make it. My nostrils quivered, and next thing I knew, tears were streaming down my cheeks. It was one of those moments meant to outlast us. My little boy and I connecting to each other and to all of creation!

I fought and managed to stop the tears. With my free hand, I was pushing his stroller on its wobbly wheels. Rolling over the small cobbles, it gave off a rattling sound. Christ almighty! The guy wasn't more than two and a half. If all went well, he would be ready to stand on his own feet in fifteen years or so. Fifteen years! It made me dizzy just thinking about it. On the other hand, it wasn't the first time I was faced with a task that made me doubt my own strength. And more importantly: it was already too late. Something never happened and now that something was never to be. There was a reality I had to face, without regret, grief, despair and bitterness. Without hope even, but with trust. Trust in providence.

In the beginning, here on this island—as long as everything was still new, yes, and as long as I was busy making a home and settling in—it was still easy to persevere. It's only lately that it has become difficult. I have to tell myself every day why I'm here, what it is I have done and why. And what the deeper meaning of waiting is. I mobilize my forces. I get up in the morning as I am supposed to. I do my exercises on the floor, see to the needs of the boy and am there for him twenty-four hours a day. For three years now, I have paid my dues, kicked a habit or two and generally done the things I judged were right. It may be that my motivation has changed, but my desire to live is the same.

And this I must say: I'm being richly compensated. Not a day passes without me getting bunches of big old happy smiles. Not just from Amiel but from all around. There's no need to hide things from the boy. He knows full well that we are shipwrecked and on our own. Sometimes he looks at me like a very wise old man who has lived, taken stock of the content of the human soul, and assessed the possibilities of life, and yet most of the time, he is the happy-go-lucky kid, who cheers his Papa's heart by being healthy and strong and in great spirits. By simply being the little daredevil with the shiteating grin that he is. He will cut himself, or he will sprain an ankle; he will get a splinter under his thumbnail, insects in his eyes, and fish bones stuck in his throat. With him, it's disasters without end. But see if he's fazed by it. No. He bounces right back. A couple of months, ago he fell off a fence and broke his right arm. Now, he hardly remembers.

The boy is exactly as he should be, no more and no less. Had I been God himself, I would not have been able to do a better job. Which is all the more reason I don't understand my own sadness of late. Has it to do with the great decisions lying ahead? Or is it because of what is happening to our world, and what it will mean to both the boy's life and mine? However much I would like to do so, I can't protect him from the madness and the destruction. If I stay here, he'll become like the natives and live the life that is theirs, yet there will always be something missing. And this nebulous "something" will remain hidden from him. He will only have little contact with schools, the newest technology and the whole scheme that has grown out of European rationalism, and which his father with all his resistance and disgust is a product of.

On the one hand, I think that life on the island will be good, or good enough. Still, I can't help doubting it. It's one thing that *I'm* disgusted with European born civilization, and quite another thing how it will affect the boy if I keep him isolated from it all. Who says he's not the primitive who has been prophesied, who, precisely because he has grown up under bluer skies, will rescue the remaining bits of our race in his ark? Who says his wild and unschooled background will not enable him to bring the raging madness to a halt and reverse it?

But enough of this too! What is needed is action—the action that brings change, as we used to say in the old days in Christiania. I still hail this credo, even if in time, I have come to include in it the action of thought. If you're unable in your daily practice to live alternatively to whatever it is you don't approve of, then you should keep your mouth shut. It's not what you have but what you *are* that counts. Now is the time of my life, and if I must choose any specific moment over another, then let it be this one. Let the sky open and rain flood the Earth, let glaciers melt in high places and tsunamis wash my wagon from memory—still I will grow gills and put on fins. By hook or by crook, I will survive. The future will have to fend for itself.

When I look up from this miserable skyblue garden table and the paper held in place by rocks on it, when I look toward the palm trees bending before the strong wind out by the coastal road perhaps a hundred meters away, yes, and when I let my thoughts circumnavigate the globe in one huge bend in the direction of the wagon I had in Christiania, I realize the importance of two very different accounts from the world of letters, accounts that, each in their own way, brought the same message home to me:

The first is the section from Petronius' "Satyricon" known as "Dinner with Trimalchio". Trimalchio is this unbelievably rich Roman fart in love with extravagance. For him, happiness is the sum total of all the sensual pleasures that can, in any way, be heaped on a mortal human being. In other words, Trimalchio and I had absolutely nothing in common except one thing: in the wagon, I, too, had all that *my* heart could possible yearn for, and all of it was within reach of my two hands and feet. With me, it was a bit like with Trimalchio when, in the middle of the orgy, he shouted: "It's Mother Earth in the middle, round like an egg, with all good things inside her like a honeycomb!"

On good days (and of those there were a great many), I, too, felt like in a celestial honeycomb. I was in fat city, and what is more: I knew it. Right from the start, I had wisely followed Trimalchio's instruction to always "drink cold and piss warm". For me, who had long had trouble taking leaks publicly, these words, spoken by this fat old geezer, had become the mantra from which I lived.

"Here I am pissing warm and drinking cold," I would mumble to myself, when I—deep in snow and on legs wide apart—stood behind my house pissing holes in the white and starry and astoundingly clear February night. "Ahh, that was good!" I would go on thinking as I took in the cloud of silent steam emanating from my mouth. Now, let's see if old Trimalchio's friends are still there," the voice would say in my head, while I was buttoning my fly and bending my head back as far as it would go. "Let's see if they're all up there and blinking their eyes to me: Aldebaran, Rigel, Sirius, Betelgeuze, Castor, Pollux and…Orion." And what do you know! Just as I am thinking the name of Orion, I look down and see the black holes I have pissed in the white snow. There are three of them in a slanting row. And right there in the darkness that reigns in Christiania at night, it seems to me that three black eyes are staring up at me from inside the Earth. "The notches in Orion's belt," I conclude a little later, when I'm banging the snow off my boots against the wooden doorstep leading up to the wagon.

And…miracle of miracles! The mantras and incantations had had an effect on my bladder. As I have already hinted, I had hardly moved to Christiania, when I was cured of my ailments. No longer was I speechless in public. And neither was I paralyzed in my private parts. The evil spell was broken, and the world had shriveled up into a ball the size of a green pea, something I had to be careful not to step on when I issued from the door of my house. Christiania had become my entire horizon: the honeycomb where I had all I needed and desired for my sustenance. At the same time, the world I had left behind had become distant, hostile and even foreign. My circles had shrunk to a point identical with the ring of granite rocks that made up the fireplace and central meeting point of The Wagon Village. It was here, within this ring of stones, that the fire blazed that held me spellbound. And while I spent more and more of my time in the immediate vicinity of the fireplace, and while the days melted and mingled into a mass of raw time, I stopped going out into the city except to drive my taxi for big-time taxicab owner, Torben Nielsen, on Halmtorvet square. Only on rare occasions would I venture into the city to meet a friend or buy a book. And when I did, I could never wait to get back.

Had anyone told me that something like that would happen, that I would be actively avoiding the places I used to go to, I would have laughed in their faces. But there it was: I had lost my taste for being in the city of Copenhagen with its shopping malls, music halls, theaters, restaurants, movie palaces, galleries, pedestrian streets, entertainment parks, bars and cafés. Not for a moment did I miss the automobiles, the exhaust, the noise, the mindless rush and wholly demented atmosphere of consumption and stress—not to mention the eerie feeling of the regulation and the remote control of my every impulse and function. Of faceless repression and personal impotence. Of the power of fashion, money, drugs and medicine. Bicycling back into Christiania, I would give a sigh of relief. Crossing the border, it was as if a giant hand let go of my soul so that it could fly into the open air. Not that this was something I thought deeply about or explained to myself. As a matter of fact, I don't think it even baffled me much. But that does not mean it didn't matter or make an impression on me. It sure did. So much so, in fact, that to this day, the feeling has not left me entirely. Sojourns into the city were bearable only to the extent that The Freetown existed and was within reach. The best place to be was at home in Christiania.

The other account from the world of literature that comes to mind is the one that Henry David Thoreau has given us about building a cabin with his own hands near Walden Pond in Massachusetts in the mid-nineteenth century. Like my wagon, Thoreau's residence was made of wood, the area of habitation small and—most importantly—removed from organized society with its courthouses, power plants, state departments, prisons, hospitals and military installations. In order not to be polluted, not to lose ground and fall into the trap of standardization, in order to live deliberately and in accordance with our own perceptions, to get and to remain within sight of ourselves and gain control over the essential elements of our lives, we had both chosen to step aside. Aside and outside. Ours were not presumptuous residences, but modest places that contrasted sharply with a materialistic civilization's dream of million-dollar homes complete with all modern amenities. So much the more remarkable is the golden halo that has hovered above Thoreau's cabin in the woods ever since its inhabitant drew his last breath in 1862. This renown has its roots neither in an extravagant way of life, nor does it depend on being plugged into the local power plant. It's not due (as in the case of Trimalchio) to some sublime author hired for the purpose of immortalization. No, whatever immortality has befallen the cabin by the waters of Walden Pond and its builder is due entirely to the personal energy of a single self-reliant man carrying out his own existential experiment and thereby—indirectly through his example—diagnosing a fear-ridden and godforsaken material civilization. From the hand of the creator, every living organism partakes of the spirit that makes life worth living. And man is no exception. Yet, since the secret is simple and man delights in complications, he suffers from the delusion of being different and set apart. Of all animals, humans today are unhappy since they believe that the ability to live freely, find meaning and experience happiness is augmented, in the same degree, the material standard of living is raised above a certain elemental minimum. That which most individual men work so hard to gain is precisely what leads to

31

their destruction.

In the proportion that more and more people in this world are being alienated to ever greater degrees, the need for Thoreau's *Walden* has grown. As a result it has been reprinted countless times and translated into many different languages. I am sure that I'm not speaking for myself only when I say that my life would have taken a different direction had it not been for this book. *Walden* was among the first books I read after moving into my wagon. Or 'reread' I guess I should say. Hitch-hiking zigzag across the United States from East to West five years ealier, I had run into a blond, bearded guy at a truck stop outside Baltimore who let me have his ragged copy to take along.

"It was great talking to you. Hope it'll serve you as well as it did me". This is what he said when he gave me his freckled hand, because I was going west with the truck-driver we had shared a table and chili con carne with. He himself was on his way to Tibet.

And the wish of the blond American was soon to come true. A couple of weeks later in Illinois, by the bank—not of Walden Pond, but of the Mississippi river—I was confronted for the first time with the philosopher's statement that: "The great majority of men live their lives in quiet desperation." Not to mention the passage a bit further down in the same paragraph. "Even in what is called mankind's games and entertainments, there is hidden a stereotype and subconscious desperation."

Having read these statements for the first time, I got up and started to march back and forth on the riverbank. Later, I stopped to swear that nothing like this would happen to me. If I were ever to become desperate, I would cry out. Rather than keeping my mouth shut, I would starve by the banks of Esrum Lake in my native Denmark.

As I was standing there looking out over the swirling

waters of the mighty Mississippi, resolved but also ignorant as to what awaited me around the next bend, I had the feeling that if, in the future, it became clear that it was not possible for me to live freely and with integrity, if it turned out that it was not possible to adorn my life with a certain greatness and grandeur, yes, if it wasn't possible to make it fertile, joyful and fit to create a new and stronger life, hell, then, it was not worth the trouble, and I might as well put an end to it.

"Simplicity, simplicity, simplicity!" To this day, I need only close my eyes, and I hear Thoreau's cry ringing between the trees, urging the world to come to its senses, before it is too late. "Look at me! If I can do it and be happy, so can you! I listened to the voice within and found heaven right here in my own breast and by this pond! Look!" And if I wish to see the words of *Walden* as they were actually written, I need only get off my butt, go to the bungalow and pick it from among the books on the shelf in the bedroom. For example I can open it at random (an old habit of mine), like one opens the *I Ching*. When I do this, more often than not, the first passage my eyes focus on takes on prophetic proportions. As a matter of fact, that's how my son and I were removed from this island where we have sought shelter from a world defunct. Once again, I find myself on a riverbank in Illinois or…in a little shack at the foot of the fortifications in Christiania. Or Thoreau's wake-up call spanning a hundred and fifty years makes me sit down to write again. Since it happened last, the scene has changed. Essentially, however, I have not become much wiser than when I first opened *Walden*. It may be my life has become somewhat dented, and I no longer want to improve the world. Still, what I want to show is that Thoreau did not live in vain. It's to this end, I have reopened the photoalbum on the page with pictures of the wagon. I want to break the evil spell, do as I once promised Melanie and…liberate myself.

It's low tide. The sea has pulled back. As I'm writing this, son is roaming barefoot down by the little harbor, showing his lose tooth to the fishermen. Five years old, a friend of weather-beaten fishermen and with no thought of his father in the back yard with his fillings, bridges and lurking paradentosis. The boy has a voracious hunger for life; he's learning how to mend a fishing net and eat raw squid while his old man steps gingerly into the garden to dawdle away his afternoon. Light and shadow race across the sheets of paper before him on the table. Immobile in the dead still hub of the spinning wheel. The revolutions along the periphery tearing more and more holes in space. In about an hour's time, Daisy, the young maid, will have lunch ready for us. Fish if I am to make a guess. Daisy comes to our house every day, but I live alone. It was not always like that. For almost thirty years, I shared bed with women. Four long relationships—not to mention the odds and ends. Two children brought into this world one of whom recently, at the age of twenty-six, emigrated to Australia.

The other day, I had my fortune read in coffee grinds. The fortuneteller was Daisy's great grandmother. The woman, who is well over ninety and blind as a bat, enjoys a tremendous reputation here. Daisy claims she's never been wrong. It was a funny feeling to be sitting there with coffee grinds on the table and my palm in the old woman's bony hand. All of a sudden, she raised her free hand and stared with her blind eyes into the air between us. After some time, she began to mumble. "The Earth is shaking" under my feet, she said. My feet and Amiel's too. And to illustrate further, she shook the hand from side to side, lowered her voice to a whisper and said that "a great earthquake" would occur and tear us away.

I looked at her, and as if she felt my eyes on her, she repeated: "Away, far far away!"

Normally, I don't take this kind of mumbo jumbo seriously. But this was different because the declaration seemed in harmony with the last time I opened "Walden" at random to read a few lines. This time, I can't seem to shake it. Above all, it's the image of the Earth shaking that strikes me. What does it mean? Why move? And where to?

It has always been like that: I find for myself a safe haven and a friendly face. And the next thing I know, it's gone.

It's part of my daily routine to spend this noontime hour with Daisy. Not today. I didn't mention it yet, but a letter has arrived from Melanie. When Daisy came down here a while ago with her head cocked quizzically, I waved the envelope in the air. I don't think she got it, but she left without a word. Sometimes, I prefer to be alone.

In a local newspaper in New Mexico, Melanie has read about the Danish authorities' policy to "normalize" the Freetown of Christiania.

To me she writes: "I dare say, I rubbed my eyes when I read that. I read it twice and still didn't get it." A little further down, she added: "It seems that the tolerant and liberal minded Denmark I knew thirty years ago has turned totalitarian. Once upon a time, I believed that the conditions of life progressed and improved with time. I don't anymore. Most of the so-called improvements have only made conditions worse, and progress has become just another word for devastation. If I were not in such a fine mood, I would surely sit down and cry."

Coffee grinds or not, I feel a storm gathering. It also has to do with our mutual friend Coyote Saël Shunk Manitu, who has returned to the States and will stop in Las Cruces en route to the Oglala Pine Ridge Reservation in South Dakota. It's not that he wants to revive the old "Bimbo brigade," the three New Mexican chicks with whom he made his first online cooking show back in Prague, but rather that he's in a hurry to record "A Lakotah Life" and "The Last Buffalo Hunt" in the sound studio of Melanie's friend Larry Hill in Silver City. Before it's too late I mean. "The Last Buffalo Hunt" is the story of how in 1942 the two old Lakotah Indians—the shaman and Washtay the storyteller—and the three eight-year-old boys Grey Hawk, Little Deer and shaman grandson Coyote set out on horseback from the reservation to find Tatanka, the buffalo bull. What they want to do is make the gravity of the global situation known to him and get him to offer up his heart in sacrifice. A ritual expedition to save Life's Great Circle from destruction and so avoid the extinction, which such a disaster would lead to.

Just before she wrote to me, Melanie had spoken to "El Coyote" in New York. He had flown in from Europe the day before (even though he hates airplanes and has sworn never to set foot in one again). Melanie could not tell why it was—if it was the shock of being back in the US—but he did not sound well. His deep and rusty Gauloises' voice sounded tired. But the fact that Coyote called her just as she had put down the article on Christiania planted the "utterly fantastic" idea in her head that the Freetown in Copenhagen, without being aware of it, was the Eighth Campfire of the Lakotah tribe. Whereupon she proceeded to remind me of what I already knew: that the tribe consists of seven so-called "Campfires", Oglala being the one Coyote was born into...

At first, I found this idea of hers really farfetched. But now I don't think it is as crazy as it sounds. Coyote *had*, in point of fact, traveled East in the year 1967 to settle in the place where he found the sign from his peyote dream. Melanie is not sure exactly when he arrived in Denmark, but he must have been present in 1970, when the camp in Thy was established as a sort of precursor of the Freetown itself. After all, Coyote had more than once mentioned how he had met John Lennon, when the Beatle visited the village Hust with Yoko Ono. That was in the winter of 1969-70. He had even told her how they had talked about The Circle. Lennon had wanted to write a song that was circular and carried the hope and meaning of the indestructibility of life to people all around the world. He asked Coyote if he was able to imagine such a tune: something radiant and softly rocking that the remains of suffering humanity could send into space as an SOS from the planet Earth.

It could be that all of this was beside the point, Melanie says. But in her opinion "it really is quite possible" that Coyote served as something like a "subterranean offshoot from the ancient Lakotah tribe". Who could tell if it had not been his fate and purpose to plant the seed of the "Eighth Campfire"—spiritually speaking of course?

Thus spake Melanie, along such lines I mean—her tone clearly an octave above its normal pitch. Slowly but surely, she clears the way for what she is really leading up to:

Because I had lived in Christiania in the early days, because I was a friend of Coyote's, because so much depended on it *and* because I had promised her to do so, it was my "holy duty" to get "off my ass" and WRITE ABOUT IT. The wagon. Who would do it, if I did not? What man alive is better equipped? Had I perhaps forgotten my promise? Well, if I had, then she was still alive to remind me. Melanie is "amazed," she says, nay "downright dumbfounded." Why on earth have I let the story of the wagon remain untold for so many years? I…a writer? And then… Christ almighty! Then I had even stopped writing. How could I do it? How could I even think of it—the way things were going nowadays both in Denmark and all over the place? Including the island where I had hidden in order to "lick my wounds in peace." It was "unreal." Could I not see it myself: that there was a reason for my stay in that wagon? This is something, Melanie says, which she feels "very deeply and sincerely." So deeply in fact that the thought of the book I would write "tickled her all the way down to her crotch." There, I had it. A shot from the hip. Ugh! "A shot of warning in the air, bended knees in the desert sand, hands folded in prayer… amen!" She, Melanie, had spoken. It was now up to me.

Is it an example of telepathic communication between connected souls in the Northern and the Southern hemispheres, or is it a coinciding of mutually independent— and fortuitous—circumstances that just before Melanie got all worked up to make me pull the wagon from oblivion, I decided to dig up the battle tomahawk, sound the war whoop and get on the move? Who can know about such things? As far as I'm concerned, it was a dream that got me started. I dreamt that I saw Tatanka, the buffalo-bull. Except in my dream, it was more like a wild boar. I was prostrate on the ground, and the boar impersonating Tatanka was driving its horns into my side. With their symbolic act of sacrifice, the little band of Indians, allies of old with Tatanka, beseeched a future, which had ceased to exist—for the red man and the white man as well. Was it ordained that Tatanka would rip open the leg of Coyote's grandfather's so badly that the little group had to make a hasty getaway with no time to take the necessary precautions? Like erasing all signs of the campfires in order that the "G-men" of the FBI and the white police would not know about the killing of the bull? Was it so arranged that eventually the government people would come for grandfather and take him away? Both he and his grandson Coyote? Was that all meant to be in order to prepare Coyote for "the road that lies open and leads East?" The one his grandfather had told him he would travel one day?

Waking from my dream, there remained the image that has haunted me ever since: that of the old shaman cutting Tatanka's great heart from his chest. At first, I did not know what it meant. Now I do. It was an order for me to take up the pen again.

How was I to know that Melanie in the shape of a wild boar was getting ready to ram her horns into my flesh, tear her head from side to side and rip me till I spilled my guts in a steaming heap? There was no way I could know that. Waking I realized I was not in control. Did Tatanka sacrifice his life in vain? For a long while, I kept staring at the ceiling. Somehow I knew the question would go on haunting me and that I would not enjoy a moment's peace until I too had committed the act. I might as well get down to it.

That's one thing. The other occurred when I turned around and saw that, through all the years, the wagon has followed close on my heels; which just goes to show that at the moment something happens to us or some thought flits across our minds, we have no idea what it's going to mean—or how it's going to affect our lives. Except, of course, if your name is Coyote Shunk Manitu, if you have had peyote dreams and happen to be the only grandchild of an old shaman of the Oglala Campfire.

The game is up. I have received a clear message: do and die. By surrendering Tatanka showed the way. Everything comes at a price, and here I am pulling my wagon from oblivion. There's no turning back any more, and it's too late for literature. From this point on, I take my orders directly from Tatanka. From this point on raw biographical content is all there is time for, its redhot heat making its own form. For all I care, literature can rot in the libraries of the city. I am cured of my forgetfulness. I know what my duty is.

I give myself up and open new frontiers. I'm a man who took up position behind ancient fortifications. I grew alongside everything that draws sustenance from photosynthesis and that does not collect dust. I took the law into my own hands. To this day, its paragraphs are written on my palms. I return to pay homage. Once again, I kiss bark and piss in the dark. Had it not been for Christiania, instead of surrendering, I would most likely have succumbed to the city's offer of salvation in consumption. To protect myself against calamity, I would have had an insurance policy instead of a life. I would have slaved to pay my creditors and never written a line worth reading. The installments would have been fixed in advance. And so would I. Thanks to the wagon, I am still ignorant as to what awaits me around the next bend. Thanks to the wagon my desperation was not without a voice and neither was my joy. Even if I have no hope, there's still hope for me. Thanks to the wagon…

It's early dusk. The sky is red, lilac and orange. Children's voices fill the cool air. As far as I'm able to make out from the sounds, they are running around playing soccer again. It's how it's supposed to be. Amiel roams freely with the other kids in the neighborhood. The evening belongs to him until Papa appears on the scene and calls him to bed. He sleeps until he wakes up. His *childhood* belongs to him. Here he's allowed to grow into adulthood at his own pace. The only force he has to obey is the lifeforce itself. Somewhat like the urchins back then on the island of Christiania. The adults sometimes had difficulty sleeping at night: like when the Danish state set a date for the closing of the Freetown. That was in 1975-76. But this didn't disturb the kids—Christiania kids surely being the most ragged, dirty and carefree bunch of brats in the kingdom of Denmark. Glittering islands of life adrift in the dark seas of death. Yes, in a way Christiania, too, was an island in the sea. Life prevails where there are living people to live it. What matters is not the state of the world but the state you wake to in the morning—if you feel mellow, at ease and ready for the new day. Between victory and capitulation there's no neutral ground. The Gods bless the self-willed man. Joy is just another word for his harvest.

And now, it's about time I present myself to you. My full name is Andreas Stein, but people just call me Les. The story goes that it was Aunt Gudrun who—when she first encountered newborn me—clapped her hands together and exclaimed: "Oh my, what a cute little Les he is!" The question why I'm called what I'm called if it's not my name has been asked so often it has ceased to make any sense. Aunt Gudrun came, Aunt Gudrun saw, and Aunt Gudrun named me. To Aunt Gudrun, all credit is due. Blessed be her name.

Now, I don't want you who are reading this to think that I'm using cheap tricks to make myself more interesting. In my opinion, the only proper way of making oneself interesting is by being and doing something authentic—not through something as superficial as a name, a nationality, a dress, a uniform or a membership to a club. It has happened to me only once that I became conscious of being different from my surroundings: when I moved to Christiania. But no wonder! I mean, Christ, when I told people that I had moved out there, they would stare at me as if I had taken up residence in a lunatic asylum. The most prejudiced were those who had never even been there. In reality, it wasn't such a big deal. At the time, there were lots of people who made the move. And there were lots more, who would have done it if there had been more room. So what was all the fuss about! Hang on a bit longer, and I'll tell you…

It was a hot and humid summer's day many years later in Stromovka Park in Prague. Coyote and I were leaning our backs against trees and telling each other the stories of our lives. When I was done telling him about my move to Christiania, he said something that I have never forgotten. It *was* a big deal, he said, because by doing so, I had reconnected with the Circle. Deep down in my "poor and lost white man's soul," he went on, I was fed up with being "God-less, isolated, lonely and damned." Like a moth being drawn irresistibly to light in the night, I had sought "manitou," which aside from being his name was also the name of the life-giving force.

But to get back to what I was saying, once upon a time, there was a young man who moved into a tiny wooden box-like shack on wheels in the Freetown of Christiania. His new home was situated at the foot of age-old ramparts that in the days of the absolute monarchy had been part of the city of Copenhagen's fortifications. On the other side of the rampart, the waters of a moat reflected the sky between its rush-grown banks where coots built their nests.

Until the day Melanie showed up out of the blue and told me the reason, I had often wondered why *I* happened to land in such a legendary place, where historic events had taken place and were now taking place again. In this self-same place where once young men had fallen in war for their king and country, a rainbow-colored army of marginalized men and women had gathered to defend what was left of freedom in the absolute democracy that succeeded monarchy. The stage had been set not long before my arrival on the scene. I don't know why I sometimes had the feeling that my function was to be a kind of a rear guard to a long procession with roots reaching back to a time when gods like Thor and Odin roamed these parts. Sometimes my heart would pound, because I fantasized how in a former life I had been a soldier and had defended king and country against its bloodthirsty enemies. In mud to my neck and all through the long night, I was shooting Swedes with a blunderbuss. The weapon was heavier than shit, and without fail, I would wake the next day with an aching left side from the recoil the damn thing had pummeled me with.

These days, the enemy was not Swedish, German, French or English anymore, and he did not come charging wearing a uniform. He was not even made of flesh and blood. One could not take aim with the damn blunderbuss and shoot him dead. These days, the enemy of freedom had become invisible; it was something intangible and infamous, which surrounded every living soul on all sides and contaminated the air and water. The piece of earth where my wagon was situated was not defended any longer by the king's uniformed army of soldiers, but by a motley bunch of civilians from pretty much all over with only one thing in common: their aversion to a society that reduced people to objects and where the only legal freedom left was to hoard riches and stuff oneself with expensive wine, food and consumer goods; a society where all other venues were, if not closed up and shut, then at least looked upon with suspicion and intimidation. It was a nasty form of (disguised) tyranny, which forced everyone to conform to manipulation by the media, the corporations, the authorities and the demands of the so-called free market economy. Together these forces formed a hydra that stood guard against anyone escaping to his or her own wagon.

When Christiania was born in September 1971, the hydra had been at large and had intimidated the population for sometime all ready, and, seen from an historic perspective, the phenomenon was on the verge of entering its final electronic stage. Artificial intelligence was in the offing, robots on the march. Those who had not succumbed already to the disturbing pressures were going out of their minds and frantically looking for a way out. If there was anything "wrong" with these people, it was only that they refused to pledge allegiance to the hydra and submit to impotence. They were dying to find some obscure, neglected corner where they would be able to get on with what was left of their own lives. I dare say that if there had appeared on this stage some Christopher Columbus who had discovered a new continent, most of these souls would not have hesitated to pack up and leave. They would rather risk their scalps on the farthest frontier of the wilderness than spend one more day as a living cadaver dancing around the golden calf of egotism.

But...when need is at its greatest is also when you want to watch out for help. Right when the trap seemed sealed and escape a hopeless dream, right when the future as an instrument seemed all but inevitable, just a short walk from parliament in the center of Copenhagen the Danish state's department of Defense vacated the eighty-four acre Boatman street military garrison and left it empty and up for grabs. And since for weeks following general elections there still was no government in place it was fair game.

Now, a run down, heavily polluted former military garrison is not exactly a virgin continent, but the fence around it was no Atlantic ocean either. Journalists from an underground squatter's newspaper who had heard of the vacated chunk of "prime property", climbed the fence, took a good look around and returned to write a centerfold article entitled: "A Sunday on Amager or emigrating with bus number eight." Before anyone realized what was going on, the pent-up frustration and longing for freedom in the youth culture metamorphosed into a material reality. What took place was a peaceful occupation. Denmark held its breath. The boil had burst, and its pus become visible. How would the authorities react? Squatters kept trickling out of Copenhagen. Entering through the hole in the fence, they turned the newfound asylum into their home. They established communes in the large buildings and brainstormed euphorically to find a name for this, their new hope. Together, they agreed on the name…Christiania. Inadvertently and to their own chagrin, the authorities had, for once, obliged the part of the population that was in direst need of more personal freedom. A former military camp located in a previously obscure corner of the city had been liberated and opened up for local autonomy, that is for a shared user's right to soil and property that was technically owned by the Danish state. The dream of a less authoritarian *alternative* society based on values other than constant economic growth and manipulation had gained momentum.

Even though it was only a dwindling part of what was in itself a tiny minority of the Danish population that succeeded in breaking out, right from the start these few individuals divided the remaining majority into two camps: the camp that congratulated the emigrants on their good fortune and the camp that detested them fiercely for having escaped. The few had taken a liberty that was not permitted the many, and the evil plant of envy sprouted its poisonous leaves.

Christiania: a case of schizophrenia become visible. Either the hole in the fence was forcibly closed, or the entire country would enter a prolonged state of inner conflict. It was a clash of cultures. A dilemma was born.

The Wagon Village in which my shack became an appendix was situated in one of the central parts of Christiania called "The Dandelion". It consisted of half a dozen six-and-a-half meter long and two-and-a-half meter wide caravan wagons raised on blocks. In those days, these were generally flat roofed wooden boxes with fat little wheels, one in each corner. Their original purpose was to provide road construction workers with dry places to eat their lunches, so that they could toil and make money for the investors behind the entrepreneurial companies. Deflated and seemingly atrophied the wheels were now curious rudiments only. One look at them and the visitor knew that the wagons were not going anywhere any more, that they had reached their final destination. Hanging there so uselessly the wheels looked funny to strangers, especially if they had smoked a bit of hashish and were a tad high themselves. Sometimes, they would sit there for a long time and ogle one of the wagons. Watching them I couldn't help but wonder what they found so damn interesting, until one day, it dawned on me. It was the wheels hanging in the air. To the "oglers" it was a case of communal levitation pure and simple. The reason they stared was because, to their subconscious minds, our wagons were charged with such strong transcendental energy that they'd let go of solid ground and gone off the deep end.

Except, nothing could be father from the truth. Our huts were neither flighty nor footloose. And they were very far from going nuts. Instead, the raised wheels were an indication that they had settled on higher, more solid ground and were a testimony to something human that had dropped out in order to turn on and tune in to a more ethereal frequency. A new order of being! It really was pretty touching, the sight of them so close together. For, at the same time as the wagons were liberated, still each and every one bore the marks of a past full of greedy developers, course gaffers, hungry road construction workers and hardly a break in their drudgery and sufferings. With their little

46

dry knotholes, half rotten bottoms and their bruises from blows, bumps and kicks the wagons told a tale of violence, exploitation and the thirst for profit. Before Christiania was born and they were ransomed and transformed into human habitations, the wagons had been mere tools of servitude and degradation. They had always been dragged around by their poles, always been on the move going nowhere, always been kept in ignorance as to their wherefores and whereabouts, and about what tomorrow might bring. Yes, and they had always been deprived of a say in the matters of crucial concern to them. Rain, sleet and frost. Hobbling along on half empty tires, squeaking loudly in their ball-bearings, exhausted and hopeless and living out their fears in clouds of diesel and asphalt fumes, it was only after they had taken their full beating that these wagons succeeded in ganging up together and making a village with a circular fireplace in its center.

The outer circle of wagons and the inner circle of granite rocks placed in their middle was the frame around our lives. It was here, on the long green plank table next to the fireplace that the sun took aim every morning and shone warm rays down on leftovers and cold ashes after the night's fire. Up among the tall ash trees on the rampart, a guy named Brian Logcabin was building his own… logcabin, and a bit further on, Jakob had his summer residence: an Indian tipi made of hides and skins, with a smoke hole at the top where the rafters met. Everywhere one looked, life was going about its business.

Jakob, by the way, was *the* real thing. With his scraggly beard, he was a thoroughly imperturbable young earth dweller, who at the time of the birth of Christiania had been squatting houses all over Copenhagen. He had also played a part, when the Camp in Thy, which I mentioned before, was established. From the tender age of sixteen (well, probably even from when he was just sixteen *weeks* old), Jakob had been out of institutional reach. Rumor had it that he and "a big-bearded and flipped out topnotch sportsman" had been in the middle of performing "Death of a Swan" without a stitch on out on the beach in Thy, when the blind Tibetan lama Geshe Tsakpuhwa came running down the broad beach bringing them the glad tidings that The Boatman Street military garrison in Copenhagen had fallen into the hands of "civilians". "We will run when the drum sounds and run, when the smoke rises!" Thus panted Geshe, whereupon he, for good measure, added the holy syllable "HUM".

Imagine! A *blind* Tibetan lama brought Jakob the great news! And so happy were Jakob and the flipped out and big bearded topnotch sportsman that they started hugging each other and Tsakpuhwa as well "right on the spot." Now, it was only a question of finding some clothes, scraping up the dough necessary for the train tickets and heading back to the capitol to turn up at the garrison and enlist under the flag of the Freetown.

Even to this day, it beats me how Jakob managed to get his gear back to the capitol. The railway personnel probably rubbed their eyes one extra time when on the platform they spotted a longhaired hippie lugging an entire tipi with the obvious intention of taking it on the train to Copenhagen. But that is Jakob in a nutshell. He's as stubborn as a mule. Once he gets it into his head to do something, he does it regardless of the obstacles, very slowly but very surely too. When he travels, he is a match for the ant in that he carries his own weight three or four times over. Either he travels light with nothing at all, or he travels heavy with goddamn everything; that is with skin and bones and reindeer hides and rafters and smoke flaps and snowshoes and God knows what else.

On that epic day at Thisted station, the tipi was irrevocably headed east towards Christiania. It was to be set up high on the ramparts where it could be seen from far and wide and serve as a landmark: Here on this spot of soil, original man had reclaimed what had always belonged to him. As a symbol of man's native and inalienable right both to the soil and to his own life, the tipi was destined to make the city of Copenhagen renowned throughout the world. It was going to be, or so Jakob explained it to me later, "sort of like" when on the moon Neil Armstrong weightlessly planted "The Stars and Stripes." To set up a Native American tipi on the ramparts in Copenhagen in 1971, during the darkest days of The Cold War, at the threshold of disaster and just a stone's throw from the heart of the hydra, was a symbol of the same order. Anyway, that is how Jakob looked at it. And I tend to agree with him.

Christ all mighty, was he a character that Jakob. I dare say he had his own way of dealing with people and things, or of not dealing with them, as the case might be. Sometimes one had to be really patient with him. But that was all. Patience was all one needed when dealing with Jakob. Being a sort of sociable loner, he loved the company of others both to a fault *and* to a certain point. For days and weeks, he would take in inordinate amounts of society and then, all of a sudden, he'd had enough, and his brow would cloud. Just as people were sitting around the campfire shooting the bull, he would become quiet, and soon, he would get up to leave without saying a word to anybody. Most likely, he would go up to his tipi to light a small ritual fire of kindling and sticks, place himself in a cross legged position on a reindeer skin from Lapland and hold private powwow smoking the tiny conical bee-dee cigarettes with a thin red thread around them. The cigarettes had been imported from India and he had bought them a couple of days before in the grocery store on Langgade Street. If Jakob was ever in a hurry, it never showed. But it did happen that he got angry. At such times, he would frown and take on the aspect of a thundercloud. Even so, he did not lose his temper. He never allowed loss of control to mess him up.

For my part, *I* never understood how Jakob managed to keep a straight face and control himself. Somehow, he was able to take things in a stride—even the many deadbeats, wayfaring scroungers and importunate intruders that were always showing up out of nowhere. Without batting an eyelash, he would show them a mattress some place and let them share our meals. Then, there they were—sometimes for weeks on end. In general, they neither disturbed nor contributed anything. Without saying very much, they came and went or sat on one of the tree trunks and stared into the fire. It was only if they started to do something that Jakob interfered. "Hey jack, stop that!" he would say to a guy who kept poking at the fire, and he would say it very calmly and deliberately too. Or he would say to a guy who was a bit too greedy at dinner: "Leave something for us too will you!" It was kind of like a shepherd calmly walking around poking the animals with his stick. No way I would have been able to stand it. I would have gotten pissed and asked the nuisance to leave. But not Jakob! He was not just a shepherd. He was a goddamn saint.

But I must not forget to mention the one thing Jakob cared about more than anything else. It was to compose, play and sing as many songs as humanly possible on his old guitar. Night after night, he would sit by the campfire and sing for the black, moonlit or starry skies. Come morning, he would be taking it real slow and easy. Taciturn and concentrated he would go about preparing the ritual pot of tea. Seeing him at it, you would think he was some hippie chemist in a secret laboratory concocting some highly potent potion. If someone happened to enter the room at a time like this, he would not notice. To go with the tea, Jakob wanted two slices of buttered rye bread and a soft-boiled egg. Eventually, he would appear on the doorstep carrying a tray. Stepping out, he would make himself comfortable with his back against the doorpost, raise his head to the sun and think of Ragma, the woman he had met half a year before in a sweat lodge deep in the Swedish woods, and who—supposedly—was returning from Lhasa to join forces with him.

In the wagon next to mine, resided Melanie's friend from Rhode Island USA. Douglas, who with his skinny figure and narrow dark face looked a bit like a gunslinging Frank Zappa, was a sustainable Freetown intellectual and vegetarian. Sharing the wagon with him was his Danish wife, Line, who besides being blessed with a great bush of black hair, sometimes meticulously arranged in tiny braids, was also blessed with a great old belly containing what was soon to be their first child. Next to this couple and their happy circumstances, in a soggy and half rotten sky blue wagon that looked like it suffered from some horrible disease in its lower parts, lived John and Hanne with their three-year-old son Rune, an urchin who was never seen, not in summer, nor in winter, spring or any other damn season, without long dirty nails and a splotch of greenish snot in varying stages of hardening or softening as the case might be. Hanne was a former junkie with lots of henna in her hair, who aided by all sorts of fetish and weird mumbo jumbo was trying to forget her former life in the city. And then there was John, her mate. Well, I never did find out exactly where John hailed from or what he had been up to before he wound up with Hanne in that rotten wagon of theirs. But what I saw was a heavyset man with lots of hair growing all over the place. In the middle of all the hair on his face, there would appear, at times, a hole from which bursts of loud laughter would issue. A laughing troll—that's what John was, a species of extinct Icelandic troll straight out of some lost saga. Three people still overshadowed by a difficult past and squeezed into a six-meter long wagon made up the family. No wonder little Rune spent practically all his waking hours outdoors.

If one continued on past John's and Hanne's family wagon, one arrived at a wagon where a woman by the name of Elvira had recently moved in with her six-year-old daughter Zobeida. Then there followed a pink and peeling wagon with faded yellow and lilac lotus flowers painted on its sides. Of all the wagons in the entire circle, this was the most vaginal. Don't ask me what I mean by this, because I don't know. It just was, and that's all. Here, Gurli Elizabeth resided with her castrated tomcats, her guitars, percussion instruments, tarot cards, incense and god knows what else. Just like Rune, the kid next door, was never seen without the greenish blob of snot under his nose, one rarely saw Gurli Elizabeth without the conical and pointed Laplander bonnet complete with lose flaps and jingle bells, which she wore pulled tightly down over the top of her head. It's hard to say what she looked like in that thing. It really is. But whatever it was, it was not like anything I had ever seen before. I used to wonder if she also slept in the damn thing. She probably did, because somehow that makes more sense, at least to me. Anyway, it was really quite endearing in all its eccentricity. I won't deny that. For example, on dark moonless nights in winter, when I was sitting alone inside my cozy and warm little space, there it would be: the thin sound of a tiny pastoral jingle approaching. Then, I would raise my head from the book I was reading and listen, knowing that it was no one other than Gurli returning home.

After Gurli Elizabeth's residence, there followed a gap on the other side of which Jakob ran his hostel for the homeless in a blue and wellkept wagon. The next point in the circle was the communal caravanserai, where we cooked and ate our meals during the winter, or in the summer if it was cats and dogs outside. Finally, completing the circle, there was the shack of Old Knud. Even if it *was* a wagon, I hesitate to call it one, because it was shorter than the other four-wheeled habitations in our village. Still, it had been big enough for Old Knud back when he was about to drink himself to death and needed to remove himself from the general debauchery of the lower downtown regions around Pusher Street. Knud's part in this story is a great one, but since everything has its time and place, I will save the rest for later.

So much for demography and ethnography. As far as the psychic and social environment is concerned, we—the inhabitants of The Wagon Village—shared a common trait in that we had all run away from something. I, for one, had run away from the mundane desperation in the affluent north Copenhagen suburb I hail from. "So what are *you* doing?" I can still hear this question, and it still sends shivers down my back. It's downright perverse, if you want my opinion. And so is the phoney grimace that usually went with it. Until you had told people what you were "doing" they had no idea how to deal with you, indeed whether to have any dealings with you at all. For starters, they didn't give a shit about who you might be. Oh no! But if you had a well-paying job or were on your way to one because you studied law or economy, whew! did they like to get to know you then. Just thinking about it makes my stomach turn. There was no way I could see myself putting up with that kind of shit the rest of my days. Trust me! It's nasty stuff. I would even say it's a form of disease, a tricky one, because

53

you don't know when you suffer from it, and you feel right in your mind thinking that the ones who *don't* have it are the ones who are really sick. Like all that crap about how it's necessary and O.K. to smirk and kiss ass and select the right people and be cautious. The subconscious panic when truth is felt to be near. The concern about, what others think about you and the compulsion to express phoney happiness! It's in the same class with dementia. Only when the victims are very drunk or on drugs—or perhaps hospitalized after one of their suicide attempts or something, is it possible to get a feeling for what they're really like as human beings. Obviously, I had no desire to live surrounded by this. Like the fish that try so desperately to get away from the oxygen deprived shallows of the fjords of Denmark in the summertime, I tried to escape collective death on the dry land.

And in Christiania, I was not alone. The neighbor to my left, Douglas, was, among other things, running from a USA that locked up its best men if they refused to blow innocent Vietnamese to smithereens. Just as these poor Vietnamese were going about their business in the rice fields down on Earth, bombs would fall out of the sky and blast away whatever life had been in that place. Then there was Jakob, who like me detested the phoniness and its cover-up strategy using sweet smelling soaps, lotions and cortisone cream—the entire set up where you were encouraged to amass money at other people's expense but prosecuted if you settled in a tree in the forest and called it your home. Brian Logcabin who wanted to build a house and home with his own hands had naturally left the restrictions laid down by an all-regulating bureaucracy and gone where he could make his dream come true. Hanne, of course, was fleeing her heroin addiction in the city plus something else, which I never found out about. With her poems, songs and homegrown Lapland rhythms, Gurli Elizabeth was on a mad stampede away from anything that smacked even remotely of authorities and a lower middle class lawn-mower idyll. And finally, there was Old Knud. Knud was special in many ways but especially so because he was no longer running from anything material and outward; if he was running at all, it was from the asbestos he inhaled, when, in his younger days, he had worked for Aalborg Portland Cement. The stuff was in his lungs, and sometimes in the wee hours of the morning, I could hear him coughing violently. The sound of these attacks used to unnerve me. At the same time, the birds were merrily chirping along. Old Knud and the birds made up an uncanny duet that would keep me awake until it gradually subsided. I am sure Old Knud knew that the days we were living together then were numbered. You could tell from the way he tried to take with him into the grave as much life as he could possibly lay his hands on.

That is how we lived, and that is how we wanted it— fugitives the whole bunch of us, runaways into our little wooden shacks on blocks. As if in obeisance to some common impulse, our wagons had turned their backs on a sick world. From the village fireplace in the heart of the Freetown, in a place where rumor had it a meteor had once hit the Earth, radiation waves spread on all sides forming ever greater circles. As these waves spread wider and wider, eventually they collided head-on with the city of Copenhagen, embodied by the macadamized veins of motorized traffic: Bådsmandsstræde street, Prinsessegade street and Refshalevej street.

From a bird's eye view or from any place on the ramparts, our wagons looked like a cross between an Indian village, a pioneer's corral and a hippie commune Copenhagen style. Jakob's tipi signaled Indian village; the circular shape signaled a cosmic harmony bordering on its opposite. On the one hand, a band of emigrated souls had found here a sort of shelter; on the other hand, they had also found an uncertain pioneer's existence in hostile territory. The long hair, the beards, the beads and cheap bijouterie; the hashish, the naked breasts, the poems, lyrics and guitars, the blob of snot stuck like a weird omen under Rune's little nose, the homegrown ballads sung around the campfire when the moon breathed its pale light on the immovable figures staring into the flames, the twinkling stars—all of this signaled that a band of hippies had taken up position for the night. On hushed snow covered days, thin blue columns of smoke would rise from the chimneys, and three-year-old Rune would freeze his red and black fingers in the pockets of a grimy snowsuit. At intervals, the snowy air would resound from axe blows, followed by the dry sound of wood splitting and the chopped off pieces tumbling onto the hard ground. In the summer, the selfsame air would be warmed by the sun, spiced by the growths of the soil and humming to itself around Old Knud's beehives, which—white, red, green and sky blue—were placed side by side with their backs to the rampart between Douglas' and John's wagons. That's how it was during the daytime, when one could also hear Jakob's horse, Cherie, whinny and blow at the insects swarming around its muzzle.

And now, there's no getting around them anymore: the tourists, I mean. Having heard of "the freedom high," they came in great numbers to experience it and to leave their mark on just about everything and everybody, and vice versa because Christiania sure as hell marked them too. Judging from the change that took place in the tourists you would think that by the entrance to the Freetown there were posted some big guys equipped with baseball bats and instructed to use them on the forehead of visitors arriving alone or in twos, threes and fours. I swear. It really did seem like there was some sort of sorcery at work. Something happened, and whatever it was, it was noticeable almost from the moment the poor suckers crossed into Christiania. And when it became time for their exit, it was only too painfully clear that a transformation had taken place. Back in the city the exited person was no longer identical with the person who had visited Christiania sometime before. And should the two of them ever meet again, I am not sure they would get along.

It was not long before it seemed a visitor had lost it. In no time almost all of them would get this sort of supercilious but mostly just silly, vacant expression on their faces that boded disaster. Seemingly no longer in complete control of their limbs, they were seen sailing along as if stripped of any rudder they might once have had. Judging from the mindless way they took in their surroundings and how their legs kicked spasmodically, you would have had to have a heart of stone not to be concerned. It really did not look good—especially if they had bought hashish down by the main entrance or on "The Prairie," which was our name for the muddy area right inside from the main entrance. In that case, they would either proceed to flop some place, light up and start to giggle idiotically, or they would succeed in getting lost entirely and also in losing the content of their pockets while puking behind some bush.

I don't know what it was about them, but when it came to getting in trouble, the Swedes were in a league by itself. It could be just me, but I rarely heard of any other nationalities being robbed. Not in the same way anyway. The poor Swedes somehow called it down on themselves. By the time the visiting Swede was making his way to the exit, more often than not, he would be flailing his arms in the air and yelling at the top of his lungs all kinds of curses and abominations in Swedish. At this point, he probably had a couple of teeth missing and would be stripped of whatever money, documents, hashish and faith he might have had in humanity.

No. There really was no end to the follies of the tourists. There were some among them who would wander about singing loudly and sticking their noses into things that were none of their business. This type of tourist whom we called "the singers" had a remarkable faculty for stumbling into situations that defied all logic. Once, for example, when we had dug a deep hole in the ground, what did we find in it the next day but a drunken Swede? All night long until he fell into our hole, he had been hollering Swedish songs. Now, he had a bruise on the cheekbone, a sprained ankle and was sleeping blissfully in the mud on the bottom. And this, mind you, happened despite the fact that we had done all we could to mark and fence off the place. Which just goes to show that when a drunken Swede is determined to fall into a hole, he will fall into a hole no matter what you do to stop him. And if there were no holes around, being an ingenious people, the Swedes would find other solutions like getting stuck in one of the narrow concrete storage places in the ramparts. Waking from their drunken stupor, they would find out they were stuck and unable to get out again. Yet no matter how hopeless the situation, still they would raise hell when you offered to give them a hand. Damn Swedes.

So no! There was absolutely no end to the follies of the tourists. Another time, a Lithuanian Jew stumbled straight into one of our tall woodpiles and cracked his skull. Getting back on his feet, the only thing he could think of was the skullcap he had lost. I could go on relating such incidents but I would rather not think about them anymore. It's kind of depressing, I think. What I wanted to say was only that the Freetown did something to the tourists, and this "something" was not just a joke. Still, considering the number and the gravity of calamities that occurred, it is remarkable that so few were ever fatally injured. Based on what I have seen, I believe tourists enjoy special protection from the powers that govern the universe. Most of the time, they were able to get back on their feet and stumble on. And what is more, they would often forget about their bruises, taking to the road again with a song on their lips and a taste for new accidents. Perhaps they were barely able to make their legs comply with their wishes, and perhaps they hardly had any voice left, but at the same time, they were obviously relieved of some burden. As I said, a tooth or two would perhaps be missing and a pinkie broken when finally the singer crossed back into the city of Copenhagen. That may be, yes, and perhaps somewhere along the line, blood and puke had stained a silk collar. Still, staring gleefully into the distance, our singer looked like he was finally pointed in his own direction and not on the march back to the drudgery of the ministry or political party or company or wherever it was that he was bound to by contract and earning his living.

Never before and never since, have I had such an opportunity to study the behavioral patterns of tourists at close range. Had I studied anthropology instead of history, I might have written a penetrating monograph on the subject. There was the wind in the treetops, and there were the tourists. The wind whispered in my ears around the clock, and the tourists passed my windows from morning to night. Sometimes, the wind suggested that I try to guess where the tourists hailed from. Most were North Americans, but there were also loads from other European countries, from Australia and Japan. Some few would wander about on their own, but the great majority came in groups that sometimes consisted of so many individuals I could not count them all or tell them apart. It reminded me of some demented migration or that story in the Bible where God sends out great swarms of locusts to punish the land of Egypt. Either way, rain, snow or sun, the tourists kept coming.

As opposed to the "singers," the tourists who came in groups would never misbehave. This species never smoked hash, got into trouble or got lost. It just was not possible, since, at all times, there was a guide to chaperone them and tell them what to do and what *not* to do. What baffled me the most was not so much the individual visitor getting into trouble but how well behaved these group-people were. How disciplined and obedient. Their behavior was so alike, it was almost like they had taken the same medicine or attended the same course on how to travel in a flock. Never would any of them walk faster than the rest or fall behind. On the contrary, you could tell how each one struggled to read the signs and to toe the line. They would never argue with the guide or make sudden movements. Judging from how conscientiously they stuck close to one another, you would think a mischievous God had sprayed the air between them with glue. From the way they dawdled along behind the guide, one could tell that they were not really going anywhere. Watching them file by my windows, it often struck me how beside themselves each one seemed. At all times, there were some among them who would be turning their heads inanely from side to side. It was as if they were taking turns digesting what the guide had told them, or as if they did not feel at home in their bodies, or as if they had been told to look for something and could not find it.

What do I know? Sometimes the whole group would come to a full stop to allow for little comments or exclamations. Then, they would probably start fidgeting with some object that was laying around and that happened to catch their fancy at the moment: the gear cable on an abandoned bicycle, say, an old potter's wheel, a loose bolt in a sawhorse or a battered piece of sheet metal.

Once a group came to one of these full-stops right outside my wagon. Just like a damn school of fish reacting to an electric impulse, they all stopped at exactly the same time and turned their heads in my direction. It happened so quickly and so suddenly that I had no choice but to freeze just where I was and endure the collective stare of some fifty souls. The way they looked at me, you'd think they were either hypnotized or had read about me in some brochure in Korea. God, did I detest it! It made me feel like a goddamned orangutan. The members of the group all wore the same knapsacks, which advertised some painkiller or other medication, and as they stopped, their guide proceeded to use me to illustrate some point she had been making. Barely had mademoiselle aspirin fixed me with her gaze when she poked a hole in the air above her head with her umbrella and pointed at me with her free hand:

"Now, do *you* remember," she called out to her faithful followers, "what I explained to you about the alarm system here in Christiania. How christianites keep a referee's whistle in their pockets or around their necks. And, no, it is *not* because they're soccer referees all of them. They use this whistle when they need to warn each other that the police are coming. Do you recall *that*? Well, what we're witnessing here is a fine example of the creative communication systems of the inhabitants. A christianite has connected the telephone cable to the neighboring wagon, which, in its turn, has taken its connection from the low buildings over

61

there. Do you *see* that?"

Here, the whole goddamn group simultaneously turned their heads and began to stare in the direction of their guide's pointed and lacquered finger…

"…That sort of thing ladies and gentlemen," the guide went on, "is not only cre-*a*-tive and al-ter-na-*tive*; it's also the result of great imagination. Neighbors take their signals from each other, share their meals, and warn and support each other. Like one big family. This, however, does not prevent the christianites from going about things in a personal and highly makeshift manner. Have you got that? Can we move on?" (Deep silence…)

When that made up doll in the two-bit suit (which made her look like a stewardess on a frigging airplane) had finished her speech, the group kept gaping and nodding their heads for a little while. It looked so funny I couldn't help wondering if they were now processing the information they had just received. I felt like opening my window and waving. Or sticking my tongue out. Yet I never acted on these impulses for fear it would be interpreted either as an insult or an invitation. Making of my face an imperturbable mask, I inwardly laughed at the sight of myself. What on earth did those people *see*? Judging from their expressions, you would think that what their guide had pointed out to them was nothing less than Thor, the Nordic God of Thunder, nowadays resident of Wagon number 537 Christiania.

Another time, coming back from one of the rare raids I made into the city, I found a chubby Italian tourist waiting. The guy was sitting in my desk chair taking pictures of my woodstove. Now, it was my turn to stare. Taking a deep breath, I also took a step forward, so I could lean my shoulder on the post holding the kitchen table, thinking that perhaps he would notice me. Wrong. The guy kept right on doing what he was doing. He didn't even show me the courtesy of discomfort. Nothing. And it was not like he was unaware of my presence, either. I know this because when I waved my hand, there escaped from his mouth a "prego" accompanied by one of those gestures Italian stronzoes use when they greet their stronzo friends in the cafés. All over goddamn Italy, it's the same gesture. And the same bad upbringing, I might add. "Christ!" I thought to myself, "Who do you think you are?" And all the while I was thinking that, I stared at him as hard as I could. But it was no use. That stronzo couldn't care less. Had I been the Pope himself, it wouldn't have made any difference. He, Signor Stronzo was the owner of the most advanced technology, and he would do as he damn well pleased. *Mein Gott* how that sort of thing gets on my nerves! The guy behaved just like it was his wagon. It wasn't until I cleared my throat very loud, and *especially* when I bent down and picked up Thor's hammer from the floor—just sort of casually and as if I were tidying up or something—that he got a move on. He got up, sent me a look like he was very insulted and moved past me to the door. Next thing I knew, he was gone. But you've got to admit! What good is globalization when it requires you to chase tourists out of your own house with a hammer! What is going on in the heads of such people? Do they think "free communal living" means it's okay to go into people's houses as long as there is no sign telling them not to? Hell if I know.

Now, maybe there is someone out there who thinks it must be great getting all this attention. And media attention too. To be labeled "very interesting and unique." To be ogled by dilettante paparazzies. To be made into a "unique cultural phenomenon." Maybe someone out there thinks it helped us in our search for a personal identity. My answer is: no way! If anything, it was more like a sedative, making us a little bit conceited and a little bit sleepy. For my own part, I did not at all like to be so goddamned quaint, nor did it boost my ego in any way. Instead, it depressed me to think that just because we chose to obey our primal nature and so had disengaged ourselves from what we perceived as a faceless tyranny, immediately we were stamped as something highly extraordinary and exceptional. And then, when on top of this, the society we formed was turned into a zoo overrun with the people still working the treadmill... Hell, then, I wanted to open my window and shout: "Hey, it's *the wrong people* you put on exhibit. Removing myself to Christiania hasn't made me an ounce better or more interesting or smarter or more artistic or more unique than any other guy who resists becoming an impotent cog in the wheel of the machine. Get that into your heads and shove it!"

But when all this is said, it must also be conceded that there was a great deal to be seen and experienced and wondered at in Denmark's Freetown. In the Wagon Village, there was always a great bustle. Especially, of course, in summer. Most days were slow and peaceful. But not all. Every so often, a psychopath would go berserk and beat people up or shoot at them with a gun. Sometimes, it really *was* the bloody mess that the media tried to paint. Like when the bikers in the Multi-house started snuffing each other and burying the bodies in the concrete foundation. So, sure there was violence. And sometimes, there was a bloody lot of it too. Yet there was never that suffocating feeling of deoxygenation that I have already mentioned. And since cars were off limits, there were no traffic-accidents either. The nearest we got to something like that was when two or more drunks would collide as they stumbled about in the dark. Then, there would be blood from a nose and a bit of hoarse shouting. But that was about it.

In Christiania, the props and supports of "normal"

society were missing. There, it was either swim or sink. Whether people wound up getting their act together and straightening themselves out, or they disintegrated once and for all was up to them and their creator. It was impossible to tell how a newcomer would fare. From the outset some had both capital and social standing. Their clothes were clean and their demeanor controlled. Before coming to live in Christiania, they had been successful art directors and executives earning large amounts of money. They'd had a spouse, a house to live in and kids to feed. In short, they'd had what people are supposed to have in order to be something. Six months down the line, all that was left in their pockets were the holes, and they were living like hopeless drunks. On the other hand, there were those freaks and failures, the down-and-out derelics that no one in their right mind would have believed capable of physical and spiritual regeneration, individuals who had been broken and humiliated and abandoned by the city where they were known only as nuisances and burdens to society. Against all odds, such seemingly lost causes would sometimes straighten out, reform their ways and become assets to their new community.

Except for the downtown area around Pusher Street, the atmosphere of Christiania was open, mellow and relaxed as compared to the rest of Copenhagen. People knew each other and behaved like villagers with a sense of belonging. Nobody seemed in any great rush to get away from where they happened to be. The places people wanted to go could be reached in less than forty minutes on foot. So people either walked or rode bicycles, and their speed was never so great that they couldn't stop to look the neighbor in the eye or exchange a couple words with him. Parents would use the Christiania-made carrier-bike to transport their children. And then, of course, there was the local jet-set consisting of actors, popmusicians and such for whom it was of paramount importance to be perceived as belonging to the absolute avant-garde. They put on shades, tight pants and roller skates and whizzed from place to place giving the impression they were the very picture of success. How people got around depended entirely on temperament, mood and character. One would crash through the soundbarrier on a flight to Rio de Janeiro while another undertook hazardous voyages exploring the land and seascapes of the mind mapping out every hill, dale and isle. Some smoked a pipe of hash first thing in the morning; others forced the doors of perception with the aid of magic mushrooms and LSD. Hallucinating, they would navigate unknown realms without batting so much as an eyelash. Others, still, would hammer nails or grab a brush and decorate a gable somewhere. And everywhere, people made music, which they would perform for each other in public places such as streets, campfires, bars and music halls.

In Christiania, there was no need to plan ahead of time. There was always plenty going on in your immediate vicinity. On sunny days, in the spring when the air was warm and the first flies were busy buzzing, the girl's marching band in full uniform complete with an incongruously short, plump drum majorette—would parade up and down Langgade Street drumming up support and soliciting smiles, cheers, taunts and jeers—just about anything to confirm that here, in this place, something was happening that was not happening anywhere else. It signified that in Christiania it had once again become acceptable to fall out of step with the official drummer and walk to the rhythm of your own. The marching band was a hilarious sight to see. But never were the girls funnier than when on the Queen's birthday, April 16,[th] they marched out of the Freetown, eliciting laughter from their fellow subjects waving both Denmark's and Christiania's flag en route to salute Her Majesty at Amalienborg Castle. Among other things, the charm had to do with the repetoire of ridiculous tunes, the weird hairdos and wigs, the missing buttons and the way the marchers stomped along in mock imitation of more official orchestras. Whenever this band of women was on the march, good vibes floated on the airwaves and worked directly on the senses of the public. Seeing them pass, even the worst dog of a man had to stop his growling and relax. And sometimes, when the merriment had pried people open, made them receptive and in a mood to cherish, commune and worship, the parade would erupt into a late night bonus cabaret performance at the The Moonfisher Bar.

When the "Cabaret of the Insane" was on, the highceilinged room was so crammed that not one more body could be squeezed in. The tiny balcony was packed too, and everybody was contributing to the wild sketches on the stage with shouts, gestures and general rowdyness. People were having the time of their lives, and once, when in the middle of proceedings, I took a look around, I had the sensation that the whole damn place was full of romping Pippi Longstockings.

It was all part of the same picture. Whether people killed themselves or each other or they kissed, it all somehow belonged. Being open-ended in all directions, days in Christiania bore very little likeness to the standardized days I lived before I came there. Time was mine to do with as I pleased. When there was rushhour going on without, peace was settling within. A man would open the door of his house, peer up at the sun and step out into it. Another would build a table out of scavenged wood, and, come evening, he would light a candle on it. Where the flame was, the hearth was too. That is where home had its address.

No. Things were not dull in Christiania. Horrible occasionally, but dull… no. Not even on such god-forsaken Wednesdays like the one I have told you about. On such weekdays, most Danes woke with an aching in their souls and had to do time in jobs far from home and their local communities. Shortly after waking from too little sleep, they found themselves in their cars strapped to the seats, unable to move and stuck in bumper-to-bumper traffic on the congested highways. Just like me, some christianites worked jobs outside the Freetown. But the majority worked inside baking bread, selling coffee, fixing up old stoves in the Smithy, painting murals, making and repairing bicycles, collecting garbage, setting up theater perfomances, playing music, planting trees, building houses, recycling waste, pushing hash, cooking meals, serving tables, looking after children, housemaiding for bedridden morphinists, hawking cakes and so on. Unlike most local communities, Christiania was never deserted after eight a.m. People stayed around and went about their business for which they received a small salary under the table. The so-called "users rent" was cheap, and people might have made ends meet, living off what they earned; but in order not to be called in for interrogation and fined by the tax authorities, the ones without regular jobs also had to collect social help. Collecting social help, you would receive a sum every month from which the taxes were already deducted. In this way, the State could demand of every living soul with a social security number that he or she paid taxes, even if he or she lived from hand to mouth. If somebody did *not* they would be called in. "How do you earn your keep?" was the question asked. Of course, this practice cost society a great deal of money; but since it affected only a few artists and crackpots it passed under the radar of the public eye and the media.

Since I started writing this, I have been thinking that there really was not much in The Wagon Village (or in Christiania at large for that matter) that set a Wednesday apart from, say, a Sunday. The Grocery shop closed a little earlier, and the kindergarten was not open. Maybe the Smithy decided to take a day off. If the sun rose and the sun set, we called it a day. A day was a state of mind and not primarily a number and a name arbitrarily foisted on it by a man made calendar. You woke up and the day began. It was a form or matrix that did not exist until you were there to live it. In this way, our days were unlike those numbered ones outside the Freetown: days that the market demanded be turned into money as fast as possible. Not only was that sort of thing not our objective, it was considered a despicable kind of violation and an affront to creation. In the final analysis, time was something holy and had nothing to do with either money or speed. Time was of the essense of life itself i.e. identical with the power or the process that makes the cell split and the body age. If we had an objective at all, it was to adapt to this essence, do one thing at a time and not force things. Things were allowed to take the time and the course they needed—if not for our immediate gratification's sake, then for God's.

So with us, the days had character. No two of them were alike. When the sun rose in the east and shone its light on us, it was anybody's guess what would be revealed. Then, it was *showtime* again. Summer evenings, the air resounded with voices, the songs of black birds and distant shouts as we made a fire and prepared the communal dinner. Bowls of rice and plates with fish were carried out of the wagons and set down on the long green plank table. Strangers appeared from out of nowhere and hung around. Without anybody noticing it, the itinerant hipster had perhaps settled on one of the hunks of tree trunk that served us as chairs around the campfire. It seemed our guest felt very much at home. Perhaps he had bought a super-joint on the Street, and perhaps he had taken a few tokes of it. Perhaps he was already blissfully stoned and starry-eyed. But it didn't matter. If he happened to still be around when we sat down to our meal, a plate would be set before him. Perhaps we would never find out who the stranger was, where he hailed from and what he was looking for among us. Perhaps he would not even say anything, and we never got to know his name. But who cared? If what we had before us looked like a human being, spoke like a human being, smelled like a human being and farted like one—well, then we concluded it must be a human being. And human beings got hungry and weary and needed to eat and to rest. That was all we needed to know to fill a plate and feed a stranger.

In this way, we fed and housed a wide assortment of crackpots, minstrels, dope-heads, saints, traveling artisans and downright nuisances. There was a constant coming and going. Only on rare occasions were we alone at dinnertable. Talk, too, was a constant: loose ends, bickering, backbiting, bits and pieces, jabber, gossip, wild and extravagant if somewhat fortuitous flights of wisdom and wit. People let go and let out all sorts of things. Of course it also happened that conversation was sluggish and lacking in spirit. It all depended on the company, the mood and the energy level generally. On the subject even—if what we talked about was our own little lives with all their trifling concerns, or if the subject was world politics. I liked it best when we didn't stray too far from home and local Dandelion affairs. A subject that never seemed to fail was the universe of the ethereal. We never tired of discussing herbal medicines, the meaning of meditation, organic foods, corn cirkles, reincar-

nation, ecology, astral bodies and chakras, healing and me-
ridians, cosmic energies, telepathy, the power of light, zone
therapy, astrology, Oneness blessing, tarot, Zen Buddhism,
I Ching, the interpretation of dreams, religious rites of original peoples, shamanism, the training of horses and dogs,
bee-keeping and environmental politics. All of this was a
sort of hotchpotch seasoned with Old Knud's rabbits and
the mysterious ways of love and eros. Grotesque or obscene
anecdotes taken from "real" life were also favorite topics.
And then, of course, there was always music, our likes and
dislikes, new album releases and concerts.

If utilitarianism was despised, rationalism too was not
rated very highly with us in The Wagon Village. With Old
Knud as the one exception, we were all of us more or less
esotericists, who believed in the spirit, the transcendental,
the real and invisible organs and the energies that, through
sunlight, have from times immemorial suffused plants, animals and humans. But on the other hand, we did not take
it too seriously either. Since we were unable to fathom even
the tiniest bit of those forces and processes of whose existence we were so convinced, we were prone to make a joke
out of things. It was funny if someone suffered from con-
stipation, because then the intestinal chakra needed to be
washed out and reactivated. It was a smelly and unpleasant affair that made one feel shitty at first and wonderful
when it was over. But more than anything, it was necessary.
Why this was we had no idea. Whenever something was
the matter, we would turn our gaze heavenward, draw up
a meridian circle of the spheres and see if it did not go away
by itself.

All things would pass except the need to laugh when
things got too serious. In order to endure the unendurable,
we had to poke fun at ourselves. We could tolerate almost
anything except inflated egos taking themselves and their

opinions too damn seriously. This we found utterly ridiculous. Nothing was so important it could not be laughed at, and nothing so unimportant it did not deserve at least *some* attention. The obscene was held in as high esteem as was the incongruous. If ever a professor in chemical engineering had infiltrated our little circle, he would surely have found our conversations quite unbearable if not downright laughable. For example one could never pronounce a profundity without first dressing it up as a frivolity. A naked profundity parading without a costume would have to run the gauntlet and suffer verbal abuse. Profundities should know their place, and so should professors.

"The whole thing can get so goddamn organic, it makes one puke!"

Thus spake Jakob. Ragma had made some vague and nebulous remark about something very spiritual, whereupon Old Knud had let out one of his loud, sarcastic stinkers. That is how it was. Even the astral bodies were not sacrosanct and so could only be spoken of in a light manner. Like the night the stars decided to have fun and so undressed, mingled and made new constellations: The Missionary Position, The Satyr, Thor's Erection, The Three Tits, The Cunt and the Carrot... A timely obscenity well choreographed had the effect of instantly clearing the air of tensions and impurities. People's eyes would light up, and spirits surge. Of course, this was especially true in the pre-prandial phase: that is, before the digestive processes had set in. Once that happened, the atmosphere tended to thicken until finally we could be seen staring fixedly into the dying embers around midnight. Nobody saying a word anymore. At this terminal stage, when the day's palaver had died out, the fire once again gained the upper hand. Now, it would whisper, and now it would hiss; now it would break into a series of little explosions only to flare up a moment later and throw its light on the faces staring at it. It was on nights like this, I would sometimes think to myself that this fire was an ouverture to the gigantic fire which one day—in the not too distant future—was going to devour all lesser fires: that all consuming blaze turning the world we know into ashes.

First, we sank deeper into ourselves; then as night fell, one by one we dropped out of the circle and broke it up. One after the other, we would vanish into the darkness or disappear into our wagons, only to wake the next morning to a fresh heap of dead ashes in the very place where only a few hours earlier there had been a playful family of flames.

I must have been living in Christiania about a month when I met Christian. It was early in the afternoon, and the sun was shining from a cloudless sky. I was sitting by myself at the green plank table in the middle of the village when he came walking directly towards me. No angel's song announced his coming; no trumpet blew. It simply happened and that was it. Yes, that was *it*. We did not know ourselves what it was.

The Christian that came walking up to me on that day was French Christian, the one whose name ended in the chanting syllable 'ang'. The reason I mention it is so you don't confuse him with Danish Christian, who also lived in the Freetown, who was of the same age as us, but whose name rather than breaking into song abated into the very prosaic syllable of 'jan'. As I said, it was early in the afternoon. I was sipping some leftover Retzina wine and reading the current issue of the Christiania "Weekly Mirror".

Half an hour before, when I came up to the table, I had found a worn paperback copy of Carlos Castaneda's "A

Separate Reality" lying on it. Inside the back cover (which looked like one of Old Knud's rabbits had been nibbling at it), one of its previous owners had written the address of a certain Charles Chuck, who lived on "Old Street" somewhere in the world. And maybe this same person had been writing it by candlelight because there were splotches of wax here and there. Opening the book at random a dried brown leaf fell out and then—what do you know—between the pages 148-149 a little bird's feather appeared. Intrigued I looked closer and my eyes fastened on the paragraph where Don Juan says: "What makes us unhappy is to want. Yet if we would learn to cut our wants to nothing, the smallest thing we'd get would be a true gift."

Finishing the page and deciding to return to the book later, I had started to read "The Weekly Mirror". It was the usual unedited stew consisting of adds in longhand by foreigners who would like to live and work in Christiania, people advertising their losses like a boy's bicycle, a necklace, a baby carriage etc. There was also a long complaint by a woman who lived next door to a guy who pissed up against "her" tree and not his own. If it was because he had "a secret need" to show her his dick, all he had to do was tell her so. She would be pleased to look at it and admire its size… There were minutes from the area-meetings listing the names of those present and the decisions reached. There was an enthusiastic appeal from "Magdalene" to all christianites to show their love and spread it far and wide. If they did, it would start a movement that would grow like "ever expanding circles." There were the adds for meditation courses, tai chi and yoga. And, of course, the stock tale of violence: Some bikers belonging to the "Bullshit" group had unwittingly beaten up what they had taken for a chimney sweep breaking into their house – only to find out, after it was too late, that it was an undercover cop. The cop had shown them his badge and yelled at them to stop because he was a cop. All to no avail. Later, when the uniformed cops arrived, a pit bull bit one of them in the calf. In the end, the bikers were arrested, and stones were thrown at the police. And then (again), there was a Swede who had been robbed. It had happened behind the Opera building to one "fairly young and nobly dressed person of the male sex." Or so it said in the article. As it turned out, the thieves had been so sloppy that they had not even found what was most valuable. Afterwards, when some christianites offered to help, the Swede tried to run from them. They let him do as he pleased only he did not get very far. About fifty meters down the line he stumbled on a railroad tie, shit like hell in his pants and started fumbling around with his fingers in the excrement. It was only after he found a little bag with heroin in it that he drew a sigh of relief and let his helpers lead him out of Christiania. When the christianites took leave of him, he was standing on the sidewalk bag of heroin back up his ass, pants full of shit over the arm and waving at taxis with the other.

I had just finished reading this, when I heard footsteps. As I put down the "Weekly mirror," I saw a stranger approaching me. Hanging from his neck was one of those boards hawkers use when they work festivals. On display was the day's production of chocolate cakes, which Christian was on his way to deliver to the grocery shop, The Moonfisher Bar and The Loppen music-hall and restaurant—all of which were selling the cakes at five crowns a piece. He was looking for Jakob. There was something he needed to talk to him about. But since Jakob was nowhere to be found, and his eyes fell on me instead, he came up to the table and asked who I was. I told him my name, and we shook hands. Drawing a deep sigh, Christian took the board off and set it on the table. This accomplished, he sort of collapsed on the seat opposite me. Shaking his head and placing a hand on his heart, he muttered: "I'm in shock!" And before he had even told me his name, he laid the morning's story on me.

Even if it was hours ago since it happened, Christian's heart was still pounding like crazy. It went "boom-boom-boom," he said, right there in his chest.

"Okay, but…what *happened*?" I asked.

When Christian was done sighing and shaking his head and saying he would tell me about it, out it came helter skelter fashion and with a French word or phrase here and there. His French accent was so funny I had to bite my lip not to laugh. He was telling me about a certain Minna. Minna was a "more or less bedridden" morphine addict who had employed Christian to serve as a cross between a chambermaid and a handyman. She lived in a shack out in the Dyssen area, which was the long, narrow strip of Christiania on the other side of the moat. Today, Minna had thrown an axe at him with such force that it stuck in the wooden wall behind his left ear. He was sweeping the floor when it happened. It was a little before eleven o'clock, and he had just come back from an errand he'd run for her. Morphine, chocolate milk and two bags of crackers… Yes, I had heard right. Minna had given him authorization to pick up her morphine at the pharmacy. The reason she needed the "medicine" was to ease the pains caused by a chronic intestinal disorder. Christian did not need authorization to get the crackers and the chocolate milk, but Minna was no less addicted to those things than to the morphine. To function the way she did, Minna needed lots of morphine and also lots of salt-crackers and chocolate milk.

That was one of his jobs, Christian sighed: to be "esclave" for Minna the morphine addict. Every month, Minna would receive a sum of money from the city with which to buy assistance and morphine. Out of this money she paid Christian twenty crowns an hour to clean, cook, light the woodstove, run errands, deliver messages, fix things around the house and chop and stack wood. All in all, it amounted to anywhere between twenty and thirty hours a week, but Minna was a witch, a horrible *mégère*. She could never get enough help out of him for the money. She always found more things for him to do before he left. From the moment he stuck his head in the door, she would start screaming at him, and she would keep it up pretty much until he left. No matter how long he stayed or how hard he tried to please her, it did not matter. Not to Minna. Nobody could please Minna let alone appease her. Not even for a second. Not even morphine. It just wasn't possible.

"And you know what: she really really lazy." Christian loaded the last syllables with as much French disgust, as he could. She never even got out of bed. She just commanded Christian: "Chop some more wood!" "Pour me a chocolate milk!" "Wash the dirty plates!" "Sweep the floor behind the stove!" And oh-la-la if he ever dared do something on his own! Then, she'd shout: "NO, NO Christian! STOP THAT! DON'T OPEN THAT WINDOW! DON'T MOVE THAT VASE! DON'T THIS, DON'T THAT!"

And as if this wasn't enough, Minna could screech like a seagull! He lived in constant fear of that horrible sound. It was her ultimate weapon. When she let it out, he would freeze instantly and get goose pimples all over. Christian stared at me, pursed his lips and looked like he was about to scream himself. No, actually, it was more like a parrot. Had I ever heard a parrot scream? No! Well, for that I ought to be grateful. It was insane. Like being electrocuted or something. All the while, Minna was screaming and spouting cascades of saliva out her mouth—like a goddamn gargoyle when it rained hard—her dentures would clatter. And sometimes, the damned things fell out too. Then, hell broke loose… Blind with rage and hissing horribly, she got down on all fours and felt around for her teeth. But as soon as she had gotten the dentures back in place, she would begin to accuse Christian of stealing from her. Not money so much because she had sewn her money into her mattress so a thief couldn't get it. No, the things she said he ripped off were toilet articles, mosquito repellent and moisturizers. That sort of thing. Minna was fucking paranoid when it came to bacteria and cleanliness. If there was a spot of grease anywhere, she was sure she would catch the plague at the very least. That was very nice. And whenever something was missing, Christian had stolen it! Why wasn't she in a loony bin? The way she would make things up and throw tantrums when he wouldn't admit his crime. For example, the time he denied stealing her nail clippers. Christ all mighty, did she spout saliva! He had given them to his girlfriend and was lying about it to her face. That was what he had done, the fork-tongued little prick that he was.

Being of a kind and gentle disposition, Christian would usually bear with her. He felt sorry for her. Besides, he needed the dough. Still, it was a shitty job. The shittiest he'd ever had. I nodded. I should try to imagine, he said, how the crazed bitch would sometimes take a bread knife out of her bedside table and brandish it in the air. He had kind of gotten used to it. Of course, he never dreamed she would actually kill her chambermaid. It would be stupid even from the financial point of view. Minna got enough money from the city to pay her assistant seventy crowns an hour. She paid him twenty, and the rest she kept. He got a lousy deal. But what was there to do? He was a poor foreigner without a work permit. His girl friend didn't have money either. If only Minna would stop being so angry with him. Most days, it was bad but tolerable. Not today, though. Today, she had gone too far. *Twice* she had lost her dentures. Christian made a face, and a French sound that was something like "yhhllps" escaped him. He stopped speaking and stared at me.

For an entire minute, he just sat there and stared. Then, he went on: As usual she had wanted him to stay longer. And as usual, it was his own fault because he was lazy and slow and sloppy. He had not even taken the garbage out yet. Also, she wanted him to take the curtains down. They needed to be washed. And then, she wanted him to remove her bandage. The BANDAGE! Christian did not understand. For some reason, Minna had a running sore on her thigh up near the buttock. Christian sent me a look of utter disgust. That sore hurt his "aesthetic sense." he said. He had seen it once when he came in the door and caught her off guard. It looked like goddamned leprosy. So…nooo way! That was where he drew the line. That was not his job. Perhaps he was her chambermaid, but he was not her nurse. And it was while she was mumbling through her dentures about the wound that needed to be bandaged (because it was Thursday or some such horseshit) – and Christian was sweeping the floor by the wood stove three or four meters from the bed that suddenly he heard himself say the words, inadvertently to be sure and not loud at all, more like a whisper through clenched teeth: *"Tait toi mégère!"*

First there was no reaction. All was very very quiet. Then Minna made a sound like a parrot slamming its beak shut and turned her head his way. She looked at him. She was out of her mind with fury. "What! What did you say?" she screamed jerking herself into an upright position: "Did I hear you say 'shut up' and call me a slut and a witch? Did I?"

Christian had not been able to take his eyes off her. It was like he was hypnotized by the sheer horror of it. The narrow mouselike face, which was always pale, was *so* distorted. Her lips twitched. The light reflected in little drops of saliva in the corners of her mouth. It was so uncanny it sent shivers down Christian's spine. He'd had no idea that Minna understood French, or that there was such power in those thin arms of hers—not until the axe came flying at him with such force it was a miracle he managed to dodge it. An inch or two to the right and she would have cleaved his fucking skull. "All for twenty crowns an hour!" Christian sent me a puzzled look. He had set the broom down, dropped the dustpan and left without a word.

"Ca y est!" Christian said making a sweeping movement with his hand. But he still had not recovered. He was still in shock. His heart still pounded like crazy, and he was short of breath. That axe was the closest he had ever come to death. *La mort!* Closer than the time he was rescued from a burning building in Bordeaux. And back then he had been more dead than alive. Now, he wanted to resign from his job before it cost him his life. Unfortunately, he had to go see the witch one last time to inform her. It wouldn't be right not to do it. In a way, it really *was* worst for her…no?

"Why?" I said. "Why don't you just let her choke on her damn dentures? That's what I would do. I mean…the bitch tried to kill you!"

Christian looked at me sort of sad and not without disapproval either, as if I must be a very callous person to say something like that.

"No," he said finally. He wouldn't do that. After all, kindness *was* the one investment that never failed! It was Louis-Ferdinand Celine who had said that, and he believed it. Minna was in a bad way. She was a morphine addict and got very ill if she did not get her stuff. It was awful how she suffered. She deserved to choke on her dentures. I was right about that. But then, she was a human being, no! He would take his precautions though. When he got out there, he would disarm her first thing. He would use earplugs and even if she screamed her head off and lost her dentures, it would not do her any good. When he gave his notice, neither the bread knife nor the axe was going to be within her reach. Maybe then, it would be possible to talk to her.

"Do you think so?" I said, raising my eyebrows.

Christian waited a moment. Then, he shivered and said: "I very afraid of her." He looked at me somberly.

I nodded and said he had good reason to be. Then, I stretched out my hand: "Hey, what was it you said your name was?"

Christian smiled sort of ruefully and said his name. As it turned out, it was Jakob who got Christian the job. Minna was a relative of his—of Jakob, I mean. Before Christian, there had been some Irish dude, but he had only lasted a week. Christian would like to tell Jakob what had happened and that Minna no longer had anyone to get her medicine. He had thought that perhaps the young German singer with the flower tattoo on her butt would like to risk her life—the one who'd had polio, limped and recently moved into the small yellow dog's house facing the low garage buildings. She had what it took: She wasn't Danish. She didn't have any work permit, plus she was chronically broke. In any case, *he* was through. Not a minute longer was he going to serve.

"*C'est fini!*" Christian said making a face that left no doubt as to the finality of his decision.

It turned out Christian lived only about ten steps from me. He and his girlfriend Gitte occupied a narrow slice of the row of low Dandelion garage buildings to the north of the so-called City Hall. The garages turned their back to Grønnegade Street and my wagon. Originally, Christian came from the Ardeche region of France, but later, he had moved with his parents to St. Jean-de-Luz. He had been traveling with the Hare Krishnas in Sweden when he met the ten-year-older Gitte, who had curly blond hair and a *"tres tres mignon"* little daughter, Anna-Purna. Mother and daughter were living in Christiania and invited him to stay with them. That was about a year ago. It had been too much of a temptation for the young Krishna monk, especially after reading Hermann Hesse's "Siddhartha" about the spiritual quest in search of salvation that led the seeker away from all teachers and brought him back to himself. Had it not been for "Siddhartha," he probably would not have broken his celibacy and gone to Denmark.

Christian looked at me quizzically and asked if I had ever read it?

I said that I had not, but that I had come across the title in the work of Henry Miller.

"Ahh, oui!" Angree Mill-AIRE!" Christian looked very pleased, nodded several times and examined my face closely to see if it might be worth his while to say what was on his mind.

"Oui, Mill-AIRE!" he repeated a bit wistfully, Mill-AIRE was fine, sure he was, but… I really had to read that Hesse book. It might turn my life upside down, like it had his. The place that had made the greatest impression on Christian was where young Siddhartha met Gautama Buddha in the forest. Face to face with the Master himself, Siddhartha had declared it was not because there was anything wrong with Gautama's teachings that he had not become a disciple, no, it was because it was impossible to teach the truth—the truth being a revelation, which Buddha must himself have received ONCE WHEN HE WAS ALONE. A human being could inspire and perhaps lead someone else in the right

direction. That was all. The light could not be passed on directly. To come into the light, a man had to go the whole way alone. Only then would he achieve enlightenment and experience Nirvana. In the forest, the young Siddhartha met himself at a more advanced age and was encouraged. The older Siddhartha had not contradicted the younger one. He knew whom he had before him and that he understood time. With a smile and a blessing, he sent him on his way.

"*Ahh, merde!*" Christian lashed out with his hand. "The flies eating the chocolate cake. *Les saloppes*. Oh, well..." He rose to his feet and strapped his cake board back on. "*You eat one also,*" he said and nudged me with the board, "the tasting is good and even better than that."

"Better than what?"

"*Le vin!*" With a nod Christian indicated the Retzina bottle. "*Le vin* not is good for you."

"Hey, sannyasi," I thought. That will be my own business. But aloud I said: "Is it Vishnu, Shiva, Krishna or some other God, who told you that!"

Christian looked at me like an enlightened human being looks at someone still sunk in darkness—that is with profound compassion in his brown eyes: "If you drink the booze, the booze drink you!" And as if to illustrate what he meant, Christian made a gesture toward his crotch: "Then HE will LORD it over YOU! He fry you on his fire like fish! He make you squirm!"

I nodded: "Okay, then I'll squirm on the fire."

Christian started to walk away. Then, he stopped and turned around: "Come and visit me tomorrow evening and I'll cook for you, yes!"

I said I would love to. Christian said "*a bientot,*" smiled and turned once more.

From my place at the plank table, I followed his thin and not very tall figure as it disappeared with its mass of tangled hair held together with a red rubber band. It bobbed up and down with every step he took. "I'll be damned," I mumbled to myself and smiled, "if that isn't Siddhartha himself." There was something about the man I had just met, something spiritual, almost meditative and very sincere. There was (I can say that now) some of that uncompromising approach to life, which I was later to find in the figure of Siddhartha. Chocolate cakes or not, the man who was at this moment walking through The Wagon Village was a sannyasi. Even after Christian had disappeared, I kept seeing him before me. The emaciated face with unshaven cheekbones protruding like one would expect to find in a fanatical ascetic or anchorite.

That is how I saw Christian the first time I met him. But the next evening, it became clear that I had been wrong at least about one thing. Christian did not exactly live like the ascetic he looked like. Unlike an ascetic, Christian ate like an ox. His girlfriend and her daughter having left for a prolonged stay in The Thy camp, Christian had invited me for dinner in his slice of garage. At first, when I got there, I did not think anybody was home. I was knocking so hard the glass in the doorwindows rattled. But no one opened. After considering a while and noticing a big pot steaming on the stove with gas flames under it, I grabbed the door handle and went in.

The first thing I noticed was the sound of heavy breathing. It came from the wide sleeping platform under the ceiling. Ever so gingerly, I climbed the ladder and took a look around. Christian was meditating. He was half lying half sitting in an awkward position that pressed on his windpipe. His eyes were closed, and his face was red. It was hard to tell if he was aware of my prescence. The yogi was so concentrated he did not even once bat an eyelash. "Oh, well," I thought to myself, "I suppose he'll come down when he's done doing what he's doing."

I moved back down the ladder to a floor consisting of broad and very worn planks. The walls were whitewashed and with the exception of a little indentation just wide enough for a synthesizer, they were all covered with bookshelves. A substantial part of Christian's book collection consisted of Eastern philosophy and religion. There was a lot of Sufi literature, for example. There was also at least half a meter of Hesse's books. Opposite the living space there was the kitchen. The stove stood in the middle of the floor and made a sort of island. Next to the stove, the large yellow gas bottle had its place. And about a meter's distance from the stove, the kitchen table ran along three walls and defined the space for cooking. Hanging on the far wall, there was a huge sink full of dirty plates, cups, glasses and cutlery. Being curious, I walked to the stove and lifted the lid to see what was brewing. And no! It was not laundry. It was potatoes and carrots in such great abundance one would think Christian was expecting the entire Dandelion for dinner.

I put the lid back and once more turned to face the ladder. Its rungs were still without sign of Christian. Except for the hard breathing and the soft vaporous sound of water boiling, no sound was to be heard. I wondered when my new friend was going to join me. Perhaps he had lost all sense of time and thought I would come an hour earlier. Or maybe he was just waiting for the potatoes to be ready. I decided that this was the more probable explanation and went over to the bookshelves, where I picked out the "Siddhartha" in Danish. As was already then my custom, I opened the book at random and read the first bit of text my eyes happened to fasten on:

"He saw people living in a childish or animal-like way, which he both loved and despised. He saw them toiling, saw them suffer and grow grey about things that to him did not seem worth the price—for money, small pleasures and trivial honors;... his real self wandered elsewhere, far away, wandered on and on invisibly and had nothing to do with his life."

Another couple of minutes and Christian stuck his tousle-haired head out over the edge of the platform and looked down at me with an amused expression in his eyes. *"Bonjour Monsieur!"* he said with that nasal voice of his, whereupon his face lit up in a broad smile that he immediately shook off: *"Ahh, oui! Les potatoes!* I am forget!"

The moment Christian reached the potatoes happened to be the exact moment they'd had enough. It was no less than a small miracle that had occurred. And so was the meal...

During the course of dinner, we roamed far and wide. From Paris, we traveled to Peru, and from Peru to India where we stayed in an ashram as the guests of a guru I had never heard of before. Truly horrified at my ignorance of such matters, Christian took it upon himself to enlighten me. After telling me about the guru for half an hour, he related how he had become a Hare Krishna, complete with long orange robe, sandals and a tuft of hair in the back of his head; I listened to how he had studied The Bhagavad Gita (as it is) come down to us in the version and interpretation of His Divine Grace, A.C. Bhaktivedanta Swami Prabhupad. And when I confessed myself ignorant of The Gita, not to mention the Divine Swami, Christian got up and brought the book back to the table with him. "Look," he said opening it more or less in the middle, where there was an extraordinary picture of the Swami. Cross-legged, draped in a pink silk robe and with a flower wreath around his neck, His Divine Grace was sitting upright on a small red sofa that looked like an extremely uncomfortable piece of furniture. He was looking to one side while pretending to be hitting a cymbal ever so lightly with a small hammer studded with something that looked like pearls. Judging from his expression, the sky itself would come tumbling down if ever he farted.

"I loved eeem. I loved eeem!" It sounded almost like he was reciting some damn litany, the way Christian mumbled as he let his forefinger point out such details in the portrait that deserved my closest attention. And when he was done explaining the picture, he laid it on me just why he had loved the Swami and through him, Krishna. Among other things, he read a small bit taken from "Text nr. 13" in the Divine book:

"The first sign of a mahatma is that he is already rooted in divine nature. He is not controlled by material nature. For whoever surrenders to the godhead Sri Krishna's all mighty personality, is at once freed from control by the material nature... The living being makes up the marginal force of the Lord, the meaning of which is that as soon as he is freed from control by material nature, he is subjected to divine nature instead..."

It was relevant for me too, I said to Christian, especially the part about not being controlled by material nature anymore. That had also been my direction even if I had approached it from a different angle. In my wagon, I had a text called "The Transmigration of the Seven Brahmins." It was a photocopy, and for some reason, the name of the author was not included. So I could not be sure who had written it. Still, in my head the name of Henry David Thoreau kept popping up. Thoreau, I said, had probably made as great an impression on me, as Hesse's "Siddhartha" had on him. The reason I thought Thoreau was the author of "The Transmigration of the Seven Brahmins" was the fact that he had taken a keen interest in the religion and philosophy of the East. He had been sort of a Mahatma of the Occident. If there was ever a soul who had been rooted in "Divine nature," it was Thoreau. Thoreau was an example of an occidental belonging to our age, who had been liberated from the control of "Material Nature." Perhaps it would be a good idea for him, Christian, to look into it. If he liked Hesse, he would surely like Thoreau too. I would recommend that he start out with Thoreau's most famous book *Walden*. Thoreau was born in 1817. His grandparents were of the preindustrial world, and he himself lived to see that the "natural" world, he loved, was about to be destroyed by the very "Material nature" Krishna wanted to free us from. And sure enough! It was only thirty some years after he died in 1862, at the age of forty-five, that the first automobile running on fossil fuel burst upon the scene. From that moment on, we all know the rest of the story.

Christian rested his head on his hand and listened as if he were cogitating. And since he didn't react to my speech in any way, I came close to telling him what had made the greatest impression on me that evening. It was not so much the years Christian had spent with Krishna as the fact that he had single-handedly eaten one half of a large codfish, two kilos of potatoes, two heads of cauliflower, two loaves of French bread and five fried onions all in the course of a meal that so far had lasted an hour and forty-five minutes. At some point, while Christian was still eating (and I had long since stopped), I looked at him and said it seemed to me he ate like an ascetic who had not seen food for weeks or even months. "Absolutely!" Christian smacked his lips and wiped his mouth with the back of his hand. The "strong" appetite was the only "eritage" from his father. Nodding, I could not resist the temptation to say that if I were in his shoes, I would have a doctor examine me to make sure it was not the appetite of a monster tapeworm he had inherited. Such a huge, gluttonous and growing son-of-a-bitch that he would always have to sell more and more chocolate cakes to feed.

"What!" Christian looked at me over his raised fork with a piece of codfish hanging from it. His face one big question mark: "Tapeworm!"

"Uh-huh," I said and opened my arms as wide, as I could to suggest its length. *Exactement Monsieur*. Tapeworm this big. Tapeworm in Anglais!"

At first Christian (whose English was just about good enough to understand the word "tape") thought that what he had inside him had something to do with cassette tapes. It wasn't until he looked up the word "tapeworm" in his English-French dictionary that he comprehended. Standing by the book shelf, he turned and looked at me: "*Ahh, mais oui: VER SOLITAIRE! NON, NON,* not at all. I eat not all day and all day I use energy. Very much of energy. So…no, no!"

Christian put the dictionary back, returned to the table and sat down. After about a minute, his face lit up in that same big happy smile that he had flashed at me when he first stuck his head over the edge of the sleeping platform. And since he kept smiling, I figured there was perhaps something he wanted to tell me. That is if he could get himself to do it. I cocked my head to one side and waited.

Finally, he made a quick decision: The other day, he said, he had gone into in a new Turkish restaurant on Havnegade Street. It was around noon, and he went in because there was a sign on the sidewalk advertising a gigantic all-you-can-eat buffet. There were twenty-five courses for only forty-nine crowns. Because of the "strong" appetite he had inherited, Christian explained, he was always on the look-out for new restaurants that would open with this sort of offer. What the sign had said about the twenty-five courses turned out to be true. He knew because he had counted them. And very delicious they were too. Having the place to himself and praising his own good luck, he loaded one plate after another and proceeded to "taste a little bit of everything." Fine cook, nice waiter and loads of delicious food all tastefully arranged in round, deep and oblong dishes. What more could a heart, no...a belly ask for? Everything went swimmingly. Christian had just wiped his mouth with the white, freshly ironed and starched napkin; he had just (once again) thanked his lucky stars for leading him to the restaurant Ankara; he had just made a solemn resolution to come back soon; yes, and he had just returned from the buffet for the seventh time with a full plate when the head waiter or the owner or just some fat Turk in a black silk shirt with buttons that looked about to burst came out of the kitchen and walked up to his table. It was not because they were angry or anything, the Turk said. No, on the contrary they were honored that Christian liked their food so much. But...enough was enough. Christian had now filled his plate nine times. NINE TIMES! Repeating these two words, the Turk was showing Christian nine fat fingers with rings on every single one of them. "No, just seven!" Christian held up seven fingers. "Just seven!" "No...NINE!" The Turk didn't budge. And nine was a few too many. "Finish, caput!" the Turk said and illustrated his words with a telling gesture. "Finish, caput!" Christian didn't have to pay. All he had to do was stop eating and get out.

It took a few moments before it dawned on Christian what had happened, that as a matter of fact, the Turk had kicked him out. But when it *did* dawn on him, boy did he get pissed. He jumped up, ran to the neighboring table, pointed to it and said: "Is anybody sitting eeeer maybe?" He then proceeded to make a round to all the empty tables, pointing his finger at each one of them and flinging the same question at the Turk. And when there were no more tables left to point at, he had run to the buffet, where he pointed to the dish with stuffed cabbage leaves: "Is anything left eeeer... maybe?" he asked sarcastically. Well, how come then they put a sign in the street advertising that he could eat as much as he wanted to, when he could not at all? When, in fact, he was kicked out after only six platefuls? Yes, and...before he was even full yet. Was that right? No, that was not right! And he, the Turk, knew that very well himself. Was *that* a way to treat a customer? Or to advertise? No. If that was how it was, then they must advertise that people would get kicked out after the sixth refill...

Christian had argued his case well, but to little avail. The Turk was unmoved. While Christian was protesting, he had moved in close and was maneuvering the indignant customer in the direction of the door with his big fat belly.

Christian sent me an offended look: "They write that I can eat all I want, and then they kick me out... *C'est ne pas juste!*"

I had to agree. That really was no way to treat a Frenchman. The Turks were a bunch of assholes. If one could not eat as much as one wanted in their restaurant, then that is what they should tell people on their goddamn sign in the street. Those lousy Turks ought to be locked up.

The evening progressed, and we found things to do. At one point, Christian shared with me how he and Gitte practiced tantric sex following a method of ancient Hinduism. It had been "ard" in the beginning, he said, very "ard," and a few times he had spouted all over the place. But now, he had learned to hold back. Now, he could hold it as long as he wanted to. It was great because it made him "strong as an ox." During intercourse, it was almost like time stood still. In a huge Hindu book, which Christian produced from a corner, he showed me details from the erotic decorations of temples. In one place, a woman was practicing transcendental meditation with the man's cock in her. Later, Christian played some "kama sutra music" that he had composed for erotic use in the garage.

It was all very instructive and when daybreak came, it found us flat on our backs next to one another on the plank floor. It was time for me to go home to my wagon a few steps away. But before I left, Christian talked me into joining him on a fishing trip to a pond in Northern Zealand. He was going with Gitte's brother who knew about fishing. The pond was located right in the middle of a farmer's field. Still, it was worth the risk because there were some "monstrous" pike in it. The last time he had gone with Gitte's brother, they had caught one each. And the fish, oh boy, did they taste good baked with garlic, parsley, asparagus and chives...

This was more or less the lay of the land. It, the land, had made its bed and was lying on it. Christian the Frenchman, Christian the Dane, Melanie, Lili, Jakob, Old Knud, Fanny—we were all there in the very same bed we had made for ourselves and for one another. Nights when I was waiting in my wagon for the girl I was with to finish peeing out in the back. In the rain, sleet, snow or nettles all depending on the season. After making love, it felt good to imagine her ass pressed close against Mother Earth; it felt good with my inner ear to hear the hissing sound of hot pee squirted from a crack still hot and steaming from my visit. To be waiting in a cozy wagon listening to the little sounds she made, just to lie there until there was the sound of her bare feet stuck in my black clogs on the little two-step staircase and she proceeded to stomp into the middle of the room.

It also belongs to this story that I had been divorced not

long ago, and that before I bought the wagon, I had not been with a woman for over nine months. It was almost like women could smell it on me: Here was a guy who had been abandoned by one of their gender. Still, when the quarantine ended, there was no more problem. Six weeks in Christiania and my dick was pissing in public and screwing again in private. Six weeks, that's all! It's kind of strange, I think. What got into the girls? What ever did they *see* in me? I was hardly what you would call a good match. Aside from the shack I lived in, I didn't have a damn thing. And I didn't even own that! All I had was a user's right to it. According to the unwritten code of law in Christiania, if I wanted to sell my wagon the maximum I was allowed to charge was a thousand crowns, less than what I had paid for it. What I had invested along the way did not count at all. Add to this, that I lived from hand to mouth, that I had quit the university, and that I was absolutely devoid of any ambition in life, except that of becoming the author of novels that sowed strife and unsettled all things stable. And as far as this last item is concerned, my ambition, well, I don't suppose the girls would have found that very attractive, should they have known about it. What they saw was a guy who had to drive a taxi once or twice a week depending on his immediate financial situation. But who knows? If they could smell the abandoned man in me, perhaps they could also smell the glorious future awaiting him. I don't suppose it could be ruled out.

That sort of thing—like women's reasons for attraction or the opposite—will, I think, always be inscrutable. But needless to say, the interest they took in me flattered me all the more, because I ascribed it to something immaterial that had to do with my charming personality. When the women came to see me, it was because I was so irresistible, they just couldn't help themselves. Aside from Lili, who attended a private school for street performance and clowning and who worked in a café in Gothersgade Street across from the King's Gardens, there was also (at least for a short while) sixteen-year-old Fanny. When she didn't come fluttering by at any old hour of the day and night or was being serviced by other hounddogs around the neighborhood, she was saving up for a circumnavigation of the Globe by serving drinks in The Moonfisher Bar and selling Danish pastry in the bakery on Christianshavn Square. Yes, and then there was Melanie. A little bit anyway. But since she's the only one to have survived in my life to this day, I would rather save her story for the right time and place. Here, I want to speak only of the transient and the temporary. Like Kristin, for example, the redhead with the muscular calves and tufts of hair in the armpits, who after having given birth to a daughter and being abandoned by the father, an out-and-out scoundrel, began to pay me visits when her little Isabella was asleep in the rusty baby carriage with its big wobbly wheels that squeaked right until it was parked outside my door. I could just see it: how in the middle of the day Kristin would be pushing the carriage back and forth, back and forth down on Langgade Street, waiting only for "Sweetie pie" to fall asleep, so she could squeak directly down Grønnegade Street to my wagon.

Squeak, squeak, squeak. I'll be damned if I know why she did not grease those wheels, or how "Sweetie pie" managed to fall asleep to the sound of them. It was downright hair-raising. And me! Being the creep I am I never offered to do it for her. Greasing the wheels, I mean. Thing is, the god awful sound was useful to me. Had it not been for that sound, I would not have known when she was on her way. It was what put me on the alert. The moment I registered the first tiny squeak off in the distance, I would either get a hard on or panic depending on the situation. As if spellbound I would freeze and listen to it grow as it came closer and closer. Yes, the damn sound would grow in force with every step she took. But at the same time as it was horrible, it was also what was good about that old rustheap of Kristin's. Warning me when she was on the prowl, it gave me a chance to make my escape, if that was what I needed, or *thought* I needed rather, because one time when I had hurried up on the rampart and was hiding behind a tall tree, she made me suffer the disgrace of having to listen to her calling my name from *inside* the wagon. And she didn't just call in a low voice either, as she would have done, if she had thought I was hiding under the desk or behind the woodstove. No, she was downright hollering. Like she didn't even give a shit if she woke "Sweetie pie" or anything, and like she was not standing in a tiny wagon but in some goddamn mansion full of niches, corners, canapés, high ceilings and what not. It would have been insane if it were not for the fact that she knew very well what she was doing. I mean that she was torturing me. It was her way of telling me that she knew where I was and that I was a detestable little prick for not showing myself. Hell, if I knew why I felt that way, but suddenly I was ashamed. I really was. I was so goddamned ashamed in fact that I would have run down to her if only it would not have looked so stupid. Oh, well, but if I chose to stay put, to be trapped in my cage, which is what I normally did, right until the crazy squeaking sound came to a stop, I would just sit there listening to Kristin kick the carriage-break down and wait for the knock on my door. It never failed that she knocked ever so lightly, as if she was timid or chaste or bashful or something else of that sort. Or like she was doubtful of her right to intrude on me. In reality, of course, she was none of those things. She was just the opposite. But still, she kept knocking in that way, just like she was. I knew what was coming and what was expected of me. I knew it was a *fait accompli* and that it was all over with whatever I had been doing. I knew I was going to take the woman just the way she was with impatient cunt, Sweetie pie's vomit on her shoulder and a cotton diaper tucked into her bra. It was a package deal.

"Come in," I would say.

"Schyyh, Sweetie pie is sleeping," she'd whisper as she stepped in and pulled the t-shirt over her head. Kristin never stopped to find out if I felt like it or not. She pulled off the t-shirt, pressed against me and trusted her boobs to clear the way. And then, when she was standing there with no clothes on, a bit of red hair showing at the armpit, she would look at me in the swivel chair and say to me in a phoney husky voice: "If you want me buster, you better get a move on!"

That's how she would go about it, and that's what she would say. It was my lot "to get a move on." She would say it just like that and in a tone like she knew precisely what I had been sitting there waiting for. She herself had a tremendous move on, that's for damn sure. Before I could even count to ten, she would be ready. Which in a way is understandable. I mean, after all there was no telling when Sweetie pie would wake up out there in the rust heap. Sweety pie really had something to say. She had clout. A wail from the *pie* spelled the end of the proceedings. The prospect used to unnerve me like hell. Pie was the unknown quantity of the equation. No matter how hard I tried to drive the thought away, I couldn't help but hesitate a little. It had happened before that Pie had started up, just as foreplay was over and excitement was reaching its climax. And I must say, if there is any one thing that can extinguish my flame it's that: the terrible sound of a baby letting go just six-seven meters away. The effect could not have been greater if somebody had tickled my feet. Instantly, I sobered up and saw things clearly. But odd as it may sound, it used to have the effect of an aphrodisiac on Kristin. The moment she heard the first and sort of muffled little wail coming from the carriage, she knew that now was the time to bring the concert to its crescendo. She gave off a loud whimpering sound, grabbed me by the hips with her hands and started to jerk me as hard as she could towards her; and she would go on jerking and whimpering till we both came together, and…Sweetie pie, of course, was screaming her head off outside.

As you can tell, Kristin wasn't especially tantric in her approach. For her, there was a time for fornication and a time for breast-feeding. Redhot like an old wino in the face, she would jump down from my bed; and without bothering about the guided tour passing by at that moment, she would run to Sweetie pie, lift her out and shove one of her still hard nipples into her mouth. Peace restored Kristin would begin to dress. First, she put on the bra and the napkin. How she managed to dress at the same time, as she was breastfeeding I never could figure out. But five-six minutes later, she would be fully dressed. A bit messier than before perhaps, but dressed never the less. She would come to me, give me a quick kiss and be on her way again.

Squeak, squeak, squeak. Lying there wasted on the bed the sound in my head grew smaller and smaller as it moved away down Grønnegade Street. If I'd had the energy I would have been impatient for the moment it was drowned out by the other Freetown sounds and my head was once again free of it. Only then would I raise my head and look around me. What now? Even if the whole thing had only taken twenty minutes or so, nothing was the same any longer. Things could not have changed more if a hurricane had hurled everything up into the air and set it back down. Everything was in its place and yet everything was somehow wrong. I could not for the life of me remember what I had been doing before the hurricane struck. Not that it mattered much, since I didn't feel like doing a damn thing anymore anyway. All I was capable of was putting on a pair of pants, lighting a cigarette and sitting in the open door. There, I would sit and smoke and study my toes. I felt so goddamned plundered and pillaged I knew it would be at least another hour before I got over it.

I'll give her *that*, Kristin. That she was one hell of a tough cowgirl from Jutland. She knew what she wanted, went for it and...got it or did not get it. She took what she could get and did not begrudge what she could not. If, for example, Lili's bike was leaning against the side of the wagon when she arrived, and the door was bolted, she would go to the window, press her nose against the glass, cut some hair-raising grimaces, roll her eyes in their sockets, stick her tongue out at me and go away. Squeak, squeak, squeak. The old baby carriage would let out its lament for the benefit of the snails on the asphalt, the squirrels on the rampart, the rabbits in Old Knud's cages and the dreams in Sweetie pie's virgin soul. Perhaps she would stay away a week, but it also happened that she gave it a go a couple hours later. It was all somewhat hormonal, as it were. In a way, it worked out fine too. And the same is true for Frauke, the defected—and somewhat defect—East German girl I had met for the first time on the bridge leading across the moat, where she was standing with a little baby bird in her hands. I hate to say it, but without comparison, Lili was the one causing most trouble. If Lili happened to find Kristin's baby carriage outside my door when she came by on her tall grandmother bicycle, she didn't just make faces, stick her tongue out and leave. No, then the door had to be torn open, and the first thing she could get her hands on had to be smashed against the concrete foundation. Before leaving, she would call me all sorts of nasty epithets and slam the door as hard as she could.

But let's be fair. In a way, I understand her. When Lili went on the rampage, she did it because she was both the first and the steadiest of the girlfriends I'd had since my quarantine came to an end. For a short while, she was the only chicken on the roost, and so secured for herself what she decided amounted to exclusive property rights. Being the first to take pity on me after my divorce, she felt I must belong to her until death did us part. I looked at it differently. Having recently come back from the land of the dead, I was not able to commit myself. Instead, I practiced the principle of first come, first served.

Had it not been for Lili I think the principle would have worked fine. However, when it came to the rampages, principles were somehow irrelevant. Once when she caught me walking down the street with another woman, she attacked and bit me so hard in my hand that I had to go to the emergency clinic to have my thumb sewed. But again, let's be fair. When Lili loved me, she did so without limit and reservation. If I didn't always know how to behave, it was because I wasn't finished yet paying for the broken promises of the past. To Lili, the price didn't matter. To get what she wanted and what she felt her love gave her the right to, she was ready to pay anything. With no second thoughts, she gave all she had to give. If necessary, she would juggle my glasses and empty the contents of her purse on my desk. For a time, she had been a carpenter's apprentice and so knew how to use her hands. Before I moved in, she helped me build the kitchen, set up the dividing wall, make shelves under the bed, install the wood stove, put up the chimney and construct the little extra window over the bed at the far end of the room. She also offered to go fetch water in the big plastic bottle with a tap at the bottom that was standing on my kitchen table and which I used when I needed to wash my hands, get tap water for coffee and brush my teeth. Or she gladly volunteered when I needed to fetch a fresh gas-bottle in The Green recycling hall. To make an old wagon ready for human habitation in a climate like Denmark's is not a simple matter. It takes time and skill. Had it not been for Lili, I would never have been able to pull it off. I am extremely impractical and hate building and fixing things. Knowing myself, I would probably have stopped working on the wagon as soon as I was able to keep warm. I would have slept on the floor and buttered my rye bread sandwiches on the desk. I would have lived like a savage. Perhaps like a savage with literary ambitions, that may be, but nevertheless like a savage.

Even with the help of Lili, life in the wagon never got to be very comfortable. But as it always remained simple and wholesome, as it was always satisfying for the senses, there was a lot to be grateful for. Despite the fact that its wheels were hanging twenty to thirty centimeters above ground, it gave me the feeling of independence that my soul needed. It aroused a slumbering nomad in me that I never knew was there. Thanks to the wagon and The Freetown Christiania where it was chocked up, fresh shoots were grafted onto my life's tree. No longer constricted, I was open, receptive and at peace with the world. Mornings, I weighed anchor only to stay adrift on a boundless sea until the evening, when the sky turned orange and purple in the west and I was washed ashore on desert islands in my dreams. Even if my vessel did not have a rudder and was at the mercy of the elements, I still had a feeling that now it was *me* who set the course of *my* life.

Amiel's school is only a block away, and the friends never

more than a shout. Returning this morning at eleven, he pitched his schoolbag over the fence and was off to play with the kids in the street. I watched him from the window. The guy is so busy living he forgets to eat. How many of us can say the same? Now he is asleep in his room paving the way for tomorrow with his dreams. How can I even think of taking him away from this island? He has a good life here. The village school teaches him the elementary skills like reading, writing, spelling and simple arithmetic. Not to mention the singing and dancing that goes on. That only takes three—at the most—four hours in the morning. The rest of his time belongs to the street. The street teaches him the other lessons he needs to learn. A derivative of these lessons is learning to play the accordion. Besides being a fisherman, his buddy Louis' father is an accomplished accordionist who performs either alone or with his orchester at practically every celebration and festival on the coast. It was only a couple months ago that The Duke—that is what the man is called—brought an accordion to our house and told me I could have it for ten dollars. Amiel was standing right behind him, and I didn't have much choice in the matter. Not that I had any objections. The instrument was a good one, and the price a bargain. When he saw the bill disappear into The Duke's gnarly hand, Amiel rushed up to me jumped and hung on me like a monkey.

I never cease to wonder at that kid. The voracious appetite of his for raw life reminds me of my own beginnings. It fills my heart with joy. The other day, as I was standing in the big window watching his buddy Louis and him turn in the wind and race in the direction of the sea, it struck me that this was the way it ought to be. If the fire isn't raging real hard in childhood, how, then, will it survive when pitiless life begins to heap tons of refuse on it in the form of disappointment, defeat and inane demands? How, then, prevent it from producing that black and poisonous cloud that all too often blocks out the sun? Standing there by the window watching the boys, I asked myself how my own fire was faring?

Something stirred in me this morning when the carrier brought me the letter from Melanie. I was returning from my usual walk with Saroyan, my dog, when the huge black woman drove up on her moped and put the letter in my box.

I had just been *thinking* of Melanie—of how we met many years ago. There is nothing surprising in that. Telepathy is indisputably happening. I thought a lot about her in the years right after we had met, and I got a lot of letters. But I dare say that since I started in on this story, she has made one hell of a come back. I recall how on that particular morning I parked the taxi on The Halmtorvet Square, settled accounts with Nielsen the owner and rode my bike back to the wagon. At the same time, Melanie woke up in the house of her parents-in-law in Jutland. The first thing she thought of was the trip she was taking that day to Copenhagen. She was going to be away from the family three days. *Three* days. She had never been away from the kids for such a long time. But what was three days as compared with the history of time from the Cretaceous period up to today?

How was Melanie to know that she and I were destined to meet that very evening? And how was she to know what the meeting would mean for us in a future just waiting to be gobbled up by pitiless life and transformed into excrement?

Walking there with Saroyan, I saw it right away: the long white envelope in the hand of the black woman, gleaming in the sun before she stuck it in the box. I had to control myself not to walk faster. That's half the pleasure: forcing myself to keep calm and continuing at the same slow pace.

In the letter (which has been stamped in Hawaii), Melanie writes that she is visiting three weeks with her daughter, son-in-law and newborn grandchild. She is working on getting used to living with four people in a very small space. It's not easy because she's accustomed to so much room at home in New Mexico, where she lives alone with her cat and her own sweet self. How she loves her great atelier in the company of the easels, the tubes of paint, the art books and all the brushes. Not to mention the paintings, of course—the finished ones and the unfinished ones both. Just to sit there looking and being still within. It is quite trying, she writes, being grandma instead and crammed into a small and humid hut with insects so far from it all.

Having read Melanie's letter twice and taking note of the usual questions, I fell for the temptation to get on the net and have a look at the Danish newspapers. And what do I see? Why, today is Christiania's birthday. September 26th, thirty-eight years ago a group from the anarchist newspaper "The Talisman" visited the all but abandoned Boatman Street garrison later to publish a center-fold article with the title: "Civilians Conquer Forbidden City of the Military." In the article, it also said that the Danish authorities had come up with an "ultimate offer" as a "very unwelcome contribution to the festivities going on in the Freetown." The birthday present to The Freetown of Christiania amounted to an ultimatum: Either the christianites chose to normalize themselves voluntarily (giving up their local autonomy and the shared user's rights to property), or they must accept being normalized by force. To make it easier for them to reach the right decision, the "ultimate offer" was sweetened with a big bag of money to be invested on compliance. Also, the offer included a promise to provide new homes outside Christiania for those who had built their own houses on the ramparts and along the moat, since these "illegal structures" were to be torn down.

If I'd had any illusions left, I would have shaken my head in wonder at this news. The Danish authorities wanted to tear down the life-work of living people and citizens of today in order for the ramparts of a long gone absolute monarchy to be returned to their former glory—that is with no houses and only a very few trees and bushes. As for the rest of the christianites, the ones that already belonged to the Freetown's upper class, not only are these people allowed to stay, they are also tempted to betray their brethren because they stand to gain a "contractual lease" on their homes. Then, there is the offer to invest "massively" in "creative" and "visionary" housing developments in Christiania. A private fund with a purely altruistic purpose and billions in its coffers has announced its interest in buying all the building rights. If Christiania accepts, the authorities and the wealthy members of the fund's board of directors guarantee that the changes will be carried out in full accordance with "the spirit of Christiania." The objective of this entirely unwelcome agenda and the threatening rhetoric, so it is stated, is once and for all to legalize the Freetown. It is for this purpose that the shared user's rights are to be replaced by housing associations, complete with chairmen, executive committees, waiting lists etc.

Of course, the reading of this article put me in a lousy mood. I looked up from the screen and far out the window towards the blue sea in the distance. The waves were white capped and by the coastal road that runs on the other side of my yard, the palmtrees were bending in the strong wind. Why did I also have to read that crap? As if the Danish state had something to offer Christiania and not the other way around. As if the state apparatus had any right to destroy people's attempt at an alternative way of life in the name of its arbitrary law.

Sitting there staring out over the sea, I felt my curiosity increase in proportion with my uneasiness. Of all things in my homeland, Christiania is what means most to me—more than family, school, environment, parliament, constitution, Queen, Mermaid and national hymn. I really am a Dane only in so far as I was born in the country and—before I was able to protest—was given that particular nationality and personal identity number. Christianite, on the other hand, is something I chose to be when I came of age and was able to think for myself. On the epic day in 1971 when "The Talisman" encouraged people to emigrate to the abandoned garrison and establish an alternative society based on different values and an altogether different mind set, I was only sixteen. Spending a year as an exchange student with a family in Palo Alto California, I never even heard the news. But when a few years later, I was trapped back in Copenhagen and badly in need of a place such as Christiania, there it was only a short bike ride and a wagon away.

Beyond any disappointment I may still harbor, there is a realization that Christiania is as Danish as smoked eel. And above all, I am grateful that Christiania was *there* for me when I needed it. What Copenhagen is to the inmate at the city's notorious Western Prison, Christiania is to the Copenhagener. Some need the limitations imposed on them by the authoritarian state; others have to break free of them because they need to come up against their own. It was not until I moved out of the city of Copenhagen that my claustrophobic tensions eased, and I was able to piss in public again. It was not until I moved into the wagon that I learned to worship and adore a different way of life than the one I grew up in and used to accept at face value. There had been the indoctrination that is education and the so-called necessary adaptation to circumstances and bureaucratic institutions. Unaware that that was what I was doing,

I removed myself from the media-generated din in order to hear the voice of my intuition again. The transformation happened at all levels at once. It amounted to nothing short of a conversion, and my life has never been the same again. In some mysterious way, Melanie had something to do with it. If it didn't sound so damn kitschy, I would say that what happened between us was like a strong light shining through a wall of darkness. It all occurred in the matter of a split second. Was it to work this miracle that she came into my life? To bring me the light? Was it her doing that it penetrated to my innermost being? Or did I open to it myself? I don't suppose I will ever know. Every so often Melanie still appears to me like she did on that morning, when with her usual flair for special effects she stood in the narrow doorway, the morning when, from the vantage point on my bed, I took her in as if haloed by the sun.

Christiania's birthday, the so-called offer on the part of the authorities, and Melanie's letter from Hawaii—all these things had opened the yellowed photo album of my mind exactly to the page where the pictures from Christiania's ten years anniversary celebration are forever inserted. On that day, one of the items on the agenda was a dog show. This epic event took place in the open area in front of The Grey Hall. Ninety percent of all dogs in Christiania were owned by pushers, and ninety percent of all pushers owned dogs. Not known for any great cleanliness neither dogs nor pushers enjoyed much popularity among the rest of the populace. People were sick and tired of the growling and snarling monsters and the aggressive and psychopathic pushers who never kept them on leashes. Not to mention the drag it was returning home with dog shit under your shoes. The turds were scattered all over the place, and since there were no streetlights, one invariably stepped in them. Aside from being fed up with having to remove the smelly excrement stuck in every groove of their footwear, people had had enough of drooling dogs fighting at the communal meetings or when a film was shown in The City Lights movie theatre. And then, I have not even mentioned all the incidents where people had gotten bitten by the monsters.

It was like this every day except for *that* day. On the ten-year-birthday, the atmosphere surrounding the population of dogs was not so much one of violence and aggression as one of fraternization. The entire place was in a state of jubilation. "We have survived! We have survived! For ten years!" That's how people felt. Quite beside ourselves, we were euphoric with relief, joy and pride. It was the Free-town celebrating itself. It was the celebration of freedom. Even if the warring factions of the Freetown, the pushers, the gays, the heteroes and the various groups of activists, loved it for their own very different reasons (reasons that for the most part collided with one another) on this day, people were disposed as to settle their disputes. For once, they were united in their wish to pay tribute to a Freetown, which through its own unique alchemy helped its lovers to satisfy their desires no matter what these happened to be. The red flag of Christiania with its three large yellow suns was up and fluttering in the wind. And so was the general mood. People greeted one another with smiles and reached out their hands across old grudges. The miser paid a round, old debts were annulled; arguments and threats were forgotten. Even the dogs were miraculously transformed from menaces and manufacturers of shit into a charming college of cute pets and clowns. A glance at one of the foulest, scummiest and notoriously vile curs in its washed, combed and decked out state complete with a big red flower behind its ear and peoples' hearts melted. The Christiania girl's marching band was warming up with majorettes, drumbeats, fanfares and physiognomies so incongruous in their freshly ironed uniforms that the sight of them had the spectators in stitches. People were cheering and clamoring and commenting loudly on everything from the hairdos of the marching girls down to the way their buttocks or breasts sagged or bulged. The focus of everybody's attention, the prize that all dog owners had a burning wish to win was a gigantic gilded turd. The coveted trophy was set out on exhibit on a high podium from where it reflected the rays of the sun, shone like the purest gold and blinded the euphoric public to such a degree that it never—not even for a moment—dared let it out of sight. Here was something with the power to bring people together in a common endeavor: The Golden Turd! Many of the hash pushers—people who normally didn't have a great deal of control over their pets—had been training them for weeks on a daily basis. Some had even spent part of their riches on manicuring the beasts. Others had hired assistance from dog trainers and circus people. Up on its podium the turd almost outshone the sun itself; down on the ground, the "best friend" of the pusher had never looked better. Some of the ugliest mongrels had had their fur dyed and some even sported brand new breeches. A few of the bitches had make-up on. Had it not been for the fact that the event took place under the open sky in front of The Grey Hall in Christiania, one might have thought it was not a dog contest coming up but the Oscar Awards.

Expectations were sky high and so was the crowd. Everything was now ready, including a jury remarkable even by Christiania's standards. Bums, drunks, villains and dope heads. Groomed representatives of the male as well as the female genders, all displaying such dignified and solemn comportment you would think the dog contest was some international conference. Between drum rolls, the names of the participants were called: Rufus, Jack the Ripper, King Kong, Wizard, Rascal etc. And I'll be damned if there wasn't a Moses too. Every time a name was called a mad concert broke out, during which the next unbelievable participant was dragged, carried or pushed into the arena. Once in the spotlight, the proud owner would greet the audience with shouts and gestures. Then followed the number that he and his dog had prepared. There was a pusher with a wooden leg who had trained his longhaired cur to snarl and attack the leg with drool flying from its mug as soon as it heard him whisper the word "cop." Another had taught his dog to bite a hole in the butt of a stuffed version of the Prime Minister. The jaws closed and a mix of straw, goat shit and something that looked like white tablets came tumbling out pell-mell. Yet another had trained his fighting dog to smoke hashish from a long glass pipe. When it had inhaled its portion of high quality black afghan and had munched a dog biscuit, it sort of stumbled sideways a couple times and keeled over. ONE, TWO, THREE, FOUR. The owner started counting over the dog like it was a boxer that had just been knocked out. At ten, he snapped his fingers as a sign to his helpers to bring the stretcher. A little later, the stoned animal was carried out of the arena to the sound of more drum rolls, more cheering and more whistling.

There were many good numbers, but for me, the most significant, not to say harrowing, was the one where "The Fat Bastard" didn't react to the torrents of abuse that the bald owner with tattoo-covered biceps kept pouring on its head. The Fat Bastard couldn't care less if he screamed his head off and cursed it into hell itself. Ignoring him, the animal simply turned around on the spot two or three times, arched its back, made some spasmodic movements with its hind legs and (to the accompaniment of a deafening roar from the audience) squeezed out a huge turd. Apparently too preoccupied with his performance, waving and shouting inanities to the crowd, the owner was backing up in direction of the turd. "Watch out, there's a turd behind you!" a kid shouted. "Waaatch out or you'll step in it!" another kid yelled. But see if the pusher would listen. Deaf and blind to anything except his act, he kept right on until he stepped in the turd. Flying into a rage, he turned to his dog and began to hurl curses at it. Not knowing if the punishment of the dog was part of the show, the audience fell silent. It was only when the pusher after a few seconds, bent down and gave the dog a friendly slap on its back, and then, smiling to the audience, took off his shoe and hurled it into the crowd that we realized it was intended. Immediately, another deafening roar broke out, and this time it didn't seem to ever stop.

To me that was big, REAL big. With never failing sense of special effects, the Heavens had picked the exact time when everybody's eyes were riveted to the dog's asshole to tell us the truth about our hopes, dreams, longings and expectations. It could not possibly have been choreographed better. It was a case of pure suspense. The audience held its breath. It was going to happen—what we had been waiting for and longing for for so long. The turning point was so near it felt like we could almost touch it. Finally, the Heavens would reveal to us the wonderland we were born to inhabit. There would be an end to suffering and grief. The miracle of creation would be ours to behold, and there would be enlightenment and the experience a rebirth. But no! When the dog's asshole opened, all that came out of it was a huge steaming turd. Following two or three seconds of unbearable silence disappointment was drowned out by a roar of laughter. THAT was indeed a proud moment in the history of The Free State and one that was destined to leave traces in the annals.

And The Fat Bastard did not even win. It got the loudest ovation but not the coveted prize. The winner was a fluffy white dwarf poodle dog with a rose in its coiffure. It had been trained to jump through a ring of fire and walk on both its front and hind legs...with no biscuit to bribe it.

Melanie, Christiania... Maybe I should consider returning to Denmark. To Christiania. To find out what is left of the Freetown I once lived in. There's no rush. Most importantly, I have a son to take care of. And me! Well, that's it! I cannot lie down to rest just yet. There's still some unfinished business I have to see to before I leave.

Is not the important thing the same as it always was: To live dangerously and do what I'm most afraid of doing.

If the road I had taken to Christiania had been smooth up till now, I was not to get very far into the Freetown before the hammer fell, and it became painful as hell. Like everything that is good and necessary on this earth, my Christiania life was born in pain.

It was my first working day out on the Freetown. I had gone there on my bicycle to start making the old wreck of a wagon I had bought habitable. My future home was standing on its four semi-flat wheels on a little round spot of asphalt at the far end of The Green Recycling Hall. It was a guy named Bankruptcy Benny who had gotten it from a contractor on mid Zealand someplace. But besides making plans to go live in a wagon in Christiania, Benny had been scheming to make bucks big time with the result that before he could make the move, he'd been busted and gone to jail. The night it happened, he was sitting in a truck somewhere out by the coast waiting for a ship bringing in a ton of hash from Morocco. What to me was a lucky break was a terrible blow to Benny. That is anyway what I thought when I was on my way to negotiate the deal with him in jail. I couldn't make up my mind if I ought to have a bad conscience. I mean—instead of being beside myself with joy.

"Hey, is it my fault you're such a greedy bastard!" This is what I was thinking when the two of us were sitting across the table from each other, and I was contemplating the dents in his shaven skull. The loss of one guy is the legitimate gain of the other, no? Bankruptcy Benny had had his own plans for the wagon. Of course, he did, and the guy didn't try to hide it either. He was bummed out of his mind, he said, that nothing was going to come of it all. It was fucked. Before he used to "go to" bars, now he was "behind" them. It made a *major* difference. Benny made a wry face. He was in for a minimum of five years. *That* and nothing else was what he had to confront. From being a beautiful dream and a promise just a few weeks ago, the wagon had turned into just so much dead weight. He had less than zero use for it anymore. Luckily, there was somebody who wanted to buy the damn thing from him. If not, it would just rot. "One has to look at the bright side, no?" Benny turned his head and looked at the wall. Thank God, he mumbled, he hadn't spent more time and money on it before he got busted. Now it was "another sucker's" turn to tinker with the bitch. But he wished me good luck. He really did.

Benny's voice had sounded kind of thick when he mumbled those last words about how it was another sucker's turn to tinker with it and so on. I could not help thinking that if he had really wanted to live in the wagon, he would have worked on it more and smuggled less. Bankruptcy Benny could say what he liked. The fact was that the only thing he had done to the wagon in the two months it had been in Christiania was to put a bed in it, the exact same bed I now had to remove. Since I did not want to keep anything that Benny left behind, I thanked my lucky star he had been so busy making easy dough. What I wanted was not just to move. What I wanted was a new life. I needed to start from scratch in the same place Benny's bed now was. Once I was rid of the bed, I would air the place out. After that, I would build my own with materials from The Green Recycling Hall.

The bed that Bankruptcy Benny had made was too low for me anyway. Mine was going to be in the same place only twice as high so there would be room for shelves underneath it. In other words, it was not so much a construction job I had come to do, as it was a demolition job.

I reckon it must have been around two o'clock in the afternoon when I arrived on my bicycle. Entering through the main entrance of Christiania at the corner of Prinsessegade and Bådsmandsstræde streets, I passed the usual handful of pushers standing around with lumps of Afghan, Lebanese and Moroccan hash in their hands and continued across the Prairie's empty expanse of gravel and puddles. But now, what was that clanking sound behind me? A moment later, Jakob (who I didn't know yet) appeared beside me:

"Hello, there Jack," he said and gave me the look-over out of a corner of his eye. "Aren't you the new dude moving into The Wagon Village?"

"Well, ehh…" I said and looked at the guy. He wore a thin and scraggly beard and his chest was naked under the sleeveless afghan vest. What impressed me the most though was the sorry old clunker he was riding. The rack was lose and sort of hung to one side, and from the cogwheel or the crank or I don't know from where exactly came an awful slipping and breaking sound when he pedaled.

"Scritsch, scritsch, scritsch…," said the chain as it brushed against the inside of the chain guard, and…: "What'd you pay for the wagon?" Jakob asked. Or rather he shouted it in what I thought was a very impolite manner.

"And who if I may be so free to ask are *you* to interrogate *me*!"

"Now, now, I live in The Wagon Village!"

"And, now now, I live on the planet Mars!"

"We need to know how much you've paid before you're allowed to move in."

"Seven grand."

"All right. That means you can charge six for it when you move out. One less than you paid. You hear!"

"What do you mean *charge*? I haven't even moved into it yet. It's still standing at the back of The Green Recycling Hall. Today's the first day I'm out here to work on it."

Jakob made a gruff gesture with his hand across the handlebars. He was staring straight ahead. "I said: *When* you move, didn't I? *When* you move and you want to sell, you can charge six grand and not one crown more. You hear? Here, we don't buy and sell houses and apartments. This is no Clondyke for real-estate agents. We want all habitations to be free and not have owners. We each pay a small rent to use that's all."

And before I was even able to answer or nod or shake my head, Jakob stepped hard on the pedals of his old clunker and took off rattling and clanking down the uneven cobbles of Pusher Street.

"Who the hell was that?" I thought as I watched Jakob's back disappear in the crowd ahead, "the village welcoming committee perhaps…"

It offended me the way the scruffy guy had called me 'Jack'—like he didn't give a shit about my real name, and he hadn't bothered to introduce himself either. Like I was some damn sleazebag broker or something.

"Ah well! Never mind," I mumbled to myself as I concentrated on negotiating Pusher Street. The damn cobbles made it into kind of a rodeo ride. Keeping a good grip on the handlebars, I navigated around and in between people doing all sorts of things in the open street. Reaching the end, I veered to the left in the direction of The Moonfisher Bar. When I got there, I twisted the front wheel sharply to the right, so that I was now headed directly for The M-house. But...uhhhps! What was *that* over there on the ground? Hmm... A sign? Yes, sure. It was a dark-blue enameled sign with the number 537 painted on it in white. I got off the bike and picked it up. I turned it in my hand: "I have found this, and it's the very first day I'm out here to work," I mused. "And very close to my wagon too... Who knows, maybe it fell off when it was rolled out here? Maybe it's a sign from Heaven telling me I'm now living in number 537. In Wagon number 537 Christiania," and as if to confirm the validity of this thought I nodded my head.

When a little later, I parked my bicycle among some tall nettles that grew along the wall of The Green Recycling Hall, I walked over to the wagon, unlocked the door to my new home and got up into it. For a full minute or so, I was just standing there savouring the scented air of its empty interior. Finally, I opened the toolbox I had left there earlier in the week and got out four small screws and a screwdriver.

A couple minutes later, I stepped down from the rickety chair I had been standing on and took in the result of my efforts. There it was, the sign, shining its 537 down at me from its place above the door.

The reason I make such a fuss over something so trivial is because I am not much of a handyman. To tell the truth, I am really quite impossible and always have been. My shop teacher in school was a German by the name of Gustav Krämer who had biceps like a heavy weight boxer and spoke with a strong German accent. He, too, was a refugee. In his own time he had run away from Hitler's army. Somehow, he had succeeded in getting to the Baltic Sea, where he had simply begun to swim. Rather than being butchered like a sheep by a lunatic like Hitler, he would perish in the waves a free man. This is how he put it to a journalist many years later. It was a fisherman from Bornholm who had spotted him and gotten him on board, more dead than alive. Still later, Gustav Krämer had been faced with the task of teaching me to make primitive technical drawings, to saw, drill and mortise. That's when he shook his round head and said: "To swim across the Baltic Sea, my boy, is *one* thing. To teach *you* to make a shelf is something else altogether!"

For this comment, I will always remember Gustav Krämer.

Where was I? Oh, that's right. I am still standing down there behind The Green Recycling Hall admiring my sign above the door. It was one of those lingering, proud and joyful moments that don't come often in life and… don't last forever either. The sequel never waits and abomination is never far off. Now, for example, there was the bed that Bankruptcy Benny had made just before he got thrown in the can. This was today's project and its problem as well. The damn thing was wedged so hard in between the two sides of the wagon that I couldn't get it out. Standing there with sweat running down my cheeks, it crossed my mind that it would be easier if I found myself another wagon. I could just see it, I mean, how Bankruptcy Benny had been standing on exactly that same spot on the floor measuring the length of the bed. Done measuring, he had scratched his shaven neck with the folding ruler and cogitated deeply right up until he came up with the solution: a couple more millimeters added to the length, and it would fit tight. The

116

result, of course, was the damn thing had become too long. Most likely, it had been at a slant, that is, at rest where it should be on one end and raised a bit too high at the other. And here is when Benny had once more scratched his cranium with the ruler and come up with a solution. A *sustainable* solution mind you. It was plausible, I thought that after he had tried everything and nothing worked, he lost his head, got up on the bed and started stomping it down with all his weight. And it was not until the goddamned piece of shit had been rammed in there good and proper—not until it was prostrate and had ceased putting up resistance—that Benny, with sweat streaming down *his* face, got down off of it and back on the floor.

What a relief it was. Bankruptcy Benny felt like someone who has just revenged himself. Or that is what I think anyway. Finally, the goddamned bitch was in its proper place. He had seen to it personally that it would never move again. Like he had told me, it was now my turn to "tinker with the bitch." Now, it was my turn to be scratching my neck like some moron and think: "Let me see. What's the opposite of jumping up and down on a bed? Hmm. What if I got down on all fours underneath it and pushed it up with my back and shoulders…"

Pleased with my bright idea, I proceeded to carry it out. And… jubilation! The bitch actually budged. On the side where I pressed with my shoulders, she had let go so I could lift her up. But every time I pressed her up in one side and moved to the other, she would promptly fall back down on the side I had just left. And when I tried pressing in the middle, she wouldn't move. Bankruptcy Benny was right. It was a *real* bitch. For a while, I kept on trying until finally I gave up.

But alas! When the need is greatest, there is usually room for it to grow a little greater. As luck would have it, my brilliant intelligence had decided to come to my rescue. It claimed it had a good idea. At first I was suspicious. From bitter experience, I knew my brilliance was not to be trusted. But since at the moment I could think of nothing better, I mumbled: "All right, then here we go." Now that my mind was made up, the next step was to get the big hammer out of the toolbox. Equipped with this implement of destruction, I got back under the bed. Just like before, I pressed the bed up in one corner, but *unlike* before this time I used the hammer as a wedge with its head up. It held the bed up while I moved to the other side. Sitting there on all fours and glowering mistrustfully at it out of the corner of my eye, I groaned: "Here…we GO!" Next thing I knew, I had pressed the bed up with the result that the hammer – finding itself suddenly lose – performed a somersault to land with its head right on the thumbnail of my left hand. Bonk, it said.

And: "FUCK, FUCK, FUCK!" I roared while at top speed I climbed out from under the bitch. Once out, I began to rotate like a top, swinging my thumb in the air. Around and around, it went until I got dizzy and tumbled out of the door. There, I was poking my thumb at the sky and staring at it. I could not see anything clearly. My vision was as blurred as if I were lying on the bottom of the sea. The thumb seemed bloated like it was not a digit at all but some gelatinous mass of flesh. Then, my vision focused again, and I saw the thumb clearly. Not only had it been knocked flat, no, the nail had turned black all over. Christ it looked bad, like some horrible case of gangrene or something. And did it throb. THROB, THROB, THROB! At every throb, thick red pain blurred my vision and pounded my temples pitilessly.

Is this not the way it always is, that right at the worst moment something else appears to make it even worse? I

118

am standing there glowering at my bruised thumb, when a voice I know only too well reaches my ear: "Hey, hey, hey, Les me lad, what's going on here. What are you looking at? Have you seen the devil?"

Have you guessed who it was? Well, you guessed right. It was no other than the man responsible for me getting the wagon in the first place. Martin was coming towards me wearing those brand new and very tight charcoal colored canvas pants of his. The thing that was so special about those pants was that there was no fly in them, and no buttons or buckles either. Instead, there were two long straps that had to be tied around the waist in a very intricate fashion. Without the fly, the ballpark arena in the crotch seemed somehow enlarged, like the tights worn by ballet-dancers. The pants were as cool as could be *except* when the wearer needed to take a piss. If you ask me, it was really ridiculous. I mean, the way Martin first had to unwrap himself like he was some sort of gift to humanity, then hold the long straps while he rolled down the pantaloons to get his dick out. Those pants were not made for public urinals. That is for damn sure. It was the stage designer of the theatre ensemble "The Chariot of the Sun" who had designed and sewn them for him. They had cost a bundle, and they actually looked good on him, I must say. I was a wee bit envious I admit that, because the girls found him attractive and because I could not afford such extravagance myself. Add to this the fact that most of the guys in "The Chariot of the Sun" were parading their crotches in those pantaloons. If one belonged to the male sex, had the balls and was part of the absolute inner jet-set circle, then those pants were what one was wearing. And, mind you, one was *not* wearing a pair of ordinary blue jeans like the ones I had on. No way…

Martin was standing right in front of me on legs apart, so I could really enjoy the sight of him and his pants: "Tell me," he began in that soft, heartfelt and also a bit ironic tone of his. "What's going on here?"

I looked at him. Martin looked back, raised his eyebrows and shook his head ever so lightly.

"What's going on here?" he repeated.

Sighing, I showed him my finger.

"Auch…My God!" Martin shuddered, his voice virtually dripping with commiseration. *"That,"* he declared, "does *not* look good. How'd you do that?"

"Does it really matter?"

"No, of course not," Martin said and looked at me in a way that annoyed me like hell.

"It was the hammer," I sighed. "If you really want to know. It fell on my thumb."

"The hammer fell on your thumb!" Martin cocked his head, fluttered his eyelashes and raised the brows once more. "Like… by itself! A stroke of bad luck, eh!"

Martin looked me deeply in the eyes without blinking. I looked back at him until I was afraid tears would fill my eyes and said: "Maybe you don't believe me, but it's true. The hammer fell. But…really, *does* it matter?"

Martin kept looking at me for a long time before telling me it was not me he had come around to meet. It was Marie-Louise in the Little Gunpowder House. Until a few weeks ago, the two of them had lived together in there. Martin had just come by to see if maybe things had changed. They hadn't. Not even the new flyless charcoal colored canvas pants with their crotch made any difference. At no point had Marie-Louise even deigned to look at them. Martin laughed. Actually, he said, she had just about grabbed him by the scruff of his neck and thrown him out. But now, he had to get a move on. There was *so* very much he had to do. He was off, he said, had to go get the DAF car at the other end of town. Always that damn DAF car. He used it when he picked up girls and drove them to the mundane north coast of Zealand where his family owned an enormous summerhouse with a view of the sea. But today, he wasn't going that far, he assured me. He didn't have time for that sort of thing. In two hours, he was meeting with the other guys. I knew exactly what guys he was referring to. It was the male "Chariot of the Sun" crowd in flyless crotch-pants. Of course, the meeting he was going to was of supreme importance. Martin sent me a look full of meaning. He had conceived an idea for a new theater piece, he said. A brilliant one, needless to say! Today, he was going to suggest to the group that without delay he and a couple of the other guys got down to work. It would be great to have a manuscript ready for Christmas. He would very much have liked to be able to stay with me, but it just wasn't possible. It was he himself who had called the meeting, and he was already running late. Soon though, *very* soon, we would have an evening and "settle" everything.

"Hey, but make sure you go to the emergency clinic, eh!" These last words Martin shouted over his shoulder, as he turned the corner of the Little Gunpowder House.

"Fuck *that*," I thought, as I was once again alone with my thumb. At seven o'clock, I was invited to a thirty-years birthday party. The invitation was one I had received a long time ago, and I didn't want to miss it. It looked like it was going to be the party of the season. And besides…, wasn't it a little bit better already? I studied my thumb. Yes, as a matter of fact, it was. It still throbbed like hell, sure, but had not the pain gotten more bearable? Maybe the nail had started to recuperate, or maybe Martin had hypnotized me with his soft voice and piercing eyes. As if it mattered how or why. The question was simple. What did I do now? Why not just pretend that nothing had happened and dress up for the party. The clothes were waiting for me in the closet in my Østerbro apartment. All I had to do was ride home and put them on. Once I was dressed for the party, surely, the mood would come by itself.

Now, now, easy does it, I admonished myself. One thing at a time. First, lock the door, then get on the bike, and then onwards. A squished thumbnail was nothing so very unusual. It happened to people all the time. Bankruptcy Benny had hit the nail on its head when he said it was important to look at the bright side. He should know. What I had to do was look ahead. As soon as the party got going, when people were dancing to the music and there was plenty of booze—well, then I would surely forget all about my little accident. It was not the end of the world.

Trouble was, I had no way of knowing if this would happen until I was drunk. Either the alcohol did the trick and I would be fine, or it did not and I would be... well, fucked. What could the chances be? Fifty-fifty? I don't know how to say this. Somehow the pain had tampered with some limits inside of me—limits I was accustomed to and respected, even if I didn't know exactly where they were. It was as if the pain had removed these borders or moved them out so far I didn't come up against them. Somehow I was not the same person anymore as I had been before the accident. What I am saying is not that I'm the inhibited kind, but that I was not feeling the inhibitions that I normally felt. Except for the throbbing in my finger, everything seemed to have vanished. And soon when alcohol was added, even this pain would go away. Who could tell? Maybe I would be born a new, liberated and more amusing character than before. It was worth a try. What did I have to lose?

On my way to the party, I stopped at a kiosk and downed a couple strong beers. Returning the bottles for the deposit, I bought a third. I held the handlebars with my right hand and the beer bottle with my left, and every time I raised the bottle to my lips, I glanced at the thumbnail. It kept looking just like the last time and throbbed the same. When I arrived at the villa, I hid the empty beer bottle in a bush and rang the doorbell. Talking to my old friend Carl, in the kitchen I was so distracted by the throbbing I could not keep track of what we were talking about. The pain was making my feet restless too.

This was the situation when half an hour later dinner was served, and I downed the first glass of wine. The pain refused to go away. But instead of drawing the sensible conclusion that the alcohol was not helping, I figured I had not had enough yet. If nothing else, the alcohol had made me pigheaded. With his majesty King Alcohol as my ally, I would show the pain who was "*Chargé d'affaires*". And chuckling to myself finding this "*Chargé d'affaires*" that had popped up in my head very witty indeed, I decided not to allow such a ridiculous little pain to spoil my party. I would hurt it in ways it would never forget. With the lazer rays of my fiery spirit, I was going to burn it away. Not being invited to the party, bastard pain should not be allowed to spoil it either. That is where I, Andreas Stein, drew the line.

Or rather, that is what I thought I did. Drew the line, I mean. Because meanwhile there was something else, some unseen force that was drawing the line for *me*. What could it be? What did it want from me?

The beginning of the end was when we sat down to eat. Instead of being a buddy and coming to my aid, King Alcohol stabbed me in the back. Sitting there trying to swallow the *primo piati*, I felt I had been deceived by time itself. It was like Time sensed that in me it had found a fool who would do anything, no matter what, to hang on to his own misconceptions. Like all of the false battles in this world, this one, too, was lost in advance. When the bell sounded for the first round, I got as far as to the center of the ring before I was stopped by a straight right and went down. Had it not been for the tall beauty sitting next to me at table, I really don't know if I would have ever woken from my coma.

My thumb was now throbbing so badly I felt like I was going to faint. The last thing I remember with anything resembling clarity was the incomparable cleavage next to me. Owing to some sort of black magic, the crack between the girl's breasts seemed constantly where my blood shot eyes fell, as if that place were sort of a bottomless pit.

Not realizing exactly how lost I was, I hiccupped: "Excuse me for saying it, but yours are *some* beautiful tits."

The combination of pain and alcohol had done something to my tongue. It said what it felt like and didn't give a damn what others might think or if I made an ass of myself. Had the lady next to me been the Queen of Denmark, it would not have made any difference. I would still have told her she had an ugly mug, if that's what had come into my head. But the beauty on my right took it really nicely, I must say. Raising her glass and smiling at me, she said in a tone of voice like she was talking about her wristwatch: "Yeah right! Let's toast to my tits!"

Surprised and encouraged, I started blabbering away about how earlier on that very same day I had been in a situation where I had to set up a washing machine in the home of a former real-estate broker living in a shack in "The Blue Caramel" out on Christiania. Where the hell I got all that horseshit from, I have no idea. And I needed to breathe. But since I was afraid she would cut me off, I just hiccupped and plunged headlong into more nonsense about how all had worked out fine until I came across a pipe that had an internal thread with rust in it.

"An internal thread!" The girl had knitted her brow and was looking at me intently.

"Absolutely", I said and hurried to add that the internal thread was so rusted it had caused a small accident. There had been some trouble with a pump too, that's true, but it was impossible to explain it to her, because it required special knowledge on her part to understand. I was terribly sorry, but the kind of knowledge that was required was something one only had if one was in the field. Maybe if we met again some other time, I could explain it to her. Would she like me to do that?

"Oh, how I'd just *love* that!" the young lady said and shook her head. "I'd find out more about the trouble you had with that pump."

Nodding I said: "Yes, you would." And without pause, I rushed on: Now that pump. A pump was not just a pump, if that's what she thought. Not when we were talking washing machines it wasn't. Also there weren't very many washing machines on Christiania, so it wasn't every day that I was called to go there. Thank God it wasn't. All those hippies who never washed, the dope-heads, scavengers, collectivists, sponges on the social system and so on. Not to mention the terrible mess. As she could hear, I said, the so-called Freetown wasn't exactly my cup of tea. What with all its "bullshit Buddhism" etc. As an honest salesman of domestic appliances operating from a base on Sølvtorvet Square, as a man who voted in the elections, abided by the laws and paid my taxes, Christiania was an insult. A gob of spittle in the face of decency. That was "the one thing." "The other thing" was the bitter fact that being a salesman of domestic appliances, I wasn't used to associating with breasts like hers. Such gorgeous tits if she really wanted to know my opinion bordered on the impertinent. How was a man to go on fixing rusty pumps when there were tits like hers in the world? But to speak sincerely and profoundly, I blabbered and fell headlong into the cleavage once more, speaking sincerely and profoundly, I was also a sort of an *"artiste"* in my own field. And being an *"artiste,"* I'd developed a very delicate appreciation of the kind of beauty found in cleavages like hers. The problem was I had gotten off to a bad start… Could she keep a secret—because what I was about to tell her, I had never told a living soul before?

"Sure. I can hardly wait."

"Do you swear?"

"Yes, I do. Go on."

"All right then." I sighed and tried to look her in the eyes: I grew up a poor orphan who had to make do with a baby bottle, if she could imagine something like that. There'd been a time in my life when nobody wanted me. Least of all my parents. By being born, I had gotten in the way of their plans. So they dumped me. It was a wonder nobody had wrung my neck and chucked me in a lake. That's how my life had been right from the start. Didn't she think that was sad? Never to have been loved by a loving mother! No loving mother had ever pressed her soft, dripping and scented nipple into my mouth. When my diaper was full, I was told to shit in it some more or go change myself. When I screamed because I had a tooth on the way, all I got was a cold shoulder and an empty baby bottle to shut me up. No wonder I never developed a mature taste for… well, for cleavages. But *if* I had and being the true *"artiste"* that I was, I would offer her great sums of money to be my model for some studies in the nude, which I'd execute in gou…gou…ache.

"In gou…gou what?" Again the beauty at my side was looking at me with knitted brows.

"Nothing. Just forget it," I said whereupon I plunged right into some more bilge about what a pity it was that I was "tied" to the domestic appliance chain by a five-year contract. But washing machines and especially dish washing machines were not only my specialty but also my hobby. Whenever I had a holiday, I would travel to all the relevant fairs in the world. I wanted to experience the very newest models. For instance, not too long ago, I had attended a spin dryer conference in Jakarta. I simply lacked words for what an extraordinary experience that had been. "I simply have no words," I repeated shaking my head in wonder. Anyway, it had so rocket my boat I had not gotten over it yet. Still, there was a confession, I would like to make *if* she didn't mind. Did she? Good. I never got a greater kick than when I sold machines to Laundromats. I had often wondered why exactly it was, if perhaps it had something to do with the owners of the Laundromats always being such great and warm hearted people. Had she ever met a Laundromat owner? No. In that case, I could assure her she would be surprised to find what a superb group of chaps they were, generous to a fault, gallant etc. When the people one was dealing with were of such sterling caliber as this, wow what a pleasure that was. Then nothing could go wrong. One was in good hands. That was it: *good hands*. There was no better way of putting it. Had she ever been in uh-uh good hands? No. Oh, but then, she must absolutely give me a ring if ever she should feel like opening a Laundromat.

"Just give me a ring," I slobbered something like three or four times while staring at her with my bleary eyes.

Almost as if she were thinking seriously about what I had said, the beauty slowly stuck her fork in an asparagus and raised it to her mouth. But before she continued, she threw me a sideways glance and said that if there really existed such wonderful people as those Laundromat "chaps" I knew, well, then she would love nothing better than to visit them and hear more about the business. She could not wait to get my telephone number either. Would I *really* give it to her?

"No sweat!" I said and started to look for pen and paper. That was the very least I could do for her. If only I could find something to write with, I would give her the number of the biggest Laundromat mogul alive. The biggest, nicest and most powerful. And the handsomest too as a matter of fact. The one with the most clout. But, Christ, where was that damn business card. Only yesterday, I had given it to a prospective associate who had recently launched a super-modern Laundromat in Bukino Faso.

At the same time as I was babbling away like this, I was rummaging in my pockets and all over the place for a pen. And to really lay it on thick, I now started saying stuff like it would be really fantastic, in fact an exceptional honor, to drive the company car to her address, park it in front of her door, get the red carpet out for her as an "honorary" customer and then—after giving her the full sales speech—install a brand new uh…spin dryer in her uh…private uh… parts.

But the pen! Where the hell was it hiding? It had to be around *somewhere*. Oh, good. There it was, I said, finding a pen in the pocket of my jacket where it always was. "Now, here… we…go!" I jotted the number down on a hundred-crown bill, which I very carefully folded and ever so gingerly wedged in between her tremendous breasts. With bulging bloodshot eyes, I saw the bill disappear into the great and impenetrable darkness that reigned in that grand cleavage, and attempting to follow it, I disappeared myself a moment later into that perdition that enveloped my head and drowned out all remaining sound and light.

I am not sure exactly what happened. Next thing I knew, I was on the floor feeling woozy. Right before my eyes, the cleavage grew and grew until finally it lost all contour and began to spin around. At first, it spun slowly, but gradually it picked up speed. At the end, just before the blackout, it spun like some mad vortex intent on sucking me in. Later, when I regained conscience, it was still there, the cleavage I mean, but now it was jostling me and pulling at me to get me into a sitting position. Round about me, there was something resembling tumult, and I realized I was the center of attention.

"Do *you* know where you're going?" My dinner partner was now very upset with me. "You're going to the emergency clinic, that's where! Do you hear?" Her mouth was huge, and inside it, the tongue was moving, and the teeth were white fangs. How about helping her a little bit! Would I get on my feet—please? She was muttering under her breath. Oh God, how she would appreciate a little help. She had a car waiting by the curb, and she would take me there.

"Do you want to drive me?"

"Yes, I do."

"Very much?"

I didn't hear what she answered, but somehow she succeeded in getting me to the car, a skyblue Volkswagen that she had borrowed for a month from her older brother. I sort of felt sorry for her too. I mean, all the trouble she was having because of me. At first, she'd had no end of trouble getting me out of the house, down the stairs and into the front passenger seat. And then, when she had me where she wanted me to be, it still remained to put the seat belt on me. There was no way I myself could possibly hit the little slot with the buckle. "Some great help *you* are," she hissed, as she bent over me trying to get the buckle in the slot. I didn't say anything. All I was conscious of was her great breast. I knew full well it would stay right there in my face for as long as she battled with the buckle. But, alas, things of beauty don't last forever. When finally she got me belted, she backed out with her butt first. She got into the driver's seat, started the engine and the transport to the emergency clinic began in earnest.

When we got there, it was fortunately still so early in the evening that the party- and traffic casualties had not started arriving yet. It was all sort of surreal. In line before us was only this stag-party casualty sitting by himself with a T-shirt on that said: "I'm getting married!" He didn't seem very happy. Apparently, he'd had his nose broken, because every time he breathed out a bloody bubble appeared at the right nostril. And when he breathed in again the bubble deflated. For some reason, I found it a very fascinating spectacle. For a while, I even forgot the pain in my finger. Bloody nose bubble blow up. Bloody nose bubble collapse. And tomorrow the poor sucker sitting there so alone was going to get married. Some woman somewhere was going to be asked if she would take this chap with the bubble and live with him till death did them part. I don't know why, but all of a sudden, it seemed to me very touching and of great importance: that the unknown woman would say yes to *him*, I mean, bloody nose bubble and all…

"Will you quit glaring at other people!" my dinner partner said, or rather she shouted it. "Don't you have any *manners* at all?" With her hand she fanned a few times right in front of my nose, and when that didn't help any, she grabbed one of those horrible "See and Listen" magazines with all the scandals involving celebrities from the pile on the table and chucked it in my face: "I said. Would you stop it?"

That did it. I dare say I came to again. Right there on the floor before my eyes, I saw a picture of the Prince Consort surrounded on all sides by little girls with ribbons in their hair and teddy bears in their hands. This was something that I absolutely *had to* check out, but as I bent over—perhaps in an attempt to pick up the magazine from the floor—I lost my balance and fell face first into the picture of the Prince Consort. For the second time that evening, my dinner partner had to come to my assistance and help me up: "Come on now," she groaned and pulled my arm, "you can go in now!"

Once inside the clinic, the doctor needed just one quick glance at my thumbnail to know what to do about it. As for me, I was too drunk and worn out with pain to register what was going on around me.

That was soon to change. I was lying on a hard examination couch with a throbbing thumb and a soused look on my face. My dinner partner, the cleavage and the doctor were somewhere else in the room, because I could hear them speaking to each other. The sound of their voices reached me as if coming from far away. From what I have been told by Lili, the doctor had informed her, it would be quite painful for her "boy friend." However, the pain would only last a moment. After that, it would go away, and there would be no pain anymore.

But as I said, I did not really know what was going on—not until the doctor came up and strapped my arms to the armrests. What could *that* be he was holding in his hand? Something long and thin and blurred like. What *was* it? To my horror, I realized what it was. The thing the doctor held in his hand was a piece of steel wire. Just an ordinary piece of medium sized steel wire. And when the doctor walked over to a table by the wall and stuck the wire into a gas flame, a groan escaped my chest. I pulled at the straps and rolled my eyes in their sockets. Holding the redhot piece of steel wire in his hand, the doctor returned to the cot, where I lay prostrate and helplessly watching. Noticing that I had become sober and focused, he smiled at me and said:

"This'll hurt, but only a second. Then, it's over. Then, you and your girlfriend can go on partying."

With these words and without asking my permission, he drove the redhot steel wire down through the nail of the thumb and as far as I could tell clear through my entire finger.

"JAAAAAUUUUCHH!" I screamed as both my legs flew up from the cot and a fountain of blood shot out of the finger twenty centimeters into the air: "JAAAAUUUUC-CHHH. THIS-IS-TORTURE!"

Immediately after that followed the collapse. I was lying there deflated, flat and exhausted. Like a balloon after someone has poked a hole in it. It was all over. Waves of painless relief washed over me. My scalp was tingling and so were the tips of my toes. Emptied, I was so much dead weight on the couch. What the doctor had said was true. By jabbing that hole in me, he had taken the pressure away. He had heard the call of my blood and set it free. With a red-hot wire, he had turned my tense organism into a floor rag, wrung, wasted and annihilated. Crushed and with my eyes closed I gave myself over to a pleasure the likes of which I had never known before.

After a while, there was the doctor's voice saying to my dinner partner that I was now "fit for fight" once more. And it was at that very moment, I became aware of the sound of church bells ringing. This probably does not make much sense to you. And maybe it shouldn't either. Perhaps those bells were just ringing in my own head. But somehow I felt that the doctor's words and the sound of those bells gave me the absolution my soul had yearned for. To my own surprise, I now loved the doctor. In fact, I loved him so much that I only had one wish left in the world: To be allowed to stay right where I was, lying on his examination couch until the end of my days. With perforated thumbnail, bled and filled to the breaking point by that huge calm and warmth and wellbeing that had come over me. With every pore and nerve anaesthetized and voluptuously reconciled with my mortal frame. Floating in the trade winds of a great ocean, carried along on tingling billows.

When we returned to the party, the tables had been removed, and people were cavorting to Chuck Berry, Rolling Stones, Elvis Presley, Gasolin and Jerry Lee Lewis. I was standing in the double door taking in the scene when, for some reason, I recalled the question Martin had asked me earlier that same day. If I had seen the devil? Now, it seemed to me just about the most ridiculous question I had ever heard. "No, Bozo," is what I should have answered, if I'd had my wits about me. "I didn't see jack shit. And you know what? It doesn't matter, because I'm fit for fight."

But if I was fit for fight or if it was some damn asylum I was fit for that was hard to say. In any case, the fall of the hammer was now history, and in the present of the here and now, I was at the very least able to walk on water. "Do you have a name too?" I asked my table partner, when suddenly she put a fresh bottle of beer in my hand.

She looked at me out of the corner of her eye as we were drinking from our bottles. "My name's Lili," she said as she lowered the bottle.

Without really knowing what I was doing, I grabbed Lili and the cleavage by the waist and dragged her out on the dance floor. And it must have been perfect timing too, because hardly had I let go of her before she went berserk. She spun like a top, stopped, bent over and swung her long hair from side to side. And that was just for starters. Next thing I knew, she was wriggling her butt, shaking her breasts, bending over and straightening up again; she even made some long jumps forward with legs apart followed by some short jumps backwards, smiling, spinning and looking here, there and everywhere at the same time. It wasn't dance. It was performance. Chuck Berry was exploding inside of her, complete with melody, rhythm and all. She gave herself over to the sound, letting it rule every small or great movement she was making with her arms, hips, legs, head and…fingers. That's right. She even danced with her fingers. Sometimes, she would stop abruptly in the middle of a movement and perform a little sketch. Like she was charming a cobra out of a basket or something. Only a moment later to rant and rave to such an extent that I had to grab her with an arm around her waist and hold her tight, so in an embrace we reeled and lurched and almost fell. To feel her perfect body pressed to my chest was almost more than I could stand. To inhale the fumes rising from that cleavage and slowly become unhinged until Lili suddenly jumped and got hold of one of the heavy duty cross beams under the ceiling. There she was swinging back and forth so hard that other dancers had to jump for their lives, and me, well, when I stepped up to her, she slid her legs over my shoulders, sat on me with all her weight and let go the beam. There she was astride me, and riding me like I was some sort of donkey or something. "This is heavy," I groaned, "you're not exactly some little weightless nymph, you know!" "Oh, my Prince Consort you can handdle it!" Lili cried as she jerked her crotch back and forth to the beat of the music. The trouble was I was facing one way and she the other. It was awkward. My nose was deeply buried between her tights. I could not see a damn thing. I almost could not breathe either. "Okay, okay," Lili heard my muffled cry for help, and before I knew it, I had a knee at each of my ears and the crotch of the tights at a more comfortable distance under my nose. It was better, but still not good. The situation was basically untenable. Something had to be done. The question was only what? Trusting me to hold her, Lili was hanging down my front with her belly showing and the long hair sweeping the floor. Ever so gently, I swung her from side to side. There was only one thing I could do: tickle her in the armpits. Not a lot but enough for her to let go of me. If she was ticklish, I was saved, if she was not, I was lost. "Don't! Oh, don't!" she groaned, and proving what strong stomach muscles she had, she got back up into a sitting position again. Exhausted, she rested her torso on my head. Once more, I was choking between her tights. And since this time it was impossible to speak, I thought: "This is too much. I've got to tickle her again!"

Laughing and kicking her legs, Lili caught hold of the cross beam, swung her legs back and forth a couple of times and jumped to the floor.

A little later when I brought her what was left of her beer, she looked at me strangely and asked if it was really true that I was making a living selling domestic appliances.

"Making a living and making a living," I answered cryptically.

Lili grimaced like what she really wanted to say was: "What do you take me for —a fool!" But instead she said something to the effect that I ought to save that yarn for my analyst, since if there was any truth in it, then surely I also had an analyst, and then that would be the right person to tell it to. *She*, however, was not that person. What *she* wanted was the truth and nothing but the truth. Salesmen of domestic appliances didn't dance the way I did. She knew, because once she had danced with someone who really *was* a salesman. But to me, she was probably just some young and empty-brained blonde, huh! Domestic appliances her ass...

I shrugged and said that the difference between domestic appliances and her ass perhaps wasn't as great as she thought. But for all I cared, she could think what she wanted to. If she really wanted to know, all she had to do was go to Sølvtorvet Square and see if I was there. Come Monday morning, I would be there behind the counter in a full salesman's outfit. "Just come...at ten o'clock sharp!"

Lili gave a snort: Full salesman outfit! Did I really think she would make a fool of herself showing up in such a godforsaken place and ask for a certain Les Stein with a hole in his thumbnail. Did I? Did I think that! In a domestic appliances store on a Monday morning at ten o'clock! Well, if I did, I must be out of my mind. But perhaps I would reveal to her what it felt like in my "professional salesman's soul" when I had sold a washing machine. Did I get a kick out of it?

I just stood there enjoying Lili's eloquence—the flocks of well-shaped syllables that came rolling over those big red lips of hers. I was discovering what a thrill it was when she simulated being angry with me. But most of all, I was happy to be rid of the pain in my finger. Imagine, I said to myself, just imagine if it could be so arranged that every day as long as one lived, one woke up with a great pain; and then at some point later on in the day somebody or something took it away again. Would it not, then, be possible to love one's pain, if only for the daily relief it would bring? And would it not, then, be possible to cut the rope and be free? Christ almighty what a lucky Prince Consort I was—with the pain gone and the cleavage still around. At that moment, something told me that I had Lili precisely where I wanted her. Somehow, I knew she would stay where she was as long as I didn't divulge the truth about myself or she found it out by herself. That's why I just kept smiling enigmatically and let it go at that. And when Lili kept making faces, I pulled her out of the wicker chair and started to dance with her again. For some reason, I remembered the hundred-crown bill I had stuffed into her cleavage earlier on that evening. Figuring it was probably still there and working as a sort of deposit, I now got a twenty-crown bill out of my pocket, folded it and let it go the way of the first one. And after that, a fifty-crown bill. It was amazing how they all went down no problem. There was plenty of room.

Lili pulled her blouse out and looked into it the best she could. "Tell me!" she said in a voice that was a bit strained because of the way her wind pipe was squeezed. "What the hell do you think you are doing? Do you think I'm some kind of piggy bank or something?"

"No, no, not at all. Why don't you look at it as a sort of advance or down payment. Or... who knows... maybe a bribe!"

Lili let go her blouse and stared at me in disbelief. I felt my dick swell in my pants. If I'd had the strength, I would have taken her in my arms right there on the spot and carried her into an adjacent room. There, I would have put her on the big double bed, and...

"The truth," I heard Lili say, "now I want the truth, d'ya hear!" She was still staring into my eyes, but now she was also tugging at my sleeve. "Do you hear? I want to know the truth about you. I want to know *what* sort of person you are."

I looked at her.

"I'll pull your pants off if you don't tell me!"

I shook my head: "The truth! The truth! Who cares about the truth! In our day and age..."

"I do. I do. I do!" Lili cried and placing her hands on my shoulders, she moved her torso ever so slowly from side to side in a very studied way. Apparently, this was part of her new strategy, for when she did that her breasts swayed just a wee bit, like they were some kind of promise on her part. She was studying my face closely.

"You might as well give it up," I said. "This is "The Last Tango in Paris" over again."

That is how it went on. And god knows how long it could have gone on like this, if the finger of fortune had not (again) interfered. Two hours earlier, Lili had succeeded in getting me to tell her that my name was Andreas Stein. But she didn't really believe it. And anyway, it was all the same by now. The night was getting on, and so were we. We were getting it on. More and more as the hours went by. And it's anybody's guess what would have happened had not accident number two spoiled my plans.

It was towards the wee hours of the morning. Most of the guests had left, and it was light outside. Tables and windowsills were overflowing with empty and half empty bottles and glasses. The music was loud like there were still fifty people on the floor dancing and not just Lili and I. That is if what we were doing at this point deserves to be called 'dancing.' Holding each other tight, we were just sort of rocking slowly from side to side. A couple of times, I had tried to feel her breasts but every time my hand had been pushed away. "Hands off!" she said, "you touch me like I'm some sort of spin dryer." The stereo set was playing a tender tune. With my eyes closed and with very slow drunken movements, I once again sort of half danced half stumbled backwards, away from Lili and…crashed on my ass on a low table full of wineglasses and filled ashtrays.

"JAAAUUUCHHH!" I yelled for the third time in less than twenty-four hours. With difficulty, I got back on my feet. And I probably would have gone right on dancing too, if Lili had not put an end to it. "Hey, stop it!" I said and put up resistance, "Hands off my pants. I'm fit for fight!"

"The hell you are," she said and bent down, "and what

if I may ask, do you call this?"

Lili was holding a piece of bloody glass up for me to see. "This is what I just found stuck in your ass. Do you see the blood? Turn around, would you! TURN-A-ROUND!"

I don't know why, but when I did as she had told me, I thought of the "See and Listen" tabloid she had chucked in my face down at the clinic. Again, there appeared before my eyes The Prince Consort, the little girls with ribbons in their hair and the teddy bears. In the same flash, I also saw the stag party casualty sitting there alone with his bloody nose. Well, I muttered to myself, I guess this spells the end of the party for Les the salesman of domestic appliances from Sølvtorvet Square. And so it was. After that my eyelids grew as heavy as led and closed. And it came to pass that it was around this time that Lili, the Good Samaritan, started picking pieces of glass from my ass using a pair of tweezers she had found in the hosts' bathroom. I imagine that Lili, as she was sitting there picking away, also kept wondering who he really was, her unfortunate dinner partner. The guy had sold domestic appliances on Sølvtorvet Square in the morning, had had his thumb squished by some mysterious pump sometime during the afternoon somewhere in the boondocks in Christiania only to get most of a wineglass stuck up his ass during the wee hours of the next morning. All this together constituted an accomplishment of sorts. It was like a puzzle she was putting together. She had found a few of the pieces, two corners and a couple along the edges—but it was still a long way off getting a picture in its entirety. She herself had not been so sparing when it came to giving information. She had even offered details of her more intimate life. Like how she'd kicked out her boyfriend because he was "a bragging little wimp." Whenever he was to give a report of something, he would exaggerate his own role and so distort the truth. In the beginning, she had been taken in by him. But the sweet had turned bitter when she found there were discrepancies between her boyfriend's story and the stories of the others. Sometimes, they were great discrepancies too. On top of all that, she had also told me that she attended a school for street performance located on Iceland Quay, that she worked in a café on Gothersgade Street, where she earned good tips juggling the oranges, and, finally, that her mother's new hubby had a daughter named Trine who suffered from diabetes.

But right now, we were sound asleep and all of that was already nothing but dream and history.

When I woke, it was almost noon. At first, I did not know where I was. I felt sore both in my head and in my ass. The sun was streaming through the thin white curtains. It was terribly hot and stuffy in the room. Lili was asleep next to me breathing softly. We were completely alone and…

Lili was the first woman to spend the night in my wagon. Lili was the first woman to stick her naked feet in my black clogs, stomp down the two wooden steps to the concrete foundation, turn the corner, get down on her haunches, pee, wipe herself, mount the steps and cross the bouncing floor of the wagon to bring me fresh tidings on the present condition of our cosmos. Lili was the first woman to declare she thought it wonderful to *be* in the city but *pee* in nature. From my outpost on the bed, I observed it all with awe. It seemed this little trip to pee out in the back stirred some ancient and pre-Christian instinct in women, something out of a distant and tertiary past where the primordial female woke from her slumber, got up on her hind legs and drifted down to the water hole to quench her thirst.

But if the clogs were always the same, the women were

140

not. They differed one from the other. Some would fill them better than others. Unfortunately, nobody filled them out completely. The length of their legs, the width of their hips, the size and shape of their breasts, the color of their skin, hair and nails, their age and dreams for the future all varied one from the other. Not to mention the pee reports. Depending on the season, the point they had reached in their monthly cycle, their hormonal state, the events of that particular day, the degree of imagination and soberness, the preliminary love-making and the chemistry between us—each one had her own special experience and characteristic way of recounting it. When the wind tore at the treetops shaking dry twigs down on my flat roof or when raindrops hit my windows as if someone had hurled them at the panes, it was mostly about the roaring wind and cool water sprinkled against warm skin that the women reported. But when the sky was clear and dotted with stars, the reports were likely to be on the planetary bodies, rotational speeds, houses, horoscopes, times of birth, ascendants, quadratures, omens of the sun and moon, who we are, where we are, and where we are going. A recurring question was: What did it mean that we had met at just such a time in just such a place and in just such a way? There had to be a secret meaning hidden in the fact that *we* had met *each other* and not some strangers under completely different circumstances and planetary positions. When after our lovemaking, I would be lying there wasted with my cock limp and a hand heavy on her bush still steaming hot, it was often astrology that would come from her mouth. Or rather, it was language in its purest form of poetry. Sometimes, it sounded like she was dreaming out loud. And who knows? Maybe she was. The sound of her voice seemed to come from a far-away place that grew ever more distant: "This aspect signifies that there's the greatest risk not only for delusion, but also for falling victim to fraud and deceit. Tendencies of scheming and scandal or secrecy seem to characterize your present experiences. Neptun…ptun… uun…nn." The planetary bodies penetrated my mind and transported me to a place beyond the horizon. Sleep and the sacrament of intercourse. Gradually, the waves of language settled until all that was left was the soft murmuring sound of the galactic surf coming from afar, until like some foetus I dozed off. Only to wake the next morning to the accusation that I would gladly fuck her, but *listen* to her, no way. Why else did I fall asleep right when she was most awake and inspired? It really was *too* frustrating. Right when she had begun to serve me up a meal consisting of the choicest morsels of her thought, she would look to the side and what did she see: me sound asleep. Now, how did I think that felt? But that sort of thing was of course way beyond the spiritual capacity of an ox like me. What I wanted from her was just some piece of ass, some nice tits, and a bit of cunt.

"Yes, darling," I said trying to sound like I was thankful for all the good things I had enjoyed, "only you forgot to mention your lovely hips!"

"Jesus Christ, what a *bastard* you are!" she would say and jump to the floor in order to get away as quickly as possible.

Maybe all that astrology, or should I say oestrogenic astrology, explains why over time I began to prefer overcast skies. When the heavenly bodies were hidden the reports tended to be more about down-to-earth subjects such as spiderwebs, mosquitoes, dog shit and nettles, or about what fun it was when, in winter, a thick carpet of snow covered the ground and it was possible to make "butt-holes" in it. Once on a good night, I was asked if I realized that women were capable of "sniffing the Earth" with their cunts? Did

I realize that women had "an evolutionary lead" because they possessed two organs of smell as opposed to men only possessing one?

It was quite remarkable really how this nightly sojourn to pee in the open awakened the primate in women. Out there, alone in the dark by the rampart, squatting on her haunches, naked in my clogs and sniffing her own impression in the snow with her sex, the slumbering primate woke and took possession of her. And along with Miss Primate came all kinds of healing and primordial instincts for surrender, lovemaking, worship, pleasure and self-preservation. What a long-time use of glossy women's magazines had seemingly killed in her was for a brief moment brought back in full force. Just by peeing in the wilderness behind my wagon. The experience also stimulated the instinct for mating in the woman. Once late at night, Lili came stomping naked across my bouncy wooden floor. Boom, boom, boom! There was something she wanted to know, she said. Was it something I had arranged—those nettles out in the back that set her butt "so badly afire" she needed a fire-brigade to put it out? Because if it *was* me, if I was "the pyromaniac of the countess' cunt," then it was pretty damn cunning on my part! "Pretty damn cunning," she repeated, whereupon she broke down laughing so hard she had to bend over and hold her stomach. "Watch out, all you women out there. The pyromaniac of the countess' cunt is on the rampage. The serial pyromaniac is at it again, is *at it* again…" At this stage, she was hiccupping so hard she could hardly breathe. "Help me. Oh, help me, won't you! Would you come to my rescue you horndog you?" Again, she bent over laughing, but this time, she picked up my underwear from the floor and flung them in my face. It was just like Lili. She threw things when she was mad, and she threw things when she was glad.

I do not know what it was about that little shack of mine, and the rampart behind it. Only there was something about that combo. It seemed somehow bewitched. Maybe the tall trees and the wind soughing in their tops played a part too. Was it a case of magic seduction or some cunning form of rape that rendered women defenseless? Whatever it was, it made a great deal of difference. The little shack on the ramparts. I swear it did…

I also think that Melanie—if only her character had not been so strong—would have undressed and let nature take its course. Just like the others, she would have reported on the climate standing in the middle of the floor and with her feet still in my black clogs. But it was not to be. Melanie remains the exception. For a quarter century, she has kept me guessing what she might have said in the report I never got. It's a bit like a jigsaw puzzle with a thousand pieces. You have finished it, only to find there's one piece missing. You have looked all over, but the piece is nowhere to be found. In itself, it's nothing extraordinary, just some skyblue piece like so many others. It does not matter in the slightest, but since it's the only piece missing, it fascinates you more than all the other pieces put together—the ones that are in their places, form a picture and would never dream of being absent. I don't know how others feel, but, for me, it's something that needs to be taken seriously. If not, the missing piece might in time take on mythological dimensions, appear before the sun and throw a shadow.

As opposed to the majority of her gender, Melanie had a will of her own and a good idea how to use it. Or as she once put it herself: If she had given in to her "biological being" and slept with me, she would have stayed with me in the wagon until the deluge flooded the Earth for the second time, and the two of us, in our tight embrace, floated away on its waters. But, she added, it didn't exactly seem like I

144

was hard up for a woman.

Melanie cocked her head a bit to one side and fluttered her eyelashes: Was I?

"No, not anymore," I said.

Melanie nodded: "I bet you've got a lot of young damsels comin' round, don't you?"

When she said that, I used Martin's method on her and looked her deep in the eyes for a long time without blinking: What made her think so?

Oh, she said, for the simple reason that the wagon appealed to women. She could feel it in her bones. There was something about it, something terribly seductive. At one and the same time, you had the feeling the wagon was a safe cave or cavern that you could seek shelter in until you were fully hatched and that it was something like an ark one could weather the deluge in. Marrying cocoon safety with the freedom and renewal that is spiritual survival it was exactly the kind of thing a woman wanted, no, what she dreamed of, desired and longed for. It was what the restlessness of her erotic nature, what her entire being drove her towards. She was able under such conditions to be at home and find peace. By itself, the cave would have been too secure and claustrophobic; by itself, the ark would have been too exposed, too fragile and vulnerable. But a cave-ship like my caravan, located in a place like Christiania, well, *that* was irresistible. In any case, it was so for her. She didn't want me to think it was not.

"Okay. Then, I won't do that," I said.

A week ago the same Melanie who once came up with the "theory of the cave-ship" came up with the shocking suggestion that we meet again in Copenhagen in the spring. It seems to me a risky idea. After all, we have not seen each other once since the cave-ship days. "It's hazardous and it will be strange too," a little voice pipes up inside me. There is no cave-ship anymore, and maybe soon there will be no Christiania either. And even if there is, it won't be anything like the freewheeling chaotic community where we once met. What do we do then? Don't we risk screwing up a correspondence that means a lot to us both? Can you put the impression you once made on each other on repeat? Can such a thing happen *twice* in a lifetime? I think of the time Melanie woke me in my wagon. As always, when it was nice weather, the door was open towards the dancing and flickering sunlight of early morning. I woke and was looking at her from the bed like one looks at the first thing one sees waking from a beautiful dream. There she was dark against the sun, dressed in a blouse with short sleeves, and it seemed as if the sun was at the same time burning through her and framing her in its splendor. That's how I photographed her with my mind's eye, and that's the picture I have kept on the mantelpiece of my soul.

Before me on the table, there is the letter that Melanie once wrote me from Italy. It's in that letter she tells me how the day we met began for her. In the house of her parents-in-law somewhere near the town of Horsens, she woke to the sound of someone calling her from downstairs. "Mom! Mooo-om!" It was her daughter Claire, who is now a mother herself and living in Hilo, Hawaii. At the time, she was only four years old. Melanie was still married to the girl's father, a furniture maker, and…breakfast was served. That was what Claire was shouting. But then, Melanie must have fallen asleep again, because, when a little later, she sat up in bed, it was with that sensation of unreality, which sometimes came over her, and which became stronger after Claire and Jack were born. The way the sensation would come and go apparently for no reason made her feel as though there was some loose connection inside her. She had been sitting there in bed listening to the voices that reached her ears from the floor below when she did something unexpected. Ever so slowly, she started to lift the nightgown until it reached her breasts. There she let it stay, but only for a moment. She then continued the pull upwards letting the soft material caress the nipples and… feeling the breasts fall back to their normal position, ample, firm and softly rounded with the dark nipples erect from the touch of the material.

This is more or less how she described it to me twelve or fourteen years later, when in the harbor of Brindisi the sun was setting, and she was waiting for departure on the deck of the ferryboat Paloma bound for Patras. With the candor of a correspondent who is far removed in every way from the person she writes to and who she doesn't expect ever to see again, she told me how she had smiled "The Mona Lisa smile" to herself and also shuddered a little bit at the thought that had a man appeared at that moment (not just any man but almost), someone who had just the slightest bit of character and who *was* a man, and supposing that that man had pushed her back on the bed, well then she would have done anything for him. In spite of the wedding ring on her finger, in spite of her husband, the future, the parents-in-law, the children, the expectations, moral conventions, dreams and just about everything…

At 11.06 am Melanie would enter the train for Copenhagen and she would arrive a little before three o'clock. Three days and three nights, she was going to be visiting with her old friend and lover Douglas, who she had met at a seminar at The University of California Los Angeles some years before. Among other things Douglas had participated in the establishment of the Frøstrup camp in Thy. That was on the fourth of July 1970. A little over a year later, he moved to the newly founded Freetown of Christiania, "The squatters' Village" that he had then proceeded to describe in such great detail for her. Arriving in Copenhagen, Melanie was to find her way to Christiania and seek out Douglas in "The Wagon Village" where he was living with his Danish wife in a "pioneer wagon on wheels".

Taking her shower that morning, Melanie could feel how much she was looking forward to the trip. But was it right of her to do this to them? To the children, to David, to her parents-in-law? Was it all right to leave it all for three full days like that? Was it not terribly egotistic of her to go away to enjoy herself in "The ray of hope for the West" which is what Douglas had baptized Christiania? A place where the inhabitants showed disrespect for private property, where people even lived outside the law, experimented with polygamy and didn't treat sex as a taboo—a chaotic "alternative society" where women kneaded dough outside their houses naked and where cannabis was grown, sold and freely smoked…

Right there in the shower, it all came back to her, all the things Douglas had told her in his first long and inspired love letters from Denmark. Everything was still new to him then; he was still full of hope. Having a major crush on her, he mobilized all the wit and imagination he possessed in an attempt to get her to drop everything and come live with him in Christiania. She should consider that it was a historic phenomenon, he said, one of a kind and that, if she missed it, she would regret it the rest of her days. A seed had been planted that would in time be of immense significance in bringing about the change necessary if man was to survive.

It had been a regular campaign on Douglas' part. There was practically no limit to the harvest she would reap from such a stay with him in Christiania—personally, professionally, psychologically, spiritually and in every other conceivable way. Being a graduate in journalism and a skilled photographer, she could do an article for *National Geographic*.

They would take it he said, and then he had proceeded to back up this statement by giving her another dose of the laidback lifestyle prevalent in the Christiania of faraway Copenhagen. What she had to keep in mind, he (again and again) pointed out—what was so unique was the fact that it was not just a building or two or even three that had been squatted. No, it was a large area with many buildings, great and small. It really was a part of the city, an autonomous enclave, which it took three quarters of an hour to cross from one end to the other. Also it was not exactly the "ordinary run of the mill characters", who had gathered in Christiania. There were some "pretty peculiar personality types" out there. He could assure her of that. She just had to take his word for it, he wrote, when he said that he could introduce her to a handful of characters the likes of which she would never dream existed. And quite aside from this, it also happened every so often that world-class celebrities stopped by Christiania. As she knew, he himself had met John Lennon and Yoko Ono. Okay, that wasn't in Christiania but in the town of Hust up in Thy, when they did their love and peace happening. It did not make a whole lot of difference though, since the happening could just as well have taken place at Christiania.

After he moved to Christiania, Douglas had never been the same. From day one, Denmark's Freetown had been "an eye- and soul opener." The reason he had dropped so much acid in the States was not just to experiment, it was also because he had felt "lost and confused" and as if confined in a "wasteland of boredom and disease." Apart from being an attempt to liberate himself and "transcend one-dimensional and lethal materialism," drugs for Douglas had been a way of assuaging the pain and nausea that had turned his life into such a miserable affair. It had been his way of protecting himself against "the fierce ravages of devastat-

149

ing disgust" that so many of the best men of his generation had succumbed to. It was the despairing for a way out that drove people to seek oblivion. His long psychedelic flight, however, had not been a free ride, if that's what Melanie thought. Self-destruction had nearly cost him his life. So close had he come to death that he still had the smell of it in his nostrils! There had been a frozen night in Montana that he would never forget, he said. But as it happened, the low point had also been the turning point in that it ejected him from the country and landed him in Christiania where he experienced "a sort of rebirth." The place in which he found himself was "a tiny crack in the capitalistic wasteland of the spirit" where, against all odds, "some lost seeds of life" had been able to grow. Of course, the crack was far from perfect. After all, it was only "a bruise surrounded on all sides by dirt, dried blood, resistant bacteriae and hardened skin." The sky above the newborn alternative community was infested with the same "rotten wind" that was blowing everywhere. People were inhaling the same poisonous particles. And in Christiania, too, people succumbed. Sure they did. Nevertheless, the place was still an oasis for him. In Christiania, Doug met kindred souls who did not go under, even if they were stuck in the "ubiquitous quagmire," up to their necks. By their example, these souls assured him there was solid ground somewhere. If one only got in deep enough, trusted in providence, was not intimidated by the morass and held out.

If Denmark was not good for much else, Douglas wrote, at least by some "freak of fortune," it had produced "an emergency lung" by the name Christiania. He was not sure what to compare it to in his homeland. Unlike the crime-infested ghettos in the US that the government turned its blind eye to, Christiania suffered from an overdose of attention from the Danish government. The authorities never stopped meddling in its affairs. Also, there was a more or less constant outcry in the media. It was unfair. Christiania did not consist solely of the calloused dregs of society out to make an easy buck. Aside from attracting the dregs, the Freetown attracted the best men and women in the nation who had made of it a full-fledged alternative society based on different values. In Christiania, the criminal and the reformer lived side by side with the artist and formed a... community.

If life in the West, Douglas went on, had been reduced to a festering boil, the Freetown of Christiania was a needle prick in its tip. And, lo and behold! Right where the skin had been perforated and puss was oozing, fresh air had slipped in to neutralize the inflammation, heal a few cells and spread hope throughout the rest of the organism. He was forever grateful, Doug said, that he had been lifted out of "greed, poverty, extreme riches and hopelessness" and brought back to life. Perhaps Christiania was not a great big hope, but since it gave people a chance to show what they contained, gave them something to live *for* other than buying and owning things, it was worth standing up for. As far as he was concerned, he was now doing what he could to "spread the word." What else was there to do in a situation such as the one the world was in? The alternative to the alternative was down and out suicide.

It was this, more or less, that Douglas had written in his letters, knowing from "first hand experience" that Melanie too dreamt of: "spiritual rebirth in a mechanized and thoroughly materialistic West intoxicated by the 'totenmarsch' of progress towards the final destruction of all life." Today, Melanie was going to experience that "flower in the desert" for the first time. No matter how much she had shared Doug's view of the world situation and no matter how deeply she had felt that the time was ripe for change, she had never reciprocated Doug's feelings on a personal level. Perhaps the campaign to persuade her to drop everything had even had the opposite effect. Underneath all the talk about peace, love, freedom, autonomy, community feeling and shared users' rights, she had heard the voice of infatuation. That is why the visit had not been possible before. Melanie could not help smiling at the thought of their imminent reunion. Now that they were both happily married, chances were he would let her sleep in peace on the folding cot he had promised.

Sitting on the train bound for Copenhagen, Melanie looked out the window at the countryside of Funen going by. In her letter, she described how everything was lush and green compared to California. Black and white cows were grazing all over the place. Sometimes the animals were spread out over the entire field; sometimes they were lumped together in a small corner with no grass. Melanie was wondering about cows. Like the animals, she was feeling docile, at peace with the world and wide open to whatever happened. Except for a young girl reading a women's magazine, she was alone in the compartment. Melanie glanced across the aisle at the girl, pricked up her inner ear and listened. At that moment, she had a feeling like she was part of a great and undisturbed quietude. Beyond the sounds that the train was making, beyond the thoughts in her own head, beyond her breathing, even beyond time and place, her inner ear was aware of a huge and ubiquitous silence. But there he was once more, the oddball ticket taker who made a point of touching the back of every seat as he walked down the aisle. The magic of the moment was broken, for even if he didn't bother asking for her ticket anymore, he looked at her and so brought her back from the place she had been. As soon as the ticket taker had passed, Melanie turned her head and looked out the window again. A little ways off, a lake was coming into view its waters glittering in the sun. Along the shores, brightly colored rushes grew. What kind of strange anthropological phenomenon was it that awaited her at the other end of this journey? Next to her on the seat was a little knapsack with camera, pencil and paper in it. Melanie was prepared. In the back of her mind, the *National Geographic* article that Doug had suggested was already forming. So his campaign had not been useless after all. It was true that if she could get an article accepted in such a magazine, her carreer as a freelancer would indeed be launched "like a rocket"...

As it happened, nothing came of the *National Geographic*. Instead Melanie's article appeared unabridged and with beautiful illustrations in *The Sun*. There was no reason for regret. She looked at it this way: if she could not always get what she wanted, she could at least be happy for what she got. This was one of several paraphrases of a proverb that was popular at the time, and which Melanie took pleasure in taking apart and putting back together in new and improvised versions. The proverb ran: "If you can't be with the one you love, love the one you're with."

When first heard, it sounded intriguing. How could anything so simple not be true? But instead of making a disciple of her, its irresistible charm made Melanie smell a rat. Wasn't it a tad too elegant and convenient to be true? "Truth never reveals itself flawlessly attired," she later wrote to me. If there was something we humans were good at, it was to invent seductive justifications for our transgressions. Being an unruly and intelligent animal, Man was unable to tolerate what he perceived as the tyranny of nature. In this respect and others too, humans differed from

153

all other species. Our ingenuity was never so boundless as when it came to deluding ourselves. As much as Melanie was charmed by the old hippie proverb, she also mistrusted it. She sensed, she said, that hidden under the glib surface there was a "less than decent" purpose. It worked sort of like a double agent: While appearing to be in the service of freedom, it was secretly providing criminal conscience with an escape route and an alibi. And anyway, it didn't apply to us. If one wanted to formulate a proverb for the situation that she had been in with me, it would have to be phrased more like a question: "If at one point a woman feels out of love with the man she is married to, the father of her kids, is she then allowed to sleep with the man she happens to be with and… feels that she loves?"

Melanie did not think so, and that decided the situation in favor of her husband and kids in Jutland. He had stood by her in her hour of need. Together, they formed the family in which she had her life. She resisted the temptation, and when the three days and nights were over, she returned on the train.

A month or more went by before I was to hear from her again.

When I did, it was in the form of a letter (the first of our correspondence), which was handed to me by Inger, our local mailman in Christiania. Melanie's letter, addressed to Andreas Stein. Wagon nr. 537 Christiania, Denmark, arrived at the end of August 1981 and contained a request: Would I be so kind as to write her some pages about Christiania. I could write whatever I wanted as long as it was "how *I* saw it." Since I was not old enough to be a flower child and "rebel of '68" maybe I could ask Jakob or Douglas to fill me in. What she would like to know was "something about the meaning of Christiania," both in concrete terms and spiritually speaking. How did the Freetown come about and why?

Why did such things happen in a "welfare state" like Denmark where everybody was supposedly more or less well off and content? If there was such great consensus as to the blessings of the state machinery, why then did part of the populace feel a need to establish themselves with separatist flag, their own currency, local autonomy, grassroots democracy and a different set of values? Christiania was labelled an "alternative society," but what did the word "alternative" really mean? These were the things Melanie wanted to know about, and if I would also speak a bit about the background, she would appreciate it. How was life "back then?" What kind of people were they who first made a hole in the fence and settled there? What was it that drove them out of the other Denmark? Supposing it was an act of protest, what then was it a protest against? What sort of society were they dreaming to create? Etc. Etc.

I accepted the challenge, thinking that, for once, I would have some use for what I had learned at the history department. Over the following weeks and over four long letters, I told Melanie "The Story of the Forbidden City of Christiania." Essentially, I said it was the story of how an ugly military garrison established during the time of the absolute monarchy was transformed a century later into a "colorful symbol of civil rights, community spirit and liberty." The Freetown of Christiania, a stone's throw from the City Hall of Copenhagen, covered eighty-five acres. Being a former military installation that had served as part of the defense of Copenhagen, it contained factories for the production of weapons, drilling grounds, large riding houses, stables, laboratory buildings, living quarters, barracks, thick-walled gunpowder depots, storage facilities, workshops, garages, ramparts, a thatched (and very quaint) residence for the commander in chief, and a moat full of water that divided the area in two: the largest part towards the west and a narrow strip on the other side of the moat facing east. With time, however, advances in the technology of war had made the installation obsolete. Rather than serving the defense of the city of Copenhagen, it had become a likely target in case of war with The Soviet Union. In 1969-70, the authorities decided to close the garrison and open the facility for other purposes. Although no plans for the future use of the area had been made (in violation of the government's own "City-planning Act of 1938), the military proceeded to vacate the area and left it unused and virtually unguarded behind a tall board fence.

To understand what happened, I wrote, one must imagine a society with many good laws that are carefully enforced but in which it's almost impossible to live. Also, it paid off to focus on the peace movements and student uprisings of 1968. The time was one of hardcore Marxism, flowers in the hair and longhaired dope-fiends. Many people were experimenting with sexual relationships and hallucinogenic drugs; many lived in communes and travelled to India, Nepal and Afghanistan. The brightly day-glo painted VW-van was a favorite means of transportation. In the back of it, were scattered ragged paperback copies of William Burroughs' "Naked Lunch," Jack Kerouac's "On the Road," Hermann Hesse's "Demian," Herbert Marcuse's "One dimensional Man," and Ken Kesey's "One Flew over the Cuckoo's Nest." Setting out from Denmark, people drove their vans through Europe, through Turkey, Iran and Pakistan, and into India where (like The Beatles), they sought wisdom and truth with gurus living in ashrams. They studied the Zen Masters in Lhasa. The ones back home listened to Ravi Shankar, Jimmy Hendrix and The Doors. Many of the young generation were high on its newfound ideals. War was believed to be an aberration, and peace was the natural state of man who was essentially good. No longer seen as a means for fulfilling other people's (profit) objectives, the individual human being was perceived as an entity whose purpose was to live his or her own life. Breaking out of what was felt to be a confinement squatters established themselves in Christiania and shortly afterwards, in November 1971, they formulated their "manifesto": "It is the objective of Christiania to establish an autonomous society where people are able to express themselves individually and at the same time take responsibility for the community at large. Economically, this society must be self-sufficient and endeavor to demonstrate how physical and psychological pollution can be avoided."

One day I asked Jakob:

"Who are we, hm?" Jakob ran his tanned fingers through his hair and gazed at the sky. "Let me see… We're a bunch of unruly slobs, lazier than hell and powerless to boot. And *especially*, we're the ones who are too flatfooted, bowlegged and hunchbacked to fit into the lousy schematic scheme of things. Our minds are so unbelievably sluggish we don't even fear what will happen to us if we don't take the prescribed medicine. We're the ones who've had our eyes plucked out and cannot, for the life of us, comprehend that it's for our own sake that things on the ward are the way they are. We're such fools, we can't get it into our fat skulls that it's the good life, which has been so well organized and set up for us. If it's so damned good, why then do we feel forced, trapped and cheated? The way we behave you'd think we're a bunch of degenerates. Just think! We e-v-e-n go so far as to refuse to participate in the digging of our own graves like all good citizens are expected to. It's preposterous. Simply to be a nuisance and get in the way, we arrange happenings and sit-ins in the most outrageous places. We take every opportunity to throw grit into the machinery and call ourselves schitzophrenics, paranoiacs, children of Jesus, pushers, preachers, draft resisters, activists, yogis, junkies, vegetarians, micro-macro freaks, nudists and Zen Buddhists. Anything to avoid doing service. Above all, we're too stupid to toil ourselves to death in order to make a living. No amount of education can convince us it's for our own best. We're the ones who are constantly bombarded with the question: "But what *is* it that you want instead?" As if coming from one huge choir, the indoctrinated mass of wage earners and money makers vent their frustration at us. As if it wasn't perfectly clear what it is that we want: What we want is a world in which the good life is not some lousy piece of ten-cent chewing gum that has lost all its taste by the time a person reaches the age of six. We're the ones who get up and stand up for a life full and rich and lasting right until the end. To set ourselves outside and above nature is *not* what we want. We refuse to participate in the ruthless exploitation and destruction of nature. We want to respect it and be part of its photosynthesis. We embrace the trees and want to be each other's brothers and sisters. What we want to do is to make love to one another in this way and that and share the resulting children between us. We want to express ourselves freely. We want to be like a tribe in the city or maybe one big family, always close enough to be able to be there for one another. Through our daily action and interaction, we create and transform things. Our actions speak for us. They say: "All you people out there, when are you going to get it—that we're the innocent ones who believe in the possibility of a joyful existence in a different and better society than the existing one? Consequently, we no longer belong among those who believe that it makes any sense changing the system, the greed-driven economy and the overall conditions of life from within. We believe that it has gotten to a point where it's only through action on the grassroots level that deep and lasting change can happen. Because when it comes right down to it, we're more religious and philosophical than political. We're not faithful to the institutions, and to us, politics is just another word for what each of us does in the course of our days and nights. We change our minds about things, reconsider and are not consistent. When visitors to Christiania see us remove our own garbage, put up solar panels on our roofs, build outhouses so that our assholes can produce fertilizer for our gardens, when they see us scavenge used building materials, they think we're just playing at collecting garbage, playing at smoking hash, playing at shitting in the open and playing at picking rags. But they don't understand. These are—each one of them political acts that reject the status quo. Every day being election-day for us, we don't set much store on the elections organized by the authorities. When after work, the exhausted voters pencil in their cross by one of the political parties, we're at home taking our daily shit in an outhouse. The turd we squeeze out is the ballot with which we elect ourselves. In sharp contrast to what the great majority is doing *we* turn our excrement into compost. We rebel against buying indulgence by voting for career politicians organized in political parties. We rebel against high rents that enslave people, and we rebel against the crippling interest rates of mortgages that leave people at the mercy of greedy bankers. We're altogether against usury and private property. No matter where they happen to be, what we say to people is: "Go find your inner Christiania and settle there. Liberate your life and take your dumps in an outhouse. And of course, if in the mood, smoke a pipe of hash and pat a dog. That sort of revolution."

This is the speech Jakob made to me, and he even said more than that, but the rest—I told Melanie—I could say just as well myself. To understand what happened in the years 1970-71 in Copenhagen, one should remember what our part of the world looked like at the time. Mighty political, economic, technological and demographical forces were rapidly transforming societies and the different populations of Europe and in the US. The threat of an all-destructive nuclear war was felt to be real and plausible. The question was in what secret ways *that* possibility influenced people's minds.

Atomic bombs, the Cold War and an accelerating arms race. One button pressed and darkness would descend on the planet. There was war in Vietnam, and in the Middle East, no peace was in sight. In the US, Robert Kennedy had just been assassinated. Refusing to fight in the war, Muhammed Ali had had his heavy weight title taken away and was sentenced to years in prison. Millions of young Americans were marching in peaceful demonstrations shouting: "Make love not war." There had been a Woodstock Festival and from the stage Country Joe McDonald sang: "What are we fighting for. Don't ask me, I don't give a damn. Next stop is the Vietnam." Whereupon he gave Uncle Sam the finger and shouted to the massive crowd: "Gimme an 'F'! Gimme a'U'! Gimme a 'C'! Gimme a 'K'! What's it spell? What's it spell?"

Generally speaking, charged as it was with prophesies of doom and mental illnesses the atmosphere in which people in the West were then living was not essentially different from the atmosphere of the present. Democracy was no longer inspired by the same visionary energy and hope that was characteristic of Benjamin Franklin and "The Founding Fathers." Everywhere in the West, the political institutions allowed narrow political and economic elites to manipulate their populations, while shutting the mouths of the few who dared speak up.

As far as my friends and I could see, we were living

in a world gone stark raving mad and progressing head-long towards its own destruction. The symptoms of disease and insanity formed a legion. First, there was the hidden force of normalized greed. From being in former times an abnormality, an abomination and a disgrace, greed had succeeded in whitewashing itself. In order better to combat Marxism, hide its real nature and justify itself, greed had mutated into a dogmatic ideology. The living-dead apostles of profit never missed a chance to hail it as the driving force behind progress. Then, there was the ally of virulent greed, namely economic growth. From being an economic notion, growth had become an obsessive mania, an excuse for unbridled egotism and consumption. Energy had become synonymous with uranium and fossil fuel resources; investment had become another word for squeezing more and still more money out of less and less time. Global wide overpopulation and an accelerating consumption especially of fossil fuels was wreaking havoc on the ecological systems necessary for the survival of the species. Conflict over access to the world's limited resources was threatening to speed up the process of destruction. The sand in the upper chamber of the hour glass was rapidly running out. If something was to be done about it, there was no time to lose. If people did not rebel and refuse to rush along the road of suicide, the breakdown would happen soon and be of cataclysmic proportions. For the time being, life was still possible, but for how long?

Considering the situation, I wrote, it was not surprising that there were young Danes who looked at progress with a mixture of disgust, shame and horror. And neither was it surprising that a growing number of them sought ways to obstruct the road to perdition.

In 1968, there had been student uprisings in Paris and in Copenhagen, and in Czechoslovakia, the tanks of the Warsaw Pact had crushed the first tender shoots of democratic socialism. Where, until recently, the bud of fresh hope had sprouted, there was now an iron turf of hopelessness. Of "normalization." Everywhere both to the West and to the East of the Iron Curtain, on the grass roots level, there was a growing resistance to the conflicting forms of totalitarian materialism. In the capitalistic world as well as the communist one, science was able to split the atom. Soon, it would also have mapped out man's genetic makeup—all of which would certainly have amounted to marvelous advances if the objective had not been greater profits and any gain from it was offset by an equivalent loss of meaning.

Such was the world's spiritual crisis. At the same time, on the street level of "Wonderful Copenhagen," there was an acute lack of affordable housing. In parts of the city where formerly tens of thousands of working class families had been housed, by 1971 there were mostly banks, insurance companies and government offices left. Sound buildings were being regularly demolished; property owners made fortunes on speculation; there was blackmailing of the city's officials and widespread incompetence. As a result of public policy, the large generation of young people that had been conceived behind the blackout curtains of the Second World War had a hard time finding adequate housing. Many had come to the metropolis from the countryside either in search of work or of education. Some had experimented with drugs and become addicted. Meeting behind the thick walls of the City Hall, the democratic politicians were considering whether to emulate Hamburg, where paved boulevards and tall modern buildings had replaced the cobbled squares, narrow streets and low houses of the old city. For example, this was the plan for the picturesque canals of Copenhagen's Christianshavn. But no consensus had been reached. The few new housing projects were located on the outskirts of the city and consisted of cheap prefab constructions. In these satellite towns, there were playgrounds and institutions for the children. There were supermarkets, laundromats and parking lots below ground level. Taking into consideration all the mechanics of a normal workday routine the planner had forgotten the more significant needs of living people. Lacking in this respect these concrete sprawls almost immediately turned into a slum where nobody wanted to live unless they had to.

Was it a coincidence that exactly at this moment in history, the authorities vacated the Boatman Street military installation?

In the weeks and months that followed, scavengers stripped the area of its sanitary installations and whatever other valuables left behind by the military. Homeless drunks and bums found shelter in the same vacated buildings where vandals were busy tearing things apart. By the time the squatters arrived on the scene, two buildings had already been burnt to cinders.

While the authorities were passively looking on and considering what to do with such an area polluted by many years of military production, an activist movement for the rejuvenation of an ailing democracy was set in motion. Was it a paradox or a systemic error or a practical joke... that a drawn out government *crisis*, a long-time *inability* of the bureaucracy to act on its own legislation and the resulting *neglect*... together amounted to the best thing the rulers had done for the population in many many years? No matter what it was, it was happening. It existed. It was there! The squatters didn't wait for the bulldozers. The occupation completed the new occupants declared the area an "independent Freetown," set up a grass-roots democracy, put an end to the vandalism and saw to it that the dilapidated historic buildings did not suffer further decay. With its almost virginal flora and the many odd residential structures that mushroomed up all over the place, the old garrison in no time at all became a laboratory of a new and different life. Thanks to a fortuitous vacuum of power and the unique energies that become manifest at the point where nature and culture intersect, Christiania survived its own birth...

The new settlers immediately set about naming buildings and places. As for the buildings, they came up with names like "The Arc of Peace," "The Rock Machine," "The Opera," "The Flee," "Woodstock," "Nirvana," "Aircondition" and "The Moonfisher." The open area directly inside the main entrance was "The Prairie." A cluster of construction wagons became "The Wagon Village". The street where the hash dealers traded their wares was "Pusher Street." What had hitherto been a dead and alphabetized no-man's-land known on the map as "The Boatman Street military garrison," had come to life and was christened... "The Freetown of Christiania." Intoxicated by its own initial success and the promise that it seemed to hold, the liberated community declared itself a nuclear-free zone, independent of official Denmark with its prime minister, membership of NATO and contributions to the arms race. Seen from inside the liberated zone the other Denmark was a place where the dominating values had created a heartless, medicated, violent, atomized, and notoriously unhappy society. The elements of unhappiness were manifold: greed, egotism, state regulation of just about everything, and control over each individual soul. There was excessive consumption, dependence, herd-mentality, docility organized in political parties, widespread depression, high suicide rate, pollution, rampant drug and alcohol abuse, loneliness, corruption, social expulsion, discrimination and mental illness. And... above all, there was a great need for at new way.

At this point, I went into the civil, judicial and moral

dogfight between authorities and christianites, which followed in the wake of the occupation.

In the letter I sent a few days later, I mentioned the cry of outrage vented at the squatters for having illegally taken possession of a piece of government property. At the taxpayers' expense these "delinquents" had established their own community of "criminals, misfits, and sponges on the social system." And I didn't forget to mention the lawsuit that Christiania had filed against the Danish State. In vivid colors I painted how, during these months of trial, there were huge "Rainbow army" demonstrations through the streets. Finally, I even testified to the hearings in parliament: Was it true that the government paid for the electricity and gas used on the former Boatman Street Garrison? If so, was this something the government intended to go on with? Etc.

After an elucidation of the issues involved in "the dogfight over Christiania" (economic, psychological, political, sanitary, social, criminological and as pertaining to city planning) and the bewilderment on the part of authorities attempting to legitimize the entire scenario by declaring it a "social experiment", I quoted Steen Eiler Rasmussen, a well-known architect:

"For someone like me whose occupation it is to plan housing and housing developments, Christiania has been rather a strange experience. Never in my wildest dreams would I have thought that anything good could come out of such chaos. It has not only been strange but also encouraging to realize what positive strength there is in people — even in those who seemingly are the weakest — when they are allowed to show it."

In my opinion, this was both the reason that the Freetown had come into existence and the reason it still existed: the release of creative energy that occurred when people who had been patronized and subjected to tight regulation were let lose. To understand the strong appeal that Christiania exercised on people from near and far, it was necessary to highlight the values that the Freetown was based on—like the freedom of the individual to express him or herself as long as it didn't happen at the expense of his or her neighbors; the liberation of the imagination as a revolt against the ever growing conformity, *uni*formity and bureaucratization of life; the love of nature; the ousting of the automobile from the public space; an economy based on real people's real needs; an organic balance, and the "sustainable growth" philosophy.

Finally, I returned to the story of how the newborn community had been met with sabotage and threatened with demolition. Apparently, the architect Steen Eiler Rasmussen was not the only one who was surprised at the discharge of energy that took place in Christiania. So were the authorities. It had apparently come as a surprise to the authorities that side by side with the wage earner, the voter, the taxpayer, the consumer, the whole silent elite made up of complacent moneymakers, careerists, and impostors in top positions, there appeared to be a great many noisy individuals who felt themselves impotent, superfluous— even traumatized and so did not want to live any more as they were told! The strong emotional reactions triggered by the birth of the Freetown Christiania, I wrote, revealed the chasm cutting down through Danish society as well as down through each individual soul. On the one side was the objectives of a power elite pledged to eternal economic growth and progress and on the other the objectives of individual men and women whose objective it was to live, love and express themselves freely. The outrage against Christiania was, I said, essentially a cry of pain triggered by this recently opened chasm separating the sterile elements of modern humanity from the vital ones.

I think I already told you of how I was driving my taxi the night before Melanie and I met. Melanie spent it at her parents-in-law's place near Horsens. It was one of those ethereal nights that sometimes occur in the summer in Denmark. Towards dawn, the dark spires and jagged rooftops of Copenhagen were silhouetted against a colossal moon. Earlier, around two o'clock, as I was returning to the city from the north, the radio played George Harrison's euphoric "My Sweet Lord," which I had loved since I was seventeen and an exchange student in Palo Alto. I spent half my pocket money for the month on the album *All Things must Pass*. Now, I had not heard the song for a long time, and turning the volume high, I soon reached a point where I no longer knew if I was in an automobile fueled by diesel or on a flying carpet bound for Samarkand. "All Things must Pass." Yeah, yeah, yeah, that's how it was, and that's how it must be. But right here and now in this balmy night, all things were vibrant and alive: the plants, the animals, and the people. Even the rocks. Everything around me and in me lived and breathed and sang and was going to last forever. Optical illusion, prophetic transport, karmic completion, transmigration of souls, rebirth and immortality. Granite, samsara and Nirvana. The Circle. The feeling I had of the indestructibility of life seemed stronger than ever before. As sure as I was sitting behind the steering wheel, the things of this world formed an unbreakable whole and were part and parcel of the same creation. All things must pass, except life itself…

In order not to be torn out of my euphoria, I turned the radio off when the tune ended. And it was exactly at this moment I saw the lake bathed in moonlight to my left. Without thinking about what I was doing, I slowed down and stopped the car. Turning off the engine, I remained sitting there very still and listening. A couple of hundred steps away, the lake was reflecting the moonlight and the dawn both in its rippling waters. Glancing at the broken green digits of the electronic watch, I saw, before my inner eye, the narrow streets of the city center—the garbage and the broken glass and the party people yelling or waving down taxis and pissing and kissing and getting into fights on the sidewalks. Now was the time to make money in there. "Some other time," I told myself and got out.

Still elated, not to say ecstatic with love, worship and assurance, I crossed the road. On the other side, I started doing the Krishna dance along the path leading to the lake. And for every meter I danced, my ecstasy grew. "I'm a dervish," I thought, "a dervish dancing for the moon, the black shiny mirror of the lake, the fishes in its waters and the heavens strewn with stars. I'm a dancing dervish doing a jig for George Harrison, Krishna and the coots nesting in the rushes."

Had I been on drugs, I could not have felt higher, more expansive and more in harmony with the cosmos. Hare Krishna, Krishna-Krishna, Hare-hare, Hare-rama, Hallelujah-hallelujah! Even though the music had stopped, it was still playing in my head at full volume. Only Krishna and the other Gods know what possessed me. I hardly recognized myself anymore. I'm not a dreamer type at all. Normally, I have both my feet solidly planted on the ground, and here I was dancing like some Krishna-freak by a lake far from where the money was. With empty minutes ticking away in the car up on the road. What did I care? Why worry about earning my keep when I was dancing in the lap of infinite eternity. Was not my life already safe in the hand of my creator?

"My Sweet Lord and wonder of wonders!" It was less than four months since I had gotten the wagon in Christiania, and I had lived in it six maybe seven weeks. It was all still new to me, and yet I had a funny feeling like it wasn't. Strange as it may sound, it was like I had lived it all before. Going through the motions of the dance, it was like I was repeating a ritual familiar to me—the ritual of returning to the starting point. And it's not like I am your archtypical Robinson Crusoe either—at least not on the practical level. As opposed to the shipwrecked English sailor, the Danish student from the northern suburbs had been born in an age when the islands that a man could wash ashore on were all inhabited. Whereas, on his island Robinson could start from scratch and build everything with his own hands, on mine I could not touch a damn thing without asking permission or being arrested for tresspassing. Robinson did not find his island; I found mine. Robinson was knocked unconscious and found he was alone; I was conscious that I was lonely. Robinson met Friday; I met Lili, Jakob and Old Knud. Breaking out of my cocoon, I had to learn how to use my wings. Like some forgotten butterfly weathering centuries in a dusty flat, I had been brought back to life. A window opened, and I flew out of it to establish myself in a new home beyond the law. With a little help from my friends, my wagon had become more than habitable. It had become cozy. It was now insulated on all six sides. The walls were covered with light tongue-and-groove boards from the Green Recycling Hall. The little cast-iron woodstove I had found in the smithy. In the same place, I also bought the chimney. There was new tarpaper on the roof, and at the end of the wagon, where the bed was, Lili had helped me put in a small window. The bed was big enough for two and with deep shelves under it for my clothes. Before my door were the steps that Lili and the others would stomp down (and back up) when they needed to pee. To the right of the door, just as one stepped up into the wagon, there was a rack where we hung our clothes upon entering. To the left, there was the narrow kitchen-table that Christian, the Frenchman, had helped me make! On it was the sink, the big plastic water bottle with its little tap near the bottom, the gasburner and the chopping board. Three short steps forward and you found yourself in the middle of the shack amid the sweet scents of fresh wood, rainwater, coffee, and foliage. Through this whole process, I had forgotten not only how impossible I am with my hands but also that I had ever been happily married. I was now happily divorced, and aside from being able to drive a nail in a board, I was able to saw straight after a pencil-line I had drawn myself.

A week has gone by since I last sat down to write. It's late in the morning of a school holiday, strong gusts of wind coming in from the sea. A moment ago, the boy took off with his friend Luis. They were going down to the harbor to see if Luis' father, the swordfish fisherman, had come in with the night's catch. I heard them shout as they ran. When their voices were drowned by the wind, I closed the door and went to my desk.

Checking my mailbox today, I found a letter from Melanie. It's the second in less than two weeks. Lately, the correspondence has increased. Of course, we could also use email. If we did, traffic would probably increase still more. It's not that we have ever talked about it or made any decision to keep scrawling on paper. It's just how it is, because it has always been that way. We seem to agree there's no reason to change something we have always been happy with—something so simple and at the same time so personal. It *is* how it should be. If you have accomplished something in a certain way, and you like doing it that way, why in God's name would you spend money, time and energy learning to do it in a different way? What matters is not the way you do something, the speed and the conveniance and so on. What matters is the satisfaction or joy it brings. Now, take these letters for example. The moment I see the envelope, I recognize Melanie's characteristically open longhand with its self-assured flourishes that, like the rhythm of her breath, sends ripples and loops in blue ink down the length and breadth of the paper. Yes…the paper, the texture and scent it carries from the place where it was filled with words and sentences. Today the stamp has the Yosemite National Park as its motive. Next to the stamp the postmark says "Honolulu HI" instead of the "Rio Grande" I'm used to. I like the river's name best, because it reminds me of a tiny used bookstore in a basement by Hjultorvet Square in Viborg. Visiting with our grandparents, who lived in a grand apartment on the square, my cousin and I used to go in there to look for Walt Slade books. On a rainy day it was great to step down into the musty cellar, to start rifling through the little paperbacks breathing the moist air and listening to the subdued sounds from the street. Over in the corner by the entrance, the bespectacled and balding bookseller, who had taken on sort of a mildewed look himself, was reading the local newspaper.

Writing this has brought it all back to me. So, for old times sake, I went to the bedroom to fetch the only Walt Slade book I have left. I have opened it on the first page and read: "Ranger Walt Slade—the man that the peons in the river villages of the Rio Grande knew by the name of El Halcon, the Hawk—leaned forward in the saddle and tried to scout the way ahead." One day when I grew up, I had told myself, I would be like that man...

As for the letter on my desk, there is really not a whole lot (other than the letter itself) to cheer my soul. Except for the ending where Melanie talks about being with her two-year-old grandchild, it is one disaster after another. First, there was a strong earthquake, which not only shook Melanie to "her roots" but also roused her from her "elemental stupor" till she could not help but contemplate the fate of our Planet and the forces that are the rulers of life on it. The quake made her think of her own mortality. And very appropriately too, because no sooner was it over, after-shock and all, than she received word that her best friend in Hawaii had been killed in an automobile accident. This last tremor was by far the worst. As Melanie is writing me, she's still unable to fathom that it has really happened. And that it cannot be changed. "What shocks me the most," she writes, "is that it's so utterly meaningless." And then, just as she, numbed by the blow, is on her way to the funeral, while having a bite at a roadside restaurant, thieves break into her rental car and take off with the radio and a dossier of important papers. Had she not been so numbed anyway, she would have been beside herself with fury and disgust. As it was, she simply took note of the theft and drove on...

No wonder Melanie could not wait to get away from "Disaster Islands" and back to New Mexico. But what do I think of meeting up again in the spring or summer in "Wonderful Copenhagen"? Together, we could visit Christiania and see if my wagon is still there...

I doubt that Melanie understands what she is asking me to do. Has she any idea what it means to be a fugitive Dane? Does she know what it would mean to cross my own trail like that? It's like having experienced children or war or parachuting or such things. Either you have been there, or you have not. Such experiences cannot be communicated to those who have not had them. Like how persecution by the "home authorities" affects a man's nervous system and entire outlook. The psychology of flight is different from that of bondage. The endless circling of the painful place, the loneliness and disillusion. The paranoia. There is a conflict in the old country that he finds so insoluble that rather than giving it another try, he prefers to remove himself and leave it behind—in order to save his life and salvage what is left of his mental health. But, alas, after the initial reprieve, comes the bill. Leaving is the easy part. It's the living that's hard. Opting out means risking it all. First and last, it's a question of survival. For company, the fugitive will have his profound disillusionment. There is no way I will ever get over being forced to leave the place on earth where I grew up, experienced the love of my parents and struck my first roots. I learned the hard way the price of flight. It's like that. Even when the fugitive does not wish it, even when he resists it with all his might, he cannot avoid being embittered about the fact that he has been burdened with so much privation and pain. Despite his apparent determination, the person who flees persecution in his homeland has never in any deeper sense made a decision to do so. The side of the scales where flight became the only way out simply one day tipped and outweighed the side, where there was the wish to stay and fight for justice. Self-preservation always gets the last word. The fateful decision dates from this moment—not from the day, half a year or a year later, when consciousness catches up and makes a note of it in its diary. Still, curiously enough, consciously or subconsciously, there usually remains a flicker of hope in the fugitive's soul that, one fine day, it will be possible to return if not in spirit then at least in flesh.

One thing is the local variety of the power elite's hypocrisy and corruption, its lying and its tyranny, another the love that a single human being feels for its place of birth and first joys. Contrary to what one might think, the reality and strength of the love only serves to augment the hatred of the former and so makes a break more of a probability.

So what am I going to tell Melanie? That I doubt a return to Denmark will be worth the price? As I see it, there are two risks that I run going back: Either the confrontation with the reality of today's Denmark strips me of my dear prejudices, or—and this seems to me more likely—the prejudices take on such proportions that I lose all control over them. Am I ready to pay *that* price? I am not going back for just one week. But will I be able to endure staying longer? And am I going to get away again without new marks on my soul?

No. What good will it do to stir up a lot of old shit? It will probably just disturb my newfound peace. And what else? Well, the countryside is pretty. At least, it used to be. And I suppose Danish is still spoken here and there. They say that the streets of Copenhagen are packed with bicycles. Sure, and there are beautiful seagulls on the rooftops and in the air, not to mention Danish flags all over the place. And what if the dark forces of the nation have poisoned the Freetown I knew? What if there has been an administrative demolition of the one original contribution to Western Culture that has come out of Denmark in ages? What, then, will be left for us to visit, other than a state regulated institution for money making and organized labor—a gigantic pig-factury and farmaceutical company fueled by countless automatons keeping the treadmill going. What on earth would make an escaped Dane like myself pack up in paradise and return to the work camp voluntarily, even if only for a short visit? Aside from Christiania and a handful of people, the one reason would be to get the perverse kick that the runaway criminal experiences upon his return to the prison where he lived through the worst days of his life. To wallow in the memory of the psychopathic wardens and the sound of their keys as they approach through long empty hallways. The ringing of the bells at dinnertime, making the inmates' mouths water against their will. The aggression and violence, the garbage and hunger strikes, the stinking heaps of rotting food in the corners, the dust, dentures, medication, constant correctional initiatives and the ever more hopeless prospect of a "field trip" that, even if it is announced every morning at nine o'clock on the invisible information system, nevertheless never materializes. The washing of laundry, the daily half hour courtyard exercise, the film shows, the visiting hours, the sweaty fucks on creaking cots, the porno, the...

But then again, all of this would not even be the worst scenario for a reunion in Denmark. The worst scenario would be if Melanie and I screwed up our intimate correspondence. Our connection is made of paper, and paper is likely to rip when confronted too directly with reality. It was not for nothing that God warned the Wife of Lot not to look back. God knows what I am talking about. What I am saying is that you pay a price for recrossing your own tracks. Certain acts are carried out best in our imagination. And, as if all of this is not enough, we will both of us be thirty years older. Seeing our older selves will come as a shock to each of us. Our meeting would not live up to expectations swollen by many years of separation. More likely than not, it will turn out a bitter disappointment.

Still, to see Melanie again. It's her intention, she writes, to go to Denmark, no matter if I will meet her there or not. Possibly in the spring. What she wants to do, she says, is to carry out a journey to "Nostalgia," which is a "land or territory" one will search in vain for in an atlas. But me! As the prosaic sucker that I am, I can't help thinking that her visit is likely to coincide with the decision of the Danish authorities to finally bribe or bulldoze what is left of the Freetown. I don't want to revisit a Christiania that has sold out and is wagging its tail in acquiescence. In that case, I would rather keep the young unruly Freetown in fond memory. The Freetown of the theater-group, "The Chariot of the Sun." The Freetown of the Rainbow Army. The settlers' and homesteaders' Freetown. The Freetown of the demonstrators. The Freetown of the heroin and cocaine blockade. The Freetown of the hash tycoons. The Freetown of the fools, the drunks, the buccaneers, bums, mountebanks, street performers, arsonists, assholes and fallen angels. The rambunctious Freetown with its homegrown consensus democracy. It's not that I want to be a party spoiler, but something tells me this is how it's going to be: In proportion with how much the Freetown obliges the dark forces to negotiate a "solution" with the government, it will diminish in value, importance and interest. In "The Prince," Machiavelli writes: "A city used to freedom is vanquished more easily by way of its own citizens than in any other way." Yes, once the authorities succeed in pitting one christianite against another, they will vanguish the Freetown.

This all happened when I was walking around in Christiania making my wooden hut on wheels fit for human habitation.

A month or so had passed since the accident with the hammer. Reluctant to let go its grip, my blackened thumbnail was still hanging on. Soon though, inexorable time would force it to vacate the premises to the new nail gaining strength underneath. My wagon had been pulled to its permanent position at the end of Grønnegade Street, and I was now spending my nights in it. Recovering from my nausea and dejection, I was open to whatever the future would bestow on me in the way of new accidents.

A couple days before, Lili and I had had our first argument. From the moment we met, we had been together almost all the time. Now, I felt like I needed to come up for air. I had tried to tell her in a very delicate way. "And *what* if I may ask," she said, "are *you* going to do with all that time alone? Do you know what you can do? You can go to hell!" And after a little pause to let the words sink in: "Why don't you want for us to get together until next Saturday? What are you setting up such idiotic regulations for? Didn't you yourself say that we've had a good time? So…what *is* it? Don't you like me anymore? Is that it? Or…is there someone else you need a little time to fool around with?"

What could I do except roll my eyes? As if Lily was not quite a mouthful for just one guy. All she had to do for Christ's sake was take one look at the black pouches under my eyes and she would see that I was wasted. There was no possible way I would be able to handle more than her. At least, I did not think there was. But what more was there to say? Did I really have to spill it all: that I was flattered that she—a beautiful woman—wanted to be with me nonstop for weeks, and that I was grateful for what she had done for me, helping me with the wagon and stuff. Like when on the first night, she took me to the emergency clinic only to wind up picking pieces of glass out of my bloody butt. Yes, and that I (right up until about two or three days ago) had enjoyed making love to her. All of it was only too true. But now I felt pooped. Was that really so hard to understand? After all I had been through. Or would she rather I gave her some crap like there was something I needed to write but could not get down to, because she was always there by my side driving me nuts with her breasts, legs and ass?

The truth of the matter is, I had this awful premonition that no matter what I came up with, no matter how carefully I picked my words, no matter how goddamn delicately I got my point across at exactly the right moment, she would still blow her top. I was in deep water, no two ways about it. One thing I knew for sure though, I liked her too much to want to hurt her feelings.

"Now, listen to me a sec, will you?" I said. "It's not like we're not going to *see* each other again, is it? We even know exactly when. But right now, my legs are wobbly and I... need... to... be... alone."

Lili shook her head. She looked like she felt terribly sorry for me, and that is where it ended: a look, a disdainful shake of the head, a slamming of the door, the sound of her bicycle lock snapping open, and...Lili was off. Standing in my window, I saw her disappear down Grønnegade Street, a strand of blond hair blowing in the wind.

In the afternoon, Martin came by with a shoulder bag full of caltrops. "Howdy Flintstone, are you ready for some action?" he said.

I looked at him gloomily. I was in no mood for company, and I hated it when he called me Flintstone. My last name means "stone," and Martin never tired of putting the "flint" before it. He thought that was funny. At least, he was not wearing his goddamn crotch-pants today. But with or without crotch-pants, there was still his never-failing sense of timing to reckon with. It was unbelievable—the faculty that guy had for catching me off guard. Only five minutes before I had sat down on a wooden beer crate outside my house to eat some green olives and bread, and it was not even a minute ago that a highly disturbing thought had crossed my mind: that it would be nice if Lili would forget what I had said about not getting together until Saturday and show up *right now*, bringing back breasts, legs and ass—the whole package. Feeling fidgety and restless, I saw her before my inner eye now serious and pushing into my embrace, now lifting her arms above her head, now biting her lip, now opening her mouth. It annoyed the hell out of me that I was obviously craving her again. It was insane. How could I be so fed up in the morning and at noon be dying to have her in my arms again? And all that talk of being worn out and in need of a break. If only she had not paid any heed to my drivel and gone for a short walk. Oh my, if only she would come riding down Grønnegade Street right this minute in her yellow dress. How magnanimous I would be. I would forgive her all the yelling and the smashing of porcelain. I would tear the dress off her and...

My thoughts were interrupted by a couple of magpies chattering like crazy somewhere close by. The sun was just touching the treetops; my dick was swelling in my pants, and it was all too much. Where was she now? What was she doing? Oh, if only she would forget all the stupid things I had said, I would screw her for as long as she liked.

"Ready for some action?" Martin skewered me with his eyes.

"That depends on what sort of action you're talking about."

"A little cop cudgeling. What else?" Martin cocked his head and looked at me in that half amused half ingratiating way he had. For good measure, he even fluttered his eyelashes. The horny magpies were chattering like mad above our heads somewhere. *They* were getting ready for some action, that's for sure.

As I didn't say anything, Martin offered a bit of further information: There was a demonstration going on up on Knippels Bridge, one of a number of small ones in different places around the city. The idea was to spread the police

179

force enough to take back the public playground in Nørre-bro that we had fought so hard to defend for the past week. People were shocked, Martin said, at the naked use of power and very frustrated. But I knew as much already, didn't I? Martin gave me a friendly slap on the shoulder. Wouldn't it be nice with some free of charge afternoon cudgeling by the cops? Wasn't it just what I was sitting there on my beer crate thinking about and longing for? Once more, Martin fluttered his eyelashes at me. Without taking his eyes off me, he opened his bag and had me check out the contents. "You can help me throw these," he said and fished a caltrop out for me to see. "I've got enough of those dudes to flatten a fucking freeway!"

That was all really tempting, I said. It *really* was. But I had no idea how to use a caltrop.

"Oh, I think you can figure it out. Look here!" Martin let the caltrop fall on the concrete foundation, pointed to it and explained that no matter how they fell, they would stand on three legs and point skywards with the fourth. He, then, fished one more out of the bag, and as he let that fall, he made a sound like a car motor followed by one like a tire with a hole in it. This instructional performance terminated in a thin and drawn out whistling of the lips. "Do you get it now?" he asked. "It's really a piece of cake. Anybody can do it."

It was unbearable. Martin was fluttering his eyelashes and cocking his head questioningly. What I wanted was to hold Lili in my arms. And if that was not possible, I wanted to go on working on my house. On the other hand, it was Martin I had to thank for living in Christiania. Besides, I admired his dedication to the cause of taking back the playground that had been lost to the police. As a matter of fact, it amazed me how Martin was always devoted to the improvement of the world. Being a freedom fighter with a righteous cause, Martin somehow never had to think about anything except staying ready for action, going to meetings and parties, carousing all night, strapping on those damn crotch-pants and roller skates and zooming down to the Sunshine bakery for his breakfast, and of course, taking women for rides in the DAF. It intrigued me, too, that he never seemed to worry about getting a formal education. That he obviously disobeyed the manual and lived according to his own rhytm. He slept when he needed to and was awake when it was more fun. It was like Martin had never known duty and drudgery. There was an aura of freedom about him an unshakeable conviction that whatever he happened to be doing was the only thing worthwhile.

What I am getting at is this: If there was a person alive in whose eyes I did not want to be a wimp, it was Martin. What won me over was not so much his argument. It was Martin himself. I admired him, sure, but how exactly it would make a difference to the world of tomorrow if today I had my backside pummeled was not obvious to me. The only thing that seemed reasonably certain was that it would make a great difference to *me*, if I finished insulating the floor of the wagon.

Staring all the harder at me, Martin kept rocking his head from side to side, as if he were some goddamned elephant. Yes, and like there was nothing in the world more amusing than calling me to arms against my will. Today, the struggle for freedom, he said, had reached a new stage. Take Cuba, for example! Martin's lips were tight as he looked at me with great resolve. But when a moment later he again began to flutter his eyelashes, I was not sure any more. With all his charms and a surface so glib and free of blemish, I never knew where I had Martin. I couldn't tell if he was sincere or just pretending to be. Like I never once caught him in the act of reading anything. Nevertheless he would sometimes refer to "The Master and Margarita" a really fat avantgarde-novel by Mikhail Bulgakov. The way he talked about that book, you'd think he had read it ten times and knew it by heart. Was he sincere or playing at being intellectual? I didn't know. The only thing I knew was that he did a bit of everything and all of it with a disarming and amused irony. That was all. For the rest, he had me guessing if his character was a large, deep and clear lake or a puddle reflecting whatever happened to be around? Like a chameleon, Martin kept taking the color of his immediate surroundings. Like a friend, I kept being fascinated.

Our roles had been fixed long before I moved to Christiania. Martin had his finger on the pulse of Copenhagen cultural life. He knew the right people and what to do. I did not. Martin belonged to the inner circle of the avantgarde. I most definitely did not. Compared with him, I was like the country bumpkin newly arrived in the Freetown. Martin was loaded with the newest and most intimate information about everything and everybody. With wings of good fortune strapped to his back, bulging balls in his tailor-made pants and the promise of a great future written in neon on his forehead, Martin could easily talk. It was not *him* who was a biproduct of the most terrible chapter in the history of Europe. Son of a university professor, he had been brought into this world by well-to-do Danes and had always lived safely in his homeland. Perhaps this explained the blind faith he had in his own invulnerability. It was as a consequence of this that he always behaved like he was protected. When the group he was in was doing something illegal, the others might get caught but not him. No matter what, he would always get away. To flatten a freeway was no exception, first because he enjoyed immunity and second, because if by some freak of fortune it so happened that he was arrested it would later turn out to be yet another asset in the curriculum vitae that he was piecing together as a springboard for what he would one day become. I admired Martin for the way he had of convincing people, of expressing himself freely and at all times giving his surroundings the impression that what they had before them was a guy headed full speed towards greatness.

Unlike me, Martin was not the product of a genealogical tree that had been blown apart. It was not him that had had the refugee burnt into his DNA from birth. For me, it was superficial and a bit childish to let oneself be pummeled by the police, when what was important was finding a remedy against the cloud of poisonous smog hanging over the country. I neither knew the tricks nor the rules of the game. When it came to making a getaway, I was not cold blooded at all. It was no coincidence that *Martin* brought the bag of caltrops, and *I* was mobilized to throw them.

As you have probably guessed, I ended up joining him.

The demonstration was in full swing on Knippels' Bridge, when Martin and I arrived on the corner of Wilders and Torvegade Streets. A black and compact phalanx of cops was moving across the bridge with their visors and shields. The demonstrators were waiting near the square. "Here!" Martin said excitedly and pushed the bag with the caltrops against my side. "You might as well grab a few to start off with!"

I fished one out.

"Come on man!" Martin was nudging me with the bag. "Grab a couple more of those cuties. Look! You see right over there in the Strandgade Street intersection? You take the cars up front, okay? C'mon. It's really nothing. I'll go down to the square and deal with the ones trying to drive towards the bridge from that side. We're gonna make one hell of an automobile barricade man!"

"My ass" is what I thought as I saw Martin disappear in the crowd. My entire being was screaming for Lili, and here I was on a street corner staring at some caltrops in my hand. What really killed me was the thought that I could have been making love to Lili and with my forefinger writing little words for that same love in capitol letters on her beautiful back; just the way she loved me to do it after the act. Christ, did I feel like an idiot. Again, I looked at the caltrops in my hand, and, who knows, perhaps I would have chucked them right then and there if, at that moment, I had not spied a Ford that came limping on a flat tire from the square. One could accuse Martin of a lot of things but wasting time was not one of them. Reluctantly, I started towards the Strandgade intersection.

When I got there, the light had just turned red for the cars in Strandgade Street. The driver of the first car, a Volkswagen, was a woman. I started when I saw her. For a split second, I thought it was Lili out driving her brother's VW. But then, I realized that the car was blue and that the woman behind the steering wheel was a good deal older and dark-haired. "All right," I thought and took a deep breath. The sooner I get this over with, the better. When the light changes, I'll throw the caltrops where she can't help running over them with at least one of her tires."

Amazing the things one has time to think about in the short interval between red and green. "But…won't it make her unhappy to get a flat tire?" I thought. And wasn't she actually quite nice looking?" YELLOW. GREEN. Forgetting my own plan and with my head God knows where, I stepped up to the VW and held up a caltrop so the woman could see it. It was only when I felt sure she would not move that I bent down and placed the sharp thing in front of one of her wheels.

If everything did not exactly happen according to plan, it was still pretty perfect as far as the VW went at any rate. The woman was sitting as erect as a chipmunk in her seat, and—believe it or not—she was smiling to me like it was some great favor I was doing her. Jesus, did it make me feel rotten. I just stood there gaping like I was seeing a miracle or something. But there was no doubt. It *was* really me she was smiling at. Like I was not some creep at all but a noble outlaw and man of honor who besides fighting for a just cause had just prevented her from getting into an accident.

"Jesus, how nice she is!" This thought had just flittered through my mind, and I am pretty sure my eyes would have filled with tears, if, at that same instant, I had not become aware of the driver of the car behind the VW. The guy had gotten out and was behaving like a bloody madman, or rather like some important minister running late for a meeting. I suppose he must have seen when I showed the caltrop to the woman, for now he charged me like a bull. Puffing and panting and with his big belly one step ahead. If nobody else was going to remove the goddamn caltrop, then he would. He was shouting this as he ran. He was red as a boiled crayfish in the face and muttering something about a bunch of assholes that ought to be shot. And somehow his reaction had been noticed, for next thing I knew, I saw two brutal looking characters walking quickly in my direction. "Under cover cops!" I thought and froze. But only for a split second. Not taking the time to process the information, I chucked the last two caltrops and took off down Strandgade Street. I am not a bad runner, and I was not in bad shape either. So who knows? Maybe I would have gotten away if a bit past Saint Annæ Street, I had not looked over my shoulder and so ran straight into an empty bike rack. It was one of those tall things with room for three or four bikes that shops keep out on the sidewalk as an advertisement. Big crash... I fell on top of the rack and hurt my elbow. The game was up. I did not even bother getting back on my feet. I just lied there waiting for the cops to arrive. A couple seconds later and this guy with a tattoo on each of his fingers and wearing a black leather jacket straddled me. He wrung my good arm to the back. "Now you're not running anywhere for a while," he hissed and pushed my arm a bit further up my back, and as soon as his partner got there, I was also frisked for weapons. Finally, I was ordered to get up.

When they were done handcuffing me, the cops pushed me in the direction of a large police car parked up on Torvegade Street. A uniformed cop opened the door in the back, and together the three of them pushed me on top of the four other guys lying handcuffed and entangled in there. They were cussing under their breath and trying to get into better positions. It seemed pretty hopeless. Instead of just four, there were now five of us squirming to disentangle ourselves. It was an anatomic chaos. It really was. There were heads and feet and legs and bellies and knees and shoulders and bulging eyes all over the place. And it kept getting worse too. The way one more person was always being added, and we were all wiggling about to get free of each other and more comfortable. Maybe it would have been better if we had just stayed the way we were, because we kept knocking our heads against each other and getting hurt. A guy was kicked in the nose and blood started oozing from it. Being right there next to him, I tried to get a pack of cleenex out of my back pocket. It was not easy. I had to twist myself around, and pulling at the handcuffs, I cut myself. But in the end, I got the pack out. "Time out guys!" I yelled. In the lull that followed I asked the guy with the bleeding nose to get a couple cleenex out and put them in my mouth. This done, I pressed my mouth with the towels to the guy's nose. "Thanks." He breathed the word into my mouth and gave me the look-over with his eyes.

But the time out did not last. Soon, it began to break up, and before long, the struggle resumed in earnest: "You guys behave like goddamn crabs in a fishing tank," the guy with the nose panted, as still another newcomer was pushed on top of the pile.

Eventually, the car was packed so full the cops could not squeeze another body in. Whether they started with the guy's head or his feet or if they turned him sideways it was no go.

"Move to the side!" they yelled.

"Hell no!" we yelled back as with one voice.

Still, the bastards wouldn't give up. They kept pushing and shoving like the guy wasn't made of flesh and bone but of plastic. I don't know what he had done, but he sure was going to be wedged in. If he broke his neck in the process, it did not matter to the cops. It was almost like it was a question of principle. Not surprisingly the guy kept bad-mouthing them. He had a real foul mouth too. Boy was he furious. Pulling himself together like a caterpillar and then stretching and kicking like mad, he kept calling the cops the worst names he could think of. So when they finally gave up getting rid of him, it was big-time relief for us—even if the door was closed and the lot of us were left in there gasping for air. After what seemed an eternity, the cops started the engine and drove the load of us to Hørhusvej Street policestation out on Amager. During the entire fifteen-twenty minute drive, none of us said a word. There really wasn't much to say. As far as I was concerned, there was no one to talk to. Instead I found myself face to face with a boot with green laces. The laces were fraying at the edges, and I counted two knots. "Just two knots not three," I thought to myself, as if that made a great deal of difference. Then, for a while, I cogitated how many knots there were on the other foot? I decided that there was only one or at the most two. And I probably would have proceeded to add up the total number of knots in my goddamn head if at that moment the driver of the van had not applied the brakes really hard.

We had reached our destination and… were left to our own devices. Somewhere in the pile, a voice was groaning quietly.

After letting fifteen to twenty minutes go by, the cops tore open the back door and laughed when two guys fell out on the asphalt. "Bastards," a voice said. When they got us all out, they made us walk single-file through a door. Inside was a table, and at the table a cop was ordering us to empty our pockets and take off our jackets, watches and belts. Stripped of everything except my glasses and my clothes, I was led by two cops into a hallway with cells along one side. The first ones were already occupied, but when we got to number four or five, the cop holding me by the arm stopped, unlocked my handcuffs and pushed me so hard through the door that I stumbled and almost fell over a figure lying across the opening right inside the cell.

"God dammit man!" I panted as I got back on my feet. "What do you think you're doing blocking the entrance like that?"

"Sorry Jake," the guy said as he got up too. "It's not like I did it to have *you* trip over me!"

"Yeah, and what if I'd knocked my head against the concrete floor. I might have fractured my skull!"

"I'm telling you I'm sorry," the guy repeated. "It was only so those assholes wouldn't be able to see me through the damn observation hole. What business is it of theirs if I pick my nose or scratch my butt!"

After my cellmate was done saying what he had just

188

said, the two of us sort of stood around for a while in the middle of the floor ogling each other.

"It's all right," I said, "I didn't fracture anything. I just had a small concussion."

"Concussion, yeah, sure!"

The guy smiled. I judged him to be in his mid-fifties with a nose as red as Rudolph's, some semi-long unkempt graying hair and a full beard that, even while it looked tangled also seemed somehow trimmed. It is hard to explain, but it seemed to me there was a bit of a Greenlander in him. Something about the way his eye sockets were sort of flat in his broad face. He was not very tall either. A little below average I would say. I don't know why it is exactly, but with those small, sly and slanting eyes of his, he sort of reminded me of a rough-haired Eskimo from Uzbekistan.

"Anyway! Hello there son and welcome. My name's Knud," my cellmate said and offered me his hand. "People—for some reason—call me Old Knud. But what about yourself?" Knud raised his eyebrows and looked at me with his small eyes: "Don't they call you something. By any chance do you have a name?"

"Yeah," I said. "My name's Andreas, but everybody just calls me Les."

I shook the hand I was holding in mine.

For a split second, I thought I saw a look of recognition in Knud's wily eyes. But then he said: "Les! Is *that* what you're telling me? It ain't no name." Old Knud grinned broadly like he'd just said something real funny. Then, he shook my hand up and down like it was some damn salt-shaker or something.

"It's all I got. And I don't reckon there's much I can do about it?"

"That's right. And now, here you are *doing* time, Jack. We've got at least the rest of the night ahead of us."

It was around seven o'clock when I was pushed into cell number five, and it was not until four forty-five in the morning that they came for me. Old Knud and I had plenty of time and nothing better to do with it than tell each other who we were, where and what we had come from and where we thought we were going.

"What a small world it is!" This is the stock phrase that people come up with whenever they run into someone they know in an unexpected place. I had used it a few times myself, but never did it fit the occasion better than in that little cell in the Hørhusvej Street Detention facility.

It turned out that Old Knud was among the first settlers in Christiania. And what is more, he was still living there. Not only did he live in Christiania. No! Of all places, he lived in The Wagon Village. This fact explains the look of recognition I had seen in his eyes when I was first pushed into his cell. I know it sounds crazy, but Old Knud's wagon was placed only about five meters from mine. The two of us were much more than just cellmates for a night. We were neighbors. But what I could not understand, I said to him, was how he had failed to notice that I was working on an old skyblue wreck only five paces from his own. Sure, he had noticed, Old Knud said, but if I wouldn't mind him saying so, the sight of me was not one to make him stop and think to himself: "Christ all mighty, how *that guy* and I are going to make a fine pair of neighbors with a lot in common!"

If the sight of me had made him stop to think at all, Old Knud went on running a gnarly hand through the long graying strands of hair, it was more like how such a "well-groomed boy from the northern suburbs," how such a "sickeningly healthy Sunday-school character" had found his way to Christiania. There was something not quite right about it. So, if anything, the sight of me had "puzzled" him. Again, Old Knud ran his hand through his hair. He was not normally wrong about people, but in my case, he had not been able to figure it out. If it was *his* preconception that was off, or what the hell it was? And now, this Sunday-school kid in his Sunday-school breeches had also been pushed into his cell in the Hørhusvej Street detention facility. "Jesus Fucking Christ! Was there no place on earth he could hide from the sight of me?

Old Knud tugged at his beard, looked askance at me and made a sound a little like a horse neighing.

After I was done telling Old Knud about how I had been arrested and assured him I was not stalking him, it was his turn. As it turned out, he had been in the first load to be taken to the detention center. But it probably would not have happened if it had not been for his dog Rolf. (Had I not noticed Rolf in the village?) Well, anyway, Knud went on: When he was going to the demonstration, he had left Rolf with some friends in the Freetown. Rolf was a smart dog. He understood a lot of things. But there was one thing he did not understand and that was what demonstrations were good for. They were not fun, especially when some of the humans started shouting and throwing stones, and when other humans in uniforms started to beat the stone-throwers up with their batons. Experience had taught Old Knud that taking Rolf to demonstrations was not a good idea. And today! He knew he should not have done what he did. But as usual, he had lost his head. He said "something" to a cop, which was not so nice and then the cop had pushed him so hard that he fell. Next thing he knew a bunch of cops were beating him up. Knud pulled up his pants leg and his shirt and showed me his bruises. He was "one big ache from top to toe," he said. And I probably would not believe what he was about to tell me now, but nevertheless, it was the truth. A friend had told him just before the cops dragged him away. Somehow with his sixth dog-sense Rolf had known that Knud was in trouble. Snoozing on the floor in The Starship, the dog had pricked up his ears. A little later, he got up from the floor and started whimpering, and before anybody could stop him, he jumped out an open window, landed on the ground three or four meters below and took off in search of his master. Like some heat-seeking missile, Rolf had found Knud between some cops' legs, and in order to get the legs to go away, he had "munched a bit" on the nearest ones.

Because of this, Knud had been arrested. If Rolf had not appeared on the scene, the cops most likely would have just beaten him up and let it go at that. Thank God for the friends who had rushed in and gotten Rolf out of the way. Without them, Rolf might have been shot. Old Knud shook his graying head. It was so absurd. Rolf was a kind and friendly animal. He always let little children ride him and pull his fur or tail. He would *never* dream of harming any-one. Not unless someone was attacking his master. If some-one hit Knud, Rolf would bite and bite hard. He was more than a good and smart dog. He was a loyal friend.

I would be exaggerating if I told you that Old Knud and I became friends over the night we shared in the detention. But if I say instead that we won each other's confidence, I don't think I have said too much. For the same inscru-table reasons that the divining goddess Fortuna had made us neighbors, she also arranged for us to spend nine or ten hours locked in a small cell together. Had it not been for this circumstance, my stay in Christiania would have been a very different one, for what two guys like Old Knud and me would never have accomplished outside the prison—

clinging as we surely would have to our friends and daily routines—this small cell accomplished in a single night. It really was something like a magical circle where we could meet separated from our normal lives.

I know! I would have met Old Knud anyway— sooner or later. But it wouldn't have been the same. Not that Old Knud and I ever touched on it with a single word. Still, it was like the cell put something between us, some special smell or air or color—something, which gave our relationship its different quality. If you think I am superstitious, feel free, but to me, there now existed a secret bond between us. Surely, what had happened was not fortuitous. In peacetime and in a society like Denmark's, people of different backgrounds and situations don't meet except by direct intervention of fate. Knowing how much it meant to me I can't help but wonder, if the night we spent together meant anything to Old Knud. I rather think not. After all, he was twice my age. I was young and green and hungry whereas he had reached a relatively sated stage in life. He had experienced more or less what there is to experience. There was not much he still wanted to do. He neither despised life nor loved it. Looking back at it, I rather think Old Knud had raised himself above life and was a taking a wide view as from a considerable height—now with a joyful eye, and now with a sorrowful one. What I was still in the process of learning, Old Knud had perfected by then.

If I had never stumbled on Old Knud, I would probably never have been called a "nice Sunday school kid from the northern suburbs." A kid who had been *homo*genized to such an extent that he'd lost the *sapiens* part. Consequently, I would never have been confronted with the meaning of those words. What it meant, Knud said, was that if people from the lower social classes were stigmatized, this was no less true of people like me who hailed from the upper middle class. Only the taint was different and had different consequences. The *size* of the catastrophe was the same. The reason people like me were crippled was because we had been fitted out with all the most desirable and most coveted advantages that a perverted society (governed by frightened individuals out of touch with the population at large and with little or no direct life experience) could possibly spoil its sons and daughters with. Before I had learned to walk, I was inoculated against tetanus, whooping cough and life itself. Such people as me had received a devastating shot of disease through the very milk of our mothers. And from the milk, it had entered the bloodstream. So thoroughly had we been poisoned that even the most advanced dialysis machine was not enough to clean our blood. For that, nothing short of a miracle would do. Old Knud's face broke into a smile. Of course, he laughed, he could not know if in my case this "very rare" miracle had occurred. But it probably had not. Ideologically, socially, psychologically and "in every goddamn respect," I was forever marked by those "insidious juices of the soil" wherein I had my roots. Even if a miracle *had* occurred, I would need another two or three in order to save my soul and be free.

And so it was: Old Knud and I belonged to very different segments of Danish society. Knud was raised on the opposite diet from mine, which consisted in healthy food, quality clothing, advantages, connections, travels abroad, protective prejudices or certain ineradicable notions pertaining to the purpose of life; indispensable comforts and a steady and strong secretion of pretensions and appearances. Knud belonged to the segment that society weeds out in advance, as it were. He belonged to the "drifters"—the "human trash" born to be thrown out and for whom there was—if little chance of worldly success and acceptance, then at least a "kind of hope" in the deeper sense of that word.

The first nine years of his life, he had spent in an orphanage. After that, he lived alone with his biological father in a small townhouse by Utterslev marsh in Søborg. The father sent little Knud to school, but Knud did not like it. As soon as he felt he had learned enough reading and writing and spelling, he ran away to hang out with the hoodlums in the marsh. By the time The Second World War broke out, Knud was thirteen and a fulltime hoodlum. He was also a talented boxer in a boxing club on Nørrebro. Returning home after practice, he would rest his aching body in his Dad's armchair and read the great "revolutionary novels" "Pelle the Conqueror" and "Ditte Child of Man" by Martin Andersen Nexø, not to mention the "Communist Manifesto by Karl Marx and Friedrich Engels. Six years later when the Nazi Germany occupational forces capitulated in Denmark, Old Knud was in possession of not only a small library of books ripped off from the local used bookshops but also of the devastating "straight left" that eventually earned him the nickname "Knockout Larsen." And if ever a boxer merited such a nickname, it was Knud. His adversaries rarely survived the first round. "Whoop, whoop, and whoop!" Old Knud punched holes in the air with his left hand. If ever one had the luck to survive the first round, he would floor "the poor sucker" with a "quick hook" immediately into the second. As a loudmouthed member of the communist party's youth movement, he loved pissing people off by shouting "all power to the people" when he had won a boxing tournament. During and right after the occupation, he spent a lot of time hunting down Nazi collaborators. It had been mean, real mean. Yet, while the "puss of evil" oozed along the city streets in stinking streams, it was still possible for a man to live somewhat freely in Denmark. There was a kind of justice. And then! Paradox of paradoxes! Old Knud had fought to beat the Germans because he hated Nazism. But as soon as they capitulated and left and everybody—even the collaborators—celebrated liberation the stymied Danes took over and liquidated freedom. When the Germans had killed freedom, you could at least kill the Germans and their collaborators, but when the Danes did the same, it was you who was killed.

It took the war six years, Knud said, to build him up, make a good fighter of him and fit him out with the necessary self-confidence. It took peace about the same time to break him down. If during the war, he'd had a bone in the ridge of his nose, peacetime was not long in crushing it. Today, there wasn't any ridge bone left in there at all.

To illustrate how there was no bone left in his nose, Old Knud flattened it with his thumb, rolled his eyes and made a few circular motions. Leaning forward, he said to me: "Go ahead and feel for yourself! The damn thing's as boneless as a cod fillet. C'mon now, gimme that finger!"

I pressed Knud's nose with my thumb.

"No, goddammit! Press the bloody thing *hard*, will'ya!"

Pressing Old Knud's nose as hard as I could, I also made the circular movement I had seen him doing…

Knud looked at me with his small beady eyes: "Now, did you feel it? Am I right or am I wrong that it's as bone-free as a fillet?"

"You're right," I said. "It's absolutely bone-free!"

"Cartilage and buggers is all that's left of my bone!" Knud said and went on with his story:

At first, everything had seemed promising. In the new peace that settled over the country, he had managed to get a job at the Aalborg Portland cement factory. The wage he got seemed fair, but the price he paid was high. Nobody said a word about the asbestos hazard that eventually ruined his health and put him on the pension the state gives to work invalids.

Wartime had made of him the warrior that peacetime had no place for. One was gain; the other was loss. First the asbestos took away Knud's boxing and the air from his lungs; then in 1956 the uprising in Hungary took away his belief in Soviet style communism. If war was mean, peace was sneaky. Slowly but systematically peacetime had filleted him. Back in Copenhagen, he read Schopenhauer, Bakunin, Proudhon and Spinoza, fought with the revolutionary communists, helped start up "rebellious" newspapers and joined the circle of anarchists. On the grassroots level, he actively resisted the lobby for nuclear power and Danish membership of the "Common Market", which he saw as a future Kremlin. In order to get some fresh air in his lungs and learn how to cook, he also signed up a few times as a cook's assistant in the merchant marine.

"But, but, but," Knud said. There was so much more than could be told in one night. Besides sailing the seven seas, he had also succeeded in getting his cartilaginous snout—both snout and cock in fact—into some shady business. A couple of times, he had paid flying visits to Copenhagen's Western Prison, not to mention the Prefect's office when going through another divorce. The two catastrophes were not so different as it might seem. Prison and marriage were two sides of the aforementioned shady business. For his instruction, a man needed both prison and divorce if not at the same time then for the same reason: to free his spirit and become truly independent. But as far as *he* was concerned, Knud said, he preferred the former. If he had not been busted and thrown in the can, he would never have gotten out of his wife's clutches—"the most dangerous monster of them all." Then, he would surely have died from cirrhoses of the liver. He would spare me the unsavory details, but it had been ugly. Real ugly. To keep out of reach of the monster, he had asked to be put into voluntary isolation.

"I didn't need to press the point either," Knud said ruefully and tugged at his beard. "They knew the bitch. It was granted me immediately."

"Oh, well!" Old Knud went on after breathing hard. He had been officially married twice and lived for longer periods with two or three others. And, of course, there had been children born out of the whole goddamn mess. He'd had *four* with the monster and eight in total. All except one, who had been killed in a traffic accident, were supposedly still alive. The monster had kept him away from the children. He had never known how they got along. Today, he only saw his first child, a daughter. She remembered him from when she was little and sought him when she was old enough. Twice it had happened that a stranger had appeared at his door claiming that he was their father. But "only twice" Knud said and sent me a sly look as if these statistics were important in more respects than one.

With the exception of the oldest child who was now thirty-two and had made him a grand dad three times Old Knud knew very little about his offspring. For instance, he did not know if they were bums or tramps. It was an odd feeling when total strangers showed up at his door claiming that he, Knud, was their father. Even if he had moved around a lot, it was not hard to find him. All you needed to do was go down Pusher Street and ask passers by. The cops did not have a problem either. Not only did they know where to find him, they also knew that he was one of the managers of "The Poppy," a nightclub where hash was consumed in large quantities. That was what gave them the pretext for paying him unexpected nocturnal visits. Last time they dropped by to say hello, they had also shown him the courtesy of breaking up the floor of his house. When he expressed his gratitude, they had brushed it aside and told him he might be keeping drugs beneath the floorboards. Of course, they had not found a damn thing. All they ever found when they came to check in was "biting sarcasm." Old Knud smoked with his friends. Sure he did. But he never stashed it at home, and selling it, he left to "the lads." Life had taught him *that* lesson: not to spoil the time he had left chasing easy money. As long as he had enough to get high now and again, he was happy. "Okay," Old Knud smiled and looked at his shoes, where one shoelace was missing and the other was too short: a pair of new shoes would not hurt either.

If life taught him the lessons he needed to learn, it could not have done so without Christiania. Christiania had set him free by placing the responsibility squarely on his own shoulders. It helped life teach him the only way he was able to understand: the *hard* way.

When in the winter of 1971-72, he broke up with the love of his life, he spent the nights gnashing and chattering his teeth in the atelier of an anarchist friend. It was on one such night that someone told him about the squatters moving into the buildings of the former Boatman Street military installation. Shivering from the cold, he went there to have a look for himself, and... well, he never returned. At first, he crashed in the Fredens Ark Building—a haven for junkies and down-and-outers. His neighbors, a bunch of derelicts like himself, liked to smoke or sniff or shoot all day long to the loud sound of Jimmy Hendrix. In their stupor, they often didn't bother to leave the building when they needed to empty their bowels. They would just do it a bit further down the hallway. Sometimes, they didn't even bother pulling down their pants. In spite of the fact that there was hardly a window left in the damn building, there was always the smell of piss and shit. *And* the sound of Hendrix' guitar. It was horrible, in a way, and yet in another it was not. What puzzled him was that even if it felt good to be out of the city, even if for the first time in his life he felt free to do as he pleased, it was now more difficult to control his consumption of alcohol. It was a real paradox, and it used to drive hin nuts. Now that he could do what he wanted and also felt much better, he was hitting the bottle harder than ever. And so…sometime later (years as it turned out) when he was hopelessly lost and thinking it was all over for him—at a time when he was barely able to drag his tattered and torn carcas through Pusher Street to the grocery shop, well right then at that moment—the girls in the Green Grocer talked Tove Birds Nest into letting him have her shack in The Wagon Village. Those girls had hearts of pure gold. They saw that what he needed was to get away from Pusher Street. Of course, in terms of distance, it was not like he was very far removed. Old Knud laughed. From The Village to The Street was only four-five hundred meters. But what I had to consider was that at the time, five hundred meters was a lot for him. Second, the atmosphere in The Village was very different from that of Freden's Ark. Now and then, people would smoke a joint, sure, but nothing harder than that. People were clean. In Freden's Ark, the first thing that met his eye when he woke in the morning was someone shooting up. Not anymore. Instead of drinking, he now raised rabbits and bees. Okay. He would still have his breakfast in the Woodstock Bar. Some habits stuck. And sometimes, he would have a joint for desert. But it was not every day. And he did not get drunk anymore.

With the years, life had gotten easier. He did not care so much anymore, did not force things and take them seriously. The only thing that could still disturb him was thinking about the children. What had happened to them? How were they faring? In a way, it was strange. After all, he had not had anything to do with them in ages. But then, whamm and out of nowhere would come a memory of a toddler crying or clinging to his leg on the floor. In a flash, he would be there again, and in another, it would go away, as if everything happened simultaneously and time did not exist.

From the moment I was pushed into the cell until a little before five in the morning when I was ordered to leave it again, Old Knud and I did not stop talking.

Being the senior citizen, Knud sat wrapped in the only blanket on a raised part of the floor, and being the young kid, I was lying on the low part with my head on one of my shoes. When we had asked the guard if we could have another blanket, we had received the stock answer: We should have thought about that before we did whatever it was we had done. Finally, we gave up and concentrated on our conversation. This was easier said than done, though. There was this guy down the hallway who kept pounding the door of his cell and screaming: "You're a bunch of assholes! Assholes, assholes, assholes!" It was insane the way he was carrying on. He kept repeating the same thing over and over. Not once did he miss a single asshole. Every five-seven minutes or so he would shut up. Then, there would be an interval of relative quiet during which I couldn't think of a damn thing except how much I hoped that *this time* he had quit for good. But he never did. You would think he had practiced it or something, because every time when he started up again after one of the breaks, he would sort of warm up and holler a bit more subdued. From there, he would work himself up to the same fury as before. Only once in the whole night did he change his tune: "C'mon in here you pigs!" he yelled. "C'mon in here if you've got the guts, and I'll beat the living shit out of you!"

But after that, he returned to the assholes bit and stuck to it...

With the cold, the screwball down the hall, and the uncertainty as to when we would be let out—as you can probably imagine, this was not exactly the nicest thing that ever happened to me. But then, there was Old Knud. It is because of him I suspect the whole thing was staged by my guardian angel. It was her job to make a man out of me, and I was not progressing fast enough. The time had come for something more drastic to be done. And so it came to pass that I was dragged to a demonstration against my will. Against my will, I was made to throw a caltrop so that, very much against my will, I could be arrested and spend a night in a freezing cell in the company of an old boxer by the name of Knud who happened to be my neighbor. The set-up was almost too obvious. But what did the angel care? I had a hunch that I'd been framed and so what. It was high time I was taught a lesson, and in any case I would never be able to prove it.

Over the years, I have sometimes wondered what the wise man meant who said, "Only the life that is lived ennobles." If I understand it right, it means that someone like Old Knud was a true nobleman. As opposed to someone like me who had never discovered much in the way of truth, Knud saw through the deceit. "The honeyed lies, the hypocrisy, the phony talk of democracy, productivity etc." Sensing it was all a hoax and that living in truth became increasingly impossible the nearer you got to the top, Knud had never desired to move upwards in the social hierarchy. For him, life was a question of "expansion in all directions at once." Maybe it sounded easy, but it was not. Expansion was achieved at a cost. In the final resort, a man was faced with the question of how much he was ready to pay for his life. If he were a true seeker, he would pay dearly for associating too closely with people. But if you did not associate enough, if you did not *gamble*, you paid just the same.

202

You were reamed no matter what. The only difference was *how* and what you learned from it. To learn was to "suffer shipwreck on the rock of humanity." In reality, there was nothing one man could teach another. To point out a direction was all one could do. The example of character was all there was. People were deluded. They strove to be indulged—in their ambitions, their notions about things, their vanity, greed and egotism. Their fear even. But by overestimating their merit and importance, they only managed to dull themselves more. There were no short cuts to happiness, and money offered no protection. What you gained by hoarding money was only a false sense of security, a comfortable bed to fall asleep in and an amputated freedom. Playing the lottery was a fool's game. That there was real gain to be made from a jackpot was one of the most obvious delusions of all. The reason Old Knud knew about "the lies of life" was because he had seen it all. It took experience to tell the difference between a gain and a loss. He also knew about the deception of drugs. Some of his best friends had been destroyed by addiction. When it came right down to it, you would be deceived by everything except your own sweet and sober self, or, as he expressed it to me in the cell:

"It may be that my sense of smell has been knocked out of my nozzles. In fact, I'm sure it has. I can't smell a fresh turd if it's shoved under my nose. But self-delusion I smell immediately."

Night had fallen in the cell. A cold starry chill filled the air when I thought I heard sadness in Old Knud's voice. He had said something or other, which I don't remember anymore, when he sighed and became quiet. After sitting a while in silence he sighed again and spoke. Kindness was an island, he said, a terribly small island in an immense sea of evil. This was the way it was and the way it had to be, since the light would not shine brightly and with a luster if it were not for the background of pitch-black darkness. A good man was neither some crazy pervert nor someone who evaded all evil; rather he was someone who recognized good as well as evil in his own self, had the courage to live it out and move beyond it. Beyond good and evil as Nietzsche said. Contrary to what most people thought, a good man was not someone who performed good deeds and avoided bad ones. No. A good man was someone who was not afraid and did not give up when the going got hard. It was as simple as that. If I didn't believe him, all I had to do was ask the women. The *best* among them, that is, for they were the ones who had taught him. When it came to infamy, men were mere novices. Even so, he could not help loving them. They did not deserve it, but what was a man to do? It was fatal, sure, but less so than if fear stopped you from loving them. It took guts. It was a bit like this guy he once knew who loved big snakes. Thinking he knew his python, he would walk up and down the sidewalk carrying it around his neck. For years, he kept it up until one day the pet decided enough was enough and strangled him. In bright daylight and right in the open street. As for him, Knud had long ago reached a point where it didn't matter anymore. He had been strangled so many times that by now it made little difference. You know, Knud said and looked at me with his small beady eyes, as long as one was only half-smothered, one was miserable. One would sweat and tremble at the thought of the queen being unfaithful. Jealousy would gather and like a raging storm rip one's heart apart. At its worst, it led to either homicide or suicide. Day and night, its victim was convulsed with an agony so intense that sooner or later it would kill. But if you had suffered and survived, if once you had been squished like a worm and found the strength to stay alive, only then did you have a chance of being cured. But, Old Knud laughed quietly, today it was all the same to him. Today, he was a glyptodont.

"What's a glyptodont?"

Once more Knud's hoarse laughter filled our cell. A glyptodont, he said, was what I was looking at right now: an extinct armadillo with an extraordinarily thick carapace. Nowadays if a woman left him, he did not start chasing her down the street. If she did not come to him on her own accord, he didn't grab her by the hair and drag her to his lair. He did not perfume his beard either. Those days were over. He didn't take things too seriously anymore. Not the police state, not the prisons, not love, not the pet pythons. Not the whole mess. What was it but a joke—good or bad depending on how you looked at it?"

Indomitable buffoon, soulful scoundrel, armadillo, bone-free proboscis and master cook. Asbestos lung, dope head, rebel and drunk. "Knockout Larsen" was all of these things and more in the same man. Even if the bell had long since sounded and ended the last round, Old Knud was still reeling around the ring. A man too big for a palace fitted into a fourteen square meter wooden hut on wheels in Christiania. Holes in his pants on each knee. A brown wide brimmed leather hat with purple band. Tattoos on his arms and in one shoe a broken red lace with a knot in it. Just like Diogenes who could have resided in a rich man's villa but chose to live in a barrel, Old Knud felt privileged to be living in a wagon in Christiania. Breathing a bit cumbersome perhaps, but free. Like the philosopher of antiquity, Knud had not known the taste of liberty until he was reduced to tatters. The material world had no reality and no power over him anymore. He had been taught to make a virtue of necessity. Nowadays, he loved his terrible fate from the moment he woke until the late night hour when he keeled over and fell asleep. He lived like the past was stone dead and the future no longer a possibility. And should a renowned king or prime minister or rich man one day show up at Knud's wagon to inquire if there was something he could do for him, then Knud would give the same answer that Diogenes gave Alexander the Great: "If you'd move out of the sun, I'd be much obliged!"

The reason I have dwelt so long on Old Knud is not only because I could not help stumbling on him that night in the cell. No. It is also because he later came to serve as an oracle for Melanie when she was in her predicament. Old Knud was of a size that allowed others to unload on him. So when he had told me his story in the cell, it was my turn to confide to him how a "well groomed Sunday school kid too big for his breeches" such as myself had wound up in a wagon in Christiania. Here is what I told him:

The day Martin phoned and informed me of the wagon in Christiania, I was probably pottering about in my kitchen on Østerbro. Perhaps I was making a cup of coffee and listening to the news, where very likely an expert was extolling the blessings of nuclear power plants and minimizing the risk to virtually nil! (This was long before the reactor meltdown at Tchernobyl and Islamic terrorism.) According to the expert, science would soon come up with a sustainable solution to the problem posed by the nuclear waste. As far as accidents were concerned, since the risk was one in a million, there really was no reason to talk about it.

At the same time, Dagmar was probably busy sweeping the back stairs landing with her broom and dustpan. Dagmar was the old lady living in the apartment next door. Out of six children, she was the only one to survive the Spanish flu after the First World War. Since she was a young girl,

Dagmar had been happily married to the tram conductor Orla. Although she never granted Orla any children, she had frequently granted him his favorite dish: bits of boiled potatoes, egg, onion, salted cucumber and pieces of cod-fish. Each serving garnished with a liberal dose of fish mustard. It was now over ten years ago that Orla had died of a tumor in the brain. However Dagmar went on missing him all the same. She would miss him in her coffin, she said. She also said that missing Orla was like having a pain in the big toe of a foot that had been amputated. For ailments such as this, life offered no remedy. Orla had been a good "man and husband."

Having poured the coffee, I gave a start at the loud sound of the big old black telephone ringing in the bedroom.

"Hey there, is that *you* Les me lad!" There was no mistaking that voice. It was pure and undiluted Martin: "Well, well, well! Haven't I told you a million times that it's time you stop crying over spilt milk, eh? How about getting your ass in gear and moving into a caravan-wagon and living next to me in Christiania? Now is the chance. There's this guy, Bancruptcy Benny, who wants to sell… Wouldn't it be great if we were neighbors?"

I told Martin that it sounded almost too good to be true. It came like a bolt of lightning though. I needed to think about it. Was it all right if I waited until the next day before I gave him my final answer?

"Sure," Martin said. "Sure thing. Only it beats me what the hell there is to think about. What *you* need is to get your head out of your own goddamn ass…now."

Even as I was listening to Martin, I knew he was right. This was indeed an offer I could not refuse. Trouble was that the misery of the past months had taken a toll on me. The dreams I had shared with Martin and Marie-Louise about a gunpowder house or a shack in Christiania had fizzled out when she left me. The fact that I was still dreaming of making such a move was not the same as wanting it to come true today or tomorrow. The woman I loved and had married five years earlier, the woman I had called "mine" and taken for granted right up until the end, the woman who had gotten tired of my infidelities and for whom my foolish heart was now bleeding, this woman had finally packed up and returned to the California she came from. Leaving me behind a lost bundle of grief and self-pity. Two things seemed clear: if I moved into a wagon in Christiania, it meant I would have to stop wallowing in my self-pity, AND it meant giving up all hope of ever seeing her again. Was I ready for *that*? "Yes, you are," answered a voice inside of me. With the help of the wagon, perhaps I would be able to make a fresh start. For nine long months, I had not lived for anything but my grief and the agonized letters I sent her. In the letters, I repented in a thousand ways and swore to reform. If only she would forgive me and come back I would love her faithfully to the end of my days. If she would only come back, I would have Dagmar teach me how to make stewed codfish, and we would live happily ever after. In fact, I had already told Dagmar of my plan, and she had agreed to it. She too was missing her…

Another letter from California informed me that it was neither a question of forgiveness nor of stewed codfish. She had forgiven me long ago, and even if Dagmar's stewed codfish was a heavenly dish, chances were she would survive without it. No. It was a question of trust. No matter how sincere I was and how much she wanted to believe, she just was not able to trust me anymore. She had given up a lot of things to come live with me in Denmark. That was all right. She had been in love, and it was what she wanted to do. But that was before I started betraying her. She could not go on the way things had turned out. Also, there had to be something wrong with us, with us *together,* when I couldn't keep my hands off other women. In a way, she would like nothing better than to come back, but she was not able to anymore. It was over between us, and it was time I realized it.

Every time I received such a letter, I would respond by sending her an even longer and more heartfelt petition back. And no sooner had the letter been dropped in the mailbox before I began to wait for the answer. Every morning at the time when the postman used to come, my ears would strain to register the faint sound of the street door slamming at the bottom of the stairwell and of steps climbing closer. When an envelope was passed through the slot in the door, my heart would start pounding like crazy. And when a split second later, I heard it drop to the floor in the hall, I would rush out, pick it up and… with shaking hands tear it open, reach for the pages and with hungry eyes scramble for the essence of its contents. Only when I had done that, only when I had once again registered the disappointing message that she wasn't coming back, I would be able to read the letter from start to finish. Three times. Four times. Ten! The telephone would ring so loud I almost fell off the chair. But I paid no heed. Nothing in the world mattered except the departed one, and in my head, I was already busy concocting the petition I would send later that same day. Oh, how I'd refute her arguments, dissolve her misgivings and put her at ease. Surely it would convince her to return when I told her it was not because there was something wrong with us together that I had behaved the way I had. On the contrary, it was precisely because we were so *right* together and doing so well that I had felt so "free and adventurous." If we had not been "made for each other," if we had felt shitty together, it would not have been possible for me to fall in love with someone else. How could she fail to see that? But no! She could *not* see that. I might have saved myself the trouble. "My God, what a sophist *you* are!" she wrote back. A lot of good it was that we were "meant for each other" when it made me run around town chasing skirts like some turkey cock. How was it we said it in Danish? It was supposed to be so good, but as it turned out, it was only bad.

"Yeah, and vice versa." I would respond. "Nothing is ever so bad that it isn't good for something else…"

But try as I might—writing her back into my arms was more than I could do. In order to pry open her heart to me again, a more potent explosive than words was required. Several times, I was on the verge of getting on a plane. But I held back at the last minute. I could get the ticket, but I could not get my ass on the plane. What would I do when I saw her again? How would I approach her? Should I just sort of casually bump into her on the street, throw myself at her feet and start kissing her hand? Or should I simply grab her by her blond hair and drag her back with me? I did not know, and neither had I the balls to let fate decide the matter. What if I found her in bed with another man? At the mere thought, sweat broke out on my forehead, and I started shivering as if from a fever. To fly around the globe only to get the cold shoulder was more than I could bear. If *that* happened, I'd be done for. I even had a dream to that effect. Or should I say a nightmare. I am stranded on some god forsaken corner in some god forsaken town in the boondocks of California, when who comes riding by on her bike but my beloved. In her right hand, she holds the breadknife she brought into our marriage, the one with the long blade, and as she passes the place where I am standing gazing vacantly into space with my heart in a plastic bag, she wields the knife and chops my head off.

Boy did that wake me up. Thank God my head was in its usual place. But after that dream, I was not going anywhere. I stayed right where I was with her things stashed in the corner of the living room, with my studies in the history department broken off, with an old lady next door filling me with stewed codfish and anecdotes of a tramway conductor who could not get enough fish mustard and had been the kind of guy one could depend on. For more than ten months now, I had been in limbo. After she had left me, I could no longer see myself as a history professor. As a matter of fact, I could not see myself as anything at all. It was a bummer. I could not pee in public, and in private, I could not see anything except emptiness and vanity.

The only thing I still seemed able to do (aside from writing long letters to the departed one) was to read books. First and last, Henry Miller in whom I found a sort of antidote to my condition. He too had eaten his heart out for a woman on another continent; he too had lamented the way the great promise of childhood was broken. And not only had he lived through it all, he even managed to transform his grief and despair into a new and richer life. Like an old trusted friend who knew my secret sorrows and longings, "Tropic of Cancer" kept me company on my sojourn through the arteries of Misery City. It was during the great depression that we roamed the streets of Paris together, a Paris that from Montparnasse at one end to Montmartre at the other was peopled by a strangely life-affirming sewer of expatriated Americans, bohemians, bums, whores, sleaze bags, drunks, Russians, painters, pearl merchants, and literati. Of gold digging paupers and comical degradation. As we walked and sat and talked and drank and ate our hearts out and fornicated and read and thought and schemed, Miller became my confidante. He told me of his heroes Nietzsche, Hamsun and Dostoievski and recommended that I read them...

And so, in the course of the many sleepless intervals

spent vegetating between letters, I devoured the works of these men of genius. I swallowed them bone, meat, cartilage, and teeth. The indigestible parts, I spat out in the toilet. I starved, froze, wrote, strove, despaired and was humiliated with Hamsun in his Norwegian Kristiania, a city that would oppress a man and not let go of him until it had left its mark on him. Or I mingled with the gallery of demoniacal characters in Dostoievski. With the bloodshot eyes of the insomniac, I would stalk the sick person from "Notes from the Underground" on his lonely forays through the streets of Czarist St. Petersburg, or I would shudder with Goljadkin from "The Double" when he was forced by his author to the borders of insanity and...pushed over the edge of the abyss. Incredulous, I was staring fixedly at the student Raskolnikov, when, after the killing of the old hag, he hid in his wretched room, or I drank in the stench from the "Stinker" Smerdjakov in "The Brothers Karamazov," when unctuously and ingratiatingly he dragged his slimy traces across the pages; not to mention the confirmation of my worst premonitions which I deduced from the relationship between Dmitri and his Grushenka. For weeks on end, I held my breath while Stavrogin in "The Possessed" turned his corrupted soul inside out. Likewise, I held my breath when in "The Eternal Husband," I was cuckolded with Veltsjaninov. There seemed to be neither beginning nor end to Dostoievski. The pages were virtually creeping with human specimens at the mercy of their ideas and passions—their pride. To my disgrace, I realized that not one of these fiery characters would have thought twice about getting on a plane to California. Every one of them would have gambled it all if for no other reason than being allowed the exquisite pleasure of wallowing in their own degradation afterwards. And, I may add, so as to qualify for the sublime interest of their creator. But not this poor devil in Copenhagen! That was not for him. He much preferred spending his days on a couch with his head propped up by soft pillows leaving the battleground of life to a bunch of kamikaze pilots each following their own course of disaster. Rather than staking it all in one go, I would ransack my heart with Nietzsche in an attempt to grasp the nature of art and reach for the angelic madness of the human soul that is its hero-ism.

If in those days, I was not to be seen on my way to the airport, now and again, a stranger might catch a glimpse of me as I dove into one of the many small and stuffy used bookstores scattered all over the inner city of Copenhagen. Hours later, I would reappear on the sidewalk, pale and lugging a bagful of ragged paperbacks. Following these foraging expeditions, I would bury myself anew in the world of books. For weeks and months, my only diet consisted in the grief and longing for her and whatever I garnered from the books I read. It was only when once in a blue moon Dagmar knocked on my door and kept at it for so long I could not stand it any longer that I would let myself be talked into sharing a portion of stewed codfish or meatballs with her.

That is how it was with me at the time. I had been stumbling down a staircase in the dark. Thinking I had reached the bottom, I had stepped into nothingness and crashed. Back on my feet, I was so numb I could not see anything except futility. Long before I was brought into the world and was made a citizen of Denmark, there had been set up a formula for the successful life. It consisted in a more or less universally accepted precept or installment plan claiming validity for everybody. If only you ate your oatmeal porridge and took your vitamins in the morning, if only you conscientiously minded your school and did what you were told to do, well, then the equation would solve itself and happiness be transferred to your account in the bank.

Then, the rest, i.e. the interest, followed automatically and life unfolded in the best possible way right up until retirement. Then, there would be no friction of any kind. In the first world so-called, the civilized one that I'd had the good luck of being born into reason prevailed and imposed its beneficent order. There, in this best of all possible worlds, reasonable people followed the instructions and look! With one wave of the conjuror's baton, they were turned into self-reliant members of society and masters of their lives. If people on the other hand were *un*reasonable, if like fools they insisted on following the impulses of their nature, then, needless to say, they would come to a bad end. In that case, it was their own fault if they began to inject heroin into their veins or they lost their home or they had to be put in prison or were committed to mental hospitals to be medicated the rest of their lives. In the world of reason, justice prevailed. The miserable wretches too might have followed the instructions, no?

It was this sort of diet I had been raised on and which everyone from where I hailed had absorbed into their minds, bodies and souls. My paralysis, I think, was at least partly due to the fact that my loyalty to the installment plan was rapidly crumbling. At first, of course, I did not understand what was happening to me. There seemed to be an abyss dividing the world of the fictional characters in the books from the world I was living in. Outside of me as well as inside, there was something wrong, or something missing, but what exactly it was I could not make out. Why did the characters in the novels behave in such an irrational manner? Why in heaven's name did they not just follow the manual that instructed them in the way one should live in *their* countries and at *their* times? Why did they not just make money, adapt and live happily with their jobs, their families and whatever promise their futures were holding up to them? Why did they have to fret and fume and knock their heads against invisible walls? Was it because they were freer than me? Or was it because there was some curse laid upon them? Now and again, I would look away from the pages of the book I was reading and let my eyes pan across the drab red-brick façade on the other side of the street. The white window frames placed so evenly, one after the other in the brickwork, the window panes and the mandatory potted plants breathing the dust. I could not explain it to myself: the mute horror of it all. The time warp and the *déjà vue*. Or was it perhaps the angle I was seeing it from? A too personal perspective? Now, take the poor sucker from Gogol's "The Overcoat," for example. Was it not the very air he breathed that was infected? Infected, poisoned and as if bewitched? At times, I had the feeling that the characters I was reading about were specters or distorted reflections of people I recognized in my own life. One by one, I would turn the pages of the book in my lap, and one after the other, the shadows of the characters were whirled up into the dust of the air only to dissolve and disappear. Slowly, the atmosphere would condense and become thick with signs, premonitions and the dim and ominous certainty that things were neither what they seemed to be nor what they ought to be. If life was to survive, it had to do so on a background of insanity, disease and death.

Yet, even if it troubled me, my reading was in some awkward way also liberating, as if I, at long last, was faced with whatever was to be the challenge of my life: the gathering of moments of joy and the living free in a world firmly determined to stamp out any ambition to do so. It was as paradoxical as it was true: it was in books about others, I found the way to myself.

In the cell I asked Old Knud if he had ever heard the name Bankruptcy Benny. Of course, he said. He had helped him out of The Poppy more than once. He knew all about him and his buddies and how they had been busted. He could also have been part of it if he had wanted to. But I should not be asking questions. I wasn't done telling my story yet...

"All right," I said and went on.

After Martin and I had hung up, I remained sitting on the edge of the bed with my feet on the floor. It was like I was riveted to the spot. Bankruptcy Benny. Bankruptcy Benny. Bankruptcy Benny. Like some demented commercial the name of Bankruptcy Benny kept racing through my head. That and the seven grand he wanted for the wagon. It was hard to believe that it was waiting for me like a ripe fruit ready to be picked: the caravan-wagon I had dreamed of. Perhaps it *was* true after all what I had so often heard about help being nearest when the need is greatest.

Lost in thought, I stayed where I was on the bed, until suddenly something flashed through my mind, and I jumped up. Roaring like a lion, I spread my arms wide, and in my socks, I performed an elegant piquet variation to the famous theme "Triumph of the Dentures." From the bedroom, I pranced into the hallway and from the hallway to the living room where I performed a perfect double pirouette by the window. God knows how long I cavorted like that. Only one thing is for sure: At *that* moment, I was happier than I had been for a very long time. "My goodness gracious Martin!" I thought to myself and chuckled. The words 'goodness gracious' were about the funniest thing I had ever heard. Just you wait until you hear my 'YES' Martin. It will blow you right off your damn feet. And not only you but janitors too and undertakers, bouncers and doormen—garbage collectors, bellhops and busboys. Yes. Even diseased tramway conductors will start twisting their feet in their graves. Dagmar's divine stewed codfish will fall off the table and do a tap dance. Humpty Dumpty will rush from the pages of Lewis Carroll's story and gobble flakes of codfish off the floor. But me, what about me when I have pronounced my gigantic 'YES'? Do you want to know what I will do? I will get down on my knees and say a little prayer. That's what I will do…

And no sooner had this thought detonated in my mind before I folded my hands and got down on my knees. Right there with the radiator for a witness, I thanked my guardian angel for having come to my aid in the time of direst need. Who would have thought? A fool such as I…

Not that it made a great deal of difference in the situation, but there was something else which would have made me decide for the wagon. At the time, I had pledged allegiance to two maxims that individually and together served as despotic rulers over my conduct. The first maxim I had lifted from a recording of the music that Mikis Theodorakis had composed for the motion picture "Zorba the Greek" based on the novel by Nicos Kazantzakis. In between the music pieces short quotations from the film were inserted. The quotations dealt with eternal themes such as women and men, love and marriage, life and death, age, work, war, freedom, and loss and were uttered with force and conviction by Anthony Quinn. It was the political refugee Carlos Hurtado who had played the vinyl record for me (and recorded it on tape too) one evening when we were playing chess in his tiny two-room flat in Nørrebro. This record was the only thing Carlos had taken with him when he fled his homeland. General Pinochet had overthrown Salvador Allende and was persecuting anybody who dared speak or even think critically of his rule. Later that night, Carlos told me how he had been present at the football stadium in Santiago on the day the regime had thrown the mutilated, life and fingerless body of the poet troubadour, Victor Jara, back to the people. It was then he had cried and sworn not to rest until the murderers were removed. But to save his life, he soon had to flee the country and continue the struggle from abroad. The reason he had taken the record with him was because the philosophical bits spoke directly to his heart. They told him it was possible to love life despite the horror. Like when Zorba tells his young English poet-friend: "God has a very big heart. But there's *one* thing he will not forgive, and that is when a woman invites a man to her bed, and he won't go!"

Carlos smiled ruefully. Maybe that was not such a good example. There was no danger of him refusing a woman. In fact, he was so starved for a woman he wished God had pronounced the opposite.

The other maxim that ruled my life at the time was a line from the song "I'd Rather be Sorry" in which Kris Kristofferson does a duet with Rita Coolidge. "I'd rather be sorry," they sing, "for something I've done than for something I didn't do!"

According to this, my second doctrine, it was no less than my holy duty to move out of the comfortable, spacious, solid, secure, centrally heated, cheap apartment complete with plenty of stewed codfish next door and a shower, in order to break new ground in a twelve square-meter caravan-wagon with no amenities, located in the Freetown of Christiania.

At the end of a two-hour high, I found myself near the window in the living room, when I remembered some words I had read the night before: "What joy to write like an organ in the middle of a lake!" The words were Henry Miller's. Now, they unfolded above me like some kind of magnificent parachute with a delayed opening device. Looking down, I felt dizzy. To write like an organ in the middle of a lake! An Aztec lake perhaps with temples all around it. To write from the solar plexus: turbulently, impetuously, sincerely. But…wait! Could it be for this reason I had been offered the wagon in Christiania? Was *it* a means to this end: to help me give myself wholeheartedly to writing, making it my calling in life? Was it perhaps because the time had come to pay back the debt I owed Henry Miller, Knut Hamsun, Fjodor Dostoievski, Friedrich Nietzsche, Henry David Thoreau and the others? Just thinking about it, my head spun so hard I had to sit down. I leaned my back against the radiator, which was cold because it was almost springtime, and my apartment was on the third floor getting heat from the apartments below. So that is how it was. When the water level inside me reached the point where it threatened to break the dikes, drowning out all inner and spiritual life, Martin phoned and waved a wagon in the Freetown before my nose. What could it be but the celestial powers intervening on my behalf? As a matter of fact Martin wrote too. With the others from "The Chariot of the Sun," he was working on a piece to be called "The White Castle." If *he* could do it, why shouldn't I be able to?

Today, it seems clear to me that fate picked Martin to help me out of the mess I was in. Aside from Martin and Marie-Louise, I did not know anybody in Christiania. Sitting there in my apartment, leaning against the cold radiator slats and breathing the dust of the day, I felt a wave of relief surging through me. It was time to turn the page.

No. My Christiania did not begin with a bunch of squatters knocking a hole in a fence and occupying some empty buildings. My Christiania began when I was so caged and unhappy I had to break out. My Christiania is not so much a geographical location as it is the hole in the enclosure you need to find when all else has failed and your life is in jeopardy. Had Christiania not existed when I needed it, I would have had to come up with something else—that or bite the dust decently the rest of my days. Alice lucked out when she stumbled on the hole into wonderland, and so did I.

Leading up to my entry on the stage of the Freetown, there had been the usual chain of so-called coincidental events. Apparently, the first link in this chain was when Marie-Louise, the girlfriend of my high school friend Martin, wound up in Christiania. One night another Martin crossed her path and abducted her to his little thick-walled gunpowder house behind The Green Recycling Hall. This new Martin, agent of my fate, held the door of his DAF car for her and watched her get in. Once she was in, he shut the door, got in the driver's seat and took off for the Freetown.

Lost in the material world of predictability, boredom and nausea as I was, Marie-Louise became the link I needed. Not that I was aware at the time of plotting any sort of getaway, but it's a fact that during the last two or three years of my marriage, I had spent as much time in Christiania as my studies, my job as a taxi-driver and finally (but not least) my wife would allow me to. It's a moot point I know, but it's not impossible that I would have moved to Christiania earlier had it not been for my wife. Subconsciously, but also somewhat consciously, my wife thwarted the fascination I felt for the Freetown and the strong need I had for spending time there. Like the paranoid neurotics of society's political and economic power elite, she sensed that the Freetown was a rival for my loyalty. Yes, crazy as it may sound, she perceived a chaotic squatter's village a threat to our marriage. Deep down, she was unsure about my motives for going there? Judging by her reactions, you would think it was her best looking girl friend I went to see. In any case, I left her for something that made me forget to call home.

In a way, it was kind of strange, I think, for when it came right down to it, *she* loved to visit with Martin and Marie-Louise in The Gunpowder House too. It was obvious. The moment we arrived, she became more cheerful. If it wasn't such nonsense, I would say the Freetown loosened some mental corset she wore under her clothes. And when we got home at night, and the door was closed behind us, she would lie on her back on our big double bed and make eyes at me. Those visits to Christiania had the effect of an aphrodisiac on her. Out there in The Little Gunpowder House, in the company of Martin and Marie-Louise, she was transformed into a happier and livelier person. Sometimes, she would talk for minutes on end, or she would start to "rock 'n roll" in the middle of the floor to some music only she could hear. And it always happened so spontaneously it cheered the rest of us. But if later I tried to compliment her on her transformation, she would not hear of it. She did not like to admit it, not even to herself that Christiania was the mood medicine she secretly craved. A tiny square interior dating back to the time of the absolute monarchy and protected against a menacing outside world behind thick masonry, hidden away in a Freetown far removed from her former existence and upbringing in the US. Even if it was only for a few hours at a time, it was not until my wife found herself out of sight and outside of law and order that she was able to let go. But, as I said, God help me if I ever so much as hinted at that. If I did, she'd get pissed as hell and refuse to go to Christiania for a long time.

Just like me, my wife had been raised on claustrophobic middle class tastes and misconceptions about life and liberty. As the only daughter of a Presbyterian theologian and a linguist who had written her Ph.D thesis on the relationship between verbs and nouns, she'd had her fill of horseshit. All considered, it is no wonder she had turned into the nice upper-middle class girl with the nice upper-middle class values that she was supposed to.

If it was difficult for me to fit a phenomenon as Christiania into the picture of the world that I carried around, it was nearly impossible for my wife. Where she came from, there were not any gunpowder houses with tall pointed red brick roofs dating back to the days of an obsolete monarchy. Pizza huts. Sure. There were lots of those. And adobe missions! There were some of those too. Parking lots and gas stations! With such things, her background was jam-packed. But an architectural relic of a past long dead with a wood stove inside and occupied by two freewheeling young people, a man and a woman, performing their dance with one another outside of organized society and having fun... No way. This was something so outrageous it really ought not exist at all. And if in spite of all logic it did in fact exist, it ought not have any impact on the notions one was raised on. And when on top of it, the "thing" was located smack in the middle of the capitol of a foreign country—no more than twenty minutes walk from the parliament building—well, that did it. *That* made the scandal complete. Not to mention that when you stood in the doorway of The Gunpowder House, you did not see anything even remotely normal like carports, automobiles and lawn mowers. All you saw was an anarchistic squatters' village occupied and heretical and lawless and a huge thorn in the eye of educated respectability. What on earth were you to make of it? What were you to believe? What was true? and what was false? What was right? and what was wrong? What was nice? and what was awful? What was clean? and what was dirty? If something like that existed, how, then could you be sure of anything anymore? How, then, could you *trust* anything?

To my wife, the Freetown Christiania was about as utterly fantastic and cock-eyed as anything could possibly be, and I don't think it would have surprised her one bit if during one of those visits with Martin and Marie-Louise, there had been a knocking at the door, and lo and behold who should appear before us when we opened up but the soldier from Hans Christian Andersen's fairytale "The Tinder Box." Tall and handsome, he would be standing there in his soldier's boots with snow on them inquiring if, by any chance, she (with a nod he would indicate my wife) was the princess he was looking for. Had that ever happened, I think she just might have gathered her things and walked out the door never to return.

She did not deny it either, and I could tell the thought of it amused her. She smiled to herself and said: "But Denmark *is* a fairy tale country. You should know. You're the one who was born here!"

I was never able to drive the notion about Denmark being a fairy tale country out of her mind. In fact, the more I tried, the worse it seemed to stick. My god, did it irritate me! Somehow that fairy tale business existed on a different plane and so was beyond argument. Confronted with it, all I could do was grit my teeth and swear ugly oaths. That's all. In my wife's mind Hans Christian Andersen, fairy tale and Denmark were synonomous so help me God. And if *I* did not know that, it was because I was an imbecile. Period.

But then again, it didn't really matter. To this day, I count myself lucky to have been in *that* place and at *that* time when we were there together. All I have to do is close my eyes, and it's there before me. In the January darkness of a heavy snowfall I see us arriving at The Gunpowder House disguised as snowmen on bicycles. It's all right there for me to touch. The way we dismount and park the bikes in the snowdrifts. The way we lock them, raise our heads, breathe in the cold evening air tinged with the smell of wood smoke. The scent that comes from The Little Gunpowder House where it is dry, and we can thaw our frozen toes. The way we laugh as we slap the snow off of one another. With most of the snow off, we move towards the yellowish glow that emanates from the cyclops-window and from the thick green door formed like an arch, which happens to be open, because Marie-Louise is out in the back melting the snow with her hot pee. There is the thrill of stomping off the snow from our boots, setting them to dry by the wood stove and pulling on our hosts' thick knitted socks with holes in them. The first volleys of welcoming remarks and looks. There is Martin by the gas burner cooking his usual omelette with potatoes, chanterelles, shrimp and onion. At the same time, he is gesticulating with a spatula in the air and elaborating on the perfectly mind-boggling and downright revolutionary perspectives looming on the horizon for the next play by the "Chariot of the Sun" theatre group. And, across the room, there is Marie-Louise who has heard the song too often before. She is sitting in the worn plush sofa rolling her eyes to my wife, who, axe in hand, is preparing kindling for the next morning. To listen to the sound of Martin's voice that goes right on in spite of the massive onslaught of Marie-Louise's scorn and sarcasm—expounding with humor on the "chemical chain-reactions" that will inevitably occur and spread from among the dregs of society and later on terminate in an explosion at its very top. What is coming, Martin says, and what we must prepare ourselves for is something that will turn everything that is dead upside down. This something will put the torch to all habitual thinking and wake time itself from its slumber. And, mind you, it will start ever so inconspicuously. One day in the street by the Grocer, a pair of drunks will tug at each other's whiskers. From there, and with the inevitability of a law of nature, what is set in motion will spiral upwards until in the second act, the stage exposes the Chairman of the Treasury, who grunting with glee, his green hunters' breeches down on his heels, is getting whipped on his fat behind by some whore in an Amazon outfit. And finally a few weeks later (when everybody thinks that the whole affair is over) it culminates with the Prime Minister letting out a huge and TV-broadcasted fart from the speakers' lectern in Parliament.

After his speech, Martin turns to me, waves the spatula like it's some kind of conductor's baton, sinks his blue eyes deep into mine and implores me to give the scenario a thought. I should keep in mind, he says, that it would be such an epic stinker of a fart it would have the grassroots gasping for air and make the opposition smell—if not exactly blood, then at least shit in such quantities that it would surely drive the government out of office. And the fart, what was going to happen to the fart? Well, we all know *that* part of the story. Dressed in fine clothes, it would soon be elected to different important directional boards where it would serve as a stand-in for its maker; pretty soon it would run for reelection and be interviewed for prime time news on national TV; it would appear in a limo at the premiere of a new show by a celebrity and travel the world with its lecture on morality only to finally wind up in the history books.

"And *that* was a true story," Martin said and prodded the onions on the pan with the spatula.

Yes. We would both have a good time when we visited Christiania. But when it was hard for me to tear myself away again, when I wanted to stay the night and sleep on the sleeping platform with Martin and Marie-Louise, my wife had always had enough. She preferred that we negotiate the blizzard and return to the centrally heated, dried-up decency we inhabited on Østerbro. Wouldn't it be nice to let ourselves in at home, frozen to the bone, throw off our damp clothes still smelling of wood smoke, just sort of romp a bit until we got warm again and then make love in the eiderdown-normality of our great double bed, a place that no one begrudged us and we could not imagine anybody ever dreaming of taking away from us? Wouldn't it be nice?

I never stopped hoping that, to my wife, Christiania would cease to be a kind of illicit affair or holiday resort away from the "reality of life." But it never did. It used to confuse me. How could other people, how could *she*—the one closest to me—fail to see what was so crystal clear to me: that the fate of Christiania was bound up with that of our entire culture? Faced with my wife, though, I felt like Galileo must have felt when the Pope condemned him for claiming that the Earth is round. The way she dismissed Christiania as a playground for immature adults infuriated me. Without being aware of it, I would raise my voice, one word getting louder than the previous one until, before I knew it, I would be shouting at her a description of the vision I saw before my mind's eye.

Then, all would be lost for a long time to come. If there was something my wife loathed with all her heart, it was when I became "fanatic," "foamed at the mouth" and bad-mouthed the so-called "prevalent features" of our Western civilization. When, for example, I said that nowadays people were only valued in so far as they could be used as fuel for its "economic machinery." Or when I said that organized society in our age systematically disemboweled people, emptied them of their living contents and filled them with consumer contents instead such as greed for money, status, security and comfort. As far as I could see the aim of this madness was to turn human beings into organic computers programmed to compete and grope for possessions. Instead of writing a novel called "For Whom the Bell Tolls," I once said, old man Hemingway should have written a novel called "For Whom the Wheels Turn?"

When I became sarcastic, my wife would always tell me not be so negative. "White laboratory mice" was really a very derogatory thing to call people. No matter what, people always remained *human beings*. And what about her? Then she, too, was probably just a "thing"…or what? Also, I really ought to stop using words like "national lobotomy program," "stock speculation behavior," "pseudo-democracy," and "money delirium" and so on and so forth. When I did that, is when I would get that "staring" look in my eyes, which was, well…yes, very unpleasant. If there was something sick somewhere, it was not that "normality" which I was always harping on, but me. *I* was plain nuts, and an indication of it was that I was "pathologically" unable to see it myself. It seemed to her I was blind as a bat to myself.

Feeling sure that she had now definitively floored me, she would say "Take that!" whereupon she would fold her arms across her chest and lean back in a very preemptory manner.

"So much the more reason to make our getaway," I would say. "If we don't, and I have to stay here, hell, then I'll probably blow something up."

"All right, that's a great idea. You just go right ahead and do that. I'm not visiting you in prison. And not in the bug house either. You can be sure of that!"

This is how we talked about these things. There was nothing to be done about it. For as long as we were married,

Christiania remained a touchy issue. The Freetown opened a split in my wife's personality that was a source of pain. Yet, as I have tried to point out, the pain was not pure. Things were complicated by the joy mixed in with it. She readily admitted it was fun when we visited our friends in The Gunpowder House provided it only happened once in a while (*and* there was a safe haven we could return to). Not that she ever mentioned it when we were in Christiania, but at home, it never failed that she complained about the junk scattered everywhere in the Freetown. It was because of the "visible chaos," she said, that she would not ever dream of living there. It was dangerous too. You could easily get into trouble, especially in the winter when it was dark, like when it froze after a thaw and the ground became glazed with ice. But, of course, she would say, I had probably already suppressed all memory of the time I stepped out of the Moonfisher Bar, slipped and almost cracked my skull open. And she was right too. Accidents like mine were not unusual. People were slipping and sliding and banging their doped and drunken heads into things and each other in the dark; bicyclists were crashing all over the place, and there was a constant traffic of bruised bodies and broken bones to the emergency ward. All it took was a rain shower, and people were wallowing in the muck. Walking down the grimy street you would try to dodge one dead drunk and drowning human after another. And if people were not stoned out of their minds, they would probably have staring eyes just like me. Uahh, the *faces*! My wife rolled her eyes and crossed herself. Had I ever stopped to take a close look at them? If one studied them, one by one it was scary. Like they had just escaped a detox institution or closed ward or something. And this—I had to admit—was not far from the truth...

There was something to it. I did not deny it. Many of

the people who had wound up in Christiania belonged to the category of social driftwood, lost souls who dreamed of escaping their past lives, kicking their self-destructive habits and making a fresh start. They came with all sorts of backgrounds. There was the respected academic whose life had been blown to smithereens when the wife left him and their four children to live with a Moldovian gypsy. There was the former politician and incorrigible drunk whose carrier derailed when his teenage daughter committed suicide. But then, there was also the Argentinian architect and grassroots activist fed up with corruption at home in Buenos Aires and charmed by the homegrown structures of the Freetown; or the American lawyer who had worked for CBS in New York but who, during an unscheduled twenty-two hour stop-over in Copenhagen, had fallen in love with a French rastafari woman and settled with her in Christiania. Not all were lost souls. Not by any means. But it was a common ambition among the ones that were to drown in the pool of humanity and kick the bucket with a vengeance. There was the rock musician, artist, womanizer, and pusher who—half purple and half red in his swollen mug—hung out in the street outside the grocer. To the broken souls with a past, Christiania offered a reprieve in the present, a place where they could mingle with each other and the random passers by. Had they not found the spot by the Christiania grocer, most likely they would have been stuck away in psychiatric hospitals and forced to subsist on the products of the pharmaceutical industry. The Freetown was a kind of melting pot where all sorts of people merely by their physical presence in the open street were able to communicate their plight to others. With its international mix and colorful social fabric, with drunken losers on the rampage and flamboyant winners socializing directly, Christiania was a strong, nourishing and dangerous broth.

There was something to it when my wife said that you could never be sure what would happen in Christiania. *She* certainly never felt quite secure there, she said. And I said that if she depended on police patrolling the streets for security, she should examine that security more closely. Could she mention one spot on the map of Copenhagen where nothing ever happened or might happen? As for me personally, I added, I liked the feeling I had in Christiania of being protected only by my wits, awareness and mental power to read people and situations and to react. I enjoyed being on the alert. No doubt people got hurt. She was right about the Freetown being lethal when it was iced over and there were no streetlights. There *were* indeed stories of people getting hit by runaway horses. Sometimes, a dog bit a child, and you might get stabbed or hit over the head with a bottle. Sure. There *were* bar-room brawls. All it took was being in the wrong place at the wrong time. There was no way of knowing when the odd mad man would strike. You might even get burned on one of the huge bon fires that were so often blazing out in front of The Factory, if, say, the raving fire dervish hopping around with soot in his face took you for a beam or door post and threw you into the flames. Or, added my wife, you risked being raped just because you were dressed in clean clothes and did not look like something dipped in tar and rolled in a Salvation-Army clothes bin…

Or, I would remark, you risked being invited for a roll and a cup of coffee by some total strangers sitting out in front of The Cosmic Flower having their breakfast.

The problem, I think, was that my wife did not share the picture I had of myself. In her eyes, I was not so much the visionary and intrepid rebel I saw myself as being, but more like a spoiled brat whose head had been turned by naïve ideas. Just because the state authorities would like nothing better than to bulldoze Christiania, that did not mean they were by definition evil. And just because the christianites played at being NATO soldiers, or if at Christmas time, they dressed up as an army of Santa Clauses giving away merchandise to shoppers in the department stores, that didn't mean they were good by definition. Things were not black and white. A single unprejuciced glance at the Freetown, and it would be clear to anyone but me *how many* emotional cripples were in circulation out there. Psychopaths of every shape and form. If you walked down Langgade Street on a November afternoon in the drizzle, you met almost nothing but monsters. Yes, I heard right: monsters! But in the befuddled state of permanent rapture that I was in I probably only saw Santa Clauses and angels living in lovely harmony. It was enough to drive her up the wall. She ought to record me. It really was a pity I could not hear myself. When I spoke of Christiania, it was like I was drunk. And ugh… (Here my wife would pretend to shiver). When my eyes got that rapturous shine, she felt like she was going to puke. The "oh-gee-how-lovely-everything-is" look. It was all right to be enthusiastic about something, in fact that was quite charming, but it was not all right to be downright idiotic.

Sometimes, during these conversations, she got so carried away she would stick her index finger into her mouth, bend over and make rasping sounds in her throat like she was really going to puke. Oh, how wonderful it was, she would wail, the dirt and grime and junk everywhere. And oh, what wonderful demonstrations with people showing off their solidarity, Icelandic sweaters, suspenders and "clogged" feet while marching through the streets with torches in their hands chanting songs like the one about how "they" can't kill the christianites, because "they" are part christianites themselves, etc. What was that but castles in the air and a way of buying cheap indulgence? What was that but a naïve way of keeping the dream of a better world alive? Or what about those ridiculous collective meetings that I loved so much! Wasn't it just great though how the chair person was bleary eyed, had bad teeth and halitosis from smoking too much hashish? Yeah. And wasn't it great how the pushers' dogs growled and barked and got into fights? And the way people shouted and pushed each other while herds of pea-brains sabotaged proceedings. And oh, how charming it was to listen to the lovely couple humping in the corner. Not to mention the drunken wreck wallowing in his own puke. That was *true* civilization. She could see *that*. She *really* could. Or what about that new fashion among the "artsy" women where you had to wear a boiler suit with a narrow belt glittering with cheap tinsel and tall working man's boots. It really was *very* feminine the way make-up in any form was banned from lips, eyelashes and nails because that sort of thing was counter revolutionary and bourgeois. And, oh, how could she forget the cute pusher dogs with slime and drool swinging from their mugs. With their intestines and rectums full of stinking shit. Of course, they too were very *alternative. Of course,* they were. I should make no mistake, she said. She really could see that. And when on top of all this, after having *seen* all of this, she happened to turn her head to the side and what did she see but the rapturous expression of her husband! Well, then... that topped it all off. No. That was *beyond* the top. That was just *too* much...

And then, the finger would go down my wife's throat, and the puking sounds would begin.

Thus spake my wife. She didn't understand me. But then who can blame me for falling for the girl in the boiler suit and the belt of cheap glitter that had sailed around the globe on a sailing ship and with her great pair of tanned legs had no problem understanding my love for the Free-town of Denmark? Once more I betrayed my wife, and once more I was caught. And that was it. Deaf to my pleadings, she packed up and left. What was supposed never to end had ended before it had really gotten started. No sooner was I free to go my own way than I longed for my chains. With nobody stopping me from going to Greece and set-tling I had lost all desire. I could sail across the Atlantic. I could move to Christiania. I could have affairs. I could do just about everything I had always wanted to do and had talked so much about. And I did not want to do any of it anymore. The woman who once in the dawn of our time together had listened to every word I said, who believed in me like I were the Prophet himself—this woman had overnight changed into one huge deaf ear to me. Maybe it was the time we lived in. Something in the air we breathed. What do I know? At any rate, it was around this time that Marie-Louise decided to kick Martin out. That made two of us, and because Martin had to find someplace else to live, he stumbled on the wagon belonging to Bankruptcy Ben-ny. In short, everything seemed to conspire to make us the neighbors we were soon to become.

The morning after Martin had called, I rode my bike to Christiania. It was ten in the morning when I arrived burst-ing with curiosity and expectation. Marie-Louise's bicycle was nowhere to be seen near The Gunpowder House and the arched green door was closed. Walking my bike and thinking that she had probably gone to clean up and make coffée in The Poppy I passed The Gunpowder House and—there it was. Right before my eyes, neither worse nor any better than I had expected: a weather-beaten light blue car-avan-wagon with paint peeling off its sides big time.

I can't tell you what I felt at that moment, if I was disap-pointed or pleased at the sight. What struck me more than anything was the stark reality of the thing! It seemed so utterly real it sent a shiver down my spine. Like something inevitable placed in my way, which I would have to swallow whole and digest! So what if its paint was peeling and it was in a sorry state? Was I not the same? Hadn't I also been neglected, abused and left out in the rain? So what if its metal pole was half hanging half lying abjectly on the ground? So what if its tires were flat? That just showed that nobody had had any use for it. None of it mattered. The only thing that mattered, was the feeling I had that we belonged together. I did not formulate it to myself in this way. Nevertheless, it was perfectly clear. I was the guy fated to take the wagon's pole in his hand and walk off with it...

I told Old Knud how I had stepped forth, bent down and taken the metal pole in my hand. "This is it, Jack!" I told the wagon. "From now on, it's the two of us hitting the road together. You hear?"

Knud and I talked nonstop until I was ordered to leave the cell a little before five in the morning. Following a short interrogation during which I saw the caltrop again and the indictment was made known to me I ran the whole way back to the Moonfisher Bar where I downed two strong beers in rapid succession.

No matter what Melanie might think of Martin (and that after only ten minutes acquaintance), it was Martin who made it possible for me to move to Christiania. And had it not been for Martin's father who, as a professor of anthropology, had taken his family to live with an Amazon tribe

234

in the Bolivian jungle when Martin was little, Martin would probably never have wound up in Christiania. In this way, you can go on digging in the archives of destiny. (What was it, for example, in Martin's Dad's background that made him choose the profession that later brought his family to Bolivia?) The list of all the "ifs" is endless, and there is no getting to the bottom of life's mystery. On the one side, the explanation vanishes like a morning mist before the sun; on the other, there is something called intuition. As opposed to me, who was blinded by infatuation, Melanie immediately became aware of the other side of Martin's personality, the one that was hidden to me and she considered to be the predominant. But that was later. On the day when I was sitting on the floor with my back against the cold radiator in the living room of my apartment in Østerbro, Martin was still the adventurer and shining knight of social rebellion that he pretended to be. The portrait he had given me of himself had just been validated by the phone call about the caravan; it was not yet marred by revelations of future events. No wonder then Melanie's first impression of him came as a shock to me. Proudly, I had introduced her to this gem of a friend, and the next thing I knew she dealt my friendship a devastating blow. At first I brushed it aside, but I never forgot it.

When I opened my eyes that day after the party on Frederiksberg, the first thing I saw was Lili sitting on a chair just out of my reach and wearing the borselino hat that the hostess of the party had worn the evening before. She had pulled one leg up on the seat of the chair and was looking at me kind of askance. Like she wanted to call my attention to how lovely she was.

I closed my eyes and in a voice that was almost a whisper, I asked where she had found the hat.

Instead of answering my question, Lili asked how I felt in my hind quarters. At first, I did not understand what she was talking about. But then it dawned on me, not only where I was but also what had happened. With my hand, I felt my butt. "Sore," I whispered like it was a tremendous hardship to speak that one word, "I'm sore like hell in my butt!"

Lili laughed under the borselino: "You look the part too, let me tell you!"

I was trying to hold my head in a way that it didn't hurt. I did not succeed. No matter what I did, it felt as if my cranium was about to crack like a coconut. It might happen any second now.

"Why," I moaned feebly, "are you sitting so far away from me? Couldn't you pull the chair a little closer?"

Lili raised her head and looked at me from under the brim of the hat: "You'd like that, huh?" And when I attempted a nod, she smiled and added: "*Would* you like that?"

"Yes," I panted. "I would."

Slowly, Lili pulled her foot off the seat of the chair and stood up. It seemed to me that she too looked hung over. Two steps and she towered above me. I am not sure about this, but it was like the world had grown very quiet. The sensation lasted only a split second. I was looking at her knees. Why didn't she bend down or move or something? Somehow, it didn't make any sense. I let my eyes climb the towering figure before me. In order to do this, I had to move my entire head. It was a laborious and rather painful process. Slowly, my eyes made it passed the thighs to the crotch. From the crotch, they dragged themselves up to the belly, the bosom, the chin, the hair. Finally, they got to where the nostrils were under the hat. The two black holes were staring down at me making me feel woozy as hell.

"Get me a bucket will you!" I blurted out when I realized I was going to throw up. "Quick!"

Next thing I knew, Lili had pushed a blue bucket under my nose, and I was puking into it. Once more, she towered above me. She did not speak. The only sounds left in the world were the ones my stomach made when it contracted. And finally these too died away. I rolled over on my back. Lili left with the bucket. "If you need it again," she said when she returned, "let me know. We keep it near by. Here's a glass of water and some paper to whipe your mouth with."

"Thanks," I said and emptied the glass. "Would you mind bringing me a another?"

Lili left again, and when she came back, it was with a bigger glass in her hand.

"Here," she said. "Drink!"

I drank and sank back on the couch.

I don't know how long I was lying wasted like that. But I know that I was feeling better. At some point, I even made it to the toilet where I pissed and drank some more. When I came back, Lili was standing at the other end of the room looking out the window, the hat dark against the grey daylight that was seeping in. A distant ambulance was heard. Church bells. Once more, I lay down on the couch. At first, I stared at the ceiling, but after a while, I turned on my side and looked at Lili's figure by the window.

"There's something I want to tell you," I said in a voice I hoped was loud enough to reach her.

She turned and looked at me: "What is it?"

"Come here, and I'll tell you!"

Slowly Lily walked her tall full body across the room. Once more she towered above me; once more I let my eyes pan upwards past her bosom to the dark nostrils. Except this time, I managed to pull it off without feeling woozy and wanting to throw up. "I'll tell you," I said. I got up on my elbow and pulled her down to me with my free hand. As she laid her head next to mine, the hat tumbled to the floor. She looked me in the eyes, her long blond hair all over the place. I removed a strand from her mouth. It was a cloudy Sunday morning in late April. The curtains were still for the most part drawn. The air smelled of cigarette smoke, sweat, stale beer and perfume and... "What is it you want to tell me?" Lili pressed closer to me. I could feel her breasts against my chest and her lips on mine, breathing. Even if my head still felt like it was going to burst, I didn't care. My *cock* was happy. It was its selfish old self and could not care less about the head. For all it cared, the head and the brain inside it could go right ahead and split. Its moment had come, and it knew it. It would get its gratification no matter what the cost. Who needs a head anyway? it thought.

"Uhm, isn't *that* something," Lili whispered when she felt how big and hard I was. With my mouth still breathing into hers, I pressed her shoulder back until she lay flat on her back. With the other hand, I brushed stockings and panties down over her thighs to below the knees. From there on, she took over. Lili sat up and pulled the blouse over her head. Reaching behind her back, she unhitched the bra. As if she knew what I was thinking, she did not hurry getting it off completely. For a long moment, she looked askance at me and let it hang there loosely over her shoulders and breasts. I held her eyes in mine as I removed the bra. Then, it was my turn to undress. We were both naked, and things were just getting started when the door behind us opened. Out of the corner of my eye, I saw the hostess of the party standing in the doorway. I held Lili like in a vice. Lili who could not see anything was lying dead still. With my eyes, I entreated the hostess to leave us alone. And I'll be damned if she didn't just raise her eyebrows in a sort of amused manner and smile at me. But as she shut the door behind her, I noticed that she also shook her head a little.

Later, when we were dressing, I felt so faint I had to lean against the doorpost. Lili asked if I wanted a ride home to Østerbro. No, I said, but if she wanted to we could go to Christiania and take a sauna together in the new bath house. Had she ever been rubbed all over with rasul?

Lili shook her head and said she did not even know what rasul was.

I explained that it was a Moroccan soap made from volcanic soil.

Lili reached out and placed a hand on my shoulder: "Uhhm, delicioso. Just what you salesmen of domestic appliances love, huh?"

That is how it all started between Lili and I. Our first day together we spent in Christiania. And it was in the sauna of the bath house when we were rubbing each other with the mud that smells like dry earth, sun and sky and which makes the skin soft and silky that it dawned on me exactly what a tall and gorgeous creature Lili was. As I was drying her with a big white towel feeling her magnificent breasts, hips and buttocks under the fabric, the other men were ogling us incredulously, as if they had never seen a woman before in their life. At least that's how it seemed to me. One moment led to the next that led to the next. We did not part until past midnight and only after having eaten at a Pakistani restaurant in Istedgade Street and made love a couple more times at my place. Finally, when Lili was standing in my doorway without a hat on and about to leave, she asked me when she would see me again? She was good with her hands, she said. If I wanted her to, she could help me make my little wooden shack fit for human habitation. I answered that it had been great. I had loved every minute of it, but being recently divorced, I was in no hurry to enter into steady relationships. I would call her in a couple of days. Then, we would see what we felt like…

I did four things in the months after I moved into my new home: I worked on the wagon and furnished it; I drove a taxi two or three nights a week; I spent time with Lili, and I spent time without Lili. The reason I put it this way is because being *without* Lili often turned out to be no less demanding than being with her. And, come to think of it, there was one more thing: my struggle with the art of writing.

Those evenings I found myself alone, I would try to prepare myself for the calling that had taken shape in me after my divorce: to become the author not of popular novels but original works of fiction. It's amazing how quickly the scenery of the mind can change. Even if it was only a short time since I had come out of the dungeon, I already had difficulty remembering how lost I had been—how the educations and apparently useful vocations open to me had all seemed meaningless if not downright harmful. It wasn't until I came across the work of Henry Miller that I found an activity that made sense. As it turned out, it was quite simple. I decided that what Miller had done for me, was something I wanted to do for others in my own way. Something valuable had been handed down to me. Now, it was payback time. But how to go about it? I had no idea. The task I faced was truly a daunting one. Where did one begin? I stalled, perspired, hesitated and stammered. Yet, I did not doubt my new direction. Not for a second. At long last, I was doing what I was meant to do. I knew what I was about and was confident that I would not lose my way. Sure, I would get lost in the dark, and sure, I would stumble on along hidden paths. But what did I care as along as I had my self for company?

No matter what I was doing, from that time there was always the ambition to become the author of astounding novels. The raw materials such as energy and faith I had in abundance. This much I knew. Still, it did not do me a hell of a lot of good if I did not have a clue about fashioning them into concrete forms. Sitting alone in the light of the white kerosene lamp, I felt as if I were a powerful engine being revved by great emotion but roaring out of shear impotence. The engine could produce enormous amounts of sound and fury, but to move an inch forward was more than it could do. The transmission was lacking. What was there to be done? My instinct told me to stay away from teachers and schools. I was *not* going to sign up for a writing course. That much I knew. No matter what, I would go my own way. To give a sincere account of my lonely sojourn was the whole point of the endeavor. Education and schooling belonged to the so-called useful professions. Unlike mine, it was the purpose of these professions to serve society. My purpose was the very opposite: to serve the element in man that did not belong to and could never be assimilated into society. In order to fulfil this purpose, I had to stand alone and outside.

Whenever you opened a newspaper or turned on the radio or television, you could be sure to come across some economist speaking of the needs of the market. How consumption was essential for growth and how it was crucial to have a skilled and flexible workforce. How it was imperative that every living soul was, if not already employed, then ready to be. If a poor sucker was unable to find a job, then he had to register and be permanently at the beck and call of the market if he wanted his rations. Always this market brandished its whip. As for me, I refused to be part of

241

this scheme of things. I wanted to live for myself and give to my life its *own* purpose. Thoreau had not spoken in vain when he wrote that, if a man had lost his job, it meant he had never been properly employed in the first place. Either a man had his own occupation or he never had any. To look at the real needs of an individual man made sense to me. To compute everything in terms of the mass of men did *not* make sense to me. Consequently, I could not make sense of the official arrangement with its indexes, graphs and charts. If it benefitted society that I let myself be registered and was permanently at its disposal instead of my own, well, then there was something wrong with society, and it did not deserve my loyal respect. Did *I* exist for society and the market or did society and the market exist for me? What came first, man or machine, man or account, man or idea? How come I received an invoice when I had never entered into a contract? Was society really so needy that it had to charge me for something I never ordered nor expressed any desire for? Yes, it was. Society was permanently in a state of moral bancruptcy. If something worked, there was always some other thing that did not. Society was always suffering from some illness or other, and no matter how hard the educated and professional part of the citizenry tried to set things right, it kept right on ailing. To set it right was hopeless. It was calamities galore. As soon as one issue had been successfully addressed, scores of new disorders became apparent. Society was incurably ill. It moaned and groaned incessantly and was always in need of assistance. But me! Did I not have health? And what was this health of mine in need of? A true man was what I needed: some *one* free of society and the market, some *one* too big and too proud to cringe and kneel, some *one* capable of thinking freely, staying aloof and instructing me through his character alone, some *one* strong enough and with enough courage to rely squarely on his own resources. Some giant Gulliver who had survived the onslaught of the lilliputs and come out laughing at the other end! Some *one* to look up to…

I raise my eyes from the paper and stare holes in the darkness outside the circle of light defined by the kerosene lamp. It's like this I see myself at the time: sitting in the warm glow of my little lamp, staring out the window and contemplating the predicament of a modern man who can't answer the questions posed to him by his life—all in a frozen fraction of a second.

Even if something had begun to dawn on me, it was not a whole lot. It was only the beginning. I never doubted that I was born with the potential to reach any goal I decided to set for myself. Yet had I known what this calling and my general attitude would cost me in the future in the way of trouble, privations, humiliations, despair, wasted possibilities, broken friendships and shipwrecked love, I might just have postponed it a bit longer—have put up a little more resistance perhaps. As it was, I fought with my demon in the darkness that has lurked in our species from the dawn of time. What I wanted to be was a "fair-weather writer". A "fair-weather writer" was someone who wrote truthfully only when he was inspired. It was also an "outdoors writer," not some hunchbacked, near sighted and pale clerk suffering from constant colds, hemorrhoids and nebulous fears. Not that my book had to be set in the wilds of Alaska and its pages resound with roaring males in rut, but if set in the great metropolis the book would smell of garbage, exhaust, chimney smoke, summer rain on dry asphalt, burnt rubber, tear gas, barbecued chicken in the park on Sundays, morning coffee, the humming of Old Knud's bees and the freezing blizzards of winter. The sound of kids stomping on the hard jagged mounds of dirty snow along the curbs. Not to mention the recording of love sounds, the smells of the human body and its juices. Of sweat and hot blood spilled on the sidewalk. In order to be always prepared when the spirit came over me, I would make sure to carry paper and pencil at all times. If need be, I would write on the hood of a car. I did not want to be a professional who proudly declared his working hours were the same every single day—year in and year out slaving away to stoke the publishing machinery with his popular novels. That sort of thing was sheer drudgery, speculation and selling out, and I would have nothing to do with it. I would be damned if I would not be able to write and to live at the same time.

Last but not least, there was another, more tangible problem. If I checked out of the general scheme of things, how would I get the money I needed? For rent, telephone, food and transport. Like everybody, I needed shoes and clothes; I needed to invite women out for dinners and take them places over weekends. What would happen if, say, the spirit came over me constantly, never leaving me time to go to work? Goddamn money. It wasn't fair. When someone had an important calling like mine, there ought to be an open account set up in Heaven! It was insane, or so it seemed to me, how people with only a very few exceptions were faced with either sacrificing their spirits and earning more than they needed or standing by their God-given calling and, as a result, have to beg, steal and borrow. Except for a few notable exceptions, everybody got mercilessly reamed either way. All I could do was rely on faith, cut my physical needs to a minimum, stick to what I felt I should be doing and see what happened. Perhaps it would work out for the best in the end. And if it did not, and I suffered the protracted death of starvation, well, at least, I would have had a go at it. Better stake it all and stay sane than staking just a cautious bit and falling to pieces over time.

It was one of those days when the sun was shining, and I was scraping old paint off the sides of my shack that the demon of writing got hold of me. I placed a couple boards on two wooden beer crates that I found under some tarpaulin. I got out a chair and my Silver Reed typewriter and sat myself down. High time, I did too. Barely had I gotten the paper ready, and the spirit rushed in starting to dictate to me like a fiend. To keep up my index fingers worked like pistons. It was hopeless. My skill as a typist was deplorable. I could dive into the stream and catch a few odds and ends, but I could not record it all as it came. Still I kept it up, thinking of it as a surrealist experiment. I felt high like a grand vizier on speed. When neighbors asked me what was going on, and I explained that I didn't know, they looked at me like I had lost my mind and let me alone.

With the one exception of Gurli Elizabeth! She had been pottering about near her wagon wearing one of those colored robes that looked like it had been dug out of a dresser way up in Lapland. Now, she took up position behind me and did *not* go away. Perhaps she wanted to study the process of writing. Perhaps it was something else she wanted. Whatever it was, it really unnerved me. I'd like to see the writer who would be able to concentrate with someone like Gurli Elizabeth looking over his shoulder. What with her Laplander outfit and the bonnet pulled down almost to her eyes. I don't have eyes in the back of my head. Even so, it drove me up the wall the way the crazy bell on her bonnet jingled every time she moved her head. It wasn't like the sound was very loud or anything. It was just a little tinkle really, and I could well imagine it had charm in the great open spaces north of the polar circle. Nevertheless, it was quite unnerving for a wannabe writer who was experimenting with stream of consciousness in a Freetown.

Like a man paralyzed, I stared at a spot of white paint on the board before me. The spirit that had possessed me only a moment ago was gone. All I could think of was when I'd hear the next tinkle. "Next thing I know she'll be yodeling." I didn't *think* that. I *wrote* it. And then I stopped again. "Christ, can't she see that she's interrupting me?" I thought to myself. Thing is, I really didn't want her to start singing. Gurli Elizabeth had a very peculiar way of singing. I would describe it to you if it were possible. I guess you can say, it was very authentic, and by 'authentic,' I mean it didn't sound like anything you have ever heard or even imagined existed. As I sat there staring at that spot, I had a troubling premonition it was only a question of seconds. Gurli just loved to jam. Once she got started, there was nothing you could do to stop her. She would get this distant look on her face like she was in a trance, and the spectacle was some holy séance or ritual that the rest of us had to endure until the bitter end. God knows! Maybe it was to explore the possibilities of voice, percussion and…typewriter that she had taken up position behind me. She would produce a variety of sounds while I hammered away on my keyboard. Right now, she was just waiting for me to begin. It would be nothing less than the creation of instant art. Hell if I know. At any rate I had no intention of going along with it.

"What do you say…should I get my guitar?" Gurli's voice was eager.

"No, it's okay!"

"Does that mean that it's okay if I get it or what?"

"No. It means it's *not* okay. For Christ's sake! Can't you see I wanna be alone?"

And there was silence: "Gurli, I would really appreciate it if you would go somewhere else!"

I tried to say it in a nice way.

But it was of no use. Gurli's feelings were hurt: "Well, in THAT case," she said in a voice that quivered slightly, "if you want me to go away, all you have to do is say so. I will gladly go away."

"Yeah, but that's exactly what I did!" I took good care not to move my head.

Gurli Elizabeth still did not budge. She stayed right where she was, like she had not heard a word I had been saying. She didn't speak. Even the bell on the bonnet was quiet. Then all of a sudden, she stepped in front of me and said: "*You* think I'm here to pester you, but actually it's the other way around. I happen to think that it's wonderful somebody is writing finally. So many people here paint, play music and dance. You're the first person I've ever seen writing. That's what's so wonderful."

Not knowing what to say to this, I just kind of sighed: "Yeah, it's all right."

And it was then, as I looked into Gurli's eyes that she smiled at me, and I felt ashamed.

Gurli Elizabeth kept smiling and nodding in that unbearably friendly way of hers, and I still did not know what to say. I just kind of sat there staring. The bonnet flapped forwards and backwards. The bell jingled. After a little while, she turned and left. Following her with my eyes, I saw her disappear into her shack.

In the weeks and months that followed, I repeated the same exercise several times. Outdoors if the weather permitted; indoors if it did not. Spurred on by the magpies' racket in the branches overhead or hail drumming up a storm on my thin roof, I would pound away on the keyboard of my old Silver Reed traveler. Making wild sallies in all directions, I tried to nail every thought that flitted through my mind. It felt a bit like catching baby mosquitoes in a swarm. No matter how many I caught, the swarm would still be intact and beyond my reach. What did I care? Even the tiniest catch meant I had plenty to work with. I never stopped to correct when I hit the wrong key. I didn't give a shit how the pages looked when I was done. As long as I could read most of it, I was satisfied. I disliked getting to the bottom of a page, because it meant stopping to tear the sheet out of the typewriter and insert another. I always felt that while I did this, great thoughts were escaping. But just as much as I hated crashing at the bottom of a sheet, I loved setting out on top of a virginal one. It was a bit like standing on a mountain peak with great vistas opening in all directions. Heedless of the losses, I had incurred and with a war-whoop on my lips I would plunge back into the stream and paddle for dear life.

Forgetful of everything else I pounded away. It was not until afterwards when I was empty and exhausted and the pile of sheets were scattered all over the place that cringing ambition again popped up and caught my attention. It was all very well, it would whisper in my ear, to sit at some boards outside of a caravan-wagon torturing a typewriter, but what good was it if nobody ever read a word of it? Wasn't it about time I became a *real* writer? A real writer was someone who did not just write loose sheets for the wind, the passing groups of tourists and the birds on the ramparts. A real writer was someone who wrote real books that were bought and read by real readers. A real writer was someone who participated in readings, book-signings and launches. Real writers were to be found in catalogues. They read from their work at book-fairs and literary festivals and gave clever and controversial interviews right and left.

Even if becoming a popular writer was not what I envisioned for myself, recovering from my writing binges I nevertheless realized how far I had to go before I became the writer I longed to be. Having spent years on university

248

studies that had led nowhere, a part of me was impatient to show the world what I could do. I was a walking contradiction really: On the one hand, I insisted on going my own way secretly making explosives that were so powerful pieces of the world would break off and craters be formed by the blast; on the other hand, I wanted to publish books that received critical acclaim and secured me a place in the spotlight. Never for a moment did I doubt that I was deserving of success. So deserving was I in fact that I felt an aversion for the usual ways of achieving it. Either my success was going to be fabulous, or my failure was. So be it. Was not a fabulous failure in itself a kind of success? Every day, the media was full of literary criticism, politics and gossip. There were reports on books to come, reviews and interviews. There were scandals and bitter feuds, opinion pieces and announcements of which writers had received which state stipends. The newspaper, radio and television editors treated all this as if it were part of some exciting sports event. Some writers who were declared talents, received state money and had their work called "important;" others who were offensive to the reigning good taste, did not receive a penny, were whipped mercilessly and declared to be devoid of even the tiniest vestige of talent. Some were winners in the game, and some were losers. There were top-ten listings of the bestsellers, pompous award events, annual receptions held by the major publishing houses and God knows what else besides. The whole thing was so phoney it was enough to make you puke. Yet, in my weak moments, I was not above paying attention to it. I could not for the life of me understand myself. How could I despise the Danish literary establishment so much and, at the same time, thirst for its recognition? Reluctant to admit it and trying not to think about it, I was bothered by the fact that men younger than me were already publishing and making names for themselves. Sick with envy, I would sometimes ride my bike to the center of town just to read bits and pieces of these new novelists' books in the bookshops. "Christ! What asinine trash this is," I would whisper to myself and put the book back on top of the pile on the "bestseller-table." How was it possible that such mediocrity had received unanimous applause from the critics? Not to mention that he had been nominated for the Nordic "Nobel" prize? How come such a nincompoop had been awarded a three-year state stipend?

In my weak moments, I say, this is how I would think. Since I knew that one day I would produce works of lasting greatness, it irked me that the public at large did not even know of my existence. Strangely enough the fact that I had not yet written anything and published nothing did not seem to make much difference. The fact that I felt the way I did justified me. Standing in the bookshops reading the inferior but *published* shit of the acclaimed young talents, I would get really worked up. It was outrageous and a scandal. It clearly showed that the public and the publishers had lost all sense of value. It was not until I was pedaling home and the cold rain struck my face that I would come to my senses again. Humbled by the elements, I would mutter that even if it was all a crock of shit, it was nevertheless the way it should be. Of course, the art of the written word did not have anything to do with a sports event. But even if the media treated it as such why should that concern me? I did not need to compete. I did not have to compare myself with anybody living or dead. I was my own. There was the road I had to travel and the story I carried along within me. It was *my exclusive property*. If I did not loose heart and was patient, the day would come when I would be able to tell it. How long my time of preparation would be only God knew. So why worry? Novels of lasting greatness were not created overnight. Period. It made no sense to fret. I would get there when I got there even if I croaked at the age of thirty-six. "Listen Jack! Don't be such a goddamned jerk. Mind your own business. Leave the others alone. Do only what *you* must do today. Don't ask questions. Just do it!" In this way and under my breath, I would berate myself as I was struggling against a head wind sweeping across Knippels' Bridge. "*And*, mind you!" I would add as I veered left into Strandgade Street and passed the Danish Writers' Union: "Do the same tomorrow and the day after tomorrow. Easy does it. One step at a time will get you to where you want to be. And remember: Don't you worry. Your time will come..."

Strung out as I was by personal ambition and the competitive hysteria of society, I tried to keep beautiful Lili just a little bit at bay. In a way, I guess it was bad luck that we met exactly at the time when my calling had revealed itself to me, and I was dying to execute it. If only we had met six months earlier, I might have surrendered unconditionally and gleefully drowned myself in the deep sea that was her pussy. As it was, I put up resistance! Perhaps we had been together the night before and parted in the late morning. Now, it was early evening, and there she was back again unannounced. I wanted to let her in and I did not. I had asked for a couple of days to myself and thought that she agreed. She had not. There she was knocking at my door and putting my resolve to a test. I was split right down the middle. On the one side, I had a feeling that if I obeyed my cock all would be lost. On the other hand, I had the feeling that all would be lost if I *didn't* obey. And when I asked myself if it was possible to resist I did not get an answer.

"Write!" Lili snorted in disgust on the phone when one day I had again postponed a rendezvous. Did I really think that what I had to tell the world was something it did not

251

already know? Did I? If I had something to say, well, didn't I think it had already been said a thousand times and by writers a *thousand* times more talented than I? (Lili was so upset her panting got in the way of her words.) "God, it's amazing," she went on. Who did I think I was anyway? SOCRATES? Or Shakespeare maybe! And as for that calling of mine! Never had she heard anything so ridiculous. How could I be sure it wasn't just my own little bloated ego playing tricks on me? How could I be sure it wasn't just a fixed idea, an obsession? I really ought to take the time to answer these questions, since it was because of all this nonsense that the two of us were not getting together until Friday. It was outrageous. Here she was…calling me, and I was messing around with another…calling. Was I a *man* or what! Christ! In three days! But in three days, she'd probably have her period, or the flu, or…or…appendicitis. Tomorrow would never come and neither would Friday. And why? Because *I* wanted time for writing! But in that case…did I know what I could do? I could take that calling of mine and stick it. That's what. And now…GOODBYE!

I was petrified. The echo of Lili's final salute rang in my head. What bothered me most was that stuff about my "bloated little ego" and my calling being nothing but a fixation. How could she fail to see the sincerity of it, or the *grandeur* even of what I had to do? And how could she fail to see that I was crazy about her? I had even had a tremendous hard-on on the phone with her. Above all, there was the issue of making agreements. What was the point of agreeing to see each other again on Friday, if she showed up on Wednesday? Why go through the trouble of agreeing to anything? Suppose I just let her have it her way. Then I could expect her to break in on me any time. I would never have a moment's peace. I would not be able to concentrate on a damn thing. In fact, I might as well give up writing. The pinpricks she had dealt me! I kept hearing her sarcasms. And what guarantee did I have that she was not right? What did I in fact have to say that the world had not heard a thousand times before? And what made me think that I would succeed in saying it in such a way that it matched the pantheon of great writers before me? Wasn't I biting off more than I could chew?

I put on my jacket and went for a walk. I threw pepples in the water and watched the ripples. I lied on my bed with my hands behind my head. I took a piss. I chopped wood. I did all sorts of things but no matter what, the questions kept swishing around demanding answers that were not forthcoming. At least not until in the evening as I was on my way back from the vegetarian restaurant Morgenstedet! Suddenly a voice inside me spoke up: "Andreas Stein," it said. "Don't you listen to what Lili says. Sure, Plato, Cervantes, Shakespeare, Miller and Dostoievski were great. And so were a host of others. But that has nothing to do with you. You are you and different from them. Are you not perhaps the first person on the planet Earth who is living *your* life? Yes, you are, and for that reason, your story is unique and can be told only by you. Either you do it, or the story will die with you, and the seed will be lost. The question is not what the world has heard before. The question is what the world has yet to hear. Are you, Andreas Stein, able to express what is in you in such a way that the world will listen? Well *are* you? The world is ignorant. It does not even know it is waiting, and much less what it is waiting for. Only *you* know that. A man's talent is his belief in what he can do and the energy with which he forces it on his contemporaries. So don't you doubt! Your vision, the life you feel stirring in you, your *angle* on this life is unique because it is yours and yours alone. Rest assured, stop up your ears, and let her talk. Don't let it disturb you…"

By the time the voice fell silent, I was standing in the middle of my wagon. I looked from the socks soaking in the bucket to my ten-speed bicycle by the wood-stove and to the battered old wooden desk on the other side under the window. I then folded my hands and mumbled a solemn 'amen.' Returning to the door, I opened it and stood in the doorway. I looked at the first stars dotting the evening sky and knew I was determined. For all I cared, Lili could parade her legs, ass and breasts in front of me. Her tongue was sharper than a serpent's tooth. In the future when I undressed to mount her, I would keep my breeches on. With my breeches on and my eyes open, I would go right on and learn to write. Even if now and then, it cost me a fuck. It was true that Lili's bodily charms were like none I had ever known before. And it was no less true that she was a hefty and passionate woman. But that did not entitle her to judge the authenticity of my calling. I shuddered. She would probably skin me alive if I let her. She would suck me dry. Suppose we had gone on like we set out—screwing day and night. Where would I be now? What would I be? Most likely, I would resemble a bag of trampled mayonnaise.

Taking one last breath of the cool evening air, I closed the door and stepped back into the room.

One day in the afternoon, I sensed that Lili was on her way. And sure enough, there she was coming down Grønnegade Street on the old grandma bike. She was wearing a long yellow dress that flapped in the wind and looked like it might at any moment get caught in the spokes. She had found me with her eyes behind the window's glass, and the way she looked at me, I could tell it was no accident. She knew only too well what she was doing. The studied way she got off the bike was intended to make it seem like she was unsure of herself. She did it sort of nervously as if she was afraid or humble or something. When she had leaned the bike against the side of the wagon, locked it, gotten a bag of grapes and other delicacies out of the basket hanging from the handlebars, she stepped back to look at me again. There we were once more looking at each other across a broken agreement. "See… you can say what you like. Here I am… anyway! How do you like my new dress?" This is what I heard her defiant eyes say. I shook my head. She had done up her hair for the occasion and the way her perfect bosom heaved impatiently under the yellow dress, it seemed the material was about to burst. I had never before seen her so beautiful, and I think my eyes told her as much. I breathed deeply but neither nodded nor moved. I took it for what it was: a *fait accompli*. The attack had been unexpected. The timing was perfect, and my defenses were crumbling fast. All she had to do was wait a minute, and my door would be open for her. How to keep such a woman out, I thought. It wasn't possible. Henry Miller would surely have agreed. Broken agreement or not he would have surrendered right away.

No sooner had I thought this and the reaction came from my crotch. "What are you waiting for? Open the damn door and take her? Don't you know that…: "There's just one thing God will not forgive…" And when you are done, why she just might exchange her yellow dress for the boiler suit she keeps in the wagon. Who knows? Perhaps the two of you can get a bit of work done."

The door-handle moved. Next thing I knew she had climbed the two steps and her tall body was hanging limp and relieved in my arms. Realizing I was not going to reject her, she made herself smaller and sort of collapsed against my chest. After a little while we began backing down through the wagon. Reaching the bed, we took off our clothes and pulled up tight once more. Like some strange, naked and uncoordinated four-legged animal, we climbed the bed. All without a word!

When we were done making love neither of us felt like doing any work. We just sort of laid around kissing and tickling and talking until we were both famished and set out for restaurant Spiseloppen, where we each put aside a huge portion of meat-balls in curry with rice. Marie-Louise who sometimes substituted at Spiseloppen served our food, and since it was not a busy night, she found time to sit down with us.

It was pretty late when we descended the old and worn staircase and stepped into the night. Lili had stuck her hand under my left arm and clung to me. Walking in silence we were synchronizing our steps and listening to the sounds our shoes were making in the dirt. At the Opera Building, we took the direction of the Grey Hall. There was something I wanted to tell Lili. Only I could not make myself say it. She was so quiet, and I felt that words even like the ones on my lips would break the spell of the moment. Wow, did it feel good to be walking so close with a woman again. And yet, it also felt funny after five married years. It was only a short time ago that my wife and I had clung to one another in just the same way—so happy, so contented, so trustingly in love and convinced that it was nothing less than our shared future we were leaning against. And here I was, intimate among the old garrison buildings and with a woman who was not *she*. I had been married to *her*, and *she* had left me to grieve. For almost a year, no woman had looked my way. And now—miracle of miracles—here it was happening again. Who would have thought? Even if it was only a few short months ago, it seemed like ages since I was vegetating in my Østerbro apartment reading piles of books. And more importantly: who cared!

Lili wanted to pick up her bike and go home. She needed to get up early. But when we got to the wagon I invited her in for a taste of the bourbon a customer had left in the taxi. I lit a candle, put on a cassette with the nocturnes of Chopin and poured her a drink. Facing each other on the bed, we sipped from our glasses. Later we slipped under the covers and made love. At one point, Lili was caressing my face big tears streaming from her wide-open eyes. I did not understand why. Neither did I ask. Later, she apparently forgot and pulled me to her forcefully. I stayed where I was heavy on her and moved with her spasms.

The candle burned down before we were done. Wasted and soft, Lili asked me to read something to her. Saying this, she indicated the paperback on my table. It was Alberto Moravia's "Il Disprezzo" with the Danish title "I Loved You Yesterday."

"Why do you want to hear that one?" I asked. I, too, felt wasted. Also, I was not in the mood to read aloud from a book about great love transformed into bitter hatred.

Lili pulled gently at my arm, pressed her face against the side of my chest and looked up at me: "Because," she whispered, "I want you to write the sequel and call it: "I Love You Also Today Baby." But why don't you get started. We don't have all night, you know. Please read from the place you've come to in the book!"

I opened the book where the bookmark was. It was in the middle of chapter fourteen where the young script writer Molteni sees the producer Battista kissing his beautiful wife Emilia and his heart falls into a bottomless pit. Lili listened attentively right from word one. I could tell from the way she breathed. And she kept it up until the end of chapter twenty. I looked at her. She had managed to fall asleep right in the middle of the violent scene between the spouses. I closed the book and put it back on the table. Turning off the lamp, I listened for a while to the sound of her breathing near my left ear. And then I, too, drifted off.

It was around nine o'clock on a rainy evening in the Wagon Village. I was in the kitchen caravan having dinner with the other villagers. Old Knud who had once been the assistant to a ship's cook had "created" his favorite dish: mincemeat. There was enough minced beef to feed an entire village of christianites; and *not* with the "goddamned rabbit feed" which certain personages habitually served us. Old Knud was always teasing Douglas about his vegetarianism. When Douglas cooked, he made a point of not being home. In his own words, Knud was a "meat eater." But what I wanted to tell you was that there had been a visitor. It had been rather rowdy and fun but even so, I had torn myself away in order to go to my own shack and…write. Now there, finally alone with nothing to disturb me, I could not concentrate worth a damn. I just sat there dawdling with a pen on a torn envelope. The way the rain was coming down on the roof you would think it was trying to drown me out. Water was streaming down the windowpanes, but instead of calming me, it made me restless. One moment I looked at the torn paper, the next I stared into the dark beyond the curtain of water. What good was it that I had the strength to tear myself away from the party, when I didn't have the strength to make my thoughts come with me?

Just when we started to eat who had appeared in the open door but a pretty fifteen-year-old gypsy girl. Apparently she knew Old Knud because no sooner was she in the room before he went to get her a plate. Looking sternly at us over the rim of his glasses that he had repaired with tape, he said: "Will you stop stuffing yourselves for a moment and make room for Fanny here!"

With Fanny's arrival on the scene, the riotous atmosphere became even more unrestrained and below the belt. Gurli Elizabeth hurled a potato at John who ducked so it broke against the wall. Old Knud bawled them out and called them "barbarians." That was when I decided it was time I got down to some writing. Getting up, I gave the other villagers some bullshit about having something "important" to do. As I was passing behind her chair, Fanny tilted her dark head back: "Is it really necessary that you leave now?" her black eyes asked me. Or at least that's what I thought they asked me, when, a while later, I was sitting by myself regretting the way she had looked at me. I kept seeing those big eyes of hers before my inner eye. Christ how that black had contrasted with that white! The image just refused to go away. Whew, was she pretty—and a riot too.

I had made myself a pot of tea and sat back down at the desk. But aside from that, not much had changed. I was still restless. I still just sort of sat there. The minutes went by like so many silent slugs racing. Feeling like a fool, I kept asking myself why I had left the party? Yes, to write. Sure! But how write when my head was elsewhere? I was thinking the question over when I had an idea. Of course! How come I had not thought of it before? What I would do was paint a portrait of that girl Fanny. Fanny with skin the color of milk chocolate. Fanny with black curly hair and ivory eyes. Fanny with fat cherry lips. The portrait I would paint would capture Fanny at the moment she stepped into the room. Congratulating myself on my creative wit, I wanted to get right down to it. But before I could get started, it came to me how at one point Fanny had looked at me across the table, folded up that thick upper lip and asked out loud so nobody missed a single syllable:

"And who, if I may ask, is *that guy* over there?"

They all turned their heads to look at me, but no one made a sound. It was sort of awkward, and in the end, I had to answer her myself.

"Guess!" I said and met her eyes.

"Well, you can't be one of Knud's friends."

The conviction with which Fanny said this I found both insulting and cheeky, as if Old Knud was some sort of king and one had to belong to the nobility to befriend him. I felt like asking her a question back: "What makes you so sure I'm not a friend of Knud's?" But I did not. Perhaps because at the bottom of my heart I knew that I was exactly the well-groomed kid from the stuck-up suburbs of northern Copenhagen that Knud had once told me I was. It's possible. I don't know.

Fortunately, Old Knud came to my rescue: "Les and I met in a prison cell. Now, we're neighbors."

That did it.

Fanny flashed me a big white smile: "So you and Knud are *prison*-pals!"

"You might call us that," Knud nodded.

If before the mood had been riotous, the atmosphere in the room now became positively charged with lecherous abandon. Everybody seemed to feel a need to share their own impressions about who I was. Jakob, for example, suggested that, instead of Les, my name ought to be Don Casanova von Caravan, and as if that was not enough, he added that instead of driving a taxi I ought to take a job as a dish washer in "The Soup Bowl." "The Soup Bowl" was the soup kitchen for homeless people and bums that The Army of the Church's Cross recently opened at the far end of Pusher Street. I looked at him in disbelief. I *knew* that place. I had, in fact, tried to eat there once and did not fancy going back any time soon. Actually, the soup had been all right. But as I was eating, there was this Greenlander woman who walked through the room from one end to the other with a bucketful of excrement. I am not kidding. It really *was* a bucket full of shit. From where I sat, I could not see what was in the bucket, but since it stank like shit, I figured perhaps that's what it was. When later, I asked the guy bussing the tables he confirmed it. However, it was the woman's *own* shit, he pointed out. Right as if it made a difference whose it was. She lived in a room upstairs and had no toilet. For weeks, they had pleaded with her to take her dumps in the Green Recycling Hall where there was a toilet. But it was no use. She was used to shitting in the bucket and that was that. If they didn't like her shit for all she cared, they could choke on it. She had bawled them out. Swearing like a trooper, she even told them that if they didn't stop pestering her, she'd dump her shit right into their fucking Soup Bowl. She would do what she damn well pleased.

They stopped pestering her.

Well anyway. Where was I? Oh, that's right. Don Casanova von Caravan. The entire place was rocking with laughter. Fanny looked questioningly at Jakob, who said: "It's because of some extremely eschatological escapades he makes that we have nicknamed him Don Casanova von Caravan."

It was obvious that Fanny had not understood a word he said.

Now, it was Old Knud's turn to pitch in: "Will you stop giving the girl all that bullshit Jakob!" And then, he leaned towards Fanny and whispered very loud in her ear: "He *does* have escapades though!"

Fanny looked at me: "What's escapades?" she asked into the room.

"An escapade," Gurli Elizabeth said, "is when somebody is doing something to somebody and also doing the same something to somebody else. Get it?"

"Do you mean," Fanny did not get a chance to finish her sentence, because suddenly the whole place was rocking with laughter again. "Ha! Ha! Don Casanova von Caravan as dishwasher in The Soup Bowl. Ha! Ha!"

Sitting by myself in my little room, I was going over it all in my mind. But enough was enough. It was time my thoughts were called to order. Who would have thought it would be so difficult to get started on a portrait of that gypsy girl Fanny!

Not that there was anything wrong with the idea. There really was not. Only the damn restlessness kept getting in the way. I just could not seem to get down to it. My thoughts were out of control and roaming where they had no business. Yet, through it all, I could see Fanny clearly before me. I could hear her voice too. But every time I tried to capture her person in a few words, it sounded utterly inane. I would grab the paper, crumble it and hurl it in the wastebasket. It happened three or four times. All I had to show for my troubles were the seven or eight lines lying on the desk before me. I was now being punished for leaving the party. If only I had stayed, everything would have been all right. Perhaps it was not too late. But what would I tell them if I came back? No matter how much I thought about it, I couldn't think of anything even remotely plausible. I could not very well tell them the truth, could I? That what I wanted was to find out more about Fanny. Like if she by any chance was interested in getting to know Don Casanova von Caravan...

At any rate, in the end, it turned out for the best. Just as I was sitting there fretting over my mistake, I heard the sound of steps on the gravel outside. Next thing I knew, there was a knock on my open door, and Fanny appeared: "What are you doing?" she asked and hesitated. "Is it something…important?" She looked at me with an expression I find hard to describe. I didn't say anything. It was not necessary either. Without waiting for my reply, Fanny came up the two steps and entered the… wagon.

"What *are* you doing?" she said again and looked around the room.

"Look!" I said as she came up to me, "I've written something!"

Fanny bent over as if to see better, but instead of reading, she turned and jumped onto my lap. From the way she smiled, I could tell she was amused at my surprise.

"Will you stop it? Do you really need to look so confused?" Looking into my eyes, Fanny ran her hand through my hair a couple of times.

"Uh…is that…uhh, what you're writing?" With her free hand, Fanny pointed to the six-seven lines on the torn envelope.

"Yeah, I guess so," I nodded. "That's what I'm writing. Why don't you read what it says?"

Fanny leaned forward and started reading from the sheet: "The skin is… the color of milk chocolate. The teeth are like ivory. The upper lip has the hue of a ripe cherry. It folds upwards in a way that gives her face an open and curious expression. In the places where she is not milk, she is lickorice."

Fanny turned abrubtly around: "Oh, my God, it's *me*!" She blurted out. She laughed in my face showing her full set of white teeth. "I see! So it's me you're writing about, huh! You prefer sitting here alone *writing about* me instead of *being with* me for real in the kitchen wagon…"

I wanted to say something, but before I could, Fanny grabbed my head with both hands, pulled my face towards hers and pressed a big kiss on my mouth. She pushed me away again: "But in that case, wouldn't you like to get some more to write about?"

We looked into each other's eyes. Instead of answering, her I stuck a hand inside her blouse and squeezed her left tit. And then I got some more to write about.

It was late at night when Fanny got down from the bed and started to dress. She wanted to know if I would go with her to The Moonfisher Bar. She worked there, she said. A couple free drinks, wasn't that just what Casanova needed now? After that nice big escapade! A pinacolada perhaps! Or a tequila sunrise! Or what about a gin and tonic with lime? Fanny was standing in the middle of the floor pulling at her tights. There was a hole on the right leg just above the knee. When she pulled, it got bigger, and when she stopped, it shrunk. I stared at it in fascination. At that moment, it was the hole that spoke to me. "She knows how to make a pinacolada," I thought. "Not bad for a fifteen-year-old."

Water was still dripping from branches and eaves when we stepped out into the open. It did not rain any more. At first, we walked without touching. But when we got to The Omelet, Fanny stuck her hand under my left arm. And it was this little gesture that got me started again. How strange everything was in this world. The night before I had been walking the same way with Lili. It seemed a clear case of Don Casanova von Caravan. Who would I be with tomorrow? No, that's right! Tomorrow, I was driving the taxi. But then, the day after tomorrow? What a world! One was divorced, and there was a drought for something that seemed forever. You thirsted for love and sex and suffered all manner of humiliations. You got a kick in the pants, lost your self-confidence down to the last iota and were moaning and groaning like a fool. You locked yourself up with piles of dusty books for your only company. You felt the days slipping by without a trace. But see if the world paid any attention. See if it cared. No way. As if nothing had ever happened, the old world kept right on turning. Imperceptibly, winter turned to spring, and before you knew it, you had dropped a hammer on your thumbnail only to wake the next day with a woman in your arms. Then after the first came the second and the third and… As if by some stroke of magic, your fortune had changed. Still, wasn't it too good to be true? Wasn't there something fishy about it all? When your need was greatest, the possibility of satisfaction was totally absent. Was that what Christ meant when he said that to those who have shall be given, and from those who don't have, even the little they possess shall be taken away? If so then, who the hell had arranged it that way? What sense did it make that you either got too little or too much, but never just right. Oh, but why speculate so much? If my time had now come, then I'd be an ungrateful bastard if I didn't go forth and fatten myself. There was a time to fish and a time to dry nets…

A couple hours later, I stepped out of the noisy bar and started home. Fanny did not see me leave. She was hanging on to the leather jacket of some broad-shouldered mulatto dude. To be more precise, she was holding on to his arm and laughing so hard it made her cough. It was all the same to me. Outside the black birds were singing from gables, woodpiles and trees. It was getting light. With the four double tequila sunrises Fanny had poured down my gullet, I was in the mood to sing from a gable myself. "Bird on the horizon, sitting on a fence, he's singing his song for me, at his own expense. And I'm just like that bird…" Yes, like Dylan and like the birds I, too, felt like climbing some high place and singing my song to the world. Just for once in my life to empty myself in worship and gratitude! Whether the world listened or not was not my concern. My concern was to sing—not to speculate if there was an audience. Once in the early days of The Freetown, an Australian hippie for no apparent reason had built a strange structure out of painted beams. Even if faded and dilapidated, his creation still stood on the ramparts not far from The Wagon Village. I cannot tell you what it looked like exactly. All I can say is that it looked like something you never thought existed, and that it was *high*. From the top, you had a great view to the East across the moat to Dyssen on the other side; to the West, you looked out over the central parts of the former garrison and past the place where the twisted spire of The Church of our Saviour goes on drilling its hole in the grey skies hanging heavily over the rest of Denmark.

With a blessing on my lips for Fanny and the four tequilas, and with one more for the Aussie who had made it all possible, I started climbing. The beams were slippery after the rains, but feeling lucid and calm despite the drinks, I made it safely to the top. Standing on the little platform with a board missing in the middle, I turned to face westward, opened my mouth and sang my song as loud as I could.

The moment I saw the mailman rummage through his bag for a longish envelope, which he proceeded to stick in my mailbox, I knew there was a letter from Melanie. I had just made a cup of tea and sat down to add a bit to this treatise of mine. Now, both tea and treatise were all but forgotten. I put on my windbreaker, against the gale and left the house. On my way down to the sea, I thought about the envelope in my breast pocket remembering how fat it had felt between my fingers. I could hardly wait for the moment when I would run the blade of my pocket knife along its upper fold. The little crisp sound it would make and the pleasurable sensation it always gave me when I reached in and got out the paper.

It was early in the day, and the heat had not set in yet. The temperature was pleasant the air smelling of seagulls and ocean water. The place I was aiming for was an old battered concrete bench shaded by some enormous bougainvillaea bushes that also offered shelter. When I got there, I sat down, stretched my legs and looked out over the white-capped sea. Just like a child whose pleasure in saving the candy for later is greater than eating it immediately, I postponed reading the letter. I guess this phase lasted about five minutes. Too impatient to wait any longer, I got it out of the pocket, cut it open and looked at it. Whew, three full pages! No wonder the envelope had been so fat. What on earth had possessed her to write three times as much as she usually did?

I don't know, but there must have been some telepathy at work. Normally, Melanie sticks to what has happened to her since the last time she wrote. Not this time. Most of the letter was about the time we met in Christiania. She had dreamt about me, she wrote, and the dream had triggered the letter. Although there had been no concrete and recognizable coincidence between people and places she nevertheless knew, even as she was dreaming, that the action was set in Christiania. And in the morning, when she woke, it all came back. There were especially two situations she remembered when she thought of the time we had spent together. The first night was one of them. It was past midnight only a few hours after we had met. We had both taken hits off the joint that was passed around. As the others had disappeared one by one into the night, we remained sitting there by ourselves, each mesmerized by the fire, which was crackling, hissing and creating series of explosions that sent sparks flying. It was then that I had begun to speak. I did not even turn to look at her or anything. Melanie was so stoned or lost in thought that at first she thought it was the voice of the fire talking to her. Sort of like when Jehovah spoke to Moses out of the burning bush. Did I remember this? No, surely not. Not only was that *her* experience but until she had the dream, she, too, had forgotten it. The dream was what brought it back and made her dig out the diary she kept at the time. In the wee hours of the morning, after we had drifted each into our lodgings, she wrote down what I had said from memory:

"Do you know," I had supposedly said and in a totally deadpan and toneless voice, "what makes so many of us ill in our minds and our bodies? It's that we're not sitting around campfires anymore. Staring into the flames at night is a sort of meditation that we have lost. And since we are no longer there serving him, the Fire god does not do us any good. Only when, once in a blue moon, it happens that the spirit recharges our pre-Christian souls then we feel rejuvenated. Our ancestors knew this and so worshipped fire. They made sure to spend a major part of life either quiet or telling stories around campfires. In this way, they re-charged and reconnected with the Godhead. We moderns believe that we have progressed beyond the "superstitions" of our ancestors and that what was true for them is no longer true for us. We believe that our life is different from theirs. But it isn't. Not in essence. We are the most recent shoots on the same old tree, that's all. Like our ancestors, we live off the sap that was there from the beginning and made the tree grow. Fire represents the life force within us. The will and power to live. It speaks to us by way of shooting sparks, glowing embers, the light, color and heat of the flames. Its language is the hissing, fizzing and sputtering—the crackling sound and the explosions.

And something in us understands and responds. Fire is the image of our elemental substance. In the beginning was a spark. Before the beginning, the spark had been asleep in the stone. At first, the flames are small and cautious, timid even. But with time, they grow big and hungry and voracious and consume anything that gets in their way. It's the same with us. In order to grow, we must consume whatever there is of nourishment in our surroundings. It's because we recognize ourselves in the fire that it has the power to hypnotize us. Fire is that substance in the deepest recesses of our being which renews our life. Instead of worshipping and building campfires, modern man fights fire as if it were an enemy of civilization. Fire is no longer holy. It's no longer the image of the primal spirit. Fire is physics and a formula and nothing else. It's something to be exploited for practical purposes and put out again when the job's done. We have gotten everything upside down. Believing we are its masters, we treat fire like a servant. We take pride in the myth about man stealing fire from the Gods, yet we don't understand that the Gods live in flames of fire. Like its source, fire lives at all levels at once. From the moment it is born a spark until the moment its dying ember turns to ashes, fire consumes itself. At one and the same time, it is the first spark, the greatest flame and the last flame and ember. For fire, all moments are created equal, unique and new. It is pure and distilled presence and awareness. It is *real*. Yes, it is real. Imagine what the world and life would be like if we would understand what it is we really need, if we would only *get* this for ourselves and *forget* all the perverse substitutes we fill our empty souls with. When will we see that it's all in vain what we are doing, that we are impoverished by the way we try to enrich ourselves, that in trying to salvage what we mistake for our lives, we are really throwing them overboard—that what we take for our salvation is really our doom? To judge from the way mankind behaves, you would think it brings a man more pleasure taking his fellow man's life or making him miserable than leaving him alone and living a life of joy oneself. Who knows what the future brings? Imagine that one day when we are sitting by a campfire staring into the flames, we suddenly become aware and decide to live for a gratification that isn't bought at the expense of our fellow man. Imagine a world where estrangement is no longer the rule. Imagine that one day we will connect again to the truth of our being, that the circuit is reestablished and the fire inside us rejuvenated!"

According to Melanie, I should take all of this with "a grain of salt." What she had just told me was probably more like an "amalgamation" of what I had said and her own dream. But even so, it was still food for thought.

The second most memorable situation arose, Melanie said, when we came back from our "tour of Christiania," and I was sitting on my swivel chair by the desk, and she on the bed. Asking me to write something for her on the little orange Silver Reed she had run next door for her camera and taken a photo of the writer to be.

Today, the photo had been lost. It existed only in her mind as a sweet memory reminding her how it was my "burning" words by the campfire that had made her fall in love with me. It was in those two *glimpses* she had seen the writer I would one day become. The lost photo showed the man of twenty-seven with his high hopes, his ambition and great hunger for life writing her a couple of lines on his Silver Reed. Wow! By the way, was I still writing on that old machine? Or did I now work on a P.C.? Had I kept up with progress? It was hard for her to believe. Would people like me try to keep up with an age that was doing its best to stamp out exactly such types of character? In vain, Melanie had weighed for and against. So would I please enlighten her! She was waiting eagerly for my answer. Love Melanie.

Last night, after son and I returned home from a musical performance put on by the children of the local church, I poured myself a glass of the island's aquavit and stepped out on the veranda.

When the glass was empty, I went back inside to answer Melanie's letter. She has asked two things of me: She wants to know if I'm still unplugged and writing on the old Silver Reed, and she wants me to tell her what I did the last twenty-four hours before we met in the Wagon Village. The latter was what I had been thinking of on the veranda, the former is what I choose to begin with. (Now you are probably thinking: "Hey, I'm not Melanie. I didn't ask you anything. What I want to know is what happened in Christiania."

If this is your reaction, I can't blame you. You are right. It isn't nice of me to interrupt the narrative with any more detours. I'll make it as short as I can, but feel free to skip a page or two if your patience is used up. It's all right.)

Normally, I write Melanie in longhand, but to show that my Silver Reed has not yet retired, I got it out of its box. Of course, I still wrote on Old John Silver, I tapped. How could she even doubt it? In thirty years, it has been cleaned, oiled and tightened five or six times. The box is worn, sure, but inside it the machine is as good as new. I have taken good care of it, and it has never let me down. Never once! I bought it to write on and that's what I have done. I have enjoyed that. And joy is joy. Times change, new technology replaces the old, but that does not mean that Man in the Stone Age did not derive as much joy from carving runes in rock as contemporary man gets out of word-processing on a P.C. and printing his text out on a printer. Who knows: maybe he even enjoyed it more since he was outside moving and breathing the air?

The subject got me so wound up that I wrote a whole lot more. The same thing happens every time I'm asked why I still write on a typewriter. Last night, it got so bad I had to go into the bedroom to look at my son's sleeping face. His calm features have a soothing effect on me. Amiel was lying on his back breathing through his open mouth. His eyes were not closed all the way and through the narrow slits, I could see that he was dreaming. Quietly, I left the room and returned to my desk. If ever I should want a new writing tool, I tapped, it would not be a computer but a hammer and chisel. And for my material I would choose granite. I would bring the monolith out of the Earth's boiling belly and transport it to the city hall square of my hometown. And while people sniffed coke and smoked and fixed heroin to the deafening sound of electronics blaring from everywhere around, while people were busy screwing each other right and left, masturbating in public and having fun shooting at targets at the carneval, I would ever so discretely begin to chisel the dormant message out of the stone and make it visible. And this is how it would read:

Stay calm. Don't despair or get carried away by the mad rush. Don't go mad. Love your neighbor as yourself. Stop idolizing the golden calf. Don't take or pay interest on loans. Keep your place. Shrug your shoulders and go on your way. Think for yourself and stick to your own values. Let your deed match your word. Love what is, embrace your fate. Be yourself. Believe in yourself. Don't sell out. Don't confuse thinking with speculation. Don't invest your fortune in paper. Don't lose yourself in inferior endeavors. Live simply and pay in cash. Don't take out insurance policies and don't be "online" more than necessary. Don't drive

272

a car when you can get where you want to go by foot or bicycle. Don't work too much. Don't wish for easy profit. Don't gamble...

Just such simple maxims in the imperative! And when I was done chiseling, I would put my tools on the flagstones and return to the temple on the hillside in order to continue my prayer. There I would be at peace with myself knowing that the monolith was in its place and would remain for all time. Majestic, alone and silent like Stonehenge on the (by now) empty and windswept square, patiently waiting for life to recover.

The night was all around me. My fatigue had vanished. Just like in the days of old my fingers tapped up a storm on Old John Silver's keyboard. Sentences kept tumbling out of me until finally I had to go to the toilet. And later—when I was standing with the bedspread in my hand—there it was back again: the dictation. Like some galley slave who has just received his orders, I grabbed the paper I always keep near the bed and wrote: "Who gives a shit what the age he lives in is like? To be a man is to be a time and an epoch in oneself. To be a man is to not give a damn about any other progress than the one that leads to God."

This last little bit did not make it into the letter for Melanie. I had already closed the envelope. Turning out the lamp on the bedside table, I pulled the cover over me. I closed my eyes. Except for a drowsy cricket all was quiet. When I opened my eyes again, there was a star in the sky I had not seen before. It listened to me breathing and twinkled. Twinkled and twinkled. It was going on morning when I fell asleep.

Looking back on it, I wrote to Melanie, it seemed a little strange that Douglas had not touched on the subject when

I spoke with him that afternoon. It must have been on his mind that she, Melanie, was coming to visit him that evening. But maybe he did not think about it, what with the unusual events of the day and the daily chores of the happy threesome?

As for me, I had been out driving the taxi the night before. A full moon was hanging huge over the earth glowering at me through the windshield. The earth looked like a place populated with fairies. On the radio, they played George Harrisons's "My Sweet Lord." Feeling high, I parked the car by a lake and like a mad Krishna monk, I danced down the path to the shore. In hindsight, I wrote, one might say it was the moon, Krishna and the tambourines that formed the prelude or overture to our meeting. At any rate, it was a little past six a.m. when I got on my old black clunker of a bike and rode home to Christiania.

The city streets were all but deserted. The air was warm and balmy and hardly a wind stirred. The weather was perfect for bicycling. The weight of my red taxi purse inside my jacket reminded me I was coming back with money, and even if I was tired, it felt good to be out of the taxi seat, rolling through the open streets of Copenhagen and headed for dream land. Passing the main train station on the Tietgensgade Bridge, I saw a bum with his head buried in a garbage bin. He was yelling something to himself and looked up as a police car drove slowly by. A bit further on a young woman was leaning over the railing and staring at the tracks below. That's all. There weren't any other people in sight. And soon I too was gone from the scene.

I took the same route as I always did: Tietgensgade Street with the long view over the broad band of railway tracks that led out and away from under the bridge, disappearing in the distance. The pale red brick central post building where in the early morning hordes of young people sorted mountains of new mail. Tivoli Gardens coming up on one side and Ny Carlsberg Glyptotek on the other. Stormgade Street and the National Museum with the long colonnade discolored by exhaust of automobiles. Frederiksholms Canal, Gl. Strand, the statue of the aproned fishwife holding a huge flounder in her upraised hand. Christiansborg Castle and the empty windswept square before it—main seat of fossilized political power and pompous symbol of incompetence and corruption. And there it was: the always closed, longish, low, ornamented, secretive, tarnished former stock exchange. As much as I wanted to look the other way, I could not help staring at this building with its twisted dragons peering at passers-by. I had never seen a single human being entering the building or leaving it. It was always dead and dark and menacing in an enforced silence, which gave me the creeps. What a contrast to the Knippel's Bridge a few pedal steps away. Even if it meant going a bit uphill, the bridge always mercifully wiped away whatever ominous images the former stock exchange left in my blood. This morning it was up, and I had to wait for a Russian cargo ship to pass. Five minutes later, the bars went up. Erect on the seat and without hands on the handlebars, I freewheeled down Torvegade Street, crossed Christianiashavn's Canal and hung a left into Prinsessegade Street, which led me straight to the main entrance of Christiania on the corner of Bådsmandsstræde Street. Entering The Freetown of Christiania I heard the voice of Kris Kristofferson in my head: "When you're headed for the border, Lord, you're bound to cross the line!" Here is where the ride gets bumpy. The Prairie. The low barracks of Psyak and the Opera Building. Riding the Milky Way. The building housing the hairdresser and the bathhouse. Langgade Street and coming up ahead the narrow gate to The Dandelion leading me past The Omelet and to my door.

The sensation of being home again is so strong it's almost unbearable. I lean my bicycle against the side of the wagon, bend over to lock it and stand up straight. I breathe in the morning air. Even if I can hardly wait to get to bed, I just sort of linger to take a look around and watch a porcupine sniffle and shuffle its feet over near Martin's shack. Prolonging the moment, I turn the corner of the wagon, unzip and take a long leak.

Yes! How good it felt to be home. Sometimes, when I stepped into my wagon after a long taxi-night, I thought of it as a spaceship. The air inside is not quite like the air outside. But it isn't exactly like inside air either. Mixed up in it, there is the little dry sound a twig makes when it falls on the roof. There's the song of birds, the sound of raindrops against the window and of the wind in the treetops. The thin walls seem more like membranes than walls. Then, a moment later, there is the bouncy feeling when I cross the floor. Home is neither a solid house nor a sailing ship. In some weird squirrelly way this morning the bouncing floor reminds me that my life is ephemeral. "It's the scent of wood," I mutter to myself as I savor the sight of the quilt on the bed, waiting for the moment when I will crawl under it. But if it is the scent of wood, it's also the fragrance of another newborn summer morning, of dead and fresh leaves, of sawdust, paint and tar. In short, it's the scent of life. After cruising the city back and forth sitting in a soft upholstered car smelling of stale smoke, perfume and halitosis, it feels like paradise to bounce barefoot across my own floor, brush my teeth and climb into bed. Pulling the quilt up over my ears, I don't have a care in the world. With my head on the pillow, I close my weary eyes and let sleep engulf me. At that moment, I don't give a damn should all humankind disappear without a trace. But *if* the world is still there when I wake, it will find me ready for it. If it shows me its pretty face or its ugly mug is all the same to me. I will take what comes and strangle Medusa if I have to. Hurrah for death. We the living are all dead or dying. Only some of us sing as we go to sleep. I am twenty-seven, and the blood of life surges through my veins. I live in a wagon on wheels. I may still wake to find another tomorrow.

"Hey, hand me the basket and the net will you!"

The sound of Jakob's voice.

And a bit later: "Where'd you put it?" This time it was Douglas shouting.

Then followed the raspy voice of Old Knud. I couldn't make out what it said. After some minutes' silence, I again heard Jakob cry out: "And the gloves. *I* need the gloves. I'M READY. ARE *YOU*?"

It seemed the world was *still* there and that I was still in it. "So be it, and so help me God!" I thought to myself and felt like laughing.

At the same time as I was thinking this, I was also trying to hold on to the dream I had just woken from. Something about a well known women's lib writer of popular novels. Though I had never cared for her in waking life, in my dream, I took her on the rack of my bicycle and together we rode off to a meadow somewhere with butterflies. Later, we ended up in the house of her grandmother, of all people. I was invited for dinner and spilled a bowl of soup on the floor. Ashamed, I threw myself on the floor and started to wipe up the soup with a paper napkin. I woke because the women's lib writer was letting out horrible screams and pulling my arm.

Since I moved into the wagon my dreams had changed. Somehow, they had become crazier, funnier and less scary—less *unbearable.* I used to feel relief waking from my nightmares drenched in sweat, now I hated to wake from them and often spent the first minutes groping to salvage the juicier parts. Along with the after taste of the crazed and funny, there was also the pinch of sadness and regret the dream left behind in me because I had been torn out of a brand new world where exciting things happened and people were freer and more true to themselves.

Floating on the last great swells of the vanishing dream, my waking mind being increasingly preoccupied with the sounds reaching my ears from The Village, I also became conscious of an itching in my crotch. Instantly, the remaining fragments of dream disappeared. Now, there was only itching. I lied as still as I could. There was no doubt. Not only was the itching real, it was also worse than any I could remember. And the itching was not restricted to the crotch area either. It itched throughout the entire hairy regions of my body, which pretty much is all over the place. Oddly enough, my scalp did not itch. But in my pubic hair, there was an intense creeping and crawling. Down there in the dark, was where it was! Getting up on my elbows, I pushed myself into a sitting position. I now had my back against the wall. With the tips of my fingers, I pushed the hairs aside in what seemed the epicenter of my itching crotch and looked down. And…lo and behold! What was *that*? What my eyes saw was like a flat little whitish flake that moved on legs. Without a moment's hesitation, I gave the tips of my thumb and index finger orders to seize the bugger. And…what do you know! A split second later, there it was creeping merrily along the skin of my forefinger. I ogled it fiercely. Like a crab, it had legs on both sides of its body. After indulging my curiosity for some time, I grabbed the book I was reading from the desk and squished the bug against the cover with my thumbnail. There! I held the book up before my eyes and inspected the dead body of the insect vivid against the dark material of an umbrella.

And so it came to pass that by crushing an insect, I became aware of the cover of the book I was reading. It was a paperback edition from 1964 of Richard Brautigan's novel "A Confederate General from Big Sur." Despite the fact that I had read this book at least three times before, I had never taken note of the picture on the front cover. Now, I did and so much so that, for a minute, I even forgot the itching. The picture showed a detail from Hokusai's painting called "The Hollow of the Deep-Sea Wave." Somewhere in the universe, a giant wave is breaking—not on defenseless open boats with little insignificant men in them (as in Hokusai's painting) but on a man and a woman standing in water to their waists. The man (who I supposed was identical with the author of the book) is holding an umbrella over both their heads as protection. His hair reaches almost to his shoulders and not only is he wearing glasses but also a sizeable downturned mustache. The woman is the image of what every lonely man is dreaming of. Obviously, these people are in imminent danger of annihilation. In a moment, the wave will fall on them with all its destructive might and wipe them off the face of the earth. And yet there is no panic in their faces. Their faces are calm and radiate joy. They *are,* however, concerned about something. The woman's soft expression is tinged with slight reproach, and the way the man frowns it seems he wants to bring a mad world to its senses and ask of it: "What do you think you're doing? Don't you see what is happening? Where do *you* think you're headed? Don't you understand that *your* life too is in danger?" It's all there in his glare and the presence of the umbrella. Had it not been for the umbrella, the onlooker would not know the couple is aware of the wave about to engulf them.

"To see the world in a grain of sand," I mumbled to my-self and crushed another insect on the cover. This time the dead body stuck to the woman's Barbie-doll coiffure. "For all I care, you can itch in *her* hair," I thought gloomily and dove into my crotch in search of more of the little devils.

But as it soon turned out it was an unequal battle. Even if I took a million pale-faced scalps, it would not slow their advance in the slightest. The little white flakes existed in huge numbers, and they kept right on multiplying as they pushed along the entire frontier from the crotch in the South across the great expanse of belly and into the less overgrown regions to the North.

Yet, even if it was hopeless and doomed to fail, still I went right on putting up resistance. SQUISH, and Brauti-gan's dark jacket was ornamented with yet another crab-like pale-face. The next three or four I crushed against the blue waters of the wave. From there, I moved up and deco-rated a neat little circle on the umbrella. I kept it up as I say, but reaching the number of thirty-eight, I decided it was time for unconditional surrender. What good did it do that I was the strongest, boldest and most courageous if the enemy existed in limitless numbers? With no hope of stem-ming the tide, it was a waste of my time. So I put on clean underwear, pulled on my jeans and taking the book strewn with dead insects with me, I went out to ask advice from Old Knud, the undisputed wise man of the Village.

In front of Knud's shack, a small crowd had gathered. Hanne, John and Rune were there too. Rune, the snot-nosed kid, was pressing one of Knud's rabbits to his chest. The animal hung almost to the ground. Its ears covered its eyes, and it probably wasn't able to see a damn thing. It was just

280

hanging there as limp and as secure as if it had never been more comfortable. The soft skin of its belly was exposed. Just like it could care less if somebody came by with a knife and slit it open. "What guts it must have," I thought and went up to Knud.

"What's going on here?" I said. "Where's Jakob?"

"Up there." Knud indicated the direction by tilting his head back a little.

And sure enough! High up in the crown of the tree behind Knud's shack, Jakob was sitting astride a thick branch holding a net and a wicker basket. I felt a cold shiver run down my back.

"What's he doing?"

Old Knud threw me a sideways glance: "It's my bees. They've taken off. Jakob is trying to get them into the basket and bring them down. I'll teach the suckers to desert!"

"Can he *do* that?"

"I sure hope so," Knud said. And he was just about to look up again, when I held the cover of "The Confederate General from Big Sur" before his glowering little Eskimo eyes. Instead of a bunch of escaped bees, what he saw was a battlefield strewn with dead and dying insects.

"Can you tell me what these are?"

Old Knud got his reading glasses out of his shirt pocket and put them on. I was looking at the place where they had been taped on the left side of his head, when his face broke into a broad grin: "That there… I'll tell you what that is!" He lowered his head a little and turned to look at me over the frame of his glasses: "Them there things are crabs, and no two ways about it. *Plithirius pubis* in the Latin lingo. Yours is a bad case and to get rid of them, we'll have to dip you in strong acid." Once more, Knud stopped. This time it was in order to shake his head slowly from side to side: "Look at yourself! You've got hair all over the place. Where'd you get them?"

I was about to answer, when Hanne broke in: "Would you *cut that out* Knud. What are you giving him that bullshit for? Just because they probably had to dip *you* in acid, when *you* were young and had crabs doesn't mean they have to dip him too. Nowadays, you just go to the drug store and buy a little bottle with some crab juice in it. Then you go home and douse yourself with it. You rub it in with your fingers. It's a nuisance but it's not as bad as all that. I know what I'm talking about because I've had to do it myself a couple times. But…" Hanne stopped and looked at my hairy chest: "You Les better get *two* bottles. And don't forget to find out *where* you got the creeps. Think who you've been with this last week or so and make sure they get the treatment too. If you don't, well, it'll be all over the place!"

"Well," I thought to myself and brushed the thirty-eight corpses off "The Confederate General from Big Sur," "let's see now!" This last week, it could be Lili and the skinny German girl Frauke with the big tits and the baby bird. I had run into her crossing the moat bridge and been with her in my shack less than an hour later. Since it seemed unlikely that Lili had given me the crabs, Frauke was the main suspect. At first, I had thought that it was because she was a dope-headed hippie that she acted so weird. Then I realized she had a screw lose. As I said, she was holding a baby bird when I ran into her. It was the tiniest ball of down you had ever seen. It must have just fallen out of the nest. And so had she it seemed. Thinking back on it, I could not make out which of them had looked more lost, the bird or the girl. I had never seen her before in my life. Even if there was that lost air about her, she also looked very sweet with her soft brown eyes and tousled dark hair. Somehow, it touched me too the way she was standing there looking rapturously at the young bird. You'd almost think she identified with it or something.

It wasn't until the next day I found out a little more. I was told that Frauke loved "all living things both great and small." And this, I was told, was to be understood quite literally. In that case, I now concluded, she probably loved crabs too. Nobody knew from where she came in Germany, if from the West or from the East. One day she appeared in Christiania where she lived from hand to mouth and day to day. Nights, she spent anywhere she could find "a bit of animal warmth." I had been told that she never spoke much. But when she was with me, she sang. Apparently, the *lieder* of Schubert were a favorite. I figured she probably came from what is called a "good family." And she was pretty too. There was only one little hitch: the extent to which it was necessary for me to ignore her filthy toe nails. On the other hand, she made no secret of the fact that she adored my looks: *"Du bist aber sehr sehr hübsch,"* she said and studied my face. *"Ein sehr hübscher hippie."* And as if she had just said something very funny, she began to giggle. And she went right on giggling when she put the tiny bird on a tree stump and threw her arms around me. Maybe, there's something I have misunderstood, but it felt strange to have my looks praised one moment only to be laughed at the next. It was almost like *I* was now the fledgling. She pressed herself to my chest so that I could not help feeling her magnificent and firm breasts with no bra. And since she didn't seem to want to let go, I finally removed her arms and told her I was going home. In German, mind you. She was beside herself with joy. She grabbed my hand, started tugging at it and cried: *"Was gibst zu hause? Was gibst zu hause?"*

I thought perhaps she would stay where she was if I started walking, but I was wrong. She tagged along at a little distance with the bird in her hand. And the moment

I looked back, she started running. She caught up with me just before the trail turns in the direction of the Wagon Village. I looked at her, and she looked back at me. She kept shifting her feet like she was bashful or something. But then I don't think she was, because all of a sudden she smiled disarmingly and took my arm. It was just as simple as that. There, we were walking along like we had known each other since the dawn of time. I looked at our feet. I was wearing the old tennis shoes, and she was in her dirty feet. I wondered what would happen when we reached my wagon. What if she wanted me to take her? Wouldn't that be sort of like steeling money from the blind beggar? I don't mean to make it sound like it worried me a whole lot, because it didn't. Yet it did *a little bit*. She was not ugly, and she was not what you would call beautiful either. She was pretty, and there was something special about her. I think the thing she had is called *mien*. Her *mien* had that soft and vulnerable quality that I have always found irresistible in women, and if it had not been for the bare feet and the black toenails, I'm not sure I would have thought her nutty at all. Of course, there was the whole issue of the bird. Not to mention Schubert and his *lieder*. But hell, who was I to judge? Even if the general surroundings seemed sad, there was nothing wrong with being in a good mood. As we were walking along, she was singing that German *lied*. She wasn't singing it loudly or anything, but she sang it directly into my right ear like it was some endearment meant for me and me only. Frankly, I do not know if it was Schubert. It just sounded like something Schubert might have composed. I didn't know much about those things. For all I knew the song could have been composed by Haydn or Brahms. When I suggest it was by Schubert, it's only because of a certain *"müllerin"* that kept popping up. I know it sounds like a lot of horseshit, but in my mind *"müllerins"* were associated with Schubert. In any case, it was really quite pleasant to listen to. There was something comforting about it, something soothing as though if she would only go on singing, things would eventually turn out all right.

But what was going to happen when we reached my door? By now, I was pretty sure we were headed for my bed. The way she breathed and whispered the lines of the song into my ear told me that it was mother nature's child I'd met. A tempting elf girl! Or maybe a Freetown fairy? What did one do in such a situation? "God has a very big heart." Anthony Quinn's voice was croaking into my other ear. "But there's one sin he will not forgive, and that is if a woman asks a man to her bed, and he will not go!" Only in this case, the bed was mine. Sure, but using that as an excuse would be a despicable thing to do. And what is more: God would not buy it. The fact that the girl had no place to live and did not own a bed anywhere in the world made it even more unthinkable to disobey the commandment. Jesus, I thought, what kind of world is this where a man may be forgiven the worst atrocities if only he repents? But if he once refuses a woman, well, then *that* is a capitol sin for which he must burn in the flames of hell forever.

It turned out more or less the way I had predicted. In the wagon Frauke set down the little downy ball of feathers on some scrap paper lying on my desk. She then looked sideways at me and started taking off her dress. Not a word had been spoken between us the whole way back from the bridge. And here, she was taking off her clothes… I went to the door and shut it. By the time I was back in the middle of the floor, Frauke was standing before me without a stitch on. "When a woman," bleated the voice and then I, too, began to undress. I watched Frauke climb the bed and get under the covers. I liked the way she moved, the whiteness of her skin and the frail figure. By the time I was ready to join

285

her, she was covered to her chin and was looking calmly and very seriously at me with her brown eyes. But when I wanted to lift the quilt and lie down alongside her, she pressed herself into the far corner. Now I was where she had been a moment earlier, and she was holding her legs and resting her chin on her knees while looking intently at me. "What's this," I thought, "is she playing cat and mouse with me?"

I was lying on my back when Frauke snatched the quilt off me: *"Warum kann ich dich nicht sehen?"* she said as she bent forward and caressed my cock. Immediately, it jumped into an erect position. *"Mein Gott!"* Frauke exclaimed and caressed it a bit more.

"What if the little bird gets jealous?" I thought and glanced at it.

Well, that is how I got crabs. While I got them, the bird was quiet, and for my own part, I did my best to ignore the black toenails down at the other end. It wasn't too hard really. Frauke made it easy by loving me just like a woman with all her screws tight and in their place. When she came, she moaned and pulled herself up with both arms around my neck. I'm not kidding when I say that loving her was easier than anything I'd ever done before. It was so simple and straightforward. And when it was over, it was over. No talk of tomorrow or the next time. Not a word about crabs… That was by far the hard part: I would have to find a way of telling Lili. It was only the day before that she had gone to Sweden to visit her father, who was recently remarried to a Swedish opera diva. When Lili returned itching like hell the day after tomorrow, I better have a plausible explanation ready. And what would I say? I could not very well tell her that one day as my cock was on its way across the moat bridge, it was turned into a baby bird that contracted crabs the moment it was picked up by Franz Schubert's *müllerin.*

I couldn't help but smile at the thought of it. If I gave her a yarn like that, whew would she go on the rampage. You might say that Lili lacked the finer sense for magical realism of this sort. She would not be the least bit amused.

I was interrupted in these thoughts when a longhaired Greenlander I had never seen before appeared over by Douglas' wagon. As soon as he caught sight of Old Knud, he started towards us. Without taking the least interest in me or my crabs, or in what was going on with the bees, or in anything else for that matter, he said to Knud: "You've got to come down. It's Laurel and Hardy banging heads again!"

Old Knud wrinkled his brow and nodded his graying head. It was clear that he understood the gravity of the situation. He knew exactly why *he* was summoned and not someone else. Laurel and Hardy were two aggressive and dim witted pushers who had formed a sort of companionship smoking their brains out together. As a former boxing champion with a legendary straight left that earned him the nickname "Knockout Larsen," Old Knud was greatly respected by the Pusher Street pushers. Whenever there were disputes and fights, Old Knud's presence had a sobering effect. Usually, all he had to do was appear and tell the combatants to stop their nonsense. If that was not enough he could also threaten to ban them from "The Poppy." That probably would not be necessary today. Neither would the straight left. To Laurel and Hardy, Old Knud was sort of a Christ figure. Stretching the term just a bit, one might well call them his disciples. Once they were pissed off, Knud was the only person on the planet who could calm them down.

His reading glasses still on his nose Old Knud turned to me: "I don't want to shout," he said. "Tell Jakob that I had to go to The Poppy to punch the usual nuisances in the nose. The fools don't know how to behave. I'll be back as soon as I can."

"No problem," I said and nodded, "I'll tell him it was an emergency!"

As I was watching Old Knud, the Greenlander and the dog Rolf walk away, I thought of that Poppy-place in Pusher Street where Knud was one of seven managers called "the caps." According to Marie-Louise who worked there, it was about the seediest place in all Christiania (and probably the whole of Copenhagen too). It really deserved, she had told me, the reputation it enjoyed as *the* terminal stop on death row. Pushing three or four in the morning, the casualties of the night would slowly trickle in to help give one another the final push into blessed oblivion. Personally, I had only spent a few minutes there. It was in the morning before it even opened. For some reason, I needed to get hold of Marie-Louise! From her neighbor in The M-house next door, I learned that she was in The Poppy. It was where I figured she would be too. Marie-Louise loved to talk about her job. In the job-announcement in the Weekly Mirror, she once told me, The Poppy had sought a person who did not mind getting HER hands dirty, who had "strong nerves," a healthy sense of humor and was competent when it came to brewing the strong coffee needed for "The seven great caps." "But," she had laughed, "the only thing those caps looked at was my boobs." As a rule, the board of directors would begin to show up around ten or ten-thirty a.m. Before that, it was Marie-Louise's job to sweep the floors, clear the tables, prepare two thermos cans of strong coffee and set them on the caps' table with fresh rolls and pastry from the Sunshine Bakery. When that was done, she could leave.

"Oh my God! Oh my God!" I could still hear Marie-Louise's groans. She had laughed so hard she nearly peed in her pants. If only the coffee was strong and ready when the caps showed up, there could be fresh shit on the floor, for all they cared. She was sorry, Marie-Louise said, but she really could not do the place justice. She lacked words. Somebody, an anthropologist say, ought to sneak in around noontime and watch the seven great caps eat. Then that somebody ought to tape their conversation, take photos and exhibit the result in parliament. If *that* did not open the politicians' eyes to the condition of our culture, then *nothing* would.

When Marie-Louise said that about The Poppy deserving to be immortalized in photos, I urged her again to *try* and tell me more about it. But, no! She couldn't do that. If ever there was a spectacle you had to see for yourself, The Poppy was it. She could shit on the floor, and the caps would probably promote her. But if she opened a window, she'd be sacked on the spot. At the first meeting, the caps had taken great pains to explain how such an act was really a felony because it would screw up the reputation of the place as the only joint in town where a guy could get high even if his dog had run away, his wallet had been ripped off, his lump of hash gotten lost, and it was five in the morning. That the joint they ran was not just your ordinary run of the mill dive was testified by the opening hours. Never open until ten-thirty, eleven o'clock in the evening The Poppy never closed until the last wreck had been scraped off the floor and shoveled out into the morning light.

When I got there, it was a little after ten in the morning. The place was exactly like when the last wreck had been "scraped off the floor" and "shoveled" out into the morning air. Having overslept, Marie-Louise had arrived only a few minutes before me.

The room was furnished with wooden benches and plank tables on which there were a great number of large cast iron ashtrays. Another remarkable feature was an assortment of whitish things of varying forms and shapes that lay scattered all over the place. In the dungeon-like light, I could not make out what they were. Stepping up to one of the tables, I touched one of the shapes with the tip of my finger. Twisted paper towel is what it was. Marie-Louise explained how the clientele used paper towels to remove sticky yellow-brown cannabis-juice from their smoking gear. If I looked closely, she said, I could see where the smoker had held the paper and how it became smeared with the stinking substance. To judge from the number of twisted paper towels left on the tables and floors the place must have been packed that night! Thinking to myself that an evil snow had fallen, it struck me that this entire interior belonged in the National Museum. I mean it would be a damn sight more instructive than the iron-age collection. On the wall above the hashish den, there ought to be a sign that said: "Danish hashish club interior from the late twentieth century".

I asked Marie-Louise how she could stand starting her days in that place?

She looked at me reproachfully: "Hey, aren't we being a bit too delicate now? It's not as bad as all that really. Don't you think it has its own charm?"

Was she serious or was she teasing me? Tilting her head slightly to one side Marie-Louise said the job was not at all as horrible as it seemed at first glance. In the *beginning* it was, until she got used to it. It was hard coming from the fresh air outside, opening a door and being struck by the stench. At first, she almost fainted. Human kind, however, is extremely adaptable. I knew *that*, didn't I? There was practically nothing we could not get used to. Like making easy money. Here addiction set in real fast. So from almost fainting the first couple times, it soon became something she just needed to get over with. Apart from the compliments they paid her boobs, the seven great caps also paid her a hundred and fifty crowns a day. And nobody checked if the corners were clean. She could be done in about forty-five minutes. When done, she was a hundred-and-fifty crowns richer.

For a crappy job, this was not bad at all. Without exhausting herself, Marie-Louise could earn four thousand taxfree crowns a month and have plenty of time for her work with "The Chariot of the Sun" theater.

In short, I knew very well where Old Knud was going when Laurel and Hardy were banging heads again. In Christiania, contrasts were sharp. When the sun was shining, and you were among friends in The Wagon Village; when Old Knud's bees were swarming and Jakob sitting astride a branch trying to lure them into a basket; well, then it was a bit hard to conceive that only five hundred meters away there was such a place as The Poppy.

After some time and a hell of a lot of trouble, Jakob succeeded in getting the fugitives into the basket and lowering it to the ground. It was a grand feat, and we applauded like mad. And since Old Knud was not back yet, John saw to it that the swarm was returned to the hive. When a few minutes later Knud showed up, he gave the poor bees an earful. If ever they dared take off again, he told them, he would personally see to it that they would regret it. "You do *that* again," Knud said and brandished his misshapen boxer's fist in the air, "and I swear you'll taste this!"

A little later when I left home with my hands in my pockets, Old Knud was still swearing in his beard. Crabs and all, I was headed for the drug store up on the square. The little suckers were taking a break from itching. What do

I know! Maybe, it was crab *siesta* time. At any rate, it was such a relief that I decided to stop at the Sunshine Bakery and get a fresh roll for lunch.

The sun was shining from a clear and cloudless sky when I returned through the old gateway into The Dandelion with two small bottles of crab-juice, a half-liter milk carton and three fresh rolls in a paper bag. In celebration of the lovely weather, I chose to go left of The City Hall and see if Christian was on his veranda taking sunshine in one of his old deckchairs. There seemed to be something special in the air over Copenhagen that day, something like atmospheric disturbances that affected human activities down on earth. No, something *was for sure* different even if on the surface everything was just like on any other day. As usual, the Dandelion urchins were playing among rusty old clunkers, rotting planks, stacks of firewood and other unspecified junk lying around. As far as they were concerned, the world was exactly like it should be and always was. With me it was different: with a crotch full of crabs and my belly growling I was in a hurry to get home.

As I've already told you, the reason I had gone left instead of right around The City Hall was from a sudden irrational desire to get a glimpse of Christian. And sure enough! Right there in the middle of the row of rotting verandas, Christian was lording it in a deckchair next to Danish Christian, his friend and workmate from The Soup Bowl! At the sight of them I stopped involuntarily. What was *that*? Leaning back in the deckchairs they both wore a big white brace-like thing on the nose. Christian and Christian. Their eyes were closed, but from the way they moved their lips, I could tell they were having some sort of conversation. The white things they wore were narrow at the top and wider at the bottom. What were they for? Was it to protect their noses from the sun? Or was it something else? I was really too hungry to care, but the way the two of them were sitting there so comfortably conversing with those idiotic things on their noses made me curious. Unable to resist the impulse, I stepped up:

"Howdy guys!"

The two Christians opened their eyes, turned their heads and looked at me. Under the white brace-like contraption on his nose French Christian's face broke into a broad smile: "*Bonjour mon ami,*" he said.

"*Bonjour,*" I said wondering if it would be a breach of decorum and an embarrassment to ask about the noses first thing. Deciding that the only embarrassment would be *not* to do it, I asked:

"Why are you guys wearing those white things on your noses?"

Christian and Christian looked at each other like they shared a secret between them. Apparently they were in the process of choosing a spokesman. Finally, Danish Christian said with a nod:

"We broke'em."

"What!" I blurted out. "Did you *both* break your noses?"

Christian and Christian nodded in a way that seemed so smug it might have been choreographed: "Don't you believe me?"

Danish Christian was still the speaker.

"All right," I said breathing deeply. "So… you want me to believe that you broke your noses at the same time! How'd you do that? Was it a frontal collision?"

"Hey," Danish Christian said, "it's not funny."

It happened the day before when the two of them had been at work at The Soup Bowl. At one point, a pusher known as Erik the Red had entered and demanded a bowl of soup. As indicated by his name, Erik's hair was red. But what the name did not say was that he was also a giant measuring two meters and weighing well over a hundred kilos.

As if wanting to make sure that it was not something he had dreamed, Danish Christian touched the brace on his nose with the tips of his fingers. He nodded. Patience was not exactly Erik the Red's strongest point. And he wasn't a role model for politeness or manners either. Maybe it was because he had been on speed the last four days or something. It was hard to know. He had been edgy and aggressive from the moment he stepped in the door. His feet kept moving under the table. Still, Erik had stayed in his place until French Christian, who was serving the tables, served three Greenlanders first. Erik slammed his fist on the table so the saltshaker and the toothpicks jumped half a meter into the air. "Easy now! Easy now!" French Christian had said and added in his own language: *Tu te conduit comme un enfant!*"

Danish Christian looked down and chuckled. It was obvious that he enjoyed telling me about it. He kept stroking the brace on his nose in what seemed to me a very professorial manner. Maybe it really *was* the French, he mused, that had pissed Erik off. Not because he did not understand it, but because someone had the audacity to speak to him that way. When Danish Christian glanced at him from the kitchen, he had seen him brush the toothpicks off the table. At the same time, he was fuming, rotating and wringing his fat freckled fingers, while cursing French Christian under his breath.

"*Oui, c'est ca,*" French Christian nodded, "*ca me faisait nerveux. Vraiment!*"

"I'll be damned if this doesn't come to a bad end." Danish Christian thought as he emptied the ladle into a plate for Erik the Red. "If that guy doesn't like leeks, say, or if the soup isn't hot enough, or the spoon is greasy, he'll blow his top completely!"

And as succeeding events were to show, Danish Christian's assessment of the situation was right. No sooner had French Christian set the plate of soup on Erik the Red's table and turned his back to him than he heard the pusher yelling something about "dog-food" and that he wouldn't something or other.

It was from then on that things had become real nasty. Next thing they knew, Erik the Red had gotten up and overturned the table. Just like that. There was broken plate and minestrone all over the place. Everybody was staring at Erik fearing what might come next. "Get out of here!" French Christian said with that accent of his. "What was that you said?" Erik roared and grabbed the Greenlander's table and overturned that too. And Erik would surely have gone on plundering and pillaging had not French Christian jumped onto his back and started riding him like you would a rodeo bull. Foaming at the mouth and with the rider on his back, Erik stampeded on the slippery floor. French Christian was hanging on for dear life, and while the other customers fled, Erik managed to overturn the rest of the tables making the entire floor a very soupy affair.

The *good* news, Danish Christian said, was that the riding lessons French Christian had taken as a child now finally paid off. Instead of being thrown, he was waving one arm over his head and yelling "yippie-I-oh." Erik could not shake him off! The *bad* news was that when French Christian with one final "yippie-I-oh" let go and got off, Erik turned and socked him in the nose. As chance would have it, Danish Christian chuckled it was at this precise moment that he decided to come to the rescue of his friend. When

Erik heard him come charging through the soup he turned and broke his nose too. *Basta co si…*

Without speaking a word, Erik just sort of stood there in the middle of the floor peering at their bleeding noses. They were both sitting in the soup on the floor. The three of them were the only people left in The Soup Bowl. The world had become very quiet.

Finally, Erik spat on the floor: "My God what a pair of chickens you are!" Then he kicked a chair and spat once more for good measure. "See you later chicken shit," he said and left.

Christian and Christian had stayed where they were without moving for some time. They felt so drained and despondent they could not even *look* at each other. Not to mention get up. They just sat there and stared. Finally, at long last, French Christian woke from the stupor. He turned his head, raised his eyebrows and knit his brow. Then in his French accent, he pronounced the immortal words: "There's pain in my nurse!"

"Christ did that break me up!" Danish Christian shook his head in disbelief. "The accent pronouncing that word 'nurse'…"

Next thing he knew a little chuckle escaped him.

And a little chuckle was all it took. In an instant, both of them were rolling in the soup. Danish Christian was holding his stomach laughing and moaning: "There's pain in my nurse! Oh-Ohhh!"

After some time they succeeded in suppressing their laughter just enough to sit up. But one look at each other's bloody "nurse", and they were writhing like worms on the floor. Gradually, the laughter petered out, and they got up into a sitting position. But then, they could not help it and looked at each other, and it started up all over again. Over and over, they would hick-up and scream: "There's pain in my nurse".

It only stopped when at one point it dawned on French Christian that Danish Christian was standing up. That made him try and get up too. But with all the minestrone, on the floor, it was like Bambi on the ice. "The Soup Bowl," he yelled as he went down again. "Yippie-I-oh, this is The Soup Bowl!"

In the end, of course, life had to go on. Eventually, they were both back on their feet. At first, they avoided looking at each other for fear the storm would hit them again. But no, the laughter had spent itself. They were now able to look at each other and assess the situation. Danish Christian suggested that they make a band and call it "The Minestrone Blood-soup Boys".

"But you know what bothers me?" Danish Christian said to me. "It bothers me that I didn't have a camera. A pic of "The Minestrone Blood-soup Boys" would have done wonders to my curriculum vitae."

I nodded. "Yeah, that's an awful pity. But what did you do then?"

"What do you think we did?" Danish Christian said. "It isn't like there was a hell of a lot we *could do* eh! We locked the door, hung the 'CLOSED' sign on the nail and went to get a taxi to the emergency ward."

"I happen to be a taxi driver," I said and shook my head. "Don't try and tell me you got a cab to take a couple of bloody minestrone boys like you."

No, admitted Danish Christian. One look at them and the cabdrivers were off. Passing Carl Madsens Square on their way out of the Freetown, there had been this Indian guy who wanted a picture of them and the sadhu. "You look very-very strange," he said. At the bus stop, the driver had had his doubts about them too. It was only when Danish Christian said "emergency ward" that he decided to let them on. The whole way he kept looking at them in his mirror.

Danish Christian pointed to his nose: "So, you see, it was a happy ending."

"Yeah. All's well that ends well!" I looked from one Christian to the other.

"*Q'es-que ca veut dire!*" French Christian asked.

Danish Christian explained it to him.

"*Bon,*" I said, "I'll be on my way then. But when are you guys going back to work?"

"Me?" Danish Christian shook his head with gusto. "I'm not going back. I'm through with The Soup Bowl."

"*Moi aussi,*" French Christian said. "I through too. But soon you come to visit, no? You remember Fanny? Sure. Now she make love wif me. One time, two times, three times. *En fin... sans arret.* She love wif me and laugh. Is *l'amour* you know. But... many problems. Many, many problems. Ida, my girl-friend, don't know. She still in Jutland and I much afraid when she come back. *Mais alors. Viens chez moi.* Then we talk. Fanny oh-la-la. I crazy for her. She young for love. Only problems. When she see my nurse she laugh very much on it. *Mais, viens me voir. Pas ce soir,* but soon. *Bientot.* So I tell you more, *d'accord!*"

When I had promised to come for a visit, I walked along the wooden garage building and turned the corner into the narrow passage leading to my wagon. Home, sweet home. There it was before me just dying for me to get back. Seized with emotion I stopped and looked at it. Somehow, it was like I was seeing it for the first time. The blue paint peeling on its sides and window frames, the rusty and useless iron bar sticking out of its end. Conscious of the crab poison in my shoulder bag and the paper bag containing fresh rolls in my hand, I solemnly pledged to paint it before the summer was out. "Caravan-wagon number 537 Christiania," I whispered. And turning my eye into a mental camera, I closed it only to open it again the next second. This is how I took a photograph of the wagon, the one that I was later to put in my life's photo album.

But now, it was time to demolish crabs and get something to eat. There was always a time for this and a time for that. Just like in Ecclesiastes. A time to douse oneself with crab juice and a time to eat! A time to move bowels and a time to fill them up again! Who would have thought that in the great order of the Universe, the framework and context of the All, an itchy crotch preceded a starving belly?

An invasion of crabs! A swarm of bees on the run! Two broken noses with white braces! I shook my head in wonder. What next? Well, I would worry about that when it happened. What was the point of knowing or waiting or guessing, when everything would be revealed in due time anyway? If only the merciless wheel of destiny would give me the time of day to douse myself with crab juice and eat my breakfast, I would keep my mouth shut. I would have nothing to complain about. Nothing to *complain* about! What kind of a thought was that? As if I had any business complaining—if life was a bitch, it was my business to learn how to love it.

The door was closed and the curtains partially drawn when I took off my clothes and started dripping the content of one of the bottles into the dense growth of hair in my crotch. At the same time, I rubbed the skin with the tips of my fingers. From the crotch, I worked my way upwards over stomach and chest until arriving below my chin I stopped. Enough was enough. There was still two-thirds left of the second bottle. I would keep it in reserve in case some of the crabs survived. Yet, I somehow had the feeling the chemical warfare had finished them off. The treatment was over. There was not much more I could do except keep my fingers crossed that Lili did not return from Sweden ahead of time. Boy, would that be a bummer!

Still in my birthday suit and feeling crusty like an embalmed Pharaoh fresh from the tomb, I made myself a meal of yogurt with raisins, pieces of apple, banana and almonds. In celebration of the anti-crab campaign, I also treated myself to a soft-boiled egg and a buttered slice of rye bread to go with it. Not to mention the three rolls I had bought in the Sunshine bakery. All served with a large glass of water and a cup of coffee with hot milk. Sitting there chewing at my little table, looking out of the window at the back of the garage-buildings and listening to the sound of an axe chopping wood in The Wagon Village, consciously and subconsciously sensing the drama of life and death being performed in my pubic regions, an unexpected thought burst in my mind. "Christ all mighty Les! Do you know what's the matter with you? You are *happy*, that's what!"

Even if I was taken aback, I kept right on chewing. Happy…eh! So that's what I was. And so that's what it felt like… I had not won a million in the lottery or on the roulette. Nobody had called me to say I had been elected president. No woman had undressed and told me she loved me. All I had done was encrust myself with crab juice and make breakfast. How could that be happiness? Well, I thought, who said that happiness was a stunning parrot on your shoulder and not just an unpretentious little bird? Like that lost little baby bird of Frauke's, for example. Why not simply accept what the voice had said? One thing was for sure, I was by no means *un-happy* anymore. So… happy then! But could happiness really be completely unfounded? Did it consist only in the absence of *un*happiness? Or… did it perhaps have anything to do with the feeling of freedom I felt? Free! How free? I bit off another piece of bread, and while I chewed it, I sort of kept sermonizing to myself: Well, the reason you're free is because you're freed from the necessity of dreaming of something better for yourself. Being a re-born Pharaoh in the body of a bespectacled crustaceologist explains why there's no improving the moment that you're living right now. It's so goddamned embalmed, it will remain long after you're gone. Like the shining armor of some dead knight!

When I was done delivering this little speech, I sat and listened to the sound of the axe splitting wood. Somehow it reassured me. And so I kept musing, could this, my happiness, have anything to do with the certainty I felt at that moment? That even if humankind was incorrigible and doomed, not only was life still possible, it was even everlasting? It was my responsibility to live in the world no matter what it was like or how it was faring, not to improve it. Only in the living of the life I had been given was there salvation and hope. The discontent I had felt before had been shameful and ridiculous. Ridiculous because unnecessary. Had I not always reaped what I had sown? And had the harvest not been justice itself? All right, so happiness was to sit in my own shack in a Freetown. And it was to have a mouth full of fresh bread.

I closed my eyes. The chopping sound had stopped and in its place was the echo it had left in my mind. I opened my eyes again and moved to the other side of the table. Now, instead of looking at the back of the low garage-buildings, I was looking at Martin's wagon and the ramparts. Vaguely I wondered if Martin was in there. If so he was probably still asleep. When I had returned in the morning, he was not in yet. Maybe he was sleeping with some woman in town. Whatever it was that he was doing, he wasn't spending much time in his wagon. Or in Christiania for that matter. Where the balance in my life had tipped in favor of Christiania, it was the opposite with Martin. Since he and Marie-Louise broke up and he was no longer living in The Gunpowder House, he was spending more and more time in town. Well, the sun was shining and the foliage a shimmering light and green. And right over there, leaning against the cold wood stove was my broom and dust pan. I had to smile at the sight. What a couple they were. For all their differences, they belonged together. More than that, they were inseparable. Take away the dust pan and the broom would be lost; take away the broom and the dust pan wouldn't know what to do. That was happiness too: to belong together. To stand tall like a broom determined to sweep the dirt off the floor. To lie by humbly devoted to serving and receiving like the dust pan. Like two warriors, fighting the dust and never fearing loss, disease and death! That was all very well. But to the extent that happiness meant to be free, it also had something to do with the things one was freed from. Like dust, dependency and debt. Was not freedom in a way like magnetism? It had its positive pole and its negative. At one end was the happiness that a man felt when he was positively true to his nature. At the other end, there was the freedom of *not* having to be what he was not and doing what he *did* not want to. For example the way I didn't want to vote in the Danish democratic elections because I thereby legitimized the sophisticated form of tyranny called democracy. In order to avoid unhappiness, you had to live in truth. And to live in truth meant being true to one's nature no matter what other people thought or what happened. Like the satisfaction I had felt the night before when I kicked the rude and racist investment banker or real-estate prick out of my taxi. Taking me for a Turk, he did not want to help me find the ridiculous little street he was going to. God did he ever deserve a sound kick in the butt. Being left alone on a dark road in the middle of the night might teach him to behave decently next time. So what if I had lost a bit of money? Who cared? I had earned my solitude. Once more, I was alone in the car. And the night had been so unspeakably beautiful. All the stars had seemed to twinkle just for me. There, invisible in the passenger seat next to me was my guardian angel. She would see to it, she whispered, that no matter how many wrong turns I took, I would get to where I was destined to go.

I shook my head in awe. Wasn't it amazing how the things of this world were arranged? At the same time as I was driving a taxi through the Copenhagen night, thousands of crabs were hatching in my crotch. And deep inside Old Knud's beehive a swarm was hatching its plan to escape. Again, the dry sound of a piece of wood splitting reached my ear. So what if we were all doomed? Deep in decay the seed of life was already active.

All was transitory and vanity ruled. There was madness, and there was greed. Yet how good it felt to be chewing on a roll in a wagon, conscious that truth was at the very root of all being—of all *well*being. Even if the world was lost there was still a life to live in it.

Barely had I finished my meal, drawn the curtains and taken a piss in the nettles out in the back when I heard Douglas' voice. There was no mistaking that American accent of his: "What! Has someone taken your *shoes*?" Immediately after I heard a woman's voice I did not recognize: "Yeah, yeah! And you know what! I'd borrowed them from Morten."

Still buttoning my fly, I hurried to see what sort of a

woman it could be who had borrowed shoes from a guy named Morten only to have them stolen. The sight that met my eyes was unusual even by Christiania standards. Sitting next to Douglas' lean figure on the wide doorstep was a woman I had never seen before. She was completely naked. Since her back was turned to me, and her attention drawn to something or other on the ground, she didn't notice that Douglas raised his head and rolled his eyeballs at me.

It was this rolling of the eyes that made me stop. What the hell is going on? I thought. Is it because he wants me to join them, or is it some secret affair he is having out in the open? I could not make up my mind. Douglas was hardly the kind of guy who had extra marital affairs, but should he ever have one, the integrity of his intellectual character would probably dictate that it be conducted right on his own doorstep where everybody could see it. It didn't make sense though. If it was an affair he was having, why was he dressed and the mistress naked as a nymph? Unsure of what to do, I too started to roll my eyes in a questioning manner. The woman was busy writing something in the dirt with her big toe. She didn't notice anything. Douglas leaned against the door post behind him, tilted his head slightly back and sent me a long and (so it seemed) pleading look.

That look decided the matter for me. Convinced that Douglas needed me to join them, I started in their direction. But I had only taken a couple of steps when, reacting to the sound of my feet on the gravel, the woman turned so abruptly on the doorstep that she got a splinter in her ass. "Ouch," she said and gave her own buttock a sound slap. "And *who* do you think *you* are?" she yelled at the splinter. "Are you crazy? Who gave you the right to get in my ass?"

She said a few other things I can't remember. And then, when she was done bawling at the splinter, she lifted up her fleshy buttock again. But instead of slapping herself, she twisted around and began to inspect it in an attempt to apprehend the culprit. She was so concentrated she paid no attention to her surroundings. With his fingers, Douglas made signs for me to come around to his side of the doorstep. When I got there, he put his mouth to my ear. His voice sounded like a storm, when he whispered: "She's wacko, this one." Then he pulled away, looked me in the eyes and pressed his index finger to his temple. It was at that moment I realized that Douglas had never met the woman before. He knew no more than I did what was going on and why she had no clothes on.

Learning that the woman was "wacko", I sat up straight. For the first time, I allowed myself to take a good look at our visitor. I don't know what it is with me or why it should make a difference, but before receiving this piece of info, it was like I hadn't dared look or I had been too discreet or something. Anyway, you didn't have to be Sigmund Freud to see she was indeed wacko. The way she kept rotating that fleshy butt of hers on the doorstep in order to get at the splinter. To anyone who was not wacko, it would have occurred immediately that there were probably more splinters where the first had come from. But maybe that was what she wanted. It was crazy because even if she kept bawling the piss out of the splinter, it was like she *liked* it too and would gladly welcome a couple more. The three of them could then play hide and seek together. I can't say that I had ever witnessed anything quite like it before. When she was done bawling, she talked to the damn splinter like it was some juvenile delinquent: "Now listen here," she would say, "I know where you are, and you know where I am. And since my position is clear, you might as well come out of your hidingplace and report. Just you wait, I'll pinch ya still. No, no, no you naughty little bugger. That won't work.

You can't hide from me, *you* know that."

During all this Douglas and I were shaking our heads and exchanging looks. I shrugged and looked at the woman. How old could she be? It was kind of hard to say. Twenty-five plus minus a couple years. Her hair, which reached her shoulders, was blond and cut short in front. Her skin was very white and on her back just below her right shoulder blade she had a large birthmark. At this stage, her ass, which was definitely on the big side, looked like it had been whipped what with all the red stripes left by her nails. For a moment, I played with the idea of offering my assistance, but I gave that up. It somehow seemed impolite. After all, I had never seen her before. A close inspection of her hind parts would be going too far. Still, it was hard just to sit by while she probed, pulled and prodded that poor butt of hers. Again and again, she tore at it with all her might twisting her torso around, setting her large tits in motion. They swung merrily from side to side like she was ringing the bells. Actually, I don't suppose I ought to use the word 'tits' when speaking of her breasts. As far as breasts go, they were really quite nice. So were the nipples. Maybe as a result of all the agitation, they were now hard jutting straight out and happy like. Possibly this woman had a screw loose, but I swear there was nothing wrong with her breasts. That much is for sure.

I don't know why it is that somehow this whole scene reminded me of Frauke. And what do you know! Next thing I knew I could not help thinking about how it would be to hump this screwball too. Like Frauke would she come to or would it all just sort of go unnoticed with her? What was going on, I mean. Like what if I took her right at this moment when she was busy looking for the splinter in her ass? Would it make her stop looking or would she carry on just like nothing had happened? And if, say, she did that, carried on I mean, would that then drive *me* crazy?

Now don't get me wrong. When you see a naked girl, you will think of humping her. That's only normal. And yet for some reason it didn't appear that way in this case. I can't explain why it is, except now it was like the thought of it got stuck in my crop. It would not go away again. Nothing I did or thought could drive it out. In no time at all it had turned into what psychologists call a compulsion neurosis. Whatever it's called it's pretty sick. You know only too well that it's absurd and that you would not dream of acting on it. But see if it helps! The thought doesn't give a damn. I suppose most people know what I am talking about. You stand there with the axe above your head at the chopping block. But instead of concentrating on hitting the piece of wood balanced there, you think of splitting your own shinbone. And it's not like there is anything extraordinary or outrageous about the idea either. On the contrary, it behaves like it's the most natural thing in the world. In another moment, you will chop off your own leg. It's so vivid it's like you can almost hear the ambulance coming with its siren blaring. In the next second, your axe falls on the piece of wood splitting it in two. And whew! Was that nice! Your leg is still intact. But even so, when the axe goes back up so does the compulsive thought. Over and over again. No matter what you do to get rid of the damn thing, it keeps coming back. That's where the compulsion comes in. You force yourself to think about your dirty underwear in the laundry basket. You recall the smell of a rotting pack of liverwurst you once found deep in your refrigerator. Or you actually go and throw some cold water in your face. Or, or, or. Truth is you can do anything you like, and it doesn't help. Even after you have put the axe back in the shed the thought of splintering your shin is still there, vivid as ever. Even when you have gotten on your bicycle and are on your way to town, it is there. It's simply there with you until it is not there anymore. It comes, and it goes, and there is no apparent reason. I'd had many obsessions but never before an erotic one about a naked girl with a screw loose.

Well, to make a long story short, it turned out precisely as I had feared. No matter what I did I kept thinking what it would be like to hump the poor girl rotating there on the doorstep. Who knows, maybe she was like Frauke who forgot she had a screw loose and behaved extra normally in bed. Maybe the two case studies put together could provide both a pattern and a basis for a scientific hypothesis? And suddenly there it was before me—the result of the scientific study as it was later to be published in a journal:

"Whereas in their erotic behavior normal women often exhibit an inclination towards the abnormal and what might be termed "the perverse", mentally disturbed women exhibit a markedly less complicated and more direct preference towards what might be termed "the normal.""

Something like that.

Douglas interrupted my musing. During my absence, he had taken recourse to interrogational methods: "What's your name?" He asked the woman in a weary voice like he had repeated it half a dozen times.

"You mean ME?" The woman was laughing and stomping in the dirt with her bare feet. "I don't have a name!" And as if to give her nameless identity a physical expression, she started jumping up and down so furiously on her butt that the doorstep rocked and threatened to fall over.

"Uh-huh," Douglas grunted. He was pulling his beard the way he did when he didn't know what to do and did not want to let on. I suppose it was his way of saving intellectual face. He said: "But didn't I just hear you say that you had a pair of shoes?"

"Shoes, sure." The woman seemed almost ecstatic at the

thought of her shoes. She was nodding her head so hard I thought she might fracture her vertebrae: "They belong to Morten!"

"Morten who? What Morten are you talking about?"

"Morten! That's... Well, it's *that* guy over *there*!" And as if this statement or the situation or something else was extremely funny the woman laughed happily out loud and pointed in the direction of the tree top where earlier in the day Old Knud's bees had taken refuge.

Douglas and I exchanged looks. Then we both looked in the direction of the woman's forefinger: "But, eh," Douglas was now tugging at his beard real hard, "up there's... nobody!"

"No," the woman said suddenly serious. She was looking at him reproachfully: "You're SO right. There isn't. Morten's gone, gone, gone!"

One look at Douglas and I could tell that the imperturbable (or perhaps flegmatic?) composure he usually used for camouflage was beginning to crumble. His eyes that were normally calm and fixed were now roaming to and fro. His breathing had become shorter. We exchanged another look, and I thought to myself that it was only good if for once he was a bit unhinged. The same was true for me. The obsessive thought was messing with my mind making me feel unsure of myself. It was almost like if I didn't watch out I would come in my pants. The thought horrified me. I can't explain why it is exactly that the missing screws made the whole thing ten times worse. Screws or no screws, she was a woman—and no two ways about it. And she was as naked as God had created her. She was young, good looking and in one hell of a fine mood. Of course, I don't like to believe it about myself, but I couldn't shake it off: the thought that if circumstances had been different I would probably not have been so peevish. I might have shocked myself. If only she had been an axe, it would have made the whole thing much easier. With an axe, you knew exactly where you stood. You could put it back in the tool shed and leave it there. It was what it was and stayed where it was until it was moved. But a woman! *This* woman here! With her it was different. What in heaven's name did one do with her? She was of flesh and blood and cartilage and…sexual organs. She smelled good and had splinters in her ass. What more could a guy want? Especially when on top of it, she had a sweet voice, which was now talking to me:

"Hi fella!" she said flashing a big old smile at me. "You're *so* much nicer than that guy there." She pointed her thumb at Douglas. "And I like you *so* much better? So will you come and sit down next to me?"

She shoved Douglas with her butt in an effort to make room for me.

I bit my lip like I had done the night before when I kicked out that real-estate broker, investment banker or businessman who had taken me for a Turk. It's sort of a habit I have. Douglas tugs at his beard. I bite my lower lip.

"Come on over," the woman said and slapped the doorstep a couple of times with her flat hand. "I think you're really nice! And…really sweet too!"

I didn't know what to do. On the one hand, there was the obsessive thought. I neither wanted to reveal it nor add fuel to it. On the other hand, there was the good upbringing I had received in the Northern suburbs of Copenhagen. Like a seal in the zoo, I had been trained to behave in a certain way. The fact that the woman was a nutcase and didn't have any clothes on made no difference as far as the role I had been programmed to play was concerned. Normally, I'm not the kind of guy who loses his head and is paralyzed by doubt. But in this situation out in front of Douglas' wagon, I was not sure what was right and what was wrong. Did

310

the fact that a person had a screw loose mean that the rules for decent conduct no longer applied?

I had just made up my mind to bow to my good up-bringing when the woman suddenly yelled "OUCH".

She looked at me gleefully: "I think I got one more splinter in my butt. Now I have TWO!"

"What a thing to collect," I thought to myself. And then... so help me God... I could not stop myself from laughing. Life was such a thankless task. Here was a woman with all the best intentions. She had shoved Douglas to make room for me on the doorstep—a total stranger. And what did she get for her effort: one more splinter in her ass! The fact that she was nutty enough to jubilate as if it was the best thing that could happen— did *that* make it any better? Was the bottom line not the same: that it was all so unbearably sad it ought to make her cry? I mean, that it *had* to be that way. And later in life—if it turned out that two splinters were not enough to teach her the lesson, well, she would just get one more. And one more. She would simply keep getting them in her butt, until she caught on, realized how sad everything was and bit the dust. She and everyone else for that matter until all the screws in everybody's heads had come loose and there was a racket like in a loonybin all over the place.

It was something like this I was thinking, when I sat down next to her and felt her thigh against mine.

"It's all right," the woman said as if she had read my mind and wanted to put me at ease. "You know, I'll just let them stay there."

"Oh, that's nice!" I nodded.

"Yeah," said the woman, "I'm not *mean*!"

We sat there on the doorstep chatting about this and about that. Time passed and so did the afternoon. Our conversation was not very profound. It suited me just fine. I relaxed. Since there was no thread at all, I didn't have to worry about losing it. I would go off on one lark after another and nobody thought it odd or anything, which just goes to show you must undo a screw here and there to get the juices flowing. One moment, we were talking splinters and the great difference it makes whether you collect them in your hind parts or, say, in you feet; the next, we found ourselves hotly debating the question of how to catch eels with your hands. But no matter what we talked about, we always kept returning to the mysterious Morten and the shoes. Among other things, we learned that Morten had taken off with his shoes in an orange plastic bag with the words "Gallery Venezia" written on it.

If there was something this guy Morten knew how to do, it was to hide. He was a real artist when it came to that. Once, he hid there was no way he could be found. And if we didn't believe what she said, our new friend told us, we could just try to find him ourselves. So at one point, we were looking all over the place. First we inspected the pile of boards that months ago had been dumped behind John's and Hanne's rotting shack. Nope, he was not there. Then we looked among the rabbits in Old Knud's cages. He was not there either. We opened the flap and glanced inside Jakob's tipi. The woman was right: Morten was nowhere to be found.

There was only one plausible explanation: Morten had put on his wings and flown up into a tree, where he busied himself tying the shoelaces on the pair of shoes he had lent the woman. Besides being an escape artist he was also a terrific teaser, that Morten. He was not her older brother, but oh boy could he tease her all the same. Like when she finally found the shoes, she said, the laces were sure to be tied so tight in knots that she would have to cut them in order to get her feet in. "And," she went on, "do you know what animal is my favorite?"

We shook our heads.

"The porcupine, of course!" the woman cried out with glee. "A porcupine is an animal of reason. That's why they sniffle so much. It's because they're sad. Instead of crying, they sniffle."

"Uh-huh," Douglas grunted.

The woman nodded and looked first at Douglas and then at me: "Porcupines are so cute. I also like squirrels. And do you know why? I like them because they're very naughty. Just like in Walt Disney. It's not something they make up. It's really true."

In this way, the conversation kept skipping from one subject to another. There seemed to be a mysterious form of magnetism at work that made us return again and again to Morten and the splinters. Morten and the splinters constituted kind of a leitmotif with her. Like when we had exhausted the animal kingdom, and she suddenly said: "I once knew a young girl who had a splinter up her cunt. But how does a nice girl get a splinter up there? And real deep too. How?"

This question must have been of great importance to her, because she repeated it three or four times over. She kept shaking her head and looking at us for an explanation.

We looked at each other:

"I don't know. Do *you*?" I asked Douglas.

"No, *I* don't know either"

Again we shook our heads.

It looked like the woman was thinking real hard about something. She even knit her brow: "Maybe you can help me find out," she said. And before we had time to think of an answer, she spread her legs wide and pointed at herself with elation: "See! It was in there! Right...there!"

With her index finger pointed at her open and exposed sex, she fell silent and pulled my arm: "Maybe *you* can find it?" she suggested. "C'mon and look! No. Look closer!"

I don't know what got into me. Normally, I'm not squeemish. It's not like me to short circuit in that way. What I *do* know though is that I was daunted by the task of finding a splinter hidden deep in a cunt hidden in a jungle of red hair that had not been trimmed in a long time. Not being much of a Livingstone, anyway it seemed to me that finding the source of the Nile was peanuts in comparison to what this woman asked us to do. Or, who knows, it could also be because I was not convinced the splinter was in there. I just don't know. Maybe I'm all wrong, and it was something else entirely. Like an after shock of the compulsion neurosis, I talked about earlier—or some delicate sense of my subconscious warning me not to transgress the limits of decency.

No matter what the hell it was, I could not get myself to stare the woman up her cunt. What business was it of mine if during an acid trip she had amused herself with a corner of a tool shed, a fence post or a broomstick? A man ought to come to the rescue of ladies in distress. Absolutely. I totally agree. But as there were different kinds of ladies, there were also different forms of distress. There was a limit to what a man should get himself into.

As it turned out, Douglas was not as squeemish as I was. Being an American, he took a more pragmatic approach to splinters. Not just those in other people's eyes but also the ones in other people's sexual organs. Obviously, this was not a trifling matter to him. No. Here was something, which his wife would never allow. This was a once in a lifetime chance. He would be a fool and live to regret it if he didn't seize the moment. And my God, did he go for it. Red as a beet in the face and with eyes that bulged like they were about to pop out he knelt before the doorstep like it was some alter and stared into the woman's open sex. And it wasn't like he was satisfied with a short glance either. No! Not Douglas. He'd have his penny's worth. As for me, I was so embarrassed my head was shaking. It was all I could do to stop myself from giving his shoulder a push that would have made him fall on his back. But I controlled myself. After all, the woman didn't seem to mind. Only I did. The way he squatted there so absorbed and without even blinking. Christ you would think it was his intellectual integrity that was at stake. Or some other nonsense like that. In fact now, it was like they were both in a trance or something. Or rather the three of us were. The woman was staring at Douglas' head. Douglas was staring at the woman's sex, and I was staring at the whole spectacle. What was going on? What was he *seeing* in there? Had he found the splinter or was it the big bang and the beginnings of the world he was witnessing?

Finally, I got so frustrated I, too, bent forward and looked. But by then it was too late. The moment I moved the spell was broken. No sooner had I caught sight of the red bush and Douglas stood up. He was staring wildly at me. I will never forget that look. There was not a single grain of intellectuality left in it. He looked exactly as insane as one would expect of a man who had just witnessed the creation of the world. But instead of giving me the solution to the riddle of life or redeem me in some other way, he started giving me some horse shit about it being late in the afternoon now and not so warm anymore either and dusk would settle soon and so on and so forth. Besides today was his day to cook. He would have to get a move on if the villagers weren't to go hungry. Etc. Etc. But... he said finally glancing at the woman: the sun was now low in the sky and it was not as warm as before. If she wanted to borrow a boiler suit, he had one for her inside?

"What I want is to go home!" the woman said her voice suddenly sounding sad.

Douglas and I stared at her: "*Where* do you live?" we asked as with one mouth.

"In Denmark. I live in Denmark!"

"Uh-huh," Douglas grunted and looked briefly at me with an expression like there was something that bothered him: "But in Denmark, women wear clothes when it gets cold and dark."

"Not all women," the woman said.

Instead of coming up with an answer to this Douglas disappeared into his wagon to fetch the boiler suit.

For the first time, I found myself alone with the woman. And it was then I happened to glance at her from the side. The *next* thing I knew a strange thought occurred to me. What if she belonged to a higher order of beings and had come down to us humans from another planet? What if she had come to warn us of some imminent calamity? What if she was carrying some sort of coded message?

"So where do you hail from?" I asked in a voice as if I had seen right through her.

"Didn't I just tell you that? I come from Denmark."

"Yes, that's right. You did say that. You come from Denmark. But…where is *that*?"

"Are you telling me that *you* don't know that?"

The way the woman looked at me when she said this was not especially extra terrestrial. Still, I couldn't make out if she was amused or shocked. She *was* being facetious though. So was she having a lot of fun pulling our legs? Was that what was going on? Maybe she was not as wacko as all that. Maybe when it came right down to it Douglas and I were the wackos.

Then something happened that seemed to deny this hypothesis. Suddenly, the woman jumped up and yelled: "Denmark is out there! Denmark is *r-e-a-l-l-y* out there!" At the same time as she was yelling this, she placed her hands on her head and made clapping motions in imitation of those stupid red and white clapping caps that fanatic sports fans wear at the national games. In between the clapping, she waved one hand in the direction of Grønnegade Street and the gate at Refshalevej Street.

"Yes, but where do you live?" The whole thing was getting kind of repetitive.

"*Out* there!" Once again, her hand waved in the direction of the exit from Christiania.

"Wait a sec!" I sighed and got up. Stepping into the wagon I bumped into Douglas. He held up the boiler suit for my inspection. She could put that on in his opinion. It was an old rag with paint spots all over. But it was clean, and it would help her keep warm.

"What about the little panties?" I said. It really was just something I threw in to say something. It wasn't like I was serious. But to my surprise Douglas reacted like he had been hit with a baseball bat between the eyes.

"Yes, what about panties?" I repeated because it amused me to see Douglas' panic at the thought. "Doesn't Line have a pair of old panties that she never uses?"

"No, no!" Douglas looked positively frightened. "You must be out of your mind. Steal Line's panties! I'd never do that. What would I tell her when she asks me where they are? No, our crackpot will just have to live without panties. But…" Douglas glanced at the doorstep and lowered his voice: "What do you think we should do with her? We can't very well let her run around like that. And I don't suppose we can keep her here either, like we sometimes keep stray

317

cats and dogs."

I shook my head: "We could call the police and ask what they do in such cases. Maybe they can find out who she is, where she lives and what's happened. I wouldn't be surprised if she remembers her name and personal identification card number when she sees a uniform."

"Yeah," Douglas mused. "And they'll probably listen to us since this isn't a case of a serial killer, rapist or raving psychopath. That's our own business. But a naked woman with a screw loose! That's something else. I think it's worth a try. If it works, it works and if it doesn't, well then we'll keep her tonight and put some food in her tummy."

When he was finished saying this, Douglas placed a heavy hand on my shoulder. "Well, compadre," he said with a confidentiality that I found really annoying. "You seem to be sleeping around with just about anything that has legs and breasts. So maybe you…"

I shook his hand off my shoulder and said: "Very funny I must say. It isn't true though. I'm a lot more fastidious than you think. Anyway, the village guest bed *is* vacant. She can sleep in there, can't she? Let's call the police and hear what they have to say."

Douglas was just about to step aside and let me pass, when he grabbed my arm, pulled me close to him and whispered in my ear: "Maybe what I'm going to tell you now will make you, eh-eh a little more hospitable. Did you notice the tatoo on her pussy?"

"Tatoo on her pussy! What are you talking about?"

"Yes siree, and right on the mount of Venus too. Hidden beneath the growth of red hair! Big and very light sky blue letters."

"No, it was you who looked not me. What's it say?"

In order to savor my reaction to what he was going to relate, Douglas pulled his head back a little: "I know you won't believe this," he began. "You'll say I'm full of shit. But sure as my name's Douglas, she's got the words "FUCK ME" tattooed on her sex."

"Right," I said. "And you've got the words "I'm full of shit" tatooed on your dick."

Douglas rocked his head from side to side. "I knew you wouldn't believe me. But it *is* true. Go see for yourself! I saw it with my own eyes when she spread her legs, and I looked to see if I could find the splinter."

"Don't you think I know exactly when you saw it? You were sitting there with your nose up her twat for so long I thought you'd at least seen the creation of the world or the burning bush. And then, all you saw was a tattoo…"

Douglas nodded: "So now you believe me. And you might as well too. There was no mistaking it. I'm an American, you know!"

"Yes, you sure as hell are!" I said and started towards the table with the telephone on it. On the way, I shuddered at the thought of the things of this world in general and of tattooed twats in particular. "What a world!" I mumbled to myself as I lifted the receiver and dialed the number.

"Copenhagen police," a voice said in the other end.

I informed the person as to who I was, and from where I was calling. "It's about a young woman," I said. "She's got a screw loose and not a stitch on. She appeared some hours ago, and we don't know what to do with her."

"I see," the man's voice said in a tone as if I had just told him of a bicycle seat that had been ripped off. "Hang on. I'll put you through to the department."

I'll be god damned, I thought as the phoney piano sound of Beethoven's "Für Elise" flowed out of the receiver and into my ear. Who would have thought the police had a special department for such cases?

To judge from the time I had to wait, the department for

naked women with loose screws was a very busy one. Every so often "Für Elise" would stop and a recorded voice informed me that all lines were still busy. While I was absent-mindedly listening to the sound of the voices outside on the doorstep, I thought about what would have happened if indeed I had been reporting on a violent psychopath.

Finally after what seemed an eternity of waiting, "Für Elise" broke off, and I heard a man say my name.

Once more, I explained the circumstances.

"But where does she live?" the officer asked for the second time.

"I've just told you!" Saying this it struck me that I sounded like an echo of the woman herself. "We can't make it out. When we ask her, she just says that she lives in Denmark."

"Well, hmm…that's not very much to go on. Does she have a screw loose?"

The way the policeman said this it was like he was at the same time filling out some official form.

"Yeah," I said. "And if there's a slot in your form for splinters in the ass, you can write "two" in it!"

"Pardon."

"I said… that… she has two splinters in her ass." I was really feeling pretty damn fed up at this stage.

There was something that sounded like a deep sigh at the other end of the line: "Well, in that case, I suppose we've got to send a patrol-car."

That was it. The car would be at the Refshalevej Street entrance to Christiania in half an hour.

After we had hung up, I sat for a while without moving. I kept staring at the phone. There was no doubt. It was the splinters that had decided the matter. There must be something I did not know about splinters. And it was right there and then I felt a pang like I had betrayed the woman by mentioning them. Was it not the same police that the

Danish authorities used to protect property against christianites when they asserted their right to live in freedom? So what if the woman had a couple screws loose. Was that a crime? And what right did it give me to hand her over to cops with screws so tight that no God could pry them loose? And worse, was it for her sake or for my own that I was handing her over to the police? I dare say it was my turn to draw a deep sigh.

When I came back out Douglas had finally gotten around to helping the woman put on the boiler suit. It seemed he had asked her to turn her back to him. It was all for her own good. That's what he was telling her. Yeah right, I thought. You are exactly like some goddamned cop who has just made an arrest. Now, you are putting on the handcuffs and soon you will be pushing her into a cell. But the operation wasn't simple. No sooner had the woman stuck her feet in the trouserlegs, and no sooner had Douglas gotten his hopes up that now it would be a piece of cake getting the boiler suit up over her shoulders, when she flung her arms back, pulled his head to her back and started stomping like mad in the pants.

"Cut it out will you? Stand still!" Douglas groaned between his teeth as in his stooping position he was struggling to prevent the suit from ending up around her ankles.

"Help me will'ya!" he panted in a voice that was by now a bit panicky.

A quick assessment of the situation told me to get in front of the woman and hold her in a vice. Maybe then Douglas would be able to get the damn thing up. So while our friend was stamping madly with her feet and pulling Douglas' head, I immobilized her frontally with the result that I got one full breast squished against my face.

"Hold out. Keep it there!" I heard Douglas muttering from the other side. "I'm just about to get it. A lit-tle bit mooore and i-it's done. There!"

How he managed to get the woman's arms into the sleeves beats me. But when a moment later, we let go of her (at the same time and from both sides) she stood between us like some sea-born Aphrodite in a stained boiler suit. A fine sight it was too. It fit her to a T. Now, it just remained to button her in front. I took care of that. Six buttons and she was done.

"Perfect!" Douglas said and stepped back to better enjoy the sight of her: "If you'll follow her out, I'll get down to cooking!"

I explained to the woman that the two of us were going for a little walk together. And to my great relief she did not protest or anything. All she did was ask me if she could bring her shoes?

"Yes, of course, you can," I said, "as soon as we find Morten."

"Okay, that's a deal," she said merrily and took the hand I offered her. Hand in hand, we set off down Grønnegade Street.

Sometimes, I wonder what people are thinking about in their heads. Now that the woman had the boiler suit on, why on earth were they staring at us? What had happened to their inhibitions? Down on the corner of Grønnegade and Langgade Streets, a middle aged couple that looked like they came from Latin America some place stopped and stared, like we were hot-stuff celebrities or something. They couldn't take their eyes off of us. When the man who had a big old graying mustache saw us coming out of Grønnegade Street, he grabbed the wife by the arm and nodded in our direction. And no sooner had the wife become aware of us than she knew what to do. In a jiffy, she got out her camera and prepared to take a picture of us. I even heard the damn shutter open and close. So, who knows! Perhaps the naked woman in the boiler suit and I are now immortalized and on exhibit on some dresser or mantlepiece somewhere in Columbia? Afterwards, when we had passed them and it was too late, I regretted not having had the presence of mind to ask them to send me a copy. That is always how it is with me. I find out what I ought to have said or done when it's too late. Most things change and some just don't…

When we got to Refshalevej Street, we saw two cops talking to each other over the roof of their patrol car.

"Are you eh…Andreas Stein?" asked the tall skinny cop with the hawk nose, "and is that…?"

I confirmed that it was indeed Andreas Stein and consort.

The short stocky cop who had not yet said a word asked me if I had any ID. I shook my head. And why didn't I have any ID? Because I just didn't… The tall cop with the hawk nose looked at his colleague. "What do you think? Should we let him get away with it this time, or teach him a lesson by taking him with us to the station?" is what the look said.

"Have you got any drugs on you?" Again, it was the tall cop speaking. It struck me they were like a couple of television hosts taking turns to speak. "For your own use perhaps?"

"Jesus Christ, you are curious!" I sighed. "What does that have to do with eh… her?"

"You just answer the questions we ask. Is that clear? Do you or don't you?"

"I don't."

"Good for *you*," the tall cop said. "And you?" He looked at the woman standing beside me and holding my hand: "You don't have anything on except that boiler suit. It's really chic, I must say!"

The woman looked at the cop with a smile that was so devoid of irony and ulterior motives it would have disarmed a hired assassin. But she didn't say anything.

"What's your name?" It was still the tall hawk nose speaking.

"ME! I don't have a name," the woman said in a voice like she was talking to a five-year-old child.

"Do you have a personal identity number?"

The answer came right away: "170458-3089".

The short stocky cop jotted the number on a small block of paper: "Very well!" he said and looked at his colleague. "But I suppose we've got to get on with it. I guess you want your boiler suit back, don't you?" He looked at me.

I told him that it wasn't mine but one she had borrowed from my neighbor. For that reason, it was probably best if I brought it back with me.

"I'm sure you have something that she can wear at the station!" I added.

"Sure, we'll find something. She'll look great. Don't worry. So take off the suit, pretty one!"

This order was given by the short cop. And now he added: "Hurry up, will you! We have other things to do than to pick up naked broads in Christiania, you know!"

Without a word the woman started to unbutton the boiler suit.

The two cops studied her every move with a look on their faces like a couple used-car dealers who had just been offered a deal. By following the direction of the tall cop's eyes, I thought I caught a glimpse of something bluish in the red bush between her legs. I quickly transferred my eyes to the face of Mr. Hawknose, which at this moment broke into a broad grin. "All right," he said making a neigh-like sound… What-are-we-waiting-for? Let's get a move on! Hop in sister and let's get it over with!"

"No, not in theeeere!" the short stocky cop cried, "god-dammit no!"

But it was too late. When the tall skinny cop had asked the woman to get in the car, she had thrown herself back down on the front passenger seat and started to pummel the ceiling with her feet.

"*I* come from DEEENMAAAARK. *I* come from DEEEEN-MAAARK!" she yelled.

The two cops and I were standing there paralyzed looking at the sex and asshole of the jubilant woman.

"Do you think," the short stocky cop said gloomily, "that this is a case of… feminism or something?"

"Might be." The hawknosed cop nodded: "Could be patriotism too!"

"Yeah," the stocky cop said, "I suppose you're right. But in any case, I think it's our job to end it."

His voice was quivering, and I could tell he was trying real hard not to laugh. Here was something they hadn't learned how to deal with in police school.

The short stocky cop had bent down and was working on getting the woman out of the front seat. It wasn't easy. She held on to the back of the seat with both hands and screamed: "Help! Help!" Finally, when the cop had managed to pry her loose, she pressed his chin up with both hands. I looked at the tall hawknosed cop. Under the official mask he was enjoying the scene. I could tell by the way he blinked his eyes. It seemed for all the world that if he had only been able to get away with it, he would have given his cursing colleague a kick in the pants.

But it was too late for that too. By now, the short stocky cop had succeeded in getting the woman out of the car. "You're going in *there*," he panted. Very ungallantly, he half pushed and half dragged her around the door and sat her the back seat: "Bring those feet together and sit decently!"

The cop closed the door, got in the driver's seat and waited for his colleague to get in too. Then, he turned on the engine, put the car in gear and… in that very last second before he swung around and headed for Refshalevej Street, just as I had raised my hand in a parting gesture, what do you know but the woman smiled to me through the side window. I tried to smile back but was too surprised to do it. Or shocked perhaps! Thing is, something had changed. It was not the same smile any more. There was something else in it than the sheer joy of being free. I would not say it was sadness exactly. It was more like wistfulness. Maybe even pity? I didn't know. Nor did I have time to think about it. Next thing I knew, there was the rear end of the car before me, the blond hair of the woman, and the empty space where the car had been. The car turned left and drove off down Refshalevej Street leaving me alone in the little parking lot.

It was almost like I was reeling after having received a hard blow. I had the feeling something had happened but did not know what it was. At first, I tried to close my eyes in an effort to avoid the smile the woman had sent me, when the cops drove her away. But when it wouldn't go away and kept haunting me even worse behind my closed lids, I quickly opened my eyes again and fastened them on the yellow wall of Holmen across the moat. "The most precious thing she owns," I muttered to myself. Without my being aware of it this sentence had risen from my gut to burst like a bubble when it reached my mind. Hey, I thought, where did that come from? *What* precious thing?

Thinking about the smile and that "precious thing" I started on the way back to the Wagon Village.

It was early in the evening. The air was cool and sweetly scented by earth and fresh foliage. I shuddered in my thin shirt, stopped and… felt goose bumps all over my skin. But though I was cold, I did not feel like returning home immediately. So what *did* I feel like? What could I do? Where

326

would I go? And why? I can't explain it, but it was like something in me was in the process of contracting. The goose bumps were only the outward symptom. On the inside of my skin, it was all goose bumps too. As a result, my senses seemed to become sharper with every step I took. Already, I saw things more sharply outlined. As if I saw with my entire being. Unsure of what to do or where to go I wandered off in the direction of the horse stables and The Childrens' Meadow. Maybe if I remained calm, I would find out what was going on.

A few steps further on I stopped because all of a sudden I had understood something of tremendous importance: "The *naked* truth," I mumbled to myself. That was it! The naked truth! The most precious thing she owned: the naked truth…

In my mind, the goal I had set for myself was the remains of a bench on the ramparts in the district of The Blue Karamel. This bench was so old and so rotten and so forgotten, I always thought of it as something left over from the days of the absolute monarchy. "*That* too is… the naked truth," I muttered. Christ all mighty, why did those words keep popping up? Was it a holy sacrament of nakedness or something? What a notion! As if a human being became an emblem of truth just by appearing in public without clothes. Was "naked truth" any better or any more meaningful or, say, more important than "truth dressed"? Why wasn't I thinking the usual thoughts when going to my bench? Never before had I been headed for that bench without thinking about the old lecher of a commander who I imagined used to diddle young servant girls on it. How vividly I saw him before my inner eye, his fat arthritic fingers groping under the girls' skirts. Not today. Somehow the events of the afternoon had moved things around inside of me. It seemed a clear cut case of the old either-or syndrome that

Kierkegaard had grappled with. Either reality had moved extremely close and come within my reach, or it had moved away and was not about to happen or be within reach any time soon. Like dead paint beginning to peal and fall off the surface…

Heading for an old bench with one of its boards missing, I felt a certainty I could not explain. In a curious way, it was like I was participating in a game or play. And like all games, this one had its own rules. On the one hand, I was to select goals that I could understand, reach and touch when I got there. Something so tangible it made me get up in the morning and move. On the other hand, I was to be able to forget about it anytime my intuition told me I needed a change of direction. If I got as far as to the bench, it was fine. But if I didn't, that was fine too. The game I was playing every step of the way was both of the utmost importance and did not matter the least. I cared, and I did not care. It was very weird.

It must have looked strange too, the way I was standing there nodding to myself and gesticulating. How were the passers-by to know that what they had before them was a man grappling with the naked truth and the meaning of life? Good thing I had my clothes on and was in Christiania. I closed my eyes and then after a moment opened them just a wee bit again. I was peering out at the world through two narrow slits. There was no doubt. I was still seeing everything around me in a different and clearer light. It began when the woman smiled to me through the window of the police car. The sensation was a bit like when you have been sitting in the dim light of a bar drinking. You don't really feel the alcohol, until you are back out on the street. "Shit, I'm drunk!" you think to yourself and feel a sudden rush of euphoria as you set off down the sidewalk in the late afternoon sun. "What and where now? My God, how is it

I have never seen the sky such a bright violet before? Let's see, what was it you left the place to get on with? Oh, yeah, that's right!" And you head for the metro or the tramstop savoring the surprise rush of trust and joy swelling your heart.

"To hell with guilt, worry and the hair raising prospects of people cloning people! Of harrowing environmental catastrophes!" Declaring this out loud, I kicked a loose lump of asphalt that happened to be in the way of my foot. What I really needed was to have wings like that dude Morten. With wings, I could rise above the clouds, breathe the universal air and feast my eyes on the infinite blue. Whenever I wanted to. It would not make the least difference if I happened to be in Marseilles, Bangkok, Prague or Tokyo. As long as vast and empty space was in me, I would be fine. Each day when I got up, I would take a quick spin above the clouds spreading the good news that all things were sacred in this best of all possible worlds. I would see things the way they were and give them my blessing. I would not pass judgement. And never would I want to improve anything anymore, because I would know that what was happening, what had already happened and what was going to happen was all as it must be. Acceptance was the code of the road. No matter to what monstrous degrees of perversity man attained and how violently he would hate and murder and kill himself for it, he'd still unwittingly further the sacred purpose.

"What secret purpose?" I thought and started to walk. Why the one on the other side. That secret and hidden celestial sphere we humans could never get a clear idea about but had to approach intuitively. So what if it was our lot to be stuck wholesale in a waiting room suffused with suffering and crime, hope and longing! Suddenly, I remembered some lines I had recently read someplace about Mozart: "Meanwhile, he became possessed by the thought that someone was trying to poison him, and the requiem grew to be a sinister cloud in his mind. Had some messenger from the Other World asked him to write a requiem? He was certain of it. He continued composing at fever-pitch, frantic to get the work completed before his frail body succumbed to the poison."

Kyrie eleison. Sanctus. Benedictus. Did all that really amount to nothing more than "a sinister cloud?" Was it not rather pure and unadulterated thanksgiving under the vault of the sky? Okay, the opening strophes were a bit on the sinister side. No use denying that. Life was short and securing the valuables would always be a race against time. But then, those opening strophes swelled and swelled. Powerfully and yet hushed, they rose to heaven and burst forth in the gratitude, acceptance and surrender that was the essence of prayer. Male and female voices in unison that rose to… what? Billions of bursting umbilical chords making up the string section. Incomprehensible mortality. How was it possible that there had ever been even the slightest doubt that the universe was animated by a soul common to all living beings? How could emptiness be empty when every atom bore witness to the opposite? Rushing in on me was the disbelief with which sudden belief stares at its own former blindness. The doors of perception blown open! Vice and faith! Vice *versus* faith! Scylla and Charybdis? Didn't Waterloo and St. Helena already exist as seeds in Napoleon long before the first battle was fought?

The reason I thought of Napoleon was because I had been reading "War and Peace" the previous afternoon while waiting in line in my taxi at the Airport. Taking over the taxicab at four-thirty pm., I would always head straight for the airport to get in line and read a book. Usually, I would get forty-five minutes to an hour before I had to open the trunk and help somebody with the luggage. "Hell, just think!" I was now telling myself, if Tolstoi at that critical moment in the battle at Austerlitz when General Kutuzov is bewailing the sundered banner, if instead of letting Prince André Bolkonsky react to the General's "despairing sighs" with an insane fit of patriotism that cost him a bullet in the head, think if instead he had let the Prince send the old man a big smile and taken him in his arms! Even if psychologically that may not have been the most plausible of reactions, in a higher sense, it might be a truer one. Just think if, at this moment the author had let the two men come to their—higher—senses and take hold of each other like brothers, would that not have made for the most terrific hug in literature? I mean instead of letting the young prince loose it so completely, letting him grab what was left of the banner, like mindless cannonfodder charge the enemy with it raised high, get hit by a bullet in the head, fall on his back and in the hushed world that engulfed him finally and at long last see that all is vanity and emptiness under the sun. All except that: the infinite depth of the kingdom of God. Just think if Tolstoi instead of celebrating God's skies, mirrored in a pair of glazed eyes, had praised life and the universe by letting two spirited men grab hold of each other and laugh their guts out together. If he had let them *defy* the madness going on around them, right there while the battle was still raging and men were falling like flies. And think too if the two men besides being conscious that the war even for the victors is always lost in advance, with peace in their hearts had turned their backs to the slaughter? If they had set off into the sunset to live the rest of their lives as vagabonds on the road! If you ask me, it's a bit late to catch a glimpse of God's face when the enemy has shot a bullet in your head? It's better than never, sure, but that doesn't change the fact that life's sketch is for living men and not for the dead and dying. In case General Kutuzov was unable to pay back the Prince's horse laughter in the same coin, he, André, should have laughed the General in his face, picked up the remains of the banner and broken it a couple more times over his knee. Finally, he should have stretched his arms wide and dansed like Kazantzakis' Zorba once did on the coast of Crete. In defiance of cataclysm, death and destruction. Right there in between the explosions and on the edge of the fresh crater just opened before his feet, the Prince should have danced and laughed himself to death. Imagine the General and the Prince at long last finding compassion, freedom and laughter in what was *their* soup bowl!

I was torn out of my reverie when two boys came racing towards me on their bicycles. In passing, one of them brushed my arm. As I swung around, the guy who had touched me shouted something that made the other let go of the handle bars and swing his arms over his head. Their yells sounded happy. What could they be... eight or nine years old? "Unless you become children again..." I nodded in confirmation. Those boys were happy because they did not give a shit about things that had no importance. They hadn't yet been tamed and taught to worry about a future. They were out to have a good time and wrung each moment to the last drop. The rent was paid and in the evening dinner waited them. Even if the plague was raging all around and people were dying like crazy, *they* were *alive*. And each night when they were worn out they got under the covers of a warm bed. Having recently arrived from that other side, they were as unfettered and nonchalant as errant knights in search of adventure.

Staring after the two boys, there was a swelling in my chest, and my eyes were blinking. I was *so* out of it. All that "naked truth" and "secret purpose" was taking its toll on me. The next thing I knew, big old tears were running down my cheeks. Either I was a real mess, or I was painfully coming to my senses. What was I? What was I living for? What was I doing? And... what sort of a goal had I set for myself: an old dilapidated bench? A great and worthy goal indeed! A sea going caravan-wagon soon to be painted with fresh Bordeaux-red paint on its four sides. Distant mountain peaks with olive trees appearing above the rolling seas. Two turtledoves, a male and a female, on a mission to scout for land and bring back tidings! A movement towards something primordial and away from something assumed and superficial. Albatros alone on its air wave with the automatic pilot activated. Sailing on a summer breeze with the swishing sound of waves licking the hull. Held on its course by the two elements: air and salt water. With the anchor long since weighed. Tossed about by capricious winds...

So this was what I had come to! This happy sobbing of my heart as I was standing in the open street. Human albatros riveted to the spot, with seafoam in his hair and wet eyes fastened on tomorrow's fair coast drawing close.

Without noticing it, I had reached the horse stables. Before my eyes, a group of young girls with blonde hair under black riding helmets were leading ponies through the gate. I took a deep breath. The evening was cool and spiced with horse manure and straw. I was *watching* their voices and laughter dissolving in the molecules of air when it occurred to me that perhaps she too had once been a horse girl who shared her love for horses with her friends.

Again, I saw the naked woman as she threw herself on her back of the police car and pummeled the roof with her feet. Recalling the sound, she had made I couldn't help but smile. Kicking the ceiling, she had told me how it was: that the true moments of joy we would get, we would have to snatch from a police car. As a punishment for having a good time, we would be shoved in the back seat. Yet, strange as it may sound, instead of making me sad the thought had a salutary effect on me. What was I but a man kicking the roof of a patrol car? And I would never stop kicking, because it was the only thing left to do. As long as I was still kicking I was still alive and free.

The soothing effect of solid, warm bodies of animals moving their hooves in boxes of worn wood. The pungent smell of straw and the hollow sound of invisible horses munching. Douglas and the naked woman as they had been sitting there so chummy together on the doorstep of his wagon. As if they had only been waiting for me to come out of my shack and join them. Crosscut to the square powerful figure of the policeman as he bent over to get her out of the front seat. The warm and wistful smile on her face as they drove off with her. *That* woman! Was she a nutcase or a prophet? Hell if I knew. But try as I might, I couldn't get her out of my head. During Lili's short absence, there had first been Frauke and then this one! What was it about me that attracted that kind of people? What was the meaning of it?

Unable to answer my questions I turned around and started back in the direction of The Wagon Village. It was crazy. How was it possible that a woman without any clothes on and with "FUCK ME" tattooed on her sex could make a greater impression on me than all my university professors put together? What did *she* have that *they* did not? The tattoo? And then there was Douglas and I! Christ all mighty! For all we were worth we might as well have been a couple of professors. Or policemen, for that matter. A couple of goddamn jerks was what we had been. We with all our clothes on, buttoned up in prudence and reason and education and all the rest, we had not been prepared to meet the bird of the field when it came to us. Like a pair of lousy pharisees we had handed over the bird to the authorities to do with as they pleased. Instead of putting the woman up, we had put on exhibit our own narrow mindedness, pettiness, ignorance and fear. Automatically and without question, we had protected the self-righteous image of ourselves, which we had worked so hard to build. The last thing in the world we wanted to discover was that we too were just a couple of naked inmates in the small and stinking patrol car of our own making. Christ what a pair of stereotypical assholes we were. How did a worm like me even dare critizise Tolstoi? Just think if, instead of handing the woman over to the authorities, *I* had kept her with me in Christiania. Just think what would have happened if I had done what her tattoo told me to. Just think if I had penetrated her black hole in search of the splinter and let my seed loose. Maybe one day, she would have escaped just like the bees in Old Knud's hive. Or maybe at some point, the authorities would have found out where she was and taken her away—because the law-and-order society of normal monsters does not tolerate people being what they are and doing together what they need. All because that sort of thing is not conducive to the production of goods and services which, of course, must come before all other endeavors. Fucking her I would at least have done what I was told. I would have behaved like a man. Then there was no telling what would have happened? Perhaps the woman would have turned out not to be wacko after all. Perhaps the reason she had kept her name secret was because she didn't want to be returned to some institution. Why, the reason she had no clothes on could be that she had escaped through a window while taking a shower that morning. Not minding her naked condition, she crossed the entire city of Copenhagen to reach Freetown Christiania, where she had heard there were real people with real hearts who would give her clothes, food and a warm bed.

I bit my lip. A fine pair of lackeys and henchmen, that is what we were, Douglas and I. A couple of pitiful traitors who did not deserve better than to be kicked out of Christiania. In execution of a decision reached unanimously and in full council. Yes, that's it. For what we had *not* done, we should be dipped in tar publicly and rolled in feathers—for not being magnanimous and hospitable when put to the test.

"My God!" I thought. What a fool you are! And a coward too! You blew it so bad! Who knows: maybe it would have been the miracle! Douglas had been right. I was really not too fastidious when it came to women. But me! Oh no, not this fellow! All *he* could think of was what Lili would say when she came back, as if I would have to put up the naked woman all alone. Together, in The Wagon Village, we might have taken good care of her until she got over all the terrible things that had been done to her in the past. Who knows! Maybe an act of kindness such as this would have been the straw that broke the monster's back. It might have turned the tide and defused the looming catastrophe.

Suddenly, I felt completely sure. Such an act would indeed have changed everything. It would have let light and air into the sealed and stuffy chamber of heartless, egotistical and suicidal hopelessness that was choking us. Why, in a couple days, the woman would have turned into an enchanted prinsess or a true handmaid of the Lord. Our act would have restored love to its rightful throne. But alas, never once did we suspect that it was the two of us who had been chosen by the Godhead when it decided to give humanity one last chance. The last rescue action before the deluge! We had both been sound asleep and now that I had come to, it was too late. The patrol car was gone. The miracle (not the false and icy technological idol worshipped by the clones) the eternally new and human miracle of love powerful enough to transform dead matter into living organisms—the resurrection of the flesh and preparation for the marriage with God which had been propagated by the visionaries of our age—*that* was what had miscarried. Full of faith in the sacred nature of her mission, the naked woman had traversed intergalactic space, and finally after having reached Christiania on the planet Earth, what did she run into but a couple of faint hearted chickens who could think of nothing better to do with her than hand her over to the police… The only thing that had occurred to these two wise guys of the West was that here was something deviating from the norm and in need of being normalized without delay, and if necessary with the violence performed by the stocky cop when he got her out of the front seat and into the back of the car where ghosts of all the other deviants were crammed in and waiting for her. Against blindness, stupidity and fear even the gods struggle in vain. Instead of a kiss the cosmic princess had gotten locked up in an institution for mentally dysfunctional humans. Instead of being freed, the naked truth had been swathed and desecrated.

And now what? Well, now, the time had come for the final denoument. Now, it only remained for the water to break and Mother Earth to go into labor bringing forth— not the peak of Ararat but the peak of the Mount of Venus— complete with cunt hairs and the words FUCK ME tattooed in great skyblue letters between their gnarly roots.

Still with an echo of "the naked truth" reverberating in my mind, I put on a sweater in my shack and headed for the fire in the center of The Wagon Village. The sun had disappeared behind the tall trees, and the villagers were sitting around the long plank table talking. There were leftovers in the bowls and some cheap redwine in cartons.

"Grab a plate and go for what's left!" Jakob didn't look up and pronounced the welcoming words in that characteristic dictatorial and brusque way of his. At the sight of Douglas' famous "Confederate potato salad," I realized how hungry I was. There were two small fish cakes left, six soggy olives, a big potato wrapped in tin foil in the fire and a burnt corncob—not to mention a tiny drop or two of yellow tartare souce in a flat tube. All in all, it was a sumptuous spread for a starved infantry man just back from the battle at Austerlitz.

I had noticed her the moment I stepped into the circle of wagons. And sitting down with my plate at the other end of the table, I studied her in secret. She was a beautiful brunette with curly hair, a red dress with big flowers on it and a grey-blue down jacket still unzipped. She was engaged in conversation with Douglas, John and Hanne. Every once in a while, the boy Rune came running to his mother to stick his grimy little face with the snot nose under his mother's arm. The fire crackled, hissed, sputtered and broke into series of small explosions. Gurli Elizabeth was strumming a guitar, humming and jingling her bell. Jakob was telling Old Knud about a giant tick he had found on the dog Rolf and at the same time scattering his usual dry and droll comments right and left. People were in a fine mood, and the atmosphere was one of merriment and banter. At first, I did not feel much like taking part. The events of the afternoon had taken their toll on me. But with every bite of food and every swig of wine, my condition was quickly improving. Keeping an eye on the visiting beauty at the other end of the table, I was thinking of Lili who had left for Stockholm a few day ago. If everything went according to plan, she would be back Sunday evening. That meant I would not see her until around noon on Monday. That was all right with me.

Hanne had gone into the kitchen wagon to make coffee, and now she came out carrying the huge enamelled light blue pot we always used. Stepping down, she yelled to John to get the village tea and coffee set. A few minutes later, John appeared with the requested set on a large tray. And what a set that was. God knows how this unlikely group of cups and mugs had come together, and from where each item originally hailed. I doubt any living person in Denmark and environs had ever encountered anything like it. It was a carnaval of different sizes, forms, colors and general conditions. Each item had its own distinct personality, and the coffee tasted different, depending on whether it was ingested from of the tall, slim mug with the missing handle or the plump, cracked ceramic cup with the motif from "The Little Match Girl" painted on it. There was one thing, though, which they all had in common: they were all more or less damaged.

As the darkness grew denser and the cold increased, we moved closer to the fire. Jakob got his guitar out and began to strum on it. Our beautiful American visitor had fetched a long green scarf and zipped her down jacket up to her chin. But apparently she was still cold because now she put on a pair of long woolen stockings. Fascinated, I followed the proceedings with my eyes. The way she placed one well shaped foot on a shoe and stretched the other leg in order to pull on the stocking. And then, when that was done I admired how she placed the now-stockinged foot on the other shoe and stretched out the still bare leg. Finally, she got up and hitched the stockings as high up under the dress as she could. I noticed that her fingers were long and beautiful too. Not to mention her legs. The way the material was tight and smooth and clung to them all the way up from the tip of her toe to her crotch. The way her every movement was graceful and easy like. Sitting there gaping I thought she was as beautiful as a goddess, and so when a little later, Douglas went inside his wagon to say good night to his newborn baby, I did not hesitate but took over his slice of tree-trunk and sat down next to her.

That is how it began. Melanie was Melanie from Los Angeles. At present, she resides in New Mexico. How and where it will end remains to be seen.

It is something I have wondered about for some time now. I mean you meet lots and lots of strangers none of whom really impress you much and then one comes along and it's like all you have gone through was just in preparation to meet that person. Right from sentence one, it seems there is magic at work. There you are swimming together like fish in a liquid specially created for the occasion. At least, between Melanie and me that was how it was. There was no doubt. I could *feel* it. As it turned out, Douglas had already told her about the naked woman with "FUCK ME" tattooed on her sex. Now I was able to complete the story and relate how she had thrown herself on her back in the passenger seat of the police car and started kicking the roof. I also told her how when, looking at the woman's asshole, one of the cops had asked the other cop if he thought what they were witnessing was "a case of feminism."

Melanie looked into my eyes, and in a voice that I thought was trembling a little bit, she said that she was not sure whether to laugh or cry. In a way, she said, it was a very witty comment, *especially* coming from a cop. But in another way, it was sad too. She moved her eyes away from mine and stared into the fire. A little later when looking at her face from the side, I wondered if I should tell her how ashamed I was of the way Douglas and I had behaved. But before I could make up my mind, she looked me in the eye again and said that she thought it a fine trait that I had *not* looked, when the "poor" woman wanted us to find the splinter in her pussy. *That*, she added, told her "a lot" about me. It told her so much in fact that she already felt like she knew me. Wasn't *that* weird? Then, after she had said that, Melanie moved her head up real close to my ear: "As opposed to Douglas!" she whispered and shook her head. She had known him for ages, and yet now she was not sure anymore. Him and his high ideals! She didn't give a shit about all that. Okay, so he had deserted from the US army and seen a lot. But what good was it if a mentally disturbed woman with no clothes on was all it took to make him stare his eyes out? Did that not go to show that he had not seen nearly enough yet? On the other hand it was he who had discovered the tattoo. That was undeniably true. Only, it didn't change the fact that it was rude the way he kept staring up the poor woman's sex. Melanie raised her eyes to look at the sky where the first stars and planets were already twinkling. All of a sudden, she burst out laughing. "A case of feminism!" she hiccupped. Never in her life had she heard anything as ridiculous as that. And she so shook with laughter that she had to lean her forehead against my shoulder. Yes... and support herself with both her hands on my thigh. The attack lasted a few seconds. When it was over, she raised her head again, removed her hands and looked at me with tears in her eyes: "Help me will you! Say something to make it go away. I think I'll laugh myself to death if you don't!" Melanie quickly placed a hand on my shoulder and smiled at me with her white teeth and full red lips.

Sitting on those slices of tree trunk and mesmerized by the flames, Melanie and I were warming up to each other. Her company, the starry skies and the heat of the fire had the effect that my tongue became philosophical and roamed about freely. Among other things, I told her of the strange sharpening of my senses and the thoughts I had when the police car took off with the woman. I even told her about the battle at Austerlitz in Tolstoi's "War and Peace." Melanie wanted to know if I had finished reading the novel. I said that the novel was so long that a trip on the Transsiberian Railroad was not long enough to read it all. Anyway, it was all part of my "independent studies," I explained. "Oh, really!" Melanie exclaimed. So I studied literature? She was so eager and curious to know more that I was almost sorry to disappoint her. No, I said, I did not study literarture, not officially anyway. But once upon a time, I'd had a vision and realized it was my calling to write novels and essays. Right there on the spot, I had decided to teach myself the art. I still didn't have a clue, though, how to go about it. All I knew how to do was to read the authors I loved and learn "a trick or two." And, of course, dream about writing my own masterpieces one day. But then that wasn't really quite true either. I *also* knew that the book I was going to write was meant for such souls as were not yet settled in an outlook, a philosophy, a religious institution, fancy money-making schemes, fixed thinking, a planned carreer, etc. In other words, my future readers were the sincere seekers of a meaning and a place in the world. Also and most importantly, my book was not going to be a popular novel like a historical tale about people who had lived during feudalism, say. It was not going to be a futuristic account either, nor was it going to be a fantasy, thriller, mainstream, romance or crime novel. My book was going to be for and about courageous borderline people prepared to pay the price for freedom and truth in these so-called modern days. It was going to be a psychological, philosophical and above all personal account of the outsider's struggle to make the best of the conditions such as they are. What I was interested in was not so much the regulated and conventional fate of the educated and frightened security seekers, family persons and employees but rather the conflicts, joys and sufferings of the fearless seekers of God and the divine. My kind of stuff was such as transcended the ordinary, made people throw caution to the wind and enter into extraordinary states of woe, rebellion, harmony and daring. The effect that I wanted to achieve was similar somehow to that created by the naked woman when she threw herself in the front seat and kicked with her feet. Or something like when she, Melanie, heard the story and did not know whether to laugh or cry.

Melanie stared into the fire. For a long time, she didn't say anything, so long in fact that I began to think I had said something wrong. Then she turned her head and looked me in the eye. I was indeed a very "serious guy," she said. Her huge and chestnut colored eyes did not blink when she said it either. But her mouth was smiling and—maybe because I had taken a hit off the joint that had gone around—it now seemed as if this smiling mouth was struggling to detach itself from the rest of her face. At first, the separation was slow. But then as soon as the smile was free, it rushed towards my face and vanished.

Either Melanie did not notice that she had lost her smile, or she didn't care. She too had thought about writing, I heard her say. These words that were the first to be spoken between us for some minutes reached my ears as if on the way they had passed through an ocean of water. It was hard getting started, she said, not just because she had little children but also since she had no patience with dilletantes. What she wanted to do was something sublime like for example "Out of Africa" by Karen Blixen. If she could write something like that, it would be worth the effort. Then she would be grateful. It was such a beautiful book, and it meant a lot to her. "A lot," Melanie repeated as if deep in thought. Karen Blixen had been tremendously courageous. Maybe that is why she could write so evocatively about a night on the coffee plantation that half a century later, clear across the world, you could smell the earth and hear the cicadas. Yes, and *feel* the lion's paws as they touched the ground. Blixen's style, Melanie said, was so divine that not only could you hear the shot that killed the lion you never got over it.

Just think, she went on, now she knew *four* Danish writers: Karen Blixen, Hans Christian Andersen, Søren Kierkegaard and… Andreas Stein. "How *about* that!"

"Me!" I protested, "I'm not a writer yet! Not at all."

"What do you mean you're not a writer?" Melanie was nodding her head fiercely. "You *are*! Only you don't know it because you haven't gotten started yet. You're just as much a writer as those nettles over there in the dark between the wagons were nettles from the moment the seed hit the topsoil and started to grow. Sure as I'm sitting here on a slice of tree trunk freezing my butt off! You just wait and see. It'll come in due time. I swear. Hand on the Bible. I can *feel* it… here!" And Melanie placed a hand flat on the left side of her chest.

What could I say? It sounded promising indeed but also a bit esoteric. I was not sure how to react to Melanie's pronouncement. After all, we had only known each other two or three hours…

The moon had risen. It was now high in the night sky. Far out in the infinite cosmos, its white face shone cold pale light on a group of people sitting around a fire on a summer's night in the city of Copenhagen. I took my eyes from Melanie's face and looked at the slightly shadowy face of the moon. Wasn't it crazy though, I thought, the way one is content, and then a new person appears on the set of your life and says: "Hey Bro, look! Here I am. Who are you?"

As content as you were before, and as elated as you feel now, still there's this sinking feeling because you know that sooner or later it will disappear again and you will have to live without it.

Jakob was in the middle of a home grown ballad about early Christiania mornings when the last bar-crawlers are heading home for bed. Gurli Elizabeth was drumming away on the bottom of an empty tin bucket that she held between her knees. Not long before Douglas had said goodnight and judging from the sounds emanating from his shack he and Line were now busy making more babies. Jakob stopped singing, leaned his guitar against the table and put some more wood on the fire. Gurli Elizabeth offered us a cup of the fenugreek tea she always kept simmering in a huge cast iron pot on her stove. Now and then, a dark figure appeared on the fringe of the circle of light created by the fire only to disappear into the darkness immediately after. Old Knud who had smoked a couple of pipes came up to announce that somebody or other had abused his trust.

Some time had gone by. Already, it was a while ago that Jakob had said goodnight and left us alone. Now, we too got up and found our way to my wagon. I lit a candle and looked at Melanie. She turned her head away and said something about it being a cosy little hut. After a little while, without saying anything and also without looking at me, she made up her mind about something. Kicking off her shoes, she went and sat on my bed with her back against the wall. She pulled up her knees and leaned her chin on them. I too got into bed and sat cross-legged at the other end.

Sitting like that and without touching each other, we spent the rest of the night. It was light out, blackbirds sang from the rooftops, and Melanie yawned big-time. It was wearing her out, she said. "What?" I said. "This...," she said and smiled over her knees to me. I nodded.

Why did it have to be like this, she asked after another long silence? When all she wanted to do was snuggle up to me and have me take her in my arms. But no, she could not allow that. She was a married woman, and in Jutland, there were two small children and a father waiting for her. Trusting her. Depending on her. Together they formed a family. It would be like inviting catastrophe, like saying to it: "Hey catastrophy come and destroy us!" But, said Melanie, she wanted me to know that every molecule of her body was screaming for her to do the forbidden thing. When she was done declaring all this, she glanced at me sort of sideways, and I stretched out my hand: "Oh, no!" she pleaded, "I beg you. Don't!"

I said: "All right. Then do as I say. Go to the bed Douglas has made for you and sleep. That's an order."

"Yes sir," Melanie mumbled. But instead of obeying, she just pulled the knees harder up against her bosom and held herself folded up even more adamantly than before.

It was all up with us. There wasn't anything to be done, so after a few minutes, Melanie got down from the bed, stepped gingerly across the bouncing floor in her stockinged feet without looking at me, made it past my ten-speed, past the woodstove, through the wardrobe and the kitchen till she reached the door opening wide on the morning. Facing the dawn and still with her back to me, she hesitated one last time as if asking the divine powers permission to trade in all of tomorrow for the sorry scraps of night that were left. On the way she had put on her shoes, and now she was listening to the wind whispering in the tall trees on the rampart. It's all of tomorrow for whatever remains of tonight! It's all of tomorrow for whatever remains of tonight! I, too, heard the wind whisper its message. When she was gone, there was the faint sound of gravel being crushed under the soles of her shoes. Then I heard her press up the bolt of Douglas's door. The door closed and the bolt fell down. I couldn't hear her anymore. The blackbirds were singing.

For a while I kept sitting on the bed without moving. Aside from my bladder, which was about to burst, my body felt emptier than emptiness itself. What did I know when it came right down to it? What did I understand? Not a damn thing, except that I needed badly to take a leak in the nettles. So that is what I did. With my feet in the black clogs, I stomped down the doorstep and turned the corner. I unbuttoned the fly, got my cock out and was just about to let go, when I stopped and moved a few steps sideways to the tall and lush nettle I had been pissing on the last couple weeks. It was sort of an experiment on my part to see how much piss the king of the nettles could take. I took a deep breath, stood erect, looked at the nettle and let my hot piss slam against its great fringed leaves. It sounded like heavy-duty rain fall. A short and hefty summer shower. When I was done and was buttoning up, I became conscious that some of the nettle's leaves were withered slightly on the fringes. In other words, there was a limit to how much even the tallest, strongest and healthiest nettle could stand getting pissed on. When I started my experiment, the nettle had been healthy all the way to the very tips of its fringes. It really had been a superb specimen. It was for precisely that reason that I picked it. Now, it was fading, and it was clear to me that if I kept pissing on it, it would surely wither and die. Out of all the nettles growing behind my wagon, it was the exceptional nettle that the evil man had selected to suffer slow death by urination. Was that not an example of horrible injustice? Yes, it was. But far more horrible was the fact that the tallest, strongest and most beautiful nettle of them all, the one that showed the greatest promise—precisely that one had been condemned to leave the world it had loved and where it had been a true ornament…

The evil man was leaning back against the shack behind him. His eyes were closed and his soul busy processing the experience of the last twenty-four hours. From the reading of "War and Peace" in the Copenhagen airport to dancing for Krishna by the moonlit lake to the meeting with two broken noses sitting side by side in deckchairs on a rotten veranda. Melanie, the night by the campfire and her hesitation on the threshold of daybreak! And now finally the death throes of a beautiful nettle. It had been born, it had grown, and in a little while it would be gone…

I don't know why suddenly it all became too much for me. The whole damn thing! The gassing of my father's parents in the Nazi ovens not long before I came into the world and now… this. The naked truth! Hot tears were rolling down my cheeks. I covered my face with my hands and cried like a baby. And it went on until at some point I spread the fingers on my face. Peering bleary eyed at the nettle I had pissed half to death, I made my vow. In that instant and leaning against my wagon 537 in Christiania, I decided by all that was sacred to never forget this moment. As I say, I did not know why, but I had the feeling that what happened to me right now would turn out to be of great importance in the time to come.

That morning I left the door open. I climbed the two steps, brushed my teeth, undressed and got under the quilt. Then, I looked one last time at the quiet light in the door-opening, fell asleep at once and dreamt about the bow my father helped me make from a hazel branch when I was a little boy.

It was around noon when I opened my eyes and looked

towards the door because the light blinked and flickered, shimmered and reflected colors and liquid forms in a myriad of ricocheting rays... And there, dark and spotted against the collage of flapping shadows, soft gusts of wind and in the scent of dry wood of summer I saw Melanie surrounded on all sides by an aura of sunlight. I watched her without moving. She, too, watched me without moving. And she *was* there. I swear to God. But all of a sudden, she was gone. I closed my eyes and opened them again. Three times, I did that just to make sure. But no, she wasn't there anymore. Feeling like I had been abandoned, I turned over and began to stare at a knot in the wood. How was it possible? How could a body that was there disappear like that? That was just the thing. It could not happen. So what should I trust? my eyes or my reason? Preferably both! But in that case, what had happened to Melanie?

After a while I got tired of the knot and the associations it awoke in me. I jumped to the floor, found a pair of clean underwear on the shelf under the bed and bounced to the kitchen only to find that there was barely enough water left in the plastic jar to wash my face and brush my teeth. In order to get the last drops, I had to tilt the jar and hold a cup under the tap. I wiped the water drops off my face with the towel and looked at the empty jar. There was no way around it. Even if I didn't feel like it, I had to get some more water. If that damn jar had taught me anything, it was to economize with its precious life-giving content. Still, I could economize as much as I liked, the jar would empty nevertheless. There was no arguing the point. Since moving to Christiania, I had learned my lesson well: never postpone getting a refill of fresh water. It didn't matter if I was in the mood for it, had the time for it or was hungover and exhausted. The only thing that mattered was having water.

So... pants on, feet in flip-flops, jar off the table, and

walk down Grønnegade Street to the source. Flip-flop. Flip-flop. Flip-flop. The rubber soles slapped me softly under my feet. They even—or so it seemed to me—slapped me approvingly. So as I was walking there on Grønnegade Street swinging the jar and enjoying the loving little slaps under my feet and the air against my skin, it occurred to me that what I was really doing was performing a sacred ritual. The feet in the flip-flops, the happy slappings against my soles, the thirsting jar longing to drink and be filled... the whole damn thing was one long religious experience. My entire faith was summed up in it. Going out to get water, I was a link in an almost endless procession of humans stretching back to Mesopotamia and beyond into the mists of prehistoric times. The Euphrates and Tigris rivers hanging like a glittering necklace from the neck of the Godhead. Cupping my hands, drinking and praying on the banks of the Jordan! The implications were mind-boggling. Because I was out of step with my own time, I couldn't just turn on the faucet in my bathroom or my kitchen. For me, it was different. Carrying my jar barefoot to the well, I partook of the divine procession and was fated to meet the Samaritarian woman on the way. No sooner had this idea gotten into my head than I stopped to look around me. And what do you know! There she was, right before my eyes. The Samaritarian woman was a naked little toddler, ten or twelve months old, sitting on her chamberpot in front of Katrine's shack. At present, she was busy babbling to herself and inspecting the little piss-crack between her legs.

Everything around me breathed peace and fresh coffée. People were going about their business. From the next shack came peals of laughter followed by some indefineable thuds. Holding the jar under the faucet I let the water thunder against its bottom. Instantly, the sun drenched air filled with cascades of tiny drops and made a miniature rainbow encircling my pelvis with its multicolored halo. Spell bound, I watched the rainbow fade as the jar filled. When it was three quarters full, I turned off the water, set it down on the ground, screwed the lid back on and rested a bit. Then, I resolutely yanked the handle and started on my way back. A few steps further on, I passed the place where the little girl had made water and inspected herself. She was still there, but this time she followed me with her eyes. "You just look at me as much as you like," I thought as I went by. "For I tell unto you that bringing your jar to the well for water is implementing the will of the One who create all!"

Not a little pleased with myself for delivering this—if I may say so myself—divinely inspired sermon apropos to the situation, I reached my door and put the jar back in its place on the table. Then I held a glass under the tap, filled it and quenched my thirst—twice.

As usual, one thing led to another. Fifteen minutes later, when leaving my wagon, I found Melanie sitting facing my way at the plank table with most of the local natives for company. She was wearing the same flowered dress as the day before only *without* the down jacket. As I came closer, she sent me a look that told me that she had, in fact, been the one who had woken me. Rune, the snotty little devil, was crawling about on all fours on the grassy spot demolishing dandelions. Every time he had torn one in two, he would let out a jubilant scream and throw it over his shoulder. On the table, homemade rolls, jam, butter, cheese, yogurt, sausage, sliced rye bread, muesli, juice, coffee and tea were laid.

Celebrating that this day was more or less like any other summer's day, Old Knud had brought his worm eaten armchair out of his shack. He had put on his battered leather hat with the purple woven ribbon around the crown and also

351

his black reading glasses. He was apparently sunk in deep contemplation of his morning paper. On the ground beside him Rolf rested his head on his front paws. With eyes wide open and his two ears upright twisting and turning like radar antennae in the air, he was on the alert. Behind him, the rabbits were quiet in their cage, and here and there in the air, bees were buzzing about looking for some sweetness to suck. In other words, the stage was set for Jakob to step out on his veranda. In his arms, he held a smiling Ragma with her back pressed against his chest. The way her hair was all a mess, it seemed she had put up resistance when taken hostage by the man. Triumphantly, Jakob had slung his right arm far down over her shoulder where he was squeezing her left tit with his long nailed guitar paw. At the same time, he held his left arm stretched out towards the assembled subjects as if to exorcise demons from them or—perhaps—to prepare us for the announcement of his conditions for setting Ragma free. Douglas didn't seem to notice a damn thing. Being the village intellectual, he considered it his privilege to wear blinders. The blinders allowed him to dissect everybody and everything and to keep the single parts in little jars with labels on them. Right now, he was lecturing Melanie on "the wrong premises" behind certain dissertations on the subject of Christiania presently being written at universities around the world. The reason he knew these were being written, he said, was because he "served as a sort of consultant" for some of them.

"Dissertations my ass! If I were you, I wouldn't pay too much attention to what that guy tells you!"

Old Knud had raised his eyes and was looking out over the rim of his glasses at Melanie. To judge from the rust in his voice, it had been a while since the last time he used it: "If you really want to know something about Christiania," he went on partly to Melanie and partly to the paper on his knees, "…then why don't you go for a walk. *Without* any escort, mind you! Have a look around and see things with your own eyes. Draw your own conclusions. That is, if you're able to avoid the company of that guy. (Old Knud made a slight nod with his head in the direction of Douglas). In theory, you could stay right where you are. Except it's no use when he's here. Best thing you can do is go down to the street. When you get there, sit yourself down outside the bar called Woodstock. That's where it's happening. There are Greenlanders, drunks, three-day-old bingers, nuts, criminals, mongrels, all sorts. It's not unlikely some asshole with a hangover will be so kind as to offer you a friendly piece of advice. Don't take it to heart. It's just so much drool coming from a spit gland. But the things you'll hear down there—I guarantee you—are not like the things you're being told by your Yankee professor friend."

All the while Old Knud was speaking Douglas pretended not to hear. Oh, no, not *him*! He had more important things to do. Like the pouring of yogurt into a deep plate. He was much too "concentrated on the task at hand" to notice anything that was going on around him. Of course! But I will be damned if he did not know only too well what was being said. I could tell from the way his movements seemed even more studied and even more slow than usual. And I have to admit, it annoyed the shit out of me. It really did. I mean what good is it to be so informed of what goes on at universities in other parts of the world when you're totally unaware of what's going on right before the tip of your own goddamn nose? With all his education, diplomas, titles and academic urbanity, with his work outside Christiania and the monthly salary arriving with the reliability of a Swiss watch in his bank account, with his unshakeable composure and faith in the authorities' sincere motives and wholly benign nature, Douglas represented that element in the organism of the Freetown which would one day cost it its life. At least that was the way Old Knud looked at it. Once, I had heard him tell Douglas that there existed another and more unapproachable Christiania than the one he knew of and inhabited. Some day in the future (Old Knud told him this straight off to his face) when the soul of the Freetown had grown soft and complacent, then the voice of the regime would call on such as Douglas and the rest of the timid and mundane Christiania middle class to negotiate an agreement. And when that day came, all those with something to lose would betray Old Knud, the Greenlanders, the pushers, the bums, the artists, the activists, the homesteaders, the screwballs, the fugitives. In short, what was left of the non-conforming elements of the Freetown. With their tongues dripping sirup, disdain in their eyes, money in the bank, cars parked on the streets outside and paragraphs up their assholes together with the Danish state, they would turn the Freetown into a retirement home.

Watching Old Knud reading his paper, I saw it all happening just as he had predicted. I don't know what caused it. Maybe because Douglas pretended not to hear! Because he did not speak up. It was really kind of eerie. If it made any sense, I would say I could see the truth of Old Knud's words in the too slow and too studied movements with which Douglas prepared his yogurt and muesli. Precisely the way Douglas *looked* at that moment, so perfectly deaf and blind to what was going on around him, so perfectly composed, studied and conceited, was how the Christiania bourgoisie would appear on the day when the great bribery would come to pass. On that day, the game would be over for Old Knud, and the road cleared for the…investors.

Listening to Old Knud's words to Melanie, I remembered something he had told me in the prison cell—that you did not have to have your address in Christiania to be a christianite. And, vice versa, just because you had your official address in Christiania, did not mean you were a christianite. As a matter of fact, it was possible that one day there wouldn't be any christianites left in Christiania.

Remembering this I wanted to shout to Melanie and all the rest of them: Look at Old Knud! See him sitting there so completely himself in his old hat and shoes, with his missing teeth, his past on the seven seas and those small, blood shot Eskimo eyes. See him so alive! See him with his tattoos, asbestos lungs, sound common sense, enormous knowledge, humor and experience. Don't you see how his entire existence has been vandalized only to come out victorious at last! Yeah, take a good look at Old Knud and see him for what he is: a representative man and a walking testimony to the highest court of justice in the land of Denmark. The orphan and the boxer who made Christiania and its inhabitants his family! Here, in the little garden before his hut, he can talk to everybody and say anything he damn well pleases. The soul has not yet been born who is so perfect or so deformed that Knud becomes tongue-tied in his presence. He does not have to hide from anybody or anything and can be himself as he is anywhere. Look at Old Knud goddammit! In spite of his age, he is the very incarnation of the young, passionate and indomitable Freetown Christiania.

Had it not been for the night we shared a cell in jail, I don't think I would have had any idea what Old Knud was all about. I would not have understood what he meant to me and to many others as well, and what's more: I would not have been able to tell you. Like what he meant to Rolf his dog, for example, and Jakob his other next door neighbor. Just to mention two of the nearest! Why else would Jakob have written that song or ballad about the old man? It was not like he said it at all directly. No, it was just sort of something that was there in the spaces between the words. A vibration of sorts, I suppose. And it was not like he praised him either. In the song Old Knud is seen from the distance and caught in an unguarded moment that is hardly glorious. It's a cold and damp winter morning, one of those dastardly windless affairs that are if not frequent then very typically Danish in the way they can cover a man's heart with frost forever after. It is on such a morning that Old Knud is seen staggering down the uneven cobbles of Pusher Street. Hungover like hell, of course, and dragging his bones along in his worn out shoes and torn jacket. At once the redeemed and tarnished fugitive poet, prophet, pilgrim, pusher *and* the high priest of destitution at home in his congregation of outcasts. All of it captured in one bloody snapshot as Jakob picked his strings by the campfire. A proud man with the heart in the right place, holding his entire steaming life in his hands and sticking doggedly to the same lost-and-found course towards salvation; always reaching for the stars and being crucified through the holes in his shoes every step of the way. Balm on the wound for some, and salt rubbed in it for others. The salt of the Earth.

Of course, Melanie, being an American, had not understood a word of what Old Knud had said to her, so now she asked me across the space of four to five meters that separated us what she had been told. I walked over to her and said:

"He said that if you want to know what Christiania is all about, you should go for a walk and see for yourself. He also said that the Woodstock Bar down on Pusher Street would be a good place to start. Whatever you do, he says it's no use listening to that guy!"

So as there should be no mistake about the person Knud had meant I nodded in the direction of Douglas. Sitting by himself, he was trying not to let on that he paid attention to

356

what was going on around him. Every so often, he raised his eyes and looked around with that smug smile of his that served as a sort of camouflage. I had seen it enough to know that it was meant to communicate on the one hand a certain scholarly detachment and on the other, a deep commitment to certain controlled thought processes unfolding themselves in his mind on a more or less permanent basis. If he felt the least bit disappointed, he didn't show any sign of it.

"Well, are we off then?" Melanie didn't take her eyes from mine.

Once more, I glanced at Douglas. It didn't seem like he wanted to make good his claims as a host (or wipe off the little smug smile for that matter), and so I said to Melanie:

"Old Knud also said that he thought it best that you went alone!"

"And *I* think it's best *you* come along!"

I studied Melanie's face for a clue: "All right. I guess that decides the matter. But then, you have to promise *not* to listen to what I tell you!"

"Can't I listen just... a little bit... please? Like if it gets as... profound as last night?"

The way Melanie said this, I couldn't help but smile: "Absolutely NO. Old Knud said you must think for yourself."

"But then... if I'm not to listen to you at all you might as well not say anything. And... then, what's the point of going together?"

"Well then, let's listen to the sounds our voices are making and play it by ear. Maybe in the end, something will come up. When I've had a roll and a cup of coffee, we're off."

"That's a deal." Melanie sent me an amused look, got up and picked an apple from the bowl on one of the sliced tree-trunks.

Melanie went to get her camera, and I washed down the last bit of buttered roll with coffée. When she returned, I got up, and we left for Woodstock. We had not gone more than a few steps before she asked the first question. She wanted to know what Old Knud had meant, when he said she risked being offered friendly advice if she went into the Woodstock Bar by herself. Well, I said, surely she understood. It was not every day that a single, beautiful, young and sober looking woman entered that place. The regulars would think it fishy that someone fitting this description chose to sit down among such rabble as they knew themselves to be. It would make them uneasy and create a need for some form of release. Who had ever heard of parrots from the Amazon hanging out with city pigeons from Copenhagen?

"If Old Knud fits right in, how do you think *you* fit in then?" I said.

Melanie shrugged and said it did not bother her. She was used to being out of place where she came from. It could hardly be worse than in some sections of LA, where you risked being molested if you didn't look like a bum or a faded pop idol or something. And in any case, we had to start somewhere. So why not Woodstock? Parrots and pigeons had the initial 'p' in common. She was ready and looking forward to it... really!

Saying this Melanie stopped me with a light touch of her hand. For a split second, we stood facing one another. Melanie's full red lips twitched like they couldn't make up their mind whether to smile or speak. Or maybe it was something entirely different. Hell if I know. But I remember that little lip twitch and how her eyes shone.

"Come on," I said. "Let's get a move on!"

It was another nice day. A light breeze cooled the air and little cartoon-like clouds scooted before the sun. If you did not know any better, you would say that the Freetown knew a visitor had come to see it and so had put on its summer best. And I am not exaggerating either. It was a little bit like I have always imagined village life in places like India. No cars and all sorts of people doing all sorts of things. Some tinkered with something out in front of their houses. Others argued through open windows; some walked, and others still rode old clunkers or carried children and big yellow gas bottles in the three-wheeled box-bikes made in Christiania. Down by the Grocery the usual handful of red-nosed bums were gathered. They were holding a conversation with beer-bottles in their hands and voices hoarse from too much shouting and too much drinking. As we came closer, someone turned up the volume on a radio blaring the new Lone Kellerman hit: "See Venezia and Die".

When Melanie had been in and out of the Grocery a few times and was done exchanging remarks with the owner of one of the three huge mongrels that had rendezvoused in the door, she pushed her camera into my hands. Would I please take a picture of her with her arm around the shoulder of Heinrich, a bum in a dirty white mackintosh whose round and flamingly red face with purple potato-nose was framed by a big white beard with splotches the color of piss. I did not much like the idea because I thought it would piss him off. But I was wrong. Instead of getting pissed off, he was flattered like hell. When he realized Melanie was serious, he started swinging the beer-bottle and sort of bum-hum "See Venezia and Die." And when even *that* was not enough to express whatever it was he felt inside, he proceeded to perform something like a dance with a beer-bottle. It was really kind of moving. The dance consisted of Heinrich swinging first one leg while raising the bottle in the air, and then swinging the other. At the same time, he was keeping an eye on his Madonna who was taking in the scene with an expression of wonder. To me, he looked like you would imagine a demented Santa Claus to look. I was amazed how much energy there was in the old dude. First, he danced clear across to the playground on the other side, and then he danced back. There and back, there and back. It didn't even seem like he was tired when he finally stopped in front of Melanie. He wasn't panting much at all. And then at that very instant, he shoved his jaw so far forward that his beard almost hid the purple nose. I must say it looked rather peculiar, especially because now he started huffing and puffing like an old locomotive. Whatever it was that he was trying to do, he sure as hell succeeded. It happened so fast it was almost like it had been choreographed. Suddenly Heinrich stopped his antics, and next thing I knew the two of them were posing together. That's how I managed to get them in the—by now—immortalized instant…

This performance was such a hit with the bystanders that Heinrich had some difficulty accepting it was at an end. So now, he downright refused to let go of Melanie. Looking triumphantly around him, he announced his intention to "bless" her with a "farewell-kiss" on the cheek. There followed a moment of tension. It was hard to tell anymore if it was still fun. I could tell that Melanie didn't much like the idea. As for me, I just kind of held my breath and kept my fingers crossed. What after all is a little kiss on the cheek? If nothing else, it would sure make a fine picture. So thinking I raised the camera and caught them right at the very instant when Heinrich presses his lips to Melanie's beautiful cheek. And that is how the other famous picture was born.

When a little later, we had moved on a few steps Heinrich came running after us. Catching hold of Melanie's arm, he pulled her to him and whispered so loud that I too could hear it: "I'm awfully horny so watch out!" Whereupon, he let go, stood erect, raised the bottle to his lips, closed his little bum's eyes, peered out at her through one of them and said "cheers." Then he threw his head back and downed the rest.

"What did he say?" Melanie asked as we reached the factory building.

"I'm not sure you want to know!"

"I asked, didn't I?"

"He told you to watch out because he is awfully horny."

"Oh," she said. "But that's *so sweet* I think."

"Sure," I nodded.

That is pretty much how the day went on. It really was like there was magic in the air, *crazy* magic I might add. Even if we hadn't had anything to drink or smoke, we were like intoxicated. And it wasn't just us either. The entire Christiania seemed to be under the influence of something or other. When we got to Woodstock, we found ourselves in the eye of the tornado again. Smack in the middle of the street, opposite the dirty white, spray painted wooden barrack, Hans, a Christiania painter, was at work at his easel. The canvas was Pusher Street on its back with its legs apart and seen through a fish-lense, expanding in the direction of The Starship, The Opera and The Sunshine bakery. Perhaps it was not intended, but to me, it looked like the street's cunt turned inside out and littered with garbage like used condoms, empty liquor bottles, various implements of sanitation, bloody secretions etc. It was all very colorful—and *very* Hans. That gangrened, exploded and not quite non-figurative, but warm, earthy and sensual vision was Hans' watermark. Once, when I visited him in his atelier, he told me he painted the world as if a barbarian giant with a humungous cock was on the rampage in it. The canvas we were looking at could either be viewed as a vision of the world after the rape, he said, *or* as the inside of the barbarian giant's intestine after he had swallowed the world raw. The enzymes were transforming it into so much shit! Or maybe he was all ready done digesting it, and it had reached the final stage in his bowels. Hans wasn't quite sure. Anyway, he didn't give a damn, he said, if it looked like shit as long as it had "real balls" in it. And you did not have to be able to see either whose balls they were as long as they were obviously barbarian. The one thing that mattered was the purity of the expression, the vision. If he could transform his shit into visionary stuff, then everybody else was free to put on it whatever tag they liked. But if I really wanted to know (Hans confided this like it was some great secret of his), he had lately labelled his shit "post-mortem, multi-ballistic barbarism." When he was done confiding this to me, he looked at me like I was now the involuntary carrier of a secret so great it would revolutionize the world of art. But the truth is, I had not asked about it at all. I couldn't care less how he labeled his shit. I just nodded to please him. I did not say a word about it being very visible or anything. I mean all that post-ballistic barbarism stuff he was ranting about.

Hans had looked at me kind of suspiciously, like he was not sure if I was taking him seriously. But then I suppose he decided I was, because now he declared that he didn't paint in order to be "indexed" by art historians and curators. For all he cared, "such people" could shove their classifications up their learned rectums. If they got a kick out of administering intellectual enemas, it was their problem. For the public that was deluded by all this hokuspokus, of course it was a bummer, but from a painter's perspective, it was of no importance. To paint had always been and still was a way of life. It was to be aware and to see and to move *at the same time*. And if I thought it easy, well, he would recommend that I try it myself. To be present at the instant of perception and to execute the vision one glimpsed was no small thing. Seen from the historical perspective, what he was trying to do was capture the unique atmosphere of Christiania. His task was to chronicle the beauty of the Freetown's neuroses, its antagonisms, and—"the menstrual flow of its procreative organs..." In the end, what it came down to was a form of meditation. And *documen*tation too. With the aid of his brushes, he was letting The Freetown of Christiania make its mark in time and space.

That is more or less how Hans spoke to me when I visited him in his atelier one afternoon soon after I moved in. Today, it was not so much his creative power as his power of concentration that was being put to the test. Every so often, some drunken jackass would come sailing up to look him over the shoulder and shout an inane comment or recommendation to the leering crowd hanging out in front of Woodstock. However, Hans took it like a trooper. He accepted it as part of the game. If you were not willing to put up with obnoxious nuisances, Christiania was not the place for you. And that goes especially for the spot Hans had set up his easel today. Here he was right on the front line as it were. If he chose to paint the street from here, the street would surely *paint* him back. *He* would then become as much a part of the street's creation as *it* became a part of his. It worked both ways. I could just hear Hans saying something to that effect. All right, perhaps he would not phrase it exactly like that. More likely, he would come up with something extravagant like how he and the street were "bathing in each other's excrements." Or in case his mood was a bit less outré, he might declare that he and the street were part and parcel of the same pulsing heartbeat. A symphony in "*shit* minor" opus syphilis. And it really was not far from being the truth either. On those old uneven cobbles in front of Woodstock, something was going on around the clock. For one thing, there was a constant din from loud-speakers playing anything from The Doors to heavy metal. For another, there were the drunken voices, the arguments and the transactions. What with the hashish inhalations and exhalations clouding the air and the electrified din, things were sort of liquidified. Borders were erased to the point where everything became borderline. Every time that great old heart beat vibrated, it was followed by something like a contraction, and a soaked floor rag would throw anoth-er fistful of raindrops against a window pane somewhere. Way in the background, there was the sound of muffled or-gasms gasping in a wasteland of broken glass. Enamelled eyes moist with emotion. Raw laughter and saliva dripping drain pipes. The rabble and its rousers drumming up trou-ble. The inane comments. Profane jokes. Drunken sugges-tions. Bleary-eyed fiends passing their hash-pipes around while tourists formed huge streams of restlessness. The of-fers proffered for the work in progress ranged from a punch in the nose, which Hans could get in advance, a joke of a ten-crown bill or five thousand sincere crowns put out by some biker with his Harley parked outside and fat wads of money making his pockets bulge.

Hans was brandishing his brush, dripping paint on the cobbles and talking a wild streak. Looking at him, it struck me he was some a kind of weird fish and the street the liquid matter he was swimming in. Apart from being a painter, Hans was also an accomplished *artiste* when it came to chasing skirts. The wet and colorful canvases he set out strategically in busy public spots were like flypaper to women. Today was no exception. Hans was on his post waiting for the next victim. Having recently been fed, he was in fine form. The very instant he caught sight of the two of us coming up he switched into his womanizing mode. Putting down the brush, he produced the drawing pad that he always kept on hand just in case. Would she mind if he "immortalized" her in Indian ink, he asked Melanie? And—inveterate sleazebag that he was—he added that she couldn't very well refuse, since he, Hans, was no other than Modigliani Junior and the proffered immortalization of the "utmost importance to the future of world art." A refusal on her part would be tantamount to high treason. When finally he got done telling her all this drivel, Hans looked at Melanie with a studied expression that I found so ludicrous I almost started laughing.

Except it wasn't funny. Melanie didn't see it the way I did. She did not know Hans and so had no way of knowing it was necessary to defend herself against his charms. I could see that not only was she amused by his approach, she was also tempted to pose for that thick tusch-pen he was holding in his hand. There was the raw smell of flypaper in the air, and… Melanie did not sense it. The woman in her sensed only what so many others of her gender had sensed in that last fraction of a split second before they threw themselves mindlessly against its sticky surface: a thirty-year-old handsome and clearly talented, unshaven, tanned, slender, energetic and joyful son of a brush wearing fancy grass-green moccasins made of skin, camouflage pants with paint splotches all over and a T-shirt with some back-alley Italian automobile motif on the chest.

"Hey, what would you like to drink, while I draw you? Just tell me. I'll get it for you."

How typical of Hans. The lousy miser did not so much as think of offering *me* anything. So it was true what somebody had told me: that he only liked to spend money on himself and what he termed "vintage cunt." In this case, he did not even wait for Melanie's answer. He just raised his hand in a gesture that said something like "freeze right there," and took off for the bar to get her something. Three or four minutes later, he reappeared with a bottle of organic black current juice in his hand.

"There you are. That's for you." Hans handed her the bottle.

"And what—if I may ask—am *I* supposed to drink?" I asked loudly.

Hans glanced at me: "You're not posing, but *she* is…"

"What makes you so sure. *I* never heard her say she would. Did *you*?" I asked and turned to Melanie.

"No, but that's all right. It's not every day I run into Modigliani Junior."

"Modigliani Junior, my ass!" I said realizing the game was up.

"Take it easy Les." Melanie put a hand softly on my arm as if to reassure me. "We're not in such a big hurry, are we? Have a sip of this!"

"No, that's for you," I said and stepped back. It pissed me off. Who did that bastard think he was interrupting our sightseeing tour of Christiania with his damned Indian ink?

While Hans was drawing, a crowd gathered around us to see the work of portraiture in progress. With a few light and elegant touches, he finished his "portrait of a foreign lady," tore the sheet off the pad and handed it to her. "Excuse me," he said to her in Danish, "if I wasn't able to do your great beauty justice. It wasn't humanly possible. Faced with you even Leonardo would fail!"

Glancing at the portrait, I recognized it as being truly masterful. With no effort at all and in no time, the damned satyr had succeeded in capturing the at-once-very-soft-and-gentle but also sharply-edged-beauty that was Melanie. From her expression I could see that she was pleased pink with it too.

"Leonardo da Vinci! What's he talking about?" Melanie looked first at me and then at Hans.

I just rolled my eyes and pulled her away.

"Be sure to come back again soon!" Hans yelled this in English as we started down Pusher Street. I wanted to erase every trace of this little episode as quickly as possible. And I had a feeling that what I was going to show her a bit further on would do the trick. I had told Melanie about many of the things that I wanted her to see but I had kept silent about one intentionally. I wanted to take her there except now Melanie remembered that she had forgotten to take a picture of Hans: "Wait here," she said and stuck the drawing into her shoulderbag, "I've got to get a pic of Modigliani Junior at work."

"Is that *really* necessary?" I sighed.

Yes. It really was. But as luck would have it, Hans had already forgotten about us. For him, it was a case of out of sight out of mind. He was now busy squeezing paint out of his tubes, and he didn't even notice that Melanie took his picture.

In the meantime, I had made a quick dash down to Carl Madsens Square to check if the next item on the sightseeing list was there today. The Stoneman, as we called him, was a very Danish *sadhu* who showed up every morning around eight-thirty to play statue with a cobblestone on Carl Madsen's Square. He always dressed in a long white Indian sari. On his head, he wore a turban of sorts. So as not to get bored, he would vary his position from day to day. On Mondays, he would stand stockstill holding the cobblestone directly above his head. On Tuesdays, he would hold it at his shoulder. On Wednesdays, he would hold it away from his body in his bent arm. And so on! Every time I saw him, I asked myself the same question: what difference it made where he held the stone and when? He never so much as moved a finger or a toe. Standing there immobile in the middle of the square with his stone, the Stoneman never even glanced at the bikers in their black leather jackets who were pushing hash all around him. Amazing how little it took to become famous! Because the Stoneman *was* famous! People had heard of him in San Francisco and Buenos Aires, which I suppose just goes to show that it matters where a *sadhu* takes up position. I mean, whether it's on a square in India with a bunch of other *sadhus* or in Christiania Denmark with a bunch of hash-pushers and tourists around. At twelve o'clock when the bells in the Church of our Savior began to toll, after three and a half hours of constant cobblestoning, the Stoneman would go to lunch. I don't know if it is true, but through the grapevine, I'd heard that he went to visit with his friend Svend Aage who was a painter about his own age. Telling Svend Aage the events of the morning, he would eat the open liverwurst and salami sandwiches he had prepared at home. At a quarter to one, he took his daily shit, and at one o'clock sharp, he was back on Carl Madsen's Square for another three or four hours of cobblestoning. At the end of each day, the Stoneman walked out of Christiania, caught a bus and returned to his apartment in the city. It's anybody's guess how he spent his evenings. Maybe he had a wife who waited for him with open arms and dinner steaming on the stove. Maybe there was a toddler on the doorstep ready to greet him too…

Now, the Stoneman was going to help me free Melanie from the spell cast on her by Modigliani Junior. And I must say, he did not fail me. The moment she saw him, Melanie stopped and exclaimed: "A *sadhu*. Here in *Christiania* and in *this* place with all those pushers and *dogs*?"

Gratified that I had surprised her, I said: "Yeah. As you see. We're a mixed lot. We call him the Stoneman. But actually he doesn't live here. He's only a visitor."

As we were talking, a group of teenagers came up followed by their teacher. They all stopped and stared. The teacher said: "What you see here kids is a *sadhu*. A *sadhu* is an Indian holy man, a mendicant and a Hindu!"

Melanie wanted to take a picture and was getting the camera out when I stopped her. With my head I indicated the Bullshit bikers and the other pushers and told her they would tear her apart, if she took photos. "They're very aggressive and totally paranoid," I said.

Instead, she decided to take mental note of the scene. Or I suppose that's what she was doing when, who happened by but my friend and neighbor Martin.

After saying hello to Melanie and giving her the standard elevator inspection, Martin explained to Melanie that he had just returned from a two-day long "maritime demonstration" against the nuclear power plant Barsebäck located on the other side of Øresund, the narrow strait separating Denmark from Sweden. Just back from the seas, Martin was awash with excitement. First there had been the reaction of the Swedish police out at sea and the tumultuous scenes. But as it turned out, this was just the ouverture. All that stuff about the demonstration was only a pretext. What was really on his mind was something entirely different: the epic account of how he had run into the "beautiful pop-singer chick," Blackhaired Liza from the successful women's band "Babylon Bitches." From the way Martin studied my face, I knew that he counted on me to have heard of this band. And as a matter of fact, I knew it very well. One of the women I had an affair with when I was married loved the band. She played the new album by "Babylon Bitches" all the time. She was especially crazy about the track "Slick Dude" written by Liza. She kept telling me how "absolutely great" it was and ordered me to concentrate on the lyrics

369

or I wouldn't "catch all the nuances…"

"We met out at sea!" Martin said.

I was only half-listening. Most of my attention was on Melanie. Still, I *did* catch how the eminent sea-hero Martin had at one point jumped from his boat onto the boat where Liza was. Apparently, this action had so impressed the famous popstar that she eventually invited Martin to visit her private "summer residence" in Skagen at the tip of Jutland.

"Can you believe it?" Martin said. "She and I! We're just gonna calypso and diddle the pelicans—for an entire week." At the thought of diddling the pelicans, Martin wet his upper lip with his tongue.

"No," I said, "I can't!"

When Martin realized I was not about to say any more, he decided that neither was he. He had to go home, he said, pack his little suitcase with the "most important stuff," get in the DAF car, pick up Liza and haul ass to Northern Jutland.

Martin stepped up to Melanie, looked her happily in the face and said: "Nice to meet you. Hope to see you again sometime!"

Melanie nodded, and Martin was off.

One hundred and fifty feet! That is how far we got. When we reached the middle of The Prairie, who caught up with us but French Christian carrying a tray full of cakes. The moment he saw us his face lit up in a big smile. He was in a terrible hurry, he said, to stock The Loppen Restaurant with a fresh batch of chocolate cakes. Lately, the demand for his product had exploded. It seemed people could not get enough of the stuff. Running as fast as he could, it was all he could do to keep up with demand. It was crazy. If the demand grew any more, he would have to hire somebody. Christian laughed. Morphine Minna and her "flying axe" was now history. And so was the Soup Bowl. Finally he was independent and soon he would have his own cake company. He might open a shop in Paris…

All of a sudden, it was like French Christian remembered something. He shook his head: "It's Fanny," he said and shook his head once more. "She very very wild. She want fuck wif me all the time. And she no respect the cakes. Only fuck, fuck, fuck. She waiting for me now. First, I must fuck, and then I must make cake, fuck and make cake, fuck and make cake…"

Christian's face took on a fatigued look. But almost immediately, the happy smile from before was back: "So… must I go now. Must I do one, maybe two more chocolate cakes today, and Fanny… *Mon Dieu*! Maybe Fanny change her mind and help me!"

Before leaving us, Christian took two chocolate cakes from the tray. One for Melanie and one for me. When Melanie sunk her teeth in the brown mass and nodded her head, he flashed his smile at her, bent forward and gave her a kiss on the cheek. Then, he was gone.

That is how it was that day, enchanted somehow. I cannot speak for Melanie but to *me* it seemed we were dissolving in the very ether that we breathed. Yet our legs kept moving. We kept walking and there was gravity, and then again, it was like we were not moving at all but were rather transformed into the same material that made up the people and buildings too. Melanie had stuck her right arm under my left. Hooked up like that we cruised our zigzag course through Christiania. The Prairie, The Loppen Restaurant and music hall, The Gallopperiet Shop and Gallery, the Soup Bowl, (where we had soup and I told Melanie the story of Erik the Red and the two broken noses), The Green Recycling Hall, The Smithy, The Women's Smithy, the Health Care Clinic, the City Lights Cinema, the Moonfisher Bar, the bicycle repair shop, the Carpenter Shop, The Grey

Hall, the Children's Meadow, the bridge leading across the moat to The Dyssen area.

When we got to the other side, Melanie wanted me to teach her how to pronounce the word "Dyssen." I tried but had to give up because she kept saying something like "Deesen." No matter how hard I tried, I just couldn't make her get the first vowel right.

"All right," she finally said, "but can't you at least explain what that "Deesen" of yours *means* in Danish?

I told her I was not sure but that it gave me associations of a dolmen like structure for the burial of the dead in chambers.

"Oh," Melanie said, "that's real nice! A megalithic sort of cairn. I can hardly wait to see it. Here we come... Necropolis!"

From the bridge we took the direction east and away from the city, passing the old red tiled and angular defense buildings "The School of Fakirs," "Autogena" and "Air-Condition." Eventually, we got to the end of Christiania.

On the way, I told Melanie about the bear. In a little while, I said, what she would get to see was a real beer-drinking brown bear. Melanie stopped and stared at me like I was pulling her leg.

I looked at her: "Would *I* lie to you?"

"No," Melanie said, "I don't *think* you would. But that doesn't mean you don't. After all you *are* a man, and so I can't be too sure. Hand on the Bible: Does *that bear* really drink beer?

"Show me the Bible then!"

Melanie pointed to her beautiful bosom. "Right... there!"

"Right here in public!"

"It's only an oath. Come on!"

I placed my hand on Melanie's soft bosom, heaved a sigh and raised my eyes to Heaven: "By everything that is holy, " I said, "I swear that this bear drinks beer!"

Melanie nodded and I removed my hand: Yes, the bear drank beers. It drank so much in fact that along with the *sadhu* it now ranked among the major tourist attractions. Since the owner was not allowed to charge money, he had put up a sign on the cage saying: "I prefer 'Bear Brew' in opened bottles please!" The reason he enlarged the word 'bottles' was because it infuriated his bear when people brought cans. He even made a little platform where people could put the bottles. The bear would get on his hind legs, grab a bottle with both paws, stick it in his mouth, tilt his head back, and swallow it in one gulp. Then, he would leave the bottle on the ground and burp. People were allowed to feed him as many beers as they liked. The bear would drink until it fell over. That was the end of the show. Trouble was that he had become such a terrible alcoholic, the owner had to bring him a couple of 'Bear Brews' every morning just to get him going. If he forgot or was too drunk himself, the bear would be so hungover it was pitiful. As far as it went, the owner and the bear were two of a kind. Now, the owner was a drunk but formerly he had been a coachman. He had liked the job except it made him feel lonely to sit for hours alone on his seat. So when one of his friends stole a bear and offered him a cheap deal, he bought it to have some company in the coach.

"They say that misery loves company," I said to Melanie.

Melanie shook her head in disbelief:

"So were they sitting next to one another drinking on the seat of that coach?"

"Hell if I know all the gory details," I said.

Although the shadows were now longer the day was not over yet. It seemed intent on going on forever. Melanie was taking everything in and bombarding me with questions. Who? When? Why? How? How many and how much? Especially a whole lot of 'whys'! Even if I didn't know the answers to most of her questions, I tried to answer them all, and when all else failed, I resorted to guesswork. Like when she wanted to know the exact number of administrative sections the Freetown was divided into... or the details pertaining to the political structure... or the financial set-up of the community? "Tell me!" I exclaimed: "Isn't there something you *don't* wanna know?" Again Melanie shook her head. She was a real sucker for information. On top of it, she wanted pictures of everything. In one place it was a twelve-foot totempole that caught her attention. In another, it was the poor bear unfortunately in a coma and on its side after one of its binges. If it was not two little sparrows chirping away for dear life on a rusty bicycle rack, it was a tiny flower that had either made or found a little crack in the asphalt to grow in. Or it was a little dark haired and dirty Christiania girl of six or so standing outside the Smithy with her threadbare teddy bear pressed to her chest, or... a Christiania box-bike parked in front of the green grocer with four little blonde heads sticking out of it, or the Christiania flag with its three yellow suns signifying the three dots in its name waving from a flagpole, or... a potted hibiscus in a windowsill with sleeping cat and two postcards, one of them with love from Madeira, the other carrying the same cargo from Madrid. To Melanie everything was of equal interest. Whether it was a hippie reading in a hammock, a chimney overgrown with moss or an overturned prairie schooner with one wheel missing. Every thing seemed to vie for the attention of her insatiable camera.

"What a refreshing mess this is!" Melanie exclaimed: "And I'm supposed to be a person who loves order. When things are messy, it depresses me. But not here! Here is different. This mess makes me happy. I love how everything is so… so… down-to-earth—man-size. You know, I can re-lax!"

Melanie's eyes shone. She wanted me to know, she re-peated, that she really loved what she was seeing. Except for the drunken bear everything was so… so encouraging. Being a Californian, there was something "Cannery Row-ish" about it. Like the odd assortment of funny homes that people had built along the moat, each mirroring the per-sonality of the builder. Some looked like they had been de-signed by Steinbeck's "Mack and the boys"—the seemingly random way they were stuck together by bunglers, their only function to provide shelter. Others like that pyramid with the Nordic God of a man lying naked on a blanket outside were built for beauty and constructed with love and attention for detail. Some dwellings were examples of refined taste, others of the exact opposite. The whole place was a living jumble full of charm. Just such a little thing as people bicycling next to each other talking and gesticulat-ing! The various enterprises run by collectives and for the common good. So what if such companies could not com-pete with businesses that had money making as their only purpose. The Christiania smithy was a good example. How encouraging it had been for her to see people working in a place they felt belonged to them and producing for people like themselves, for the purpose of these *people's lives* and not for the dismal principle of profit. Did I know how many businesses that were downright destructive to the fabric of life! But even so… if they made money they were accept-ed. Even if it was obviously debilitating, the profit motive was sacrosanct. Yet, in judging the value of an enterprise it wasn't enough just to look at the accounts. The important question that ought to be asked was: to what extent does this activity serve to enhance the real needs of life in the community?

Melanie shook her head. Unfortunately that question was never the one that was asked, never. It was always the other one. So what if things were a bit messy. It allowed us to breathe. Melanie stopped abrubtly and looked directly into my eyes. Someday, she said, I must write about it. I absolutely had to. Why else did I think I had been torn from my comfortable city apartment and planted in Christiania? Would I promise her that? It was important since one day Christiania would not be there anymore. You didn't have to be a prophet to predict that even if it managed to avoid demolition in time, it would give in to the pressure and conform. One day, it would loose its fierce will to independence and a collapse of sorts would follow. It was inevitable. And the collapse would be called a solution to the conflict. Of course, but to all intents and purposes the conflict remained except now the Freetown would be done for. Then, the poet's song was all that would be left. And even if it wouldn't be the same, it would be a damned sight better than nothing, because it meant that hope lived on and freedom could happen again somewhere else. In the final resort, it was a question of grabbing a stick from the blazing fire with which to light another. No matter at what cost, hope had to be kept alive.

While Melanie was sermonizing, I was thinking about the sentences I was laboriously stringing together in the evenings. And even if I had never looked at this activity in that larger context, I now informed Melanie I was "already taking notes."

"No, hold it a sec!" Melanie grabbed my sleeve. "Where do you think you're going?"

We were standing in the middle of the dirt road looking at each other.

"Listen to me Jack," Melanie said, "and listen carefully! Either this story is told and the meaning of Christiania lives on, or it's not and Christiania dies meaning and all. You probably think I'm too excitable and that I exaggerate the importance of the Freetown. To you, I'm probably just another ignorant and starry-eyed American tourist blinded by enthusiasm and talking a wild streak. But believe me, this *is* a question of life and death. Here and elsewhere in the world, people live their lives in hopelessness, squalor and suppression. They need to know that rebellion can succeed. They need to know that it's possible even in an epoch of globalized Capitalism to create a man-sized society where each person is free to pursue his or her fortune without it being at the expense of another. Only by telling the story can these people be encouraged. At this moment as I see it, the world we live in is in desperate need of more Freetowns."

Here Melanie stopped to catch her breath. And thinking that perhaps the sermon was over, I again tried to walk on!

"NO! STAY HERE! I'm not letting you go until you've promised me to write about it."

I nodded.

"Do you promise?"

I nodded again.

"DO you promise then?"

"All right!" I sighed, "I promise."

Melanie smiled and let go of my arm. Now, she said, it was time to take a photo of the "Christiania chronicler as a young man," and without waiting for any consent on my part, Melanie started circling me holding the camera before her eye. Would I please turn my head a little to the right? Would I please lift my chin up and look directly at her... There! Melanie took the picture and removed the camera from her face.

Just think! she went on as we started to walk back the way we had come, how great it would be if Danish society would forget its fear, envy and aversion and instead try to *understand*. Just think if there were some exceptional people out there in "key positions" who would make an effort to learn from the "social experiment" that was Christiania. It would give Denmark an advantage over the rest of its neighbors in Europe. On the day in the not-too-distant future when the inevitable economic crises finally occurred, when there was mass unemployment and general depression, it was important that some record existed that documented how the people of Christiania had learned to live without becoming slaves to the market place. In a time of protracted crisis, it was of "immeasureable" importance that people had learned to build their lives from things of real value. The "market forces, growth and compulsive consumerism" was turning people into statistics and life into a nightmare. It was killing people by degrees the way they were trading in their independence as well as their feeling of personal worth for a place in the capitalist scheme of things. What it amounted to was the total surrender to depression and despondence. Vanity, fear and the groping for possessions tyrannized souls everywhere. People were losing the grip on their lives. Rich as well as poor. But hey! A human being did *not* live by bread and money alone. How was it possible that mainstream culture in our part of the world had lost sight of this obvious truth? And there were more people on the Earth than ever before. Millions and millions were starving and even more were starved for meaning. Porno, the wet dream of rank materialism, was smothering the flame of love under its foul blanket. Increasingly, people were becoming unable to feel anything. All that was left people to experience was their own little pitifully bloated egos growing more and more isolated one from the other, but…

"But… it's not like that here!" Melanie made a sweeping

378

gesture with her hand in the air. Here, the "vicious circle" had apparently been broken. In Christiania, to some extent, people had won back the right to live their own lives. That and much more was what I must write one day. And I should not wait too long either. Now, she knew why we had met. Melanie took my hand and held it in hers. Last night, she thought it was because we should fall for each other and make love. But no! What she had been sent to Denmark to do was to tell me about my responsibility. She, Melanie, was now my friend, just as I, Andreas, was now hers. She too would write about it: the phenomenon that was Christiania. Maybe even for *National Geographic.* Time would tell. But I had to bear the brunt of it since I was the one living it. Why else did I think that I had learned of my calling right before moving to the Freetown? Coincidence, said Einstein, was God's way of appearing incognito among men. This new idea of mine was no accident. If it was, I was free to call her Chunky-doll the rest of our lives.

"Why... Chunky-doll?"

"Just because." Melanie made like she jumped an imaginary rope. "I had a girl-friend once who used to call me 'doll,' and when we were kids, my older brother called me "Chunky" to tease me. So Chunky-doll..."

PART TWO

At the time we had no way of knowing that what the stars had in mind for us took them only twelve hours to accomplish. Perhaps it did not even take them that long. Perhaps it took them twelve *seconds.* In any case, it was done, and from that moment on, the rest of our time together was spent consolidating the bond between us.

In the twenty-nine years that have followed our short one-and-only meeting in Christiania, Melanie and I have written, stamped and sent letters back and forth between the US and Europe. Now and then, we have also come close to crossing each other's paths. But always some little delay or displacement has gotten in the way of our actually seeing each other. Some may say that twenty-nine years only amounts to an insignificant entry in the cosmic ledger. I don't disagree. Still, it's a long time in the brief flash that is a human life. If sometimes I have trouble comprehending this, all I have to do is look around me. During those twenty-nine years, children have been born who are now parents themselves; lap-tops and pocket-size computers have flooded the market and proceeded to suck people's brains from their heads. The cell-phone, the short message service and the e-mail have become the dominant forms of communication; the electronic keyboard has abolished writing in longhand and all but done away with the personal letter on paper; like Aldous Huxley predicted in "Brave New World," large segments of western societies, children as well as adults, are taking antidepressants; an epidemic of obesity without parallel has spread throughout our part of the world; the North and South poles are melting fast as are the glaciers of the Alps and the Himalayas; people are becoming game-addicts at an alarming rate and have to be detoxed in clinics; year by year, school shootings are becoming more common; our daily weather has changed; plastic is everywhere even in the remotest places; robots invade our homes and institutions; chromosome manipulation and artificial insemination are becoming acceptable remedies, and the internet is tightening it's grip on all. In the short time that has passed since Melanie and I met each

380

other in The Wagon Village, man has been taken hostage by technology. As far as life in its most elemental form goes, there is perhaps not much new under the sun, but as far as the terms under which it must be lived are concerned, not much remains the same. Never before has technological progress accelerated so fast and never before has the amount of human confusion and misery been greater.

Then, last fall, Melanie hatched the idea of a reunion in Copenhagen and a visit to Christiania. Of course, at the time, none of us knew what the spring would bring. Melanie had what it took in terms of time, money and enthusiasm. I wrestled with doubt and resentment. Yes, you heard right. The thing is I resent traveling. To old Hans Christian Andersen who traveled throughout Europe by coach, traveling was synonymous with living. Not to *me*. To me, traveling has no more to do with living than time has to do with money. For one thing, traveling to Denmark now would mean breaking up from this lush island in the sea where I have found a new reason to live. I also resent being a tourist. I want to be where I feel at home and not waste energy on logistics. At this stage in life, I want to apply whatever strength I have left to invoking the god of my own making. Those lawgivers, philosophers, artists, mathematicians, poets, dramatists, historians and army commanders that secured for Athens its illustrious renown did so in and around their own city. Plato's sojourn in Sicily was a disappointment, and Henry David Thoreau never ventured further than a week up the Concord and Merrimack rivers. I'm not saying that people don't have fun traveling to far-away and exotic destinations; what I am saying is that the fun they have does not do them much good. It's usually short lived and bought at a high price. And I don't mean the airfare. Awaiting the holiday maker is an account at home that needs to be settled—the same old account in fact. Only now new interest has been added and the settlement has become more difficult.

So I wrote and told Melanie not to count on me. I did not *ever* want to go back to Denmark. Not even for a short visit. And what happens? A few months go by. Then, one afternoon back in the old country, my mother breaks her hip and is taken to the hospital. I am informed of the incident by my brother. Next thing I know, Amiel and I are on a plane to Frankfurt and another to Copenhagen. And what about the woman who hatched the plan of a reunion in Denmark? Well, she has become too busy in the States to go anywhere. The reason is that Coyote, who first became my friend and then (through me) hers, well old Coyote has picked exactly this time to die in a shack on Pine Ridge Reservation where he was born some sixty-eight or seventy years ago.

As I am writing this, I am in a hospital in Copenhagen. To be exact I am standing by the windowsill in the common room adding to this legend in which I intend to bury myself. Hanging from the ceiling is a television set broadcasting a programme about heavy losses incurred on the exchanges around the world, nervous markets, re-adjustments of loans, interest rates and forced evictions—all to the edification of a demented old lady slumping sideways in a wheelchair and babbling away about some picnic she is (definitely not) going on tomorrow. In her room down the hall, Mother is asleep and snoring with her mouth slightly open. My son Amiel is playing backgammon and walking on stilts with his cousin in the cottage of my brother in Northern Zealand. And Melanie...well, she is nursing a dying Indian a million miles away on a reservation in South Dakota.

Life is a joker. It loves nothing better than to make fools of us. With a laugh, it slights all our carefully laid plans. Put a strong magnifying glass to it, and it is made up of the unexpected blows and joys, the grappling with the circumstances, the acqusition and breaking of disabling habits, the correction or cementation of false ideas, narrow escapes, sudden changes of fortune, unsuspected situations plus all the mandatory warts, boils, bunians, corns, varicose veins, infections, prostates and pains in the neck. With the few magnificent exceptions caused by love, only the platitudes and the decay materialize. Nietzsche had come to know life when he wrote: "I want to get better and better at seeing the beauty in everything that is necessary; in this way, I become one of those who beautify things. *Amor fati*. Let that be my love from now on."

I embrace such a resolution wholeheartedly. At this stage, I don't have any other wish or desire than to gain the sort of wisdom that allows one to distinquish between reality and illusion. That sort of wisdom will allow me to see my destiny and to have the courage to let it take its course. I want to pass along the good paths as well as the evil ones. Standing here writing in a smelly Danish hospital, I vow not to worry but to let go. There are the facts of life that I no longer want to look away from. I will face the horrible and the inevitable. I want to be able to look truth squarely in the face without flinching. Nothing ever really begins nor ends. There is movement and that is all. Just like Coyote was fond of telling me. That is also why I'm not going to whip myself if this book is never finished. One day something inside me, some intuition, will make me jot down the two words "THE END." It's going to happen. And yet the story goes on. It will be like after a flood, when people mark the houses to show how high the water stood. It does not signify an end. The water did not go *away*. All it did was sink a little and keep moving. There's the rising and the sinking in the same continuation. Like God's breath, the wind is everywhere and forever. I know because Coyote told me so. The air is laden with it. *Life* is forever. It is indestructible.

Melanie once wrote to me that everybody must help improve the world. I answered her that it was my responsibility to live in it. And that is how I still look at it. It's only in so far as I get better at living in the world that I improve it. That is also where this activity I'm doing on the windowsill comes in. If after all these years I still go on writing, it is because I never found a better way to collect myself and my thoughts. By writing, I remind my forgetful self of who I am and what it is I must do. Writing helps me to tell the unnecessary from the necessary and to lighten my load. It's my way of meditating. Some sit down crosslegged on the floor and hum. I'm so grounded I levitate. As I grow older and the years whirl by at an ever increasing speed, I get the sensation that I'm rushing down a runway. So as to remain sane and not be caught up in the storm, I keep both feet firmly planted on the floor by a windowsill. Stability is the code of the road. As of old, I write such words as these on the loose sheets of paper I always carry with me. I unload the ballast from my hull, to put it in nautical terms. Because this is what I have learned: To navigate safely in dangerous seas, you must not be too heavy. There are hidden rocks and reefs everywhere. Sailing the seas of these white-capped pages, I have to be careful. I glide along calmly. I'm in my right element. Every day is the same. At daybreak, I push my boat off the shore until the scraping sound is gone, and I know I'm free of the land. The whole day I sail, and when at sundown, I return with my catch I pull the boat back up on the beach, fasten it to a rock and sit down in the sand to watch the sun's disc sink into the horizon. There it is, our great planet Earth slowly revolving on its axis and taking me with it. At first, I make a small circle and then I make a larger one containing the first. As the finely attuned seismic instrument that I have become, I register even the tiniest vibrations in the crust. I adjust to the circumstances and add another syllable to the memorial I leave behind. My pen keeps tracing larger circles. Some are neat and even and some have little dents in them. The world is dancing to the tune I hear in my heart. It skips and jumps like a merry waltz. I reckon that if the sun can be happy setting then so can I.

Is it five or ten minutes ago that Mother woke up and the Polish nurse informed me she would be wheeled off to some examination?

So here I am in the empty place left by her bed. The sun is shining on the fresh red tulips that my mother's girl-friend with purple hairdo brought during visiting hours. It is warm in the room. From the flowers, my eyes wander to the closet and from the closet to her roommate's shoes in the corner. There they are, white bordering on grey, with little holes in the skin, abandoned and worn down at the heels. I don't know why those worn heels make me sad—much sadder than is warranted by the wear and tear of life. To shake the feeling I close my eyes and repeat to myself that I don't want anything to be any different from what it is. There are the flowers in the glass vase, the forlorn shoes on the linoleum floor. All of a sudden the picture freezes, nothing moves, and all is quiet around me.

As I said, I am standing in the empty place left by mother's bed when they wheeled her away. If I'm not sad, not sorry and not indifferent, what am I then? I am something that was torn up and is now dangling with its roots in the air. I'm as alone and out of step as one can possibly be. It is visible from my demeanor. Still, it would be a lot worse to be in step. Cut off, I am at least attuned to that forever vibrating tone inside myself. It's all right if I am bleeding. My blood is red and hot and shocking to my surroundings. I no longer give a damn what other people do and think. My course is set. I am the happiest man alive.

This is more or less what I wrote last night in the letter to Melanie, which is still unstamped in my pocket. After letting her in on the unexpected form that my happiness has taken, I promise to keep her ajour with everything going on here in Copenhagen. I even promise to send her the last bits of this book as I write them. In that way, she and Coyote can be involved. It's really a form of incantation on my part, a way of ensuring that it happens. I'm no angel. I made mistakes, failed people who deserved better and was hard headed in many ways. But once I give my word, I stick to it. The way I see it, giving your word is a way of depositing part of yourself with someone else. The promise ties us together with a tiny little string along which it is possible to move back and forth. Licking the back of the stamp and placing it in the top right corner of the envelope, I tell Melanie what I think about us. To me, we are two line dancers on a telegraph line suspended above the same abyss. We both know that one wrong step is fatal. A few days later, the letter arrives in her mailbox with a kiss from me on the back of the stamp. This kiss contains my DNA, and my DNA contains my word. When Melanie opens the box and takes the letter in her hand, her DNA mixes with mine and the sacred communication is consummated. Who cares that it's no longer common for two people to write paper letters to one another? As long as Melanie and I are doing it, the line has not been broken. And if Nietzsche is right when in "The Gay Science" he writes that the form and the spirit in which letters are written characterize their time and age, well, then, there's no better description of ours than this correspondence.

Melanie is the cross on the worn map of Treasure Island indicating where my treasure is hidden. She is my backup against such calamities as fire, power failure, flood, burglary, meteors, homicide, war, plague, famine and disabling disease. The fact that I didn't expect to see her any time soon, made me inclined to tell her the truth in my letters. At present, I'm back in Denmark. My return ticket is open and good for a year. I have a Danish passport. If I wish, I can stay until they put a tag on my toe and cremate me.

Let me see… How long have I been here now? Twelve-thirteen days. In the course of this period, I have visited Christiania three times. The first thing that struck me was how much it has changed. The Prairie, for example, that used to be an empty expanse with nothing but pushers and puddles, has been turned into a veritable forest of oak, cherry plum and poplar trees called "The Forest of the Future." Standing under the tall trees and listening to the wind in the treetops, the name reminded me what happens to a man when he turns his back on his place: no sooner is he out the door before the forest grows up behind him in which he will lose his way if ever he returns.

There, I was back again after all these years, and I was not sure how I felt about it. I had bent my head back. In my ears, the sound of the wind in the trees blended with the hollow banging and crashing sounds from a nearby skateboard house I had never seen before. The foliage flickering in the rays of the sun sprinkled green color on the infinite blue of the sky above my head. If I settled in the old country would I be able to integrate? It would not be easy. What had been before was no more. There was no returning, not after all that had happened. Official Denmark and its institutions were like so much dead skin to me. The only things left for me to settle back into were the trees, the beaches, the animals, the people and the language.

When a bit later, I moved on it struck me that Pusher Street was just a shadow of its old self. I only counted about a dozen pushers. The hash-stands were gone, and there was no hash on display. The closest I got to the way it used to be was a pusher who opened his hand and showed me two flat pieces of green Moroccan. Somehow, it gave me a funny feeling. Like there had been a flood before I got there. Later in the evening at the main train station waiting for a train, I read in a magazine that since the government ordered the police to break up the Christiania monopoly, the hash trade had spread to just about every neighborhood of the city. In the article, it said that the police had made "a huge effort" to impede the users' access to purchasing hash; this effort, however, had cost hundreds of millions of Danish crowns and helped create the new immigrant gangs now engaged in violent warfare with Hells Angels over the market shares. And as if that were not enough, the new "no tolerance" policy towards Christiania meant that where formerly a young person out to purchase hash was offered only what he had come for, he now had the choice of drugs like heroin, coke, amphetamines etc. Standing there in the kiosk, I could not help but think back on the time when, still married, I participated in a couple of raids on heroin pushers. It was during the "Junk-blocade" of 1979 when over several months, inhabitants and pushers of Christiania ganged up on all users and pushers of "hard drugs." The Freetown offered treatment to the former and expelled the latter. As far as I knew, there had not been "hard" drugs like crack and heroin sold at Christiania since that time. Hash, yes, and tons of it too, but nothing else. The local hash tycoons were making such enormous sums they'd had sense enough to guard their trade monopoly against other drugs, even if at times this protection meant using force and weapons.

But if there was less hash on Pusher Street than there used to be, there was also more police. In the two and a half hours I spent in Christiania the first time, I counted thirty-some cops in riot gear. They walked about in groups of seven or eight, entering businesses and bars where they frisked people at random. The first group I encountered in The Moonfisher Café where they were interrogating a young woman. After some time, they took her outside and forced her to take off her clothes behind some trees. But that was not all. Just like sharks have a pilot fish that follows them everywhere, there was this guy who followed them around filming them with his camera. The difference was that where the shark doesn't seem to care and is used to the presence of the little pilot fish, the cops were uncomfortable being stalked by that guy. Now and then, one or two of them would turn around to glare at him through their visors, and once, three cops also stepped up to him and said something I didn't catch. They probably told him to get lost or they would take him to the station. In any case, it did not help. The guy knew them, and they knew him. What I was witnessing was obviously an old story repeating itself.

Even so the atmosphere was pretty damn rotten. Most of the people the cops met on their way ignored them and went on doing what they were doing. But on Pusher Street, there were also people who yelled at them. It reminded me of the pictures from the occupation that my grandfather once showed me. Only then, the people's hatred was directed at the German soldiers. Coming from a peaceful place like I did, it felt a bit like martial law. And yet this was normal procedure now. It had been like this for years, supposedly to combat terror. Body-searching people at random no longer required a warrant, for example. Or nobody gave a damn about the warrant any more. Either way, it seemed that the cops did whatever they wanted to. The very exis-

389

tence of a citizen in the street with no apparent reason for being there warranted a search.

"Freedom of Expression," it said in big rusted letters placed across an iron miniature of The Statue of Liberty out in front of the Communal Kitchen on Pusher Street. With silent sarcasm, it was witnessing the frisking of a guy going on a few feet away. Taking in the scene, I was struck by how everything had been turned upside down. Back in 1971, the abandoned garrison was occupied sort of pel-mel by a bunch of hippies sharing their dream of a freer and more just community, and today the very same community was occupied by the state police in combat gear with only their orders and the monthly pay checks on their minds. And half an hour later, when I was relating these thoughts to a young guy out in front of The Moonfisher Café, I was told he no longer felt like a Dane. He and his little circle of friends, the guy said, felt like so many numbered inmates on a temporary parole from the correctional institution called Denmark. That's how he put it. He also said that the searchings of private homes, the friskings of ordinary people, the telephone tappings and the confiscations were all part of an effort by the Danish State to "normalize" Christiania. There was a great wave of standardization and coercion washing over the country. "Law and order fascism," is what he labeled it…

The guy seemed overjoyed to have run into a former christianite like myself who had not been around for many years. He could not wait to fill me in. The thing that impressed me the most was that he used the words 'normalize' and 'regime' about the situation. It was one thing for the regime, he said, to behave like an occupying power and quite another for it to make use of the rhetoric. The fact, that it did not even need a fig leaf any more! Twenty years had passed since the totalitarian regimes behind the Iron

Curtain had fallen and here were the rulers of Denmark making use of the exact same rhetoric. Twenty short years, I thought. If in *my* time, the time of Christiania's birth, the Danish authorities had made public a wish to 'normalize' the population or even a small part of it, people would have been outraged. Perhaps there would have been an uprising. After all, 'normalize' was the word used in 1968 by the Warzaw Pact led by The Soviet Union to justify the occupation of Czechoslovakia. Even many Danish communists were shocked. No politician in his right mind would have dreamt of taking such a word as 'normalization' into his mouth. Fourteen years old at the time, I remember how my father (who had fled Czechoslovakia after the communists came to power in 1948) was furiously wringing his hands as he watched the Soviet tanks in the streets of Prague on the family's black and white TV-set. Asking Papa what was going on, he told me that the Soviet Union was using its military might to crush an experiment in democratic socialism called The Prague Spring. Kremlin wanted to 'normalize' the Czechs. But that word, my Papa said, belonged to the vocabulary of totalitarianism. It meant that from now on, the Czechs would be forced to live the grey zombie-like existence that the rest of the Soviet Block lived.

As I was listening to this young guy sitting out in front of The Moonfisher Café, I began to feel nauseated. It started like a lump in the throat. From there it sunk into my belly where it wound up a few minutes later coming up again in the form of an ulcerous burp. Grimacing, I swallowed the burning mucus. When the attack was over, I told the guy about how the Soviets stamped out whatever was left of the freedom of the Czechs and the Slovaks. I told him of the oppressive 'normalized life' forced on the population in the years that followed the invasion. At one point, I even became lyrical and said, that "the smile had been chiseled off the Czech people's faces." Now it was *his* turn to listen. It turned out Oluf was born in 1980. He neither knew of the occupation of Czechoslovakia nor the details of the squatters' occupation of the Boatman Street Garrison in the fall of 1971. But he was very active in his "environment," he assured me. He was living in one of the houses or "structures" that the State had decided were going to be demolished. He hung on in spite of the fact that he had been evicted. He refused to move. No way was he going to budge. A few days ago, it had become too much for his girlfriend—the tension of waiting for the police. She had found a room to rent in the city. In a way, he could understand her, he said. He too hated the uncertainty of not knowing when the cops would show up with their implements of destruction. But what was a guy to do? His girl friend agreed with him but thought he was too stubborn. He was only hurting himself, she said. "But, hey!" my new friend exclaimed, "it isn't like I'm aiming to hurt anybody else, is it?" In his opinion, she was missing the point. He had to defend himself. If the law made everything he believed in illegal, then was it the law that should be changed or him? And how was he going to live with himself after obeying an unjust law? His girl friend had studied his face quietly. Then, she shook her head and said there were unjust laws all over the place. That's what *she* thought. But even if she was right, still there was no way he was going to let them dick him around. In fact, only yesterday he had decided to add a bay window to his house. The inspectors would see it as a provocation where to him it was a statement. Today, he had bought some materials. Tomorrow, he would start. He would have to watch out or he would probably fall off the roof. It made his heart pound just thinking about it. Would it take the inspectors two days, a week or a month to find out? No matter what, it was a special feeling to be building and not knowing if they were going to show up the next morning at four to arrest him and tear it all down.

"Are you serious?" I asked. "I thought that over the years Christiania had entered into several formal agreements with the Danish State. How can it suddenly have become illegal to live in a house on the moat?"

My new friend lit a cigarette and explained that it had to do with the unlawful Christiania Act passed by Parliament in 2004. According to this Act, the agreements I was talking about had been declared null and void. The Christiania I lived in was long gone, and now the Christiania we knew today was going to be destroyed. For example, the "human habitations" along the moat were going to be torn down and all the trees felled so the fortifications could be returned to their "original state!" The unique way that nature now blended with culture was of no account and would be demolished. The government could hardly wait to get started. About a month ago, he was offered a "pretty large" sum of money by the State if he would tear down his own house.

Oluf's expression was one of disgust and amazement: "But why would I?" he asked, "tear down my own house? What do they take me for? Do they think I'm as corrupt as they are? Don't they see that offering me money is like adding insult to injury? Either they—still—haven't gotten it—I mean that this is a struggle for liberty, or they really *are* just the goddamned sickos they look like."

When we had discussed this question for a while, Oluf told me how the Danish State had given all of Christiania a similar offer: Either the Freetown helped it's oppressors in the digging of its own grave and by so doing gained some influence on the result, or it was liquidated in cold blood and buried by the authorities. Christiania had a year to decide if it would accept doing away with its collective ownership and, in return, get a huge bag of money from a rich fund to start new building projects. It was a very sneaky move by the regime that left room for only a "yes" or a "no." The tempting prospect of money, private ownership of property, peace and acceptance as opposed to living with the threat of demolition was too much for a lot of christian-ites. With this offer, the regime had driven a wedge right down the middle of Christiania, dividing it into two fac-tions.

"Imagine reaching a unanimous decision on a matter like this!" Oluf said shaking his head.

I nodded: "The way you're talking about it reminds me of the Jews in the concentration camps. The insane offer made to some of them to either help the authorities fill and empty the gaschambers, or of being snuffed out immedi-ately. Some chose to do it because they saw it as a chance to survive, others decided there'd be no point in surviving even if they lived and said no.

"Does that comparison really hold water?" Oluf asked.

"Yes, psychologically it does," I said. Of course, it makes a difference whether you gas people or you just demolish everything they have, cherish and believe in. Sure! But the difference isn't as great as it seems. I mean, whether you kill people, or make it impossible for them to live the life they've chosen for themselves. In both cases, the oppressor says: "All of you folks are going to be annihilated. You now have the choice between ignominious postponement and immediate execution. If you prefer the former press one, if the latter press two! According to the Polish sociologist Zygmunt Bauman, this was how the civil servants of the Nazi bureaucracy went about implementing the decisions made by the political leadership."

Had he ever heard of Bauman's book *Modernity and Ho-locaust?*

Oluf shook his head like he would not hear of any names. He clenched his teeth and rapped his box of matches against the edge of the table.

After a minute or so he looked at me again and nodded. Yes, he said, it was hard—both because it was hard to think like that but also because of all the hard feelings fostered in the process of reaching the decision to reject the State's offer. It had ripped the population of Christiania apart causing a wound that would not heal anytime soon. Instead of accepting the so-called offer, Christiania had taken the Danish State to court claiming squatters' rights. At least now, the healing process had a chance to begin. Finally. The process had been *so* emotional. On one side, there had been the argument that Christiania needed peace with the State and would never get an offer that was better. On the other side, there was a feeling that accepting it was selling out and giving up autonomy. Deep down, people on both sides knew that accepting the offer was in fact abandoning Christiania. But for those christianites who stood to gain most from the transaction, it was preferable to trade in Christiania for a sense of security. What I had to consider, Oluf explained, was that there were a lot of people now living in Christiania who were already normalized. Some were even normalized *before* they moved there. Among them were some who had invested lots of energy and money in their houses; over time, they had also developed a taste for spending the dark part of the year in their cottages in Greece, France or Portugal. Some of them even lived off state pensions while having to pay only a small user's rent. They were adept when it came to sponging off both the welfare system and Christiania. For people like these who, say, occupied whole floors in spaceous houses, the one major drawback was the uncertainty. What they wanted was to make peace with the State and stay where they were in their comfortable circumstances. For them, the spiritual dimension of Christiania, the old hippie dream of an autonomous Freetown liberated from the State of Denmark, was only worth something in so far as it could be bargained away. Except for that, it was downright silly, even meaningless. Listening to them argue that "new times" required "new solutions," he always had the feeling that it was fear and self interest that drove them. In their own eyes, they had simply outgrown the old hippie nonsense. But hey! Truth was truth. Truth never became obsolete. So, when they said it was time to start "something new," what they really meant was that it was time that their privileges were finally secured. And another thing! As it was, they could not capitalize the investments they had made in their dwellings. But if the collective users' rights were abolished and "normal" private ownership introduced, they would find themselves in fat city with no danger of eviction. Perhaps they could even sell their property in Christiania and move permanently to Portugal. And if they chose to stay, they would no longer have to put up with their neighbors, when these neighbors complained they were living alone on an entire floor in a house and paying less for a hundred and fifty square meters than the family of three was paying for a shack of twenty. "We want legalization now!" they shouted as if in one voice. They were sick and tired of a consensus democracy where each individual, no matter how broke, stupid and drunk, had a voice and permission to use it at the common meetings. What they wanted was the permanent rule of the majority over the minority just as it was in the world outside. Dreaming of having their circumstances legalized, they wanted to establish one or more housing associations complete with boards of directors. They wanted a fund with billions in its coffers to buy the property and the building rights. If they had their way, new tall and innovative structures would be erected, and the people who were educated and understood how to run associations and desired to sit on directional boards could run the show.

Unfortunately for them, it was not going to happen. Oluf and his hardcore nay sayers would see to that. Who the hell cared for a Christiania that was no longer an alternative? Big multi-national companies certainly would not give a shit about it anymore. By the way, did I know that companies such as Coca Cola and Nike had studied Christiania to find out how it had managed to get such a megabrand? They were swimming in money, but here was something money couldn't buy. It baffled them. How was it possible that they had spent millions on their brands without achieving anything even close to what Christiania had created for itself *inadvertently?* What was the secret?

Oluf looked at me: Christiania was not corporate capitalism for Christ's sake. You didn't register living dreams on the Dow Jones, did you! Christiania was a Freetown goddammit, a refuge for outlaws. It was not for sale, and it could not be normalized. "Long live Christiania halleluja-halleluja."

Having delivered this little speech, Oluf studied my face and asked if I was not bored by all his talk. I assured him I wasn't and that he was welcome to go on if he wished. I was happy to listen.

Oluf then hit the still fresh pack of cigarettes against his finger and pulled one out with his lips. Putting a flame to it, he grinned, blew smoke out his nose and pointed at the cigarette: "Political correctness would like to make it illegal to smoke these too—and to make it illegal for boys to get into fights in school yards—and to pay a woman for sex." He sighed. As if boys had not always fought and men bought sex from women! Men bought sex in all kinds of ways either directly with money or indirectly with other things! The way it was going, pretty soon there would not be a living soul in the land who was not a criminal. A man had the right to pollute, sell shit, harass his employees, report on his neighbors for social fraud, destroy his competitors and indulge his greed for money in every way. But if in all modesty he chose to live his own life as a free human being—*that* was going too far. That was illegal. Just think what would happen to the economy if everybody did that! No, it was much better that everybody watched everybody else and suspicion poisoning the air! To him, Oluf said, it was obvious that in this dispute over Christiania there was so much more at stake than just the fate of a little Freetown in Denmark. In peoples' minds Christiania stood for the inalienable right to live your own life and not to be a useful idiot. And in that way, it really *was* the clash between cultures that a prime minister had recently introduced. The situation *was* critical. Where would we all be, if Christiania were no longer there as a place where people could go and hang out when they needed a time-out from insanity? He was serious! Outside, in the society at large, people were now so afraid, the fear was making them ill. They were fearful of just about everything and looked to the State health services for help, which was like chickens asking the wolf for protection. It was a fatal mistake really. As long as people were still willing and able to work, the regime and its economy had no interest in curing them of their fear. Helping yes, but curing no! Helping provided it with a pretext to penetrate the private sphere everywhere. Helping allow it to make demands. One way or another, the State made sure to have something on every single individual rich or poor. Oluf laughed. It would not surprise him, he said, if soon there would be a law against sleeping naked, or against *not* purchasing and not spending a minimum of two hours a day on your P.C.

More than ever, Oluf went on, it was now time to put up resistance. Evil forces were on the march, and the Freetown was called on to take the lead. If only today's Christiania were not so enfeebled by inner tensions and compromises. If only it had been its old strong self. If only it would believe in itself again, then everything it stood for could success-fully resist *any* regime. That is what he thought anyway. Standing up for what it stood for, the Freetown would not even need lawyers to defend it in the Supreme Court. In a couple days, there was going to be another grand meeting. And for the first time in six months, he was going to it. For a long time, the only thing on the agenda had been how to make Christiania perform a lobotomy or by-pass operation on itself. Thank God that was over now. Perhaps now, it would be possible to discuss what direction was best for a Christiania that still belonged to itself—what to do when the court-case was lost and the regime threatened to demol-ish it in the name of democracy and law and order? The meeting was going to be in The City Lights movie-theater, if I would like to go, or I could pay him a visit where he lived down in the Hogweed region.

I told him I would like to do both. After all these years, it would be interesting to experience a communal meeting again, to see how things had changed. But unfortunately it was not convenient. There was also my son to think about. At the earliest, I would be back in Christiania in a week.

"All right, then," my new friend said. "All you have to do is get yourself to The Hogweed Area and ask for Oluf. I'll feed you hot Indian Daal and cold water. Bring the kid along. He'll have spaghetti with garlic and organic tomato sauce."

Oluf tore a page out of a little paper block he carried in his shirt pocket, scribbled his phone number on it and handed me the slip.

"Call me," he said.

I have not been to Christiania since. It was not possible, and yesterday, there was another letter from Melanie. Now, I owe her three. It was posted from Pine Ridge Reservation, South Dakota. Besides mentioning some Indians I have never heard of, she mentions a young red haired guy, Robert Dean, who looks exactly like an illustration of the Pied Piper of Hamelin in a childhood book of hers. Robert showed up out of the blue carrying only a little rucksack and clarinet box. He had hitched from Ohio, where he was born. The last twelve years, he had lived in Prague, which was where he met Coyote. He has come all the way from Central Europe to say goodbye to his friend. "Suddenly one dusty noon," Melanie wrote, as she was making tortillas on the little gas burner and listening to Bonnie Rait's "Love in the Nick of Time" on the transistor radio, there was a knocking at the door. When she opened, Robert Dean had looked at her and smiled "that shy smile of his."

No sooner had he let out the first syllable when they heard el Coyote's voice coming from the couch: "Jesus fucking Christ... Is it...HIM? Couldn't you have warned me so I'd had a chance to make a get-away?"

This was how the two of them interacted, Melanie said. But apparently that was how it was supposed to be. Her presence made no difference. Except to her, of course! It was a bit tiring, she confessed, the way they constantly teased each other, bickered and got on each other's case. Obviously, Robert loved Coyote more than anyone on the Planet, and obviously Coyote enjoyed Robert's company. At first, Melanie thought Coyote was too hard on the young man. Then, she realized that "the redneck," as Coyote called him, was hardly defenseless. He managed to get in quite a few jabs himself.

The two men had met when, ten years before, Robert entered Coyote's tex-mex restaurant on Karlovo Namesti in Prague looking for a job. "If you know how to wash dishes, then you're my man," Coyote told him. Robert said that he did and was taken on. He was a kind and quiet clarinet player with a sharp mind and a subtle sense of humor. When Coyote teased him about something, he would wait until he was done and pay him back in the same coin. It was great that he had showed up. No. It was necessary. A necessary little miracle is what it was. For Coyote's condition was getting worse from day to day. Only a week ago, he had been visibly stronger. Now, he was so exhausted he could hardly walk any more. It was painful to see him drag himself around huffing and puffing like "an old time plains' locomotive" while smoking one Gauloise after another. Still, he refused to stop. He was not the kind who let down his friends in the hour of need. The Gauloises were helping him make the transition to the eternal hunting grounds. Bless them. And besides, there were cigarettes in stock just waiting to be turned into smoke. Coyote preferred to die from the life he had led rather than from some life of abstension that had never been his. In order to get a fresh start on the other side, he needed to wipe the slate clean here on this.

Coyote was so stubborn, Melanie said. He would have his cigs, but no way would he see a doctor. Since he had never seen a doctor in this life, he saw no reason to see one now that it was too late anyway. White man's medicine men were anathema to him. If Melanie ever brought such a person to his door, he said, he would scalp the bastard on the spot.

That was Coyote. Deadly ill with cancer, he was still

the grumpy, cantankerous, and laughing old devil he had always been. And that's how he would remain until his last gasp. But was that not why we all loved him because he was like some reprocessing plant for upgrading the atoms of life? Was that not why we honored and revered him? Alone among the millions of bound individuals he had remained free and savage, relying magnificently upon himself in every situation. A reading and writing and horseback riding Indian outlaw with no red tape attached. A fearless and independent man not mired in the same shit as the rest of us. An example!

Now, Melanie went on, just take the way el Coyote defied the grim reaper by laughing clouds of Gauloise smoke in his face. What was there to be afraid of? Did he not know himself to be an integral part of the circle? Absolutely yes! He certainly did not suffer from the lethal notion that death was some terrible end to life, something to be shunned and postponed. He didn't fear anything in this world or beyond. Not only was he allied with Tatanka he was also allied with the wind on the Great Plains. The wind that was forever! He was even allied with his Gauloises, for that matter. They were going to be forever too. In his own kingdom, he was an absolute monarch doing as he damn well pleased. If his cigs were his friends and allies, he would go to prison for them or even die. What his heart chose to associate with was as much a part of him as a kidney or an arm. A MAN THINKING is what he was. Never would it occur to him to model himself on some momentary whim hatched by the world of fashion. He wore his shirt as he pleased. And now, he had the first buffalo hunt in the eternal hunting grounds to look forward to. There was beef jerky in his saddle bags, and he would travel light in consideration of horse. The load of bitterness and complaints he carried not. Instead of wasting his time on this earth, he had devoured every second of it. He had taken his chances and paid his dues. He had fought, won and lost. Several times, he had nearly died. One time, he had crashed a small air plane somewhere in the Black Hills and broken just about every bone in his body. Still he survived.

Now, however, it was time to break camp. Behind him, Coyote had the limitless grassy plains of his childhood where Tatanka grazed in the tens of thousands. Nothing on earth surpassed the sight of such a herd in grandeur and beauty. Stretching all around him was the vast emptiness of space. He was the wandering fire point where eternities intersect and galactic sparks fly from star to star in the dusty realms of heaven. On his feet, he wore "space boot-moccasins," and in his hand, he held the wanderer's staff. The universe was one big uterus, and it made no difference if one was coming or going. Any time was a good time to die. "A man," el Coyote said looking Melanie in the eye, "could be a president, professor or pope, yes, and he might even be a poet and pen pusher like that Andreas Stein back in old Europe. That's all very well, but if he ain't a warrior too, he ain't shit!"

Contrary to what people thought, the world that Coyote was soon to depart from was more lifeless than the man dying in it. "Two billion Chinese, a western woman, and a pale-faced white man reaping what he'd sowed!" That's how it was. Sometimes, when Coyote spoke, it seemed like he had already joined his shaman grandfather, Washtay, the storyteller, and the forefathers. Yes, and Tatanka too… Tatanka the buffalo his people were allied with. "Time would tell," wrote Melanie. However, Coyote was still with us, and he still spoke. But his pains were getting worse every day, and soon, he would need morphine, so if I could spare a dime, now was the time to send it!

An hour and a half ago, I transferred one thousand dollars to Melanie's account in New Mexico.

Sometimes on a nice day, the three of them would take a spin in the Lincoln Continental. When back in America, Coyote realized that the journey to the eternal hunting grounds was drawing close he had bought the sumptuous automobile with what remained of his money. It was in "his white hearse," as he called it, that he had transported himself and the cartons of Gauloises *sans filtre* from New York to the reservation. It was parked in an empty lot about a hundred yards from the shack. Not quite as sparklingly white as in its hey-day perhaps, somewhat dusty really, but still flashy, especially in the wretched squalor that surrounded them on all sides. Its former owner was a gangster with arthritis in his knees who had been shot one day as he got out of the car on Long Island. Coyote bought it in cash from the driver who was a former baseball star and needed to get it off his hands quick. The engine had only about forty thousand miles on it. It was a real bargain.

Robert drove. On the seat next to him, Coyote sat like some spineless doll swaying now this way now that. "Why don't you put on the seat-belt?" Robert would suggest in his quiet way. "Hell no," Coyote would retort. Behind them, Melanie had the enormous red-upholstered back seat to herself. It felt funny, she wrote, to cruise aimlessly around on the horrible reservation roads in a chrome-plated Continental, right as if they were in Beverly Hills. Sometimes the Indians came out of their shacks and hogans and stared as they went by in a cloud of dust on their way to nowhere in particular. But time was hanging heavy on their hands and the little excursions in the hearse lightened the load. The main thing was that Coyote loved it. Sometimes, when they hit a hole in the road, Coyote's face would twist in discomfort. "Stay out of the ruts, or I'll scalp you," he would say to Robert with that hoarse toothless laugh of his. His sense of humor was still intact. Perhaps a tad more cynical and morbid but otherwise the same! He still enjoyed life—the little bit of it he had left.

But how was life in Copenhagen? Melanie demands to be briefed on "everything," but with special attention to the situation for that "reservation of non-conformist pale-faces called Christiania?" She wants to hear everything in detail, including the prospects for the future. And as if this is not enough, she has also ordered an account of the last year I lived in Christiania. It's something I have owed her for a very long time, she says. Why didn't I stay? As far as she knows, it's not common for people to move out of Christiania once they get a foot in the door. Not only am I requested to write her this—it's even my duty to because I promised to do it long ago. Postponement is no longer acceptable. As far as she is concerned, she's still not sure she'll make it to Denmark to join me, but *if* she does, it means that a new cycle is set in motion. And if she does not, well, then, it's all the more reason to pay my back debts.

I started when I read the sentence about she still not being sure she would make it to Denmark. I thought she had dropped the idea. Even if it's good news, I must admit the prospect makes me uneasy. For what happens if el Coyote is called to the eternal hunting grounds right now as I am sitting here in my coat writing on my brothers porch? The funeral over, maybe Melanie will get in the Continental, drive straight to the nearest airport and fly to Denmark. Then, it's she who shows up out of the blue. And even if it won't be as unexpected as Robert Dean showing up in Pine Ridge, it will catch me unprepared. The thought of the eternal correspondents physically confronted with one another makes my heart skip a beat.

What next? It's not quite noon yet, and son has gone with my sister-in-law to the library and the grocery store. Let me think! Why did *I* leave Christiania when so many did not? Did I love life in Christiania any less than my neighbors? I don't think so. It was not that. The difference was that I would never become the writer I wanted to become if I stayed. When I left the Freetown, it had done for me what, unknowingly, I had come there for it to do. I had been freed, was on my own and ready to move on. Now that the metamorphosis had taken place, there was something (my intuition perhaps) whispering in my heart's ear that it was time for me to tear myself loose even from the people and places I loved most. The close communal life we shared, its many pleasures, its responsibilities, everything. On the one hand, there was the music, the partying, the drinking, the women, the mutual interdependence and the responsibility to join, if not *all* the communal projects, then at least *some* of them; on the other hand, there was my newfound calling which made its claims on me. "My life is the poem I would have writ, but I could not both live and utter it!" Thoreau knew my dilemma and expressed it beautifully. I had moved to Christiania in order to put the past behind me, take a new direction and begin to learn how to write. It had happened. I'd found what Christian called '*joie de vivre*' again and gotten started in the occupation I have pursued ever since. Still, in my heart of hearts, I knew that if ever I was to penetrate to the deeper regions, to remove the upper layers of crust beneath which the true story lies soaked in blood waiting to be brought to light, I had to shut down activity in other areas. In order to walk down one corridor and stay in it until the end, I had to close the doors to the other corridors.

Even so, I am not sure I would have succeeded in tearing myself loose if it had not been for the interference of my guardian angel. Yes, today, I am convinced it was no other than the angel that saved me from dissipation by giving me the kick in the pants that sent me back out across the border. But that's another story, and we will save it for a bit later.

Conscious of my need to move on but not wanting to, I'm still there in the wagon. Yet, even if I lingered longer than I should have, it's something I will neither regret nor forget. It was great.

It was early fall and the leaves were turning yellow. Some had already fallen and lay scattered on the ground. Even though the calendar still showed September, we had all started to make little fires in our wood stoves. A stick or three in the mornings, when we woke, and the same in the early evenings. The firewood was something Jakob had bought cheap from the forest ranger at Tisvilde Hegn whom he knew from his days at gardening school. The load had been delivered in mid-April. For the most part, it consisted of beechwood, but there was also some oak. The truck had dumped it in sizes ranging from a half trunk to a quarter trunk. There was a veritable mountain of wood, and for an entire week, we sawed and split and piled it up into large circular woodpiles of such elegant shapes they reminded me of huge pine cones. Now that summer was over and September half gone, it was time to start using it.

What a pleasure, it was to wake in the morning and like some *Midgard* Giant, without a stitch on, walk across the bouncy floor in its short length, stick my feet in the black clogs, step into the open doorway, lean against the door post, breathe in the cool and scented morning air while contemplating the wood smoke rising out of the neighbors' chimneys. There was a quiet devoutness about such moments. I mean to be standing there like some hairy Cro-Magnon man listening to the not-so-distant palaeolithic whisper of automobiles rushing headlong down macadamized streets to their owners' work-places, immoveable stoic with the mellow feeling that Jakob, Ragma, Old Knud, John, Hanne, Gurli Elizabeth, Line and Douglas like me, had turned their backs on the workaday world and were just now waking up. Right at this moment, they, too, were probably done making fires and about to cook the morning porridge. Add to this, the visceral awareness of Lili lying warm, naked and temptingly soft only a few yards behind me on the bed where we had made love and held each other tight. To have emerged from the murky depths into one's opening, like the king-snail with its palace on its back, taking a wide view of its personal kingdom: the settlers' wagons in their circle, the smoke rising soundlessly in windswept little columns; the trees, bushes, rabbit-cages, bicycles, bee-hives and birds; the junk, the yellow metal gas-bottles Old Knud hid under his wagon; the rickety tower up on the rampart, the tipi, the sky above and the laundry suspended from clothes-lines drying in the air. The hammock and Cherie, the horse belonging to Ragma, newly back from half a year in the East. In short, to be healthy and sound, standing on my own doorstep, seeing life and creation unfold before me and declaring it all for good and right and as it should be. Every blessed thing including all the shit. The evil. The exploitation. The greed, delusion and fraud. Simply once and for all to be crying 'yes' to it all. 'Yes,' 'yes' and 'yes' over and over again like a mantra. 'Yes' to the whole package. How great it was to be twenty-eight, to have lived through a crisis, to still have the full use of your five senses, not to mention the ability to move crab-like in all directions at once. Or, for that matter, to be able to stay put right where you were. To feel that you are finally master in your own house. To have both feet solidly planted on your own bouncy floor and being your own measure for things, people and situations. To live by your own criteria and set your own standard. Like an absolute monarch to have your own fated place in the world.

But hey! What is it I see moving over there? Could it be Jakob appearing with the usual teapot and the just as usual cup? I dare say it is. And now, he sits down, bends forward and pours tea into the cup. He pushes his ass closer to his shack to make himself more comfortable. Look at that loafer. In order better to soak up the rays of the morning sun, he leans his head against the doorpost. For some reason, the sight of Jakob sitting there like that reminds me of a stanza from Whitman's poem "Salut au Monde," which I read a couple nights before. It had filled me with such ecstatic joy I didn't sleep until the wee hours. And right over there, the lines are embodied in the way Jakob nonchalantly lounges about:

"Oh, while I live to be the ruler of life, not a slave, to meet life as a powerful conqueror, no fumes, no ennui, no more complaints or scornful criticisms."

These words have stayed with me ever since. Like an echo ringing from one age to another, they are to me the very definition of earthly happiness. Even if circumstances have changed and not much is the same as in Whitman's time, they still gladden my heart; even if I am no longer the young man I used to be, they still give me courage. I like to think of myself as walking evidence that the tidal wave of time has so far thrown itself against this utterance in vain. Walt was a man, and so am I. His were the words of my youth, and to this day, they reset my mind and heart whenever I stall. It encourages me to think that when a man like Walt cries out his faith from his inner mountaintop, it will be heard in distant places a century and a half later? Newton wouldn't have known what to make of it, since indeed there is something here that defies the laws of physics.

Before my inner eye, I see myself saying goodnight to my Dad as he sits bent, grey and weary reporting his income to the tax authority. I don't like seeing him like this and pledge never to do it myself. Declaring income and filling out forms is most definitely *not* the conqueror's way. I want to live and so refuse to let the time of my life be expropriated by institutions and activities that are demeaning and unnecessary. I insist on being free of the entire catalogue of humiliating preoccupations poisoning and paralyzing the soul. I'm not born to be an accountant, and neither have I any ambition to be a cash register. I detest speculations about money and other substitutes foisted on me. I will unwrap life from its packaging and learn from Jakob, when he sits on his doorstep and enjoys a cup of tea in the morning sun.

I was looking at Jakob from my post in the open door. If I felt like it, I could at any time walk the twenty paces that separated us; I could lift my hand, say "good morning" and sit down next to him on the doorstep. Like two schoolboys with a day off, we could sit around and be quiet or talk about whatever came into our minds. And if it so pleased me, I could choose to shift my weight from one foot to the other and look on from the distance without budging an inch. It occurred to me that the situation served to illustrate the declaration of independence formulated in the early days by the Freetown's founding fathers—to establish, on the premises of the former military garrison, a self-governing society of autonomous individuals expressing themselves freely while at the same time being responsible for each other. Hell yes! There I was. I was free to create myself in my own image. I could earn my money black and largely stay free of the crippling state institutions. If I wanted to, I could disappear, and it would be like I had settled on an island in the South Seas. I could do as I wanted as long as what I did was not at the expense of my neighbors. I could even take my own life if it pleased me. It was all right. In Christiania, I did not stand accused of something I did not know what was. I accepted and was accepted in return. Christiania—an Ararat mountain peak where man could survive (at least for a brief moment) the general extinction. In a little circle of shack-wagons, I had succeeded in hearing my own voice in the cacophony. Standing there in my doorway that morning, I felt mellow, buoyant and ready for whatever the future might bring. Life was as good and sweet as it could possibly be, and if I was wise, I might be able to keep it there. But... no matter what I did, it would never get better. For material sustenance, I had the cash I earned each time I drove the taxi. I had no hope, no plan, and no wish for improvement. As far as my eyes could see from my vantage point in the open door, there was only the Great Now. I would wait for no future, and no future would wait for me. But what the hell, I thought to myself. What did it all matter? No matter what happened, I would be all right. The way I felt at that moment was that I would be able to survive even my own grave. It was like being a boy again...

I bat an eyelash, move a finger or toe. I shuffle my feet a bit. I'm like a mummie waking from a two-thousand-year sleep. I remove the sleep from my eyes. Awake I look around me and notice that I'm standing on the exact same spot only in a slightly different way. I take note of my position and decide that in this life, it is the sum of small joys that becomes the greatest of them all. Like the joy of pissing in the nettles. I stomp down the doorstep and turn the corner of my shack. I unbutton my fly and let it spout. There's the sound of urine splashing against fresh leaves. Afterwards when I am done, I catapult my penis up and down watching the little drops fly in the sunlight. In the end, I stomp back up the doorstep, shake the clogs off my feet, hear them loudly falling, cross the bouncing floor to Lili on the bed who moves back a little, points at herself and says:

"Les, will you hold me there? Yes… right there. That feels good!"

I drove my taxicab one or two nights a week, I read voraciously until a rumor was going around that I was bookworm. From near and far, the classics came to be read by me.

Outside my door a veritable crowd had gathered. There was a pushing and a shoving. They all wanted to appear before my tribunal: Hamsun, Kierkegaard, Andersen, Kazantzakis, Melville, Lautreamont, Machado de Assis, Franz Kafka, Bruno Schulz, Jaroslav Hasek, Jack Kerouac, Ken Kesey, Axel Sandemose, Strindberg, Brautigan, Andersen, Moravia, Henry Miller, Hesse, Nietzsche, Beckett, Faulkner, Camus, Tolstoi, Lawrence, Gogol, Fitzgerald, Chaucer, Thoreau, Petronius, Plato, Emerson, Blixen, Dostoievski, Singer, Whitman… Not to mention both Testaments of the Bible making themselves unpopular because they tried to bully the others in the line. Sometimes when the bustle outside got so loud, I couldn't concentrate, I would fling the door open to shake my fist at the supplicants. In that way, I managed to get an hour or two of relative peace.

In between my reading bouts I filled notebooks and loose sheets with observations, situations, words, thoughts, sentences both single and in little bunches resembling paragraphs. Scribbling on whatever flat and hard surface was at hand, I brought home episodes I witnessed on the street, in the sauna or by the automat for receiving bottles by the supermarket on the square. There were fragments of conversations or arguments overheard in the taxi. These, I jotted down on the narrow block of paper attached to the dashboard. And, mind you! I did it instantly on the spur of the moment and without waiting for the people to pay and leave. In the same place, I also wrote quotations from the books I read while waiting in line in the airport or at the main train station. Dreams I wrote in a special book that I kept ready on my desk next to the bed. And since I figured just about everything might come in handy some day, I was not particularly fastidious. I found most of what happened to me interesting and wrote as much of it down as time allowed. And little by little, I relaxed my principles and constructed pieces that were a page or two long. Eventually, these attempts lost some of their labored clumsiness and became more elegant and direct.

Days went by some of them handsome, prepossessing and proud, others modest, unattractive, even shy. Time was a chain of days seemingly without end. Meanwhile, the narrow space contained within my four walls was saturated with questions raised by the books lined up on my shelves. When I had finished with one author's work or simply tired of it, I would place the volumes on the new shelves I had put up just below the ceiling on both sides of the room, tear the door open and make a grab for something else. I was a mean reader devouring whatever fell into my hands. I would rip and tear my victims until all that was left of them was a little pile of dry bones. Meticulously, I recorded the bloody proceedings with the cyclop's eye that had appeared in the middle of my forehead. This eye enabled me to divine what was of the deepest concern to the authors. Whatever had preoccupied these people, the greatest authors of our civilization, even to the point of obsession was deserving of my attention. I had a hunch that these obsessions were destined to become my subject matter too: the human potential for good and evil, the existence of God, the nature of justice, art and morals; greed, disease, crime, magic, the spirit of wonder; the incurable longing of the soul, the meaning of curiosity, the need to worship and to satisfy the senses; loneliness, anxiety, old age and death. Faith, truth and love. Science and philosophy. If life was an amalgam or conglomerate consisting of all these things, a quest for truth, then it was my job as a writer to make sure it was to be found in every detail of my oeuvre. How to be born and live the life of a human being? And how to die as one? *These* were the million-dollar questions.

Soon I was to discover that spiritual food in the form of books have very little likeness to the food we eat and digest with our stomachs. Whereas the food I ate and digested with my stomach would make me full, the books with which I nourished my spirit never seemed to fill the hole inside of me. No matter how completely I digested a book with my acidic spirit at the end of the repast the questions haunting its author were left painfully intact on my plate. On my tape recording, Zorba asked his writer friend: "Why do the young die?" And when the writer friend answered that he did not know, Zorba exclaimed: "Then what's the use of all your damn books if they don't tell you *that*?" Considering the older man's outburst, the young poet answers that the people who wrote the books did so precisely because they were unable to answer questions like Zorba's.

Evenings in the little shack when my hungry soul would throw itself like a moth at the light in the lamp; with burnt wings and thoughts piled high behind my eyeballs, I would go looking for the exit-sign. Sometimes, towards midnight when the moon poured its eerie light over the wagon and fatigue made my eyes ache, I would put on my green Kansas jacket and set out for either The Loppen Music Hall or The Moonfisher Bar. On such nights, I would smoke, drink and dance with the women who did not prefer to dance with themselves or others of their own gender. With their half-closed eyes and dreamy movements, they reminded me of specters. So self-absorbed and contained in their own little sound bubbles! Alone in the back of the dance-floor and with a beer bottle in my hand, I watched the women wagging their heads and waving their arms in the air. Why were they not dancing at home to a stereo set? Because they wanted to be seen by other people and didn't give a shit about these peoples' feelings. There were also the border-line cases. Sometimes it *did* come to pass that one of the narcissuses opened her eyes. Then, the trick was to pretend that by pure accident at that very instant you happened to be dancing into her (still rather expressionless) field of vision. With a bit of luck (that is if you were not immediately met with an indifferent look and a cold shoulder all the harder for the bra-straps showing) you might be granted the favor of feeling you were actually dancing with the beauty. But beware! It was only an illusion. Inevitably, your hopes would be shattered. Sooner or later and without having at any point acknowledged your existence, the nymph began to drift out of sight. Slowly at first and then faster, she would disappear among the mass of bodies writhing before the long haired band that seemed forever to be finishing off the set with a half hour drum-solo. Once again, you would find yourself alone.

And when finally you'd had enough beer, smoke, narcissism, tinnitus and loneliness, there still remained the ten-minute search for your jacket in the clothes piles along the walls. Sometimes, I would find it far away from the place I had left it around midnight. At the sight of it, I breathed a sigh of relief. Even if the jacket was just an old rag I had scavenged, it was mine and I liked it. It had given me its warmth. In return, I had given it my smell. No warmth, no smell! The two of us belonged together. The jacket was an extension of my skin, which is why losing it was like losing a bit of my faith in humanity. It made me wonder if it was possible to hold on to anything of value in this life. The night my jacket was ripped off, I walked home stripped of my faith that things of beauty could last. Now, I knew why I had always breathed a sigh of relief at the sight of my jacket. Sure! Some degenerate had chucked it into a corner. And it had also been trampled on. But at least, nobody had stolen it, torn it up, puked on it, or thrown it away. Perhaps there was still a place for decency in this world.

Reunited with my beloved jacket, I descended the two floors from The Loppen Music Hall. On the way, I held on to the worn banister, careful not to fall on steps hollowed by the thousands of booted artillerists who had used them since the long storage building was built in the 1860's. There was the sinking sensation of leaving noise and turmoil behind, of volume being reduced with every step down the staircase, of stepping out into the Christiania night to breathe the air and cross the gravelled spaces between puddles that reflected the overcast heavens and led directly into cobbled and uneven Pusher Street. The dirt on all sides, the standard fire roaring out of a rusty barrel with charred and torn holes in it, the sparks rushing upward and dying in the starless dark, the black specters standing around or moving in the periphery of the glare and vanishing in the darkness, the shadows of yet another night seeping through the skin and invading the dream, the sound and impact of boot-heels against the cobbles sending waves of soft vibrations up my spine, the tinnitus and torn bits of melody lingering on, the dark form of my wagon rising up before my eyes as I step out from the narrow passage between the low garage-buildings and the ramparts, the sweet unbuttoning of the fly to piss in the nettles. And then, two steps up into the wagon, kicking off the boots, bouncing barefoot across the floor, undressing and crawling under the quilt. Head on the pillow, turn out the light, breathe deeply one last time and hear sleep coming. Sinking into a wonderland of women, friendship, adventure and bravery. Fragments of forgotten soccer-matches from my past! The adrenalin high when receiving the ball just outside the box, letting it bounce once and resolutely sending it into the far corner. The euphoria-run ending when one after the other, the jubilant teammates jump on my back, and I tumble to the ground. The ever changing visions, impressions and panoramas. The eternal companion longing whispering in my ear, the waiting and then little by little the porous awakening to the sounds of the world delicately blending with the rearguard of departing visions. Everything, the entire mirage, forever unfolding on both sides of the membrane at once. The climatic zones hopelessly shuffled. The wind that swept the Great Plains of Coyote's childhood was all there ever was. The borders falling away on all sides. Nothing but the same disfigured landscape lit up as by sudden flashes of lightning. Contours sharply delineated one moment and gone the next. The darkness and the flash. To be a human being with everything it entails and especially *does not* entail. To be equipped with a mind and a spirit craving worship, expression and most importantly: love. Harrowing mental states and upheavals, blows, quakes, collapses and signs in the sun and the moon. Transitoriness. One wrong step, and it's over forever.

Today, it is obvious to me how the books, the hunger for truth and the dance supported and encouraged each other. In Christiania, there was nourishment for both body and soul. Besides removing the tensions that were constantly building in my blood, the dance and the music stimulated the desire to express my life in words. If the philosopher was right who pronounced that learning is the soul thinking, then dancing surely was thinking with the body. To be a man who thought with both body and soul seemed to me about as close to the divine as you could get. The Freetown was wise. It knew better than I myself what I needed. And what I did not need. Like it saw to it that I did not get an overdose of books. It did not let me read myself to death. There were communal projects and activities where my participation was demanded. Things were kept in balance and there was some harmony. Technology was not yet total. Things did not happen by themselves, and a strong body and mind was still necessary. Four times a week, I walked down Grønnegade Street to get fresh water. Once a month, I borrowed a box-bicycle and fetched a fresh gas-bottle in The Green Recycling Hall. There was the new sewage system that we were going to make, the ditches to be dug. There was the playground to be built because in Christiania people were having kids right and left. Walls were going to be torn down and new ones constructed in the Dandelion City Hall Building. The kitchen was going to be renovated. When I lived in the city of Copenhagen my connection to the community had been an abstract one; in Christiania, it had taken on a human face and become both immediate and concrete. My actions had consequences. If I didn't pay my rent in the city, I would be evicted by the magistrate's bailiff; in Christiania, my neighbors would knock on my door. Living outside the law, the need for honesty and responsibility was keenly felt by all.

Sometimes late in the morning, French Christian would stop by for a bite of breakfast. If he saw Lili's bicycle parked against the side of my wagon, he would turn around, but if not he'd come in and we would squeeze into the chairs on both sides of the tiny table between the kitchen and the desk. Munching fresh rolls with butter and cheese, we would discuss the affair Christian was having with Fanny, the teenage girl who visited me a couple of times and decided she preferred the more tantric approach to sex practiced by Christian. According to Christian, Fanny had found me "a bit too bestial" for her taste. When we made love, I would get a "bestial" look in my eyes that scared her.

"Uh-huh," I said.

Christian looked at me reproachfully: *"Elle est une femme, un peut jeune, c'est vrais, mais...quant meme – je t'assure, une femme."*

I felt like saying: "Christ almighty, how wise you've suddenly become when it comes to women!" But I kept my mouth shut.

Women, Christian informed me with an expression befitting a famished sannyasin – women *also* had a "spiritual dimension." And it was precisely this dimension that he appealed to when he and Fanny sat together crosslegged and naked on his platform.

"Uh-huh," I grunted again.

Oh, yes it was. And when the weather was nice, they'd also do taichi naked on his veranda.

I nodded: "I've *seen* that! Is it some kind of spiritual foreplay, or what?"

No. One could not put it that way. It wasn't as simple as that. Of course, it eventually led to the bed where he would hump her. But spiritual foreplay, no way! At least not in the crude way I had in mind. If I had been familiar with Kama Sutra, he could have explained it to me. But since I did not have a clue about the age-old art of intercourse, it was useless going into it with me.

"Kama Sutra uh-huh!" I nodded and tried to look like I

knew more about the Kama Sutra than he dreamed.

But Christian was not taken in. He breathed deeply and looked like it cost him considerable effort to bear with me. At the end of this little act, he knitted his brows and looked at me with a sad smile: Such "raffinements *de l'amour ancient*" I would have to live more lives in order to fathom.

"Okay!" I said and raised my eyebrows as high as I could. I would remember that. But then…was there any hope for me at all—for a bestial man like me?

Christian shook his head gravely. No, there probably was not. Not in this life, the next and the one following that. But even if I would not get the gist of it the next time around either, I need not be discouraged. The oversoul was concerned with its creatures. It did not give up and never let anyone down. If necessary it would go on transmigrating endlessly. Eventually, even *I* would be born an illuminated being.

"I'm much relieved," I said, "but isn't there a way this wheel can be stopped?"

"No," Christian said, "there isn't."

Realizing that I really *was* the Cro-Magnon, I had imagined myself to be just a few days before, I could not help but smile. It was fine with me. After everything he had been through, Christian deserved the good fortune he was experiencing now. He was head over heels in love with Fanny, had broken up with his girlfriend and was now walking the streets of fat city with a big old shit eating grin on his face. At this precise point in time, all the divergent elements of Christian's life seemed to form a synthesis called Fanny: Cock, hot fish soup, taichi and chocolate mousse. Not to mention fois gras with prunes to help his bowels, snails in strong garlic sauce and frog legs in chili and served with asparagus. And even as he was concocting his various meals, the barometer went on rising until one fine day it reached his head. One night his love for Fanny grew to such euphoric heights that he got up on an overturned wheel barrow in the middle of the night and started singing his heart out, waking the entire Dandelion.

That was the climax, and at the same time, the renowned "point of no return," which (so it goes) is hidden in every story. Everything he had been cramming up the various orifices of Fanny's body now came tumbling out again: cock juices, frog-legs, prunes, and asparagus. It was a veritable deluge that carried Christian away in its flood waters, not leaving as much as a single ripple or eddy on the surface of the pool where he had disappeared out of sight. Not so much as a single *"raffinement de l'amour ancient"* was visible anymore. All that was left were the smoking coals of an affair extinguished by a bucket of water. It was a case of Nirvana transformed into a torture chamber. The interval between Fanny's visits on the platform *d'amour* had gone up from ten hours to twenty. And from the twenty, it had become twenty-eight and so on, until it finally dawned on Siddhartha that his Kamala courtisan was engaged in an amorous liaison with no other than his minestrone friend Danish Christian out on Dyssen. There must have been something fateful tying the two of them together. One day when French Christian, half dead and gnashing his teeth with jealousy lay hidden behind a pile of used boards spying on Danish Christian he, the rival himself, came out the door and calmly walked up to French Christian. He was not threatening or anything like that. No, he just approached him like one approaches a fellow sufferer.

French Christian laid it all on me sitting at my little wooden table, chewing on a buttered roll. It was the truly harrowing tale of how he and Danish Christian (whom he named his "alter ego") had both spied on Fanny when she was not with them. Sometimes, they would find her other times they did not. At such times, they asked themselves where on earth she might be. Since Fanny did not really live anywhere in particular, it was difficult to know. And at ten in the evening, she was not likely to be at work in the bakery up on the square. She was not visiting her mother either since the mother had moved to the Canary Islands. So where was Fanny? This question drove the two Christians so crazy it was a relief to them the day they met behind the boards and came clear with one another. Right there on the spot, they decided to coordinate the covert activities necessary to discover Fanny's whereabouts. From then on, they would stand shoulder to shoulder, Christian said.

"Or nose to nose?" I suggested facetiously.

"Don't try to be ferny!" Christian said in his French-sounding Danish.

"I'm not," I said.

"Yes, you are," Christian said.

"Good luck," I said.

Christian looked at me disapprovingly. It was wrong of me to think "negatively," he said. Why, if they really gave it a try, they would probably succeed. Only, they must not lose their heads. And it was important they stand by each other. The mission required that they showed some solidarity and were ready to sacrifice something too. To share their love…

"How is it," I said changing my line and trying not to be too sarcastic, "isn't it also…uhh, pretty *tantric* out there in Aircondition where your alter ego lives? Maybe it all just became a bit too tantric for Fanny. Who knows…maybe she needs a bit of bestial action again."

"Very ferny indeed!"

An awkward silence had come between us. Knowing it was my fault, I was just waiting for Christian to forgive me and say something. Anything really. I kind of regretted my sarcasm, but not too much. A few more minutes went by before Christian turned his head again. If I would only listen to him, he said and sent me a tortured look. Take him seriously. For it really *was* serious, wasn't it?

I nodded.

There was something, Christian said, that he would like to ask me because I, too, knew Fanny. Something about her "type." Had I noticed that her psychology somehow did not correspond with her physiology? As far as he could see, there was an almost visible discrepancy between her spirituality on the one hand and her desire on the other. Wasn't there something to this?

"Oh, but there *is!*" Christian exclaimed when he saw the expression on my face.

At that moment, it occurred to me that the damage Erik the Red had done the two Christians was nothing compared with the pain Fanny would inflict.

And it was not long before my dark forebodings were confirmed. As time went by and events unfolded, Erik the Red came more and more to resemble a gentle and considerate fellow. When he had broken the duo's noses he'd had enough and left them alone. With Fanny it was different. Not only did she break their *hearts*, no, she kept breaking them. And for a long time. After the last time French Christian had breakfast in my wagon, the situation deteriorated rapidly for the union of love sick tantrics. And by the time Christmas was ushered in, complete with jingle bells and phoney Santa Clauses, they were both a mess. Kama Sutra and tantra had long since been sacrificed on the altar of pain. The expression they wore was reminiscent of last years' Christmas trees. The orchester was playing the ragtime medley. Danish Christian looked like a bum. His boots were in tatters. And obviously, he could not care less. And as for French Christian, there was some sort of hunger strike going on. Every time I ran into him, he would tell me how he had neither eaten nor slept for weeks. And looking at him, I had no reason to doubt what he said. All that was left of him was skin, bones and rags. He wasn't motivated to do anything any more, he said. He had even stopped making the chocolate mousse cakes on his floor. He had run out of money, and now he was running up debt instead. At night, he twisted and turned on his sleeping platform unable to sleep. And when on the rare occasions he would actually sleep, he'd dream that his residency had expired and he was deported. Then, he woke up in a sweat screaming.

It really was no laughing matter. In spite of their unbreakable solidarity in misfortune, the Minestrone boys were now falling apart big time. Yet the more they fell apart, the more they also stuck together. And vice versa. It was an at once weird and vicious circle that needed badly to be broken.

"Why don't you come and have breakfast with me anymore?" I asked French Christian one day when I passed by his veranda and happened to catch a glimpse of him through the window.

"It's no use," he said and hung his head.

"For Christ sake Christian! Fanny *is* nice. I know. But it's time you knock her out of your mind."

Christian nodded and allowed that I was right. If only he could.

"If in the next life," he said and blinked, "I get choice to have the nose punched by Erik the Red and falling in lorve wif Fanny – *mon dieu* I then take Erik!"

Noticing that you could add 'humor' to the 'skin, bones and rags' list, I said: "Why don't you look Erik up and ask him to knock her out of your head!"

Christian smiled sadly: "Very ferny," he said.

The hollow bump and trembling little ring escaping the bell when Lili leaned her bicycle against the side of my wagon. The annunciation. On hot and humming summer days and during December's pink and silent twilight hour in the snow. The woodstove radiating warmth inside. The dimming light of the short and frosty afternoons filtered by the intricate mesh of branches on the ramparts, the day fighting its losing battle against the dark in the space encircled by our homes. An axe chopping wood in the dying dusk. The sound of the blows and the pieces splitting and tumbling off the chopping block onto the ground. Victims of gravity. Hard and indifferent earth always there to receive them. Voices reaching your ear from somewhere in the cold. The clouds of steam emanating from the speakers' mouths far away in a frozen dream. The night shadows thick with falling flakes of snow. Dogs barking. The communal meetings in the Rockmachine where the smoke from hash-pipes is so thick it brings tears to your eyes and burns your nose and throat; where the appointed chairman has left to take a leak in the snow; where there are people so stoned that only their mouths are open; yes, and where others are shouting and behaving in such a manner that it is hard to believe you are in a civilized society with mandatory schooling. If Acid Søren is not coughing his lungs out, he's sure to be kicking the stinking mongrel at his side. The animal is whimpering, and somewhere someone has overturned a chair in an attempt to get up and comment hoarsely on something no one understands. It is hard to tell what is going on. I mean what is *really* going on. There seem to be a number of different agendas simultaneouly vying for attention. From the dark recesses at the back of the room, there is the scraping sound of two people making out. Suddenly, a shout is heard above the din: "NOW WILL YOU BASTARDS SHUT UP GODDAMMIT!" For a brief instant there is silence but almost instantly the cacophony is back in full force. Now, a fight breaks out near the exit. A handful of sober activists in crotch pants rush in and go between the drunken parties and separate them. Growling like curs, the combatants slink off in opposite directions. The mess has been restored. All is back to normal. The general meeting can go on...

But on Sunday afternoon in The City Lights Cinema where the floor is covered with sand, parents and children sit and watch as Winnitou and Old Shatterhand ride their horses across the plains. The weekend partying over and the adults being slightly hungover, the atmosphere is subdued, warm and friendly.

Meanwhile, merciless time was going about its business behind our backs. Before we knew it, another spring had been ushered in. The buds on the trees were just about to break when preparations for the wood chopping camp in the forest of Tilvilde Hegn were entering the final stage. The whole thing came about because Jakob knew Jokum the Ranger. The two of them had graduated from gardening school together. The great storm in January had knocked down many trees and Jokum had no idea how to get them sawed up and removed. So when Jakob called to ask, if by any chance, Jokum would let a village of christianites set up camp in his forest and do the job for him, he readily agreed. If we would leave the trunks and only take the limbs we could have as much as we wanted for free. Jokum the Ranger rubbed his bearded chin and looked very satisfied on the evening it was decided that the Wagon Village was going to set up camp in his forest for a minimum of four weeks and a maximum of six.

In order that we could all stay dry and be cosy even on rainy nights, Jakob had scavenged an old circus tent. Of

426

course, there were a few holes in it, but who gave a damn. Those holes, Jakob assured us, were not a problem at all. Firstly, there were not very many, and secondly the biggest one happened to be in the corner where we would not choose to sleep anyway. Jakob panned us one by one with his eyes as we sat around the campfire. There was really nothing to worry about on that score, he said. We would get a good night's sleep—*every* night. Working hard from morning to evening in the open, we would even be able to sleep in a puddle if need be. For many years, Jakob added as an after thought, the tent had been used for the camels. The reason it had so many holes in it was because the animals had nibbled at the material with their big teeth. As far as he knew, there had been eleven of them. But perhaps the number was twelve. He was not quite sure…

Old Knud looked at Jakob with his little eskimo eyes and grunted: "When the tent has been good enough for eleven camels for thirty years, it's also good enough for eleven of us for fifty days in 1981? Is *that* it?"

"Yeah, that's exactly it!" Jakob looked at Old Knud with his deadpan expression.

"And in the end, we'll probably have humps just like the fucking camels!" Old Knud said.

"And teeth maybe!" Jakob just kept looking at him.

A couple evenings later, it was decided in my absence that I was to be "Camp Officer." I had been "the obvious choice."

The next morning when we were sharing a pot of tea on Jakob's doorstep, I asked him what the function of a "Camp Officer" was.

To get an understanding of what the duties of a C.O. were, Jakob said, I should imagine someone who was a "bit of a mix." Ideally, a camp officer combined the skills of janitor, kitchen hand, street sweeper, animal trainer, custodian, prison guard, bouncer and nightwatch. Chef de Cuisine too. And… not to forget dishwasher and bus boy.

"As the person in charge of the first aid and feeding units, the Camp Officer holds a most dignified position," Jakob concluded.

"I see," I said.

For some time, none of us spoke. Then Jakob went on musing: A Camp Officer never left the camp. If one of the laborers had an accident with a chainsaw say, and was in need of first-aid, there must be someone back in camp to help him. Neither would it hurt any if I kept the troops free of lice and ticks and so on. The heavy work with the chainsaws could in fact cause myotonia, so there'd be a need of massage as well. But above all else, it was the responsibility of the Camp Officer to feed the men when they returned famished in the evening. It was my responsibility to have dinner ready at seven and see to it that rations were justly divided. It wasn't my duty to wipe the mouths of the troops after the meals, but I had to get up in the morning before all others and prepare the coffee and the breakfast so it was ready to eat when they awoke. Every day, I had a half hour break, but it was expected of me that I spent it cleaning the camel tent and tidying up around the camp. Finally, I was also to look after the thieves when they were caught red handed and put in the stocks I myself had stolen from a museum in the city and set up in camp as a deterrent.

"Ya follo?"

"Follo!"

Everything progressed according to plan. Everything was ready for departure. When Jokum the Ranger had been to see us for the second time, he was served Old Knud's favorite dish: cow tongue with mustard and horse raddish. Now, we were just waiting for Jakob and Ragma to set out ahead of the rest with our gear piled high on the horse wagon: tent, blankets, chainsaws, tools, gasoline, tarp, rope, jugs, kitchen implements, sacks of potatoes and other food-stuffs. By the time, the rest of us arrived some days later everything would be ready.

For someone like me who had never been a boy-scout and was not yet a renowned writer of novels, it was both an adventure and a troublesome way to obtain firewood. It goes without saying that it was also very cheap. And very social. But above all, it was extremely time-consuming. Ever since I had received my calling in life, time had become more and more of a problem. To have time for Lili, time for the taxi, time for digging sewage ditches. And now time for weeklong woodchopping camps in the forest…

"Why don't you bring some paper and a pencil along?" Jakob said. "During your half-hour break you take a few minutes out to draw up a portrait of Old Knud—or you exercise your skill by describing a dung beetle as it goes along its way. There won't be a lack of things to write about, I can guarantee you that!"

Time was to prove Jakob right. In fact, there was so much to write about that I did not have time to do a fraction of it. I know because I really gave it a go. Every chance I had, I would grab the pencil I carried grocer-style behind my ear and jot down something or other. But the forest was bewitched. If I did not know better, I would say it set up all manner of mischievous incidents just to sidetrack me. No sooner had I sat down with my back against an old beech tree, and barely had I gotten started when some wood-mouse would get busy looking for something by my boot heels. It was fascinating to watch the energy and determination with which the little animal went about its business. For minutes on end, I could not take my eyes off it. Or I had just managed to write, say, five lines when a jay took aim from the treetops and shit right on my paper. A big old gob, it was too, followed by a loud and scornful cackle. There could be no doubt. The forest was against my project and actively obstructed my efforts. If it was not a mouse or a jay it was something else. No matter where and how I placed myself, it either itched or tickled somewhere on my skin or in my hair. Time and again, I had to spend time catching an ant up my pants leg or somewhere worse. It was crystal clear: The forest would not allow me to perform my calling.

Even the weather was against me. Exactly that year the barometric pressure of springtime in Scandinavia was not only high but extremely stable. One perfect day was followed by the next. Early every morning when I stuck my head out of the tent, the sun was already up and letting its light filter down through the fresh foliage. And so it went on, throughout the day until evening came with its gathering dusk.

With few variations each new day was like the one preceding it. Sometimes, the morning was a bit misty, but at noon, the mist had cleared, and the sun was back in full force. The same was true of the Camp Officer's duties. They, too, were the same and unchanging. To get up before anyone else and build a fire, make coffee, cut the ryebread in uneven slices and prepare breakfast for the ragged bunch of woodcutters. And when, one after the other, the men were done drifting off into the scrub to move their bowels, the group would gather and leave camp all together. Day after perfect day, I would be standing there by the campfire with my hands in my pockets watching them leave and carrying whatever they needed for the day's work. Day after perfect day, I would stand there and wait until I had seen the ass of the hindmost disappear. Once more, I was left alone in the clearing. And day after perfect day, I would think the same thing to myself: that it was amazing how everything was so perfectly arranged for the life of man. How happy man could be if he would only realize this and stop being such a damn marplot and spoil it all. If this was not the case how then was it possible that I could be standing there with my hands in my pockets and feel as free and happy as a stoneage man in love?

It was on the day when pregnant Ragma had her check-up in the city that Jakob came up with his suggestion that the two of us take the horse and four-wheeled cart to the coast for some fresh fish. Half an hour later, we were on our way along a shimmering forest path. Jakob was holding the reins loosely in his hand, and I was sitting next to him with my bare feet stuck into an old pair of tennis shoes. There had been a couple of rain showers the night before, and the depressions along the way had turned into shining puddles. Everything was so fresh, it seemed the world had been created that very morning. For a long time, neither of us said a word. We just sat there breathing the air and watching Cherie's strong hindparts carry us along towards the sea. Jakob loved to speak when he was in the mood, and he loved to keep silent when he felt like it. Every now and then, I would look at him out of the corner of my eye. From the expression on his face, I could tell he was enjoying the ride as much as I was.

At this time, we had been camped in the woods a little over two weeks. The beech trees no longer had any buds left. Dressed in their first furry green, they surrounded us on all sides like some psychedelic dayglo dream. Passing under a low hanging branch, I grabbed it with my hand and tore off the leaves. Without saying a word, I handed Jakob a couple. We put the leaves in our mouths, and for a while, we sat there chewing the slightly acidic juice out of them. The clip-clop-clip-clop of Cherie's hooves was mesmerizing in its perfect regularity. If it were not so corny to say it, I would say it felt just like we were passing through that cool cathedral, which new-leaved trees invariably invoke in poets. The huge and slightly greenish trunks rising out of the earth and reaching for the sky far above our heads. Trancelike we chewed until the forest opened up, and we looked out over the sea sparkling in the sunlight. Far out in the blue haze, there were the white sails of a sailing ship.

Down in the harbor, we ran into a big-bellied fisherman wearing overalls and black gumboots. In answer to our question, he pointed to two wooden crates in the bottom of his fishingboat. In one of the crates were flounders, in the other, codfish. We chose the latter. Counting seven medium sized codfish and slipping them into two plastic bags the fisherman told us the price. Even if it was more than we were prepared to pay, we were not about to spoil our good mood arguing about it. I found the communal wallet, fingered some notes out and paid in full. And as a sort of closing comment on the deal, the fisherman farted a big one in his overalls. Then, he wished us god speed.

"Greedy son-of-a-bitch," Jakob muttered as we walked back to the horse and cart waiting for us in the street.

"But there's nothing wrong with the fish," I said.

"No," Jakob said. And a couple minutes later, we were on our way back.

It was only a little past noon when we rode into camp and found the troops sitting on the trunks, glowering, silent and so famished you could almost hear their bellies growl.

"You sure took your time," Old Knud growled.

"Did you get some fish?" Douglas wanted to know.

"Codfish. Look!" I jerked one of the bags of fish so hard over the side of the cart that a couple of fish fell out. One of them landed at John's feet. He pushed it off.

"Johnny!" Jakob said, "that fish chose you. You're skinning them, okay!"

"Ahh, get lost!" John said. "What did we bring a Camp

Officer for if not to skin fish. And besides codfish aren't skinned."

"He's right Jakob," I said. "I'm good at preparing fish. It's no problem. I'll do it."

The seven codfish had long since been eaten and digested and squeezed out in the thicket around the campgrounds when at siesta time on the third day after our trip to the coast Lili came walking into camp wearing sandals, jeans and a skimpy T-shirt barely covering her full tits. Just like that. The whole gang was lying around snoozing and digesting. So it took awhile before any one noticed. It wasn't until Old Knud raised himself up on an elbow and said: "Are you ready to take us all on or what?"

Lili was looking at us lounging about haphazardly where we had fallen: "Why should I be ready to take you all on?"

"You don't know?" Old Knud's tone was one of surprise.

"No, I don't."

"Well. Wearing almost no clothes you come walking right into a camp consisting of nothing but sex-starved male woodcutters. How do you think *that* makes them feel?"

"Horny, I suppose," Lili said with a nervous little laugh.

"You got it," Old Knud grunted. And then as he laid his head back on the ground he added: "There ought to be a fucking law against such things goddammit!"

When the gang had gone back to work and the camp was empty once more I got out a blanket and told Lili to follow me. A couple hundred feet away where there was a small and relatively flat clearing I threw the blanket on the ground and waited for her. "What if they see us?" she said.

"They won't. They can't see us from the campsite!"

The last time I'd had a woman was almost three weeks before. It was almost too exciting. My dick was throbbing, and so the first time I held her, I came almost at once. After that we just laid around for a while holding each other and whispering in each other's ears. And then, gradually, we began to make love in earnest. This time around, I was being slow and thorough. I was huge and hard and it seemed like it lasted forever. When we finally got back on our feet, it was late in the afternoon. Luckily the camp was still empty. Lili put on some more clothes, and I pottered around with the kitchen utensils. By the time, the gang came out of the thicket both Lili and I were busy cooking dinner. The way she looked frying the meat on the grill, Lili was prettier than I had ever seen her before or since.

That night as we were lying next to each other in our sleeping bags, we held back out of respect for the others. We had moved up until we couldn't get closer and were rubbing our noses together and nibbling at each other's lips and smiling. At one point, I almost broke out laughing because it reminded me of French Christian and his tantric antics. Tantra or not, what we were doing was super exciting. The way we rubbed and pressed our bagged bodies up against each other, you would think we were two sea slugs in heat. It was all that I could do to wait for the chainsaw gang to fall asleep. But judging from the sounds made all around us, we were finally the only ones awake. Ever so gingerly we pulled ourselves out of the bags and threw our arms around each other. She didn't have a stitch on, and when I entered her, she gasped. Maybe I am only imagining things, but I don't think I had ever done it so quietly and cautiously before. But even if we scarcely moved at all, it was just about the most exciting fuck I have ever had. Pale moonlight falling through the hole in the tent. The presence of the sleeping men all around us. It excited me to know that they might wake at any moment, or that there were those among them who were not sleeping at all and might right now be spouting in their bags. Which just goes to show that circumstances are not irrelevant to sex.

In this case, they added an extra dimension. An extra *bonus* dimension… Even if my thrusts were minuscule, they had an impact quite out of proportion to the exertion. One little thrust, pause, then one more, and one more again. I was like one electrified. And so was Lili. With each tiny move I made her tense trembling increased. By now, she was pulling so hard with her arms around my neck and gasping so violently into my ear that I knew she was about to come. "Arhhh! Arhhh!" she groaned and socked me a good one with her forehead against my jaw. I had not come yet myself and was holding her like in a vice. It excited me to feel her relaxing the grip around my neck and growing heavier in my arms.

We remained immobile until something started it again. One little thrust, pause, one more little thrust, and one more. The only difference being that this time, I let myself go too; so that when Lili socked me in the jaw, I came in one long spasm.

At that moment, there was a loud "shyhhhhh goddammit" from somewhere in the dark. We froze, looked each other amusedly in the eye, tightened our lips and lay completely still.

Soon we disengaged and spent the rest of the night sleeping in our sleeping bags.

At breakfast, the next morning no one spoke except to make little sarcasms. At one point, someone said: "It was kind of hard to fall asleep last night, don't you think."

"Sure was," someone else said. "There was this strange sound. Did *you* guys notice it too?"

There was a nodding all around.

"How would you describe it?" someone wanted to know.

"Like two people humping."

"Exactly. But according to camp regulations that sort of thing must be shared, isn't that so?"

"Right. Any banging that goes on must be gang-banging!"

I could tell from Lili's expression that it didn't much amuse her to listen to all this. But no sooner was the chainsaw gang gone than we looked at each other.

Lili shook her head and grinned: "Oh man are you a horndog!"

"Yeah. I'm a man? And how can a man be anything but a horndog with a babe like you around?" As I said this, I slipped a hand inside the boiler suit she had put on and closed it around her wonderful breast.

A few minutes later, we had thrown off our clothes and were making out again on a blanket I had spread out just ten feet away. We were rapidly establishing new habits. And so the next day as we were at it again in the same spot Old Knud surprised us when he came back looking for a bandaid for his index finger. He did his best to be discrete, I must say. And perhaps he would also have succeeded in getting away without being noticed by us if he hadn't sneezed. I looked in the direction of the sound and so did Lili. There was Knud with his hat pushed back on his head. He was mopping the sweat off his forehead with a hankerchief and looking at us with those little eskimo eyes of his. When he was done mopping, he started to nod like something profound had just occurred to him. He nodded once more for good measure and said as if to himself: "It's your own damn fault. You shouldn't have let it come to this. Old men over fifty ought to be shot. It's your own damn fault."

"It's…uh, it's okay," Lili said when Old Knud had gone, and I was awkwardly trying to get into her again. "How old is he anyway that Old Knud? Do you know?"

"In his late fifties I think."

"Oh," said Lili and got up to get her cigarettes.

Three weeks spent in this way up in Tisvilde Hegn forest, and it was summer for real.

I'm writing Melanie a letter to tell her how it all ended for me. My Christiania life, I mean. Summer number three had just started when I fell in love with a long legged mulatto from the town of Belo Horizonte in Brazil's Bahia province. Her skin was the color of nougat and her posture regal. The way her full upper lip curled just wee bit upward gave her a pouting expression, which I found irresistible. Her feet and fingers were shapely as was the rest of her body. Creating Diana Silva dos Santos, the good Lord had given the world of men a true masterpiece.

It all started one Saturday night when I was driving my taxi. Around ten-thirty, I was called to an address in the Nørrebro part of town. When I arrived there wasn't anybody waiting on the sidewalk. And when I rang the bell in the doorway, no one answered. I could hear that there was some sort of party going on up on the second floor. I was trying to decide whether to wait a bit longer or just drive away when a dark haired guy in shades came down the staircase and opened the door. Seeing me standing there, he seemed to hesitate a moment, but then he wiped a long strand of hair away from his forehead, let me in and disappeared into the night. I began to climb the stairs. What waited for me on the landing of the second floor was quite a sight. Diana Silva with toenails painted red and stuck into a green pair of braided leather-shoes. Little drops of red-hot blood in the jungle.

"You don't happen to be the taxi-driver, do you?" It was the Danish woman standing next to the mulatto beauty who spoke. Utterly spellbound by her friend, it was all I could do just to nod. Any attempt at human speech was ruled out. The woman who had put the question to me turned around and said something in Portuguese to the woman in the green shoes who she called "Diana." Diana said something to her in return and then the two women gave each other a hug. I didn't understand a word of what had been spoken, but from their body language, I gathered that Diana was sorry about something that had taken place prior to my arrival. Giving each other one more hug, they said goodbye. Apparently the name of the Danish woman was Viviane…

Back on the sidewalk I held the door to the back seat for the woman in the green shoes. She didn't look at me when she got in. I closed the door and moved around to the driver's seat. "Sofiegården," she said. Just that one word. But it was enough. I had heard her accent. "On Christianshavn?" I asked stupidly. She didn't answer. There was no need to. There was only one Sofiegården in Copenhagen, and everybody knew that it was in Christianshavn. Not only had I taken many customers to Sofiegården, but I had also been to several parties there. I understood her mute refusal to answer and shut up. That is how I am. Or rather: that is how I *was*. I let it be up to the customers if they were in the mood to speak. Maybe they needed to be left alone. For this reason, I never struck up conversation with them. It was sort of a principle I had. Only weighty reasons could make me break this principle of mine. That night the reasons were more than weighty. They were overwhelming.

Driving towards the center along Nørrebrogade Street, I played the Serge Gainsbourg tape that my friend Pascal had given me before he moved back to Avignon. I had just turned it around and the song that filled the dark little space of the car was *"Le poinconneur des Lilas."* Even though I tried not to I kept glancing at Diana in the rear view mirror, it was impossible to resist. She was looking out the side window, and if she noticed my ogling her, she didn't show it. No sooner had I taken my eyes off of her before they longed back. I could force them away from the mirror but not keep them away. It was like I had a spring in my neck, and had it not been for the fact that I needed to see where I was driving, I would not have been able to tear my eyes away from the mirror at all. My entire being was focused on her, when to my own surprise I heard my voice ask about her "charming" accent. For something like a split second, I wasn't sure the beauty had heard what I said. But then she turned her head and met my eyes in the rear view mirror. She was from Brazil, she said.

Learning that she was from Brazil, I immediately thought of Machado de Assis and his novel "Dom Casmurro," which I had just finished reading. And wanting to impress her with my knowledge of Brazilian literature, I asked her if she knew the book. Rarely in my career as Don Wagon had I made such a direct hit. She met my eyes in the mirror and her voice was surprised, when she asked me if I had read "Dom Casmurro"? "Try me!" I said.

The woman leaned forward in her seat and took a good look at me from the side: "Are you…a real taxidriver?"

"Sure," I said pretending to be surprised, "do I look unreal?"

It was hardly the first time that this question had been put to me by the customers. I never did find out what it was about me that made people ask. Like all the rest I drove a taxi to make some money. But somehow I did not live up to whatever picture the customers had created for themselves of a person with that occupation. I somehow aroused their curiosity. And I kind of liked the question. Not only was it a sign that people had a hard time labeling me but it also gave me the opportunity to reinvent myself. I did not always answer it truthfully. I looked people over first, and if

439

they seemed like the perceptive kind, I would usually tell it the way it was: that I was driving once or twice a week as a substitute. The rest of the time I was preparing myself for the occupation as a novelist. But more often than not, I evaded the question either by affirming that I was in fact a taxi-driver or if that was too boring by dishing out some hog shit about selling washing machines in the daytime. In fact that is how I came up with the story I told Lili the first time we met.

"No, but…" the woman said, "Danish taxi-drivers don't know Machado de Assis."

"Oh, no?" I said once more feigning surprise.

"No, they don't!" she said. "And now it's time we find out if you're a real taxi-driver or what you are."

"How?"

"Tell me the name of the female protagonist of the novel and I'll believe you!"

"Capitu," I said making my voice as bland and disinterested as possible. "Her real name is Capitolina, but she's called Capitu for short."

There was a moment of silence on the backseat. Then I heard her voice again: She was sorry, she said, that she had not believed me. Capitolina was indeed the woman's name. And what, then, was my favorite chapter? Her's was chapter thirteen entitled "Capitu" in which the two of them were still only innocent kids.

I said that I had no favorite chapter but loved the whole book as a tragic testimony to terrestrial beauty, deception and loss.

It turned out Diana had come to Denmark two years before. She now lived in Sofiegården with her husband who besides being an Argentinian Jew was also "a small Mafioso." He did not care about anything except his own shady transactions. But maybe it was unfair of her to put it like that. The truth was that she was not sure what kind of business he was involved in. But whatever it was, it seemed pretty shady and made her uneasy. Like all the weird characters that kept dropping in for coffee and beer.

This is what Diana told me about her husband the first night in the taxi. And as she was getting out, she told me about a party in the Brazilian club the following Saturday. I was welcome to show up if I liked. If I had such an interest in Brazilian literature that was only the more reason to do it. A friend of hers, a young Brazilian writer who was a relative of Jorge Amado, was going to be there too. Did I know Jorge Amado?

I said that I had come across his name, but that I had not yet read anything he had written.

Daina bent down and looked at me through the open sidewindow. We looked at each other. Then, she stuck her hand in for me to take. That was the first time I really noticed her beautiful long and slender fingers with the blood-red nails. I said: "What's the address if I want to come to the party?"

I let go her hand, tore a sheet from the little block hanging from the windshield and handed it to her along with a ballpoint pen. Diana put her little bag on the hood, placed the paper next to it and wrote an address and a telephone number on it. Then, she crumbled the paper into a small ball, placed it between two fingers and handed it to me. Looking her in the eye, I took it and closed my hand around it. A moment later and there was the sound of her braided green shoes on the sidewalk, and she was gone.

As she had probably already guessed, I wrote to Melanie, I went to the party. And after the first time we were together there soon followed a second and a third and a fourth until the whole affair kind of got out of hand, and we were both hopelessly sunk in a quagmire of lies and clandestine meetings in the cheap hotels behind the main train station.

But life is a series of jolts. It does not bother itself with petty concerns and will go its way no matter what. Diana and I might just as well not have taken all the precautions. By this time, it was mid-August, and the situation had become way too complex and nerve racking for my taste.

It was before noon on a hot day. The christianites who had not already left for the coast were either preparing to do so or skinny-dipping in the moat. The tourists, this race of oddly restless and misplaced individuals that always manage to look like they are totally lost and superflouous, were sauntering about on the ramparts enjoying each other's company the best they knew how, ogling the naked christianites' wet breasts and buttocks and the glittering water in the moat. Some of the young ones also smoked the Moroccan hash they had bought in Pusher Street. Here and there, they could be seen lying about in twos or threes either giggling idiotically or staring up into the heavens above. Personally, I have never been much of a smoker of hashish. French Christian and I were not bored just because we were straight. Sitting out in front of my wagon on a couple of wooden beer boxes, we were sharing a meal of fresh bread, some feta cheese and green olives with pits bought in the Christiania green grocer.

In sharp contrast to my surroundings, I was feeling tense that morning. For months now, I had known that I could not stay on forever in the Freetown, that in order to pursue my ambition, I needed to move on. On the one hand, Christiania had set me free, but on the other, it demanded too much of me and was too much fun. I was very much aware that I could not go on procrastinating forever.

But then again! Why be in such a hurry to get away from a place that had given me so much, where I had found myself again and I still loved to be? And besides, where would I go? Add to this, the new complications caused by my affair with Diana, and it is no wonder I was puzzled as to the right course of action.

This was more or less how things were on that morning when Christian and I sat out in front of my wagon. A few nights before, I had come home from a rendezvous with Diana and found Lili there. She was sitting *on* my desk, her face red and swollen with tears. I tried to explain it to her in such a way that it would not make her feel too bad. But it was useless. Instead of listening to what I was saying, she just got more and more worked up. Finally, she lost it completely, grabbed the new teapot and threw it out of the — closed—window. "YOU ARE AN ASSHOLE!" she yelled. Then, she left and slammed the door.

I had spent the weekend fixing the window, and I had not seen her since.

"Mais oui. Nous sommes des salopards." Christian heaved a deep sigh and looked at me with a sad expression. *"Vraiment. C'est degueulasse!"*

If there was any doubt that we were the couple of *"salopards"* that Christian was making us out to be, there wasn't any doubt that we were both in deep shit. True—to some extent Christian had gotten over Fanny. It could not be denied. But even if the worst was over, still he wasn't all right. With his Gallic sense of the dramatic, he had just told me he had "fresh wounds on his soul." It would take a long time for these wounds to heal, he said. And now, it seemed that I too was to be counted among the casualties of love. Every five minutes, I would get the shakes. That's how nervous I was. Before returning home, the night Lili broke my window and teapot, Diana had warned me to look out for her husband. Somehow, she said, he had found out about us, and now he was hot on my trail. She did not know if he had my name and address. But it wouldn't surprise her if he did. He had his own "methods" of getting information.

Diana had wisely kept this information to herself until after we were done making love. Had she told me before, I would not have been able to get it up. We were in the same room as usual, and as I listened to what she said, I was looking at the painting of a fishing boat on the opposite wall. I was feeling naked and exposed. It was almost like I expected there'd be some thug waiting for me as I stepped out of the building. Ready to knock the teeth out of my mouth or put a bullet through my head. At home, Lili had been waiting for me, and since then, I had hardly closed an eye. The peace of mind I had enjoyed for so long was totally gone.

The game was up. That is how I felt. A month or so before, I had seen the guy with my own eyes. Diana and I were sitting behind a café window when two gangster types came walking down the sidewalk on the other side of the street. I immediately recognized one of them. It was the guy in the shades that had opened the door for me the night I saw Diana for the first time.

Diana took a hit off her freshly lit cigarette and removed it from her lips. There were traces of red lipstick on the filter. She blew the smoke up in the air and looked at me. "My husband's the one with the shades and the car keys dangling from his finger. Over there!" Saying this, she lifted a painted fingernail from the table and pointed. "I know," I said and was explaining how when all of a sudden I gave a start because the guy in the shades had just turned around and was looking up the sidewalk and across the street. It struck me that he feared something and was on the lookout for a taxi to whisk him and his companion away. "So

444

that's who I'm up against. He and I are rivals!" This inane thought was what ran through my head. A snub-nosed no nonsense type with a short and fat gun under his arm. Just the kind of guy I would love to meet in a dark alley.

Thinking back on all this, I watched Christian who was giving me an account of his first great love in the Ardeche of his childhood and youth. It seemed to him that the village girls of his past had more heart than the women he had come across since. In fact, everything seemed to have been better and more beautiful then: the landscape, the light, the warmth human and otherwise, the colors, the food. When in his fit of nostalgia Christian was done with the colors and the tastes, he started listing all the smells: the smells of lavender, of thyme, of sweet basil… And it was when he was done with the smells that I broke in and said. "Do you realize that I've never even been to France?"

Christian looked at me with an expression like he had just at that very moment thought of something:

"Ey," he said, "if you'd like to visit Paris now's the chance."

"How's that?"

"Listen!" Christian said unable to conceal his excitement. Was I ready for "this?"

And when I nodded, Christian went on to tell me his idea. He had an older brother whose name was Marc. Marc had a one-room studio apartment in the middle of a little island in the middle of Paris. Its name was Ile St. Louis. Standing in the open French balcony door on the first floor, you had at your feet the entire street. Rue St. Louis en L'ile. As he had said, the apartment was one single room, but down below, there was a creperie and so the air always smelled sweetly of pancakes and cinnamon. There was also a sleeping platform, making it possible to sleep under the ceiling. Tomorrow Marc was going to fly to New York City where he would stay the next three months. If I wanted to, he'd probably let me use his apartment while he was gone. For free. Marc wouldn't care. As it was, he had already told Wilfried, a childhood friend from Ardeche who had recently returned after six months of traveling in South America, that he could stay in his place. Wilfried was not going to be home very much. He was so deeply in debt that he had to work ten hours a day for at least three months in a company called Manpower in order to pay up. He wouldn't be in from six-thirty in the morning until ten in the evening. It would probably suit both Marc and Wilfried just fine if I were to live there too. Then, there would be someone in the mornings to look after things. Perhaps, who could tell, Diana would even come down to join me. And in any case… wouldn't it be nice to get away from it all for a little while? To get a little sleep! What did I say? Did I want him to go into my wagon and call Marc? Since he was packing for his trip, he would be home for sure…

Christian was staring at me with his eyebrows raised in expectation. And before I knew what I wanted, I heard my voice say: "Go and try!"

While Christian was inside calling his brother, I stayed put on my box. There was not a single thought in my noodle. I was only waiting. But when Christian did not show up, I started studying my toes. I wriggled first the big toe on my left foot and then the big toe on the right. The nails needed badly to be trimmed. It was not very charming with such long nails on one's toes. In Paris, I would probably be arrested and deported for having such long toenails. It would be taken as an insult on the promenades. Unlike Copenhagen, Paris was a civilized place. But the nail-clipper! Where was it? That is right. It was all because I had lost the damn nail-clipper. And because I had not taken the trouble to get another one. But maybe Christian would have one I could borrow. No way I could go to Paris with such nails. It just wasn't done.

I had taken a holy oath to trim the nails on my toes on that very day, when Christian came tumbling out of my wagon carrying the news: that I could live with Wilfried in the apartment on Rue St. Louis en L'ile while Marc was away in New York. So, what did I say?

To be honest I think that I just went on staring at my toe-nails. Or maybe I nodded and said something like: Thanks. I'll go as soon as I've trimmed my toe-nails. Not before.

Something like that.

In my letter to Melanie, I am asking her to thank the gnarly old Indian for "A Lakotah Life" which is the text and triple CD-rom I received a week ago in the mail. I am telling them they have no idea what pleasure it is for me to listen to it. It has encouraged me and confirmed a belief or conviction I was never fully conscious of before. I am telling Coyote that when he speaks of Tatanka, the buffalo bull elected by the herd to give up its life and heart, his voice looms so huge it spans the entire length and breadth of the black night bearing down on us. Accompanied by a peal of thunder blasting through the skies, "Tatanka's great heart" is invoked as life takes its last stand. I tell him that I can't find the right words in my native tongue. The experience is so new to me that I hardly know what it is I am feeling and in need of expressing. I also tell him that it's something so far removed from the downloaded on-line life of a Dane at the end of this first decade of the second millennium after Christ as to be almost unintelligible. The unity and wholesomeness of it. The rootedness in worship, gratitude and *being*. The innocence, mystery and sense of wonder. The mere absence of money gives it a mythical status. It's a tale torn out of the very womb of our race. His name, I tell Coyote, ought from now on to be Jack the Ripper, since he has ripped into *my* chest as Grandfather's "great knife" cut into Tatanka's to get at his heart. The story of the last buffalo hunt and the clash of civilizations. The seed of destruction, of the devastation to come. With this document Coyote has given us a modern myth that could have an impact on the prospect of survival for our species.

From the moment I received the package, I have been listening to the CD's every chance I had. Last night I listened to CD number two. And tonight when Amiel is asleep, I will listen to number three. I can't help seeing some mystical connection between what I am living right now, what an Indian sick with cancer is presently going through on Pine Ridge Reservation and finally what seems to me may turn out to be the last throes of the Freetown of Christiania. It goes for both reservations that the issue is one of custom, private ownership and "user's" right to the earth. Tonight, when Coyote's voice dies out and silence settles in the corners of the living room, I will see before my inner eye the little group of men and boys mount their horses and ride out of the reservation. With demeanors of grim determination and not a word spoken between them! Imperturbable faces. The eighty-something-year old grandfather and shaman, his contemporary friend and storyteller Washtay with whom he defeated General Custer as a young warrior, the grand child Coyote with his eight summers and the boy's friends of the same age Grey Hawk and Little Deer. All mounted on horses, all silent, all aware of what is at stake, and all partaking of "Shkahn" or *movement* being the innermost element of their existence. Reading the story, which is a photocopy of a manuscript Coyote wrote back in Prague, I am as absorbed as when as a boy I read

448

the novels by James Fennimore Cooper. The way he ejects the word "Shkahn" like it was a cartridge from a gun or better, an arrow from the bowstring of his soul, aimed at the heart of Custer. To be. To do. To see. To belong and be a part of movement. The fearless wisdom of life that has been forgotten in our materialistic culture and the manual for its practice and expression. The Circle with its center everywhere and circumference nowhere, forever expanding until it is reborn in another womb. Birth, life and death. Man's existence as a growing circle that from its first seed throws itself at its limitations in all directions at once. Expansion, heartbeat upon heartbeat in the endless mandala that is the karmic wheel transforming coincidence into destiny.

It somehow reminds me of the night when I was driving my taxi and the radio played George Harrison's "My Sweet Lord". (Hi Mel! Don't mind Coyote! I can hear his derisive laughter all the way over here…) I'm sure you know the song in which Harrison repeats the mantra "Hare Krishna. Hare Krishna. Krishna Krishna" etc. (Ask El Coyote to put in the place of these words the Lakotah cry: Ou-Ah-He-Yia-Ya!) The way the song ties beginning and end together, and I seemed to grasp for the first time how all is interconnected in the Circle. How "it" (Shkahn) moves endlessly in the minutest particle without ever getting anywhere. That night I seemed to grasp how power—or the energy by which we are sustained—is identical with the Universe and accessible to any one living object. The ending contained within the beginning and the beginning still active at the end. Just like in any good song.

In one place, Coyote writes:

"The Indian was not speaking of commerce (though there was a little of that) he was talking about 'Life.' The white man did not understand life. He did not understand The Circle… Was he not 'Steward of The Earth'? Of course, he was. His God had told him

so – he stood outside of The Circle. The white man was different from…the 'Other.' The white man allied with whom he chose. So he thought. For the Indian people of the Plains, however, the white man's view was seriously flawed. As a matter of fact, it was downright foolish… dangerous even. Were such a Path to be followed it would disrupt The Circle and harm The Land. All were part of The Whole, including the white man—regardless of what he believed. And The Whole formed a Circle: Within The Circle all were equal, all shared, all things were allied, including The Land. To a people who had risen from The Earth, who treasured The Grasses, who lived 'in the wind'—all was interconnected: The Animal, the Indian, The Tree, The Flowing Waters, The Things that crawled, that climbed, that swam, that flew, that jumped. And, yes, the white man too was a part. Even The Stone. All had their share of 'Manitou' or 'Life-force,' and were by definition 'allied'… due to the very fact of their existence. The name 'Lakotah' meant ally… and it was this 'allegiance' to-and-among-all-things, this Manitou that kept The Circle unbroken, that allowed Life to flow and enabled the Great Mother Planet to breathe…"

I tell Melanie how I picture her reading my letter aloud to Coyote and Robert Dean. I want you, Saël, to know that the seed you planted in this runaway pale-face is alive and growing daily. Which goes to show that you were right when you told me of the perfect timeliness of all things. I had been talking about something I wanted to do and had used the expression "before it's too late," when you showed me your one remaining—long—tooth in a grin and said: "There you go thinking like a white man again. Everything has its time. You do what you must and do not do what you cannot. Nothing is ever too late!" Then, a year later when I was going to father a child you wrote me in a letter: "You'll reap what you sow. Now that you've sown your seed, a child will be born who will transform you into an asshole."

At first, I did not understand what you meant. In fact,

the remark seemed so utterly ridiculous to me I thought perhaps by some mistake you had fished the word 'asshole' out of your vocabulary instead of the word 'Papa.' But no, you had used the word 'asshole' because that was what, in your opinion, I would become. You said that you had always been way too egotistic to think of fathering a child. It was not for nothing you had lived among white men for so long. Some of their selfish lifelessness had rubbed off on you. Yes, lifelessness! The mass of modern pale-faces was born to a joyless test tube-like existence *in* the workplace but *outside* The Circle. Having lost even the last vestiges of feeling for time and freedom, and exaggerating the importance of the so-called careers, we had convinced ourselves that it's all right leaving our children in the care of au-pairs or professional pedagogues working in institutions. Do you remember that conversation Coyote? And Mel, I'm sure you still recall the Swede by the name of Strindberg that I used to rave about, how he wrote in one of his plays that "men are to be pitied." The reason he wrote that, I think, is because he was thinking of us pale-faces—how we soon after our birth are made conscious of having to die, and how from then on we have to live without the faintest idea why. From his own experience, Strindberg knew that in order to live a man must know how to die. And there is no knowing how to die without knowing the reason we are alive. Even if we don't want it to, The Circle will be unbroken.

Don't laugh Coyote! Have some respect! Being a pale-face and a Viking, Strindberg recorded in his own blood the raids he made to get back into The Circle. It was with his help I managed to put your Prophesy to shame—that having a son would turn me into an asshole. I have not let my son down, and he has not taken me hostage. I am not living the empty, egotistical test tube-existence devoid of the spirit that you find so despicable. And as for Amiel, I endeavor to make a fearless womb-raider out of him. I am trying to wake his instincts by telling him about you and Tatanka and how you would have taught him to cry Ou-Ah-He-Yia-Ya and be free. Even if the price of living in The Circle is to stand outside of organized society with no insurance other than himself. I am telling him where the cry "catch me if you can" comes from and about the old Lakotah Indian who wanted to leave him a million dollars in his will—in order that, upon turning eighteen, he would be able to give his Papa the finger. Yes, and so he would get a better start than you who came close to being crushed before you even got started, you who later squandered fortunes only to go on living merrily from hand to mouth.

It is true then, that I planted my seed. But it's not true that I failed the boy that grew from it. Not yet anyway. Even now as harvest time is drawing close, I spread my seeds as if my life depended on it. I throw them into the wind singing in the grasses on the Plains about Shunk Coyote Saël Manitu, Washtay, grandfather, Grey Hawk and Little Deer. Crazy Horse is there too somewhere and Custer, Little Big Horn and…The Circle on and off forming hurricanes that bring death and destruction in their wake. From now on, son is to learn about "Shkahn," the being that IS and is movement. And…Coyote! You grumpy old redskin. Listen to what I say! Together let's put our ears to the ground and listen for the distant thunder of Tatanka stampeding once more in the tens of thousands across the Great Plains. Do you hear? Don't think that son made your friend in faraway Denmark the "gigantic asshole" you imagined in your letter. If anything I have remained the asshole I always was before God. And if that is how I am created, well hell, then that is how I am going to live. Do you hear me Coyote? This is from me to you. To tell you that I am here—with the wind at my back and in my lungs. I breathe in the wind, and I breathe it out. Again, I am the young man of forty-five that you met and led into The Circle. The man you initiated among the great old trees in The Stromovka Park in Prague. He is there still holding and protecting the fiery baton. We are running side by side. I swear that you will live on in me until the cry of freedom Ou-Ah-He-Yia-Ya no longer rings in the wind and my lungs collapse. Where I am, you will be there too. And when I am no longer, we will both be in son who maybe will, maybe will not settle in Freetown Christiania in a timid, anaemic and intraveniously fed land of palefaces called Denmark.

Come to think of it. Do you remember the time in your little apartment up by The Strahov Stadion when you told me the story from The Deerpark north of Copenhagen—how you and a blonde-haired editor with a womens' magazine had bought a gramme of Afghan hash in Pusher Street and smoked it among a herd of deer? The animals had surrounded the two of you on all sides and even formed a circle... At one point the editor had tried to mount you and you'd "thrown" her... Do you remember? The two of you had then struggled, until she began to cry and asked you 'why?' Expecting that what you were going to say was going to close the subject, you'd looked her in the eyes and told her you were a warrior. Was that the reason, she wanted to know, that you had turned cold? You had tried to explain but it was no use. She said that she felt "humiliated". You laughed and said that you didn't give a fuck.

It was a complete and utter fiasco. Or farce maybe? You tried to leave, but she held you back. She wanted to make it good again. She still wanted you, she said. But there was no way you wanted her anymore. She could "keep it", you told her. Keep what? The *thing* she had between her legs. You didn't want it anymore. It wasn't worth anything. BUT WHY, she wailed. Just because she wanted to be on top!

What was wrong with that? What *was* wrong with that! You laughed your "mean" laugh! Would she perhaps have your babies? No, she said. What had that got to do with it?

Disgusted like hell at this stage, you told her to go back to her job with the magazine and take the "lethal delusions" about life and love that she suffered from with her. She had a *thing* between her legs and deeper within she even had a womb—from nature's hand she was meant to give life. But unfortunately the former was no longer the gateway to the latter, which had so shrunk that at this stage it was no longer "The Womb of Wombs". Give life and nurture it. Oh, no! Not her! *She* had more important things to do than to obey the eternal commandment. *She* was on a salary. *She* was a professional. *She* used pornography!

The woman had looked at you like you were out of your mind. Never had she heard anything like it in her life. Why did you think she had gone to the best schools, taken difficult exams and gotten an education, if all she was going to do was have his baby? Yes, she was a professional. Yes, she knew how to land a good job, argue a point in meetings, work hard and efficiently, make money and be independent. And, no, she didn't use pornography! But she had friends who did. They said pornography was fun. It was their business. What was wrong with that?

You just looked at her with your imperturbable stoneface and said: "I told you. I'm a warrior. Don't ever forget that!"

And then you turned around and walked away. You never saw her again...

But here's Amiel leaning against me at the table. He wants his Papa to do something with him. So I have got to go. What I had in mind to write you was really something else. Well, to hell with it! Tonight or tomorrow, I will write the missing part. And if not, it will be the day after tomorrow. Such are the facts of life. And here I go again. I keep thinking of Tatanka reborn and thundering across The Great Plains in herds of a hundred thousand individuals. Two thousand years from now. The sun is setting and I am looking forward to the next letter stamped Pine Ridge. No matter what we will not put on mourning bands. No matter what we will keep our heads cold, our hearts warm and our backs upright. Is that a deal? Don't hide anything from me. Bawl me out when I blunder. Just lay it on me hard. I am ready.

I herewith enclose the usual ADIOS AMIGOS. And listen Melanie... Who knows? Maybe time has a speedy reunion in store for us? How does it look now? Do you think you'll make it over here?

There kept being no letter from Melanie. Seven weeks I waited until finally day before yesterday it arrived. It is now early September, and I had known it all along. The reason for her silence I mean. The 30ᵗʰ of August Shunk Manitou alias Coyote alias Säel set out for the eternal hunting grounds. And on top of it, Melanie announces her arrival in Copenhagen on Tuesday the 22ⁿᵈ of September. Four days before Christiania's birthday, which we are going to celebrate together. Later, we will go bury an amulet made of Tatanka's bone. "Some place where we know Saël was when alive—like that place '*Eremitagesletten*' In the Deer Park where it sort of looks like it does on The Great Plains."

It has all been arranged, the schedule is set...

I put Melanie's letter down, and for the longest time, I just sat without registering anything. Amiel came up to ask if anything was the matter. No, nothing was. I did not want to tell him that I needed to be alone.

Today is the first day in a while when I have a few hours to myself.

The first time I met Coyote was at the Futurum Club in Prague. That was before Amiel was born and before a whole lot of things. I was sitting at a table up front near the stage when the mother of the not-yet-conceived boy leaned towards me and whispered in my ear: "Look up there…by the proscenium! I'll be damned if that isn't an Indian!"

I followed the direction of her eyes and had to agree. Even if I had never before in my life seen a North American Indian except in motion pictures, there could be no doubt. The man in question looked like something right out of the Indian movies I used to see on Sundays at four o'clock in the local movie theater. In a flashback I saw him race across the screen on horseback, whooping and shaking his rifle above his head or with painted face and tomahawk in hand come up to the white man tied to the totempole. The same square chin and leathery skin! The long black hair and the equally black hat! The cigarette dangling from his lips! The warlike and furrowed expression of the outlaw! The kind of self-reliance that comes from a life outside of organized society!

The last time I saw Coyote was also in Prague. Like so many times before I visited him in his little apartment on the Nad Zaverkou Street near Strahov. Later, we walked together to the end station Malovanka where Coyote got in the tram that waited there and was just about to take off. Having some other business in the area, I stayed behind. It was only a matter of seconds before the tram would start. I shifted my feet uneasily, whereas Coyote standing by the door in the middle of the second car seemed as calm and composed as ever. His short figure did not budge an inch. He was not wearing a hat, and there was no cig hanging from his lips. There was nothing except the laughing eyes, the worn shoes and the no longer white shirt with the thin yellowish stripes on it. I imagined that the other shirt in his possession was crammed into the little suitcase made of imitation leather on the floor between his feet. For no reason, I also imagined that the answer to the riddle was contained in that suitcase. When the tram doors slammed shut, I knew what I had not allowed myself to know before: that this was the last glimpse of Säel I would ever have. There would never be another. Of course, he had known it all along. Only he did not show it, nor did he talk about it. He just looked reassuringly at me with those dark and smiling eyes. Like our ways would never part. Now, he opened his mouth, and once again, I saw that the last long and yellow tooth was gone from his upper gum. "That's it," I thought, "the sign or bad omen from my dream!" The car jerked and the tram started down the track. I raised my hand and looked. There he went, and it...it was gone. But what was that? I could not see him anymore, and yet I knew he was still there. Something had been left behind. I could *feel* it. My hand was raised and waving it a couple of times in the emptiness I let it drop. But...there, there he was with me again. Standing at the end of the car, he was looking at me. And it's that last long look as the tram drove away that still connects us. To this day, it remains with me when I am unsure, encourages me when I am in doubt and comforts me when I feel low. I keep it in my shrine. To my mind, it is always at hand.

The first time and the last and the two years in between. In the two days since I received word of his death, I have replayed the scenes over and over again. Not to mention the CD-rom. As I sit at this round metal table in The Moon-fisher Café in Christiania, as I converse with the emptiness of this space the departed one is still part of me no different from when he was around. I am hearing his voice so alive at this moment that even if I register the four male and two female cops who are right now entering through the narrow doorway, I cannot care less. "Let them search me as much as they want!" I think. "If they search my heart, some gadget will start to beep somewhere in their uniforms, and they'll find Saël all over the place and take me into custody for possession of explosives and disrupting the social order."

I smile at the thought. Why 'explosives'? Coyote was an outlaw, but he was not a criminal. He did not throw bombs. And he was the most honest man I ever met. Also, he was what you might call sublimely adapted. But since his adaptation was to life and not to society, it was conspicuous. Instead of making him a part, it set him *a*part. So much so in fact his mere presence was enough to make the run-of-the-mill money making person uneasy. As long as he was not around, they were able to sort of stick it out and make their money and all the rest. But the moment he appeared among them, they felt the rot that was in their marrow and did not know what to do. God almighty how they hated him for making them feel like that. It was not for what he did but for what he was.

I get up from my chair and walk towards the door. I pass through the narrow opening and realize it is suspect to leave just as the cops begin frisking people inside. But nothing happens. A moment later, I have turned the corner and am headed towards the Grocery.

My getaway succeeded. That was the easy part. The hard part is what I am going to tell Melanie in the letter I must write her. Do I tell her about the police in the Moonfisher Café, and how I always react with something like bad conscience when I encounter the law in person? It's insane really. As if I have not lived my life the only way I could. Yes, and as if a cop can see the transgressions in my eyes!

With the years, this reaction on my part has grown weaker. But it has not gone away. In a year or two maybe. Or do I comment on the vivid account she gave me of the funeral ceremony? Do I repeat the satisfaction I felt that Coyote laughed the Grim Reaper in his face? Do I tell her how much the departed one meant to me? Do I confide in her how I love the thought of her and Robert Dean cruising to Las Cruces in the white Lincoln Continental? Is it all right if I become sentimental and tell her about the tears I cried when she told me he had "stepped into The Circle"? Or do I simply say how much I would have loved to be with them in the white hearse? Do I say this knowing that none of it gives expression to what fills me at this moment? Cursed the man who feels the need to say something very exact and who cannot for his life think what it is.

That is on the one hand! On the other, I don't know how to react to the news of Melanie's arrival in Copenhagen. What is it going to be like to see each other again after so many years? So many *words*... Do I just say it like it is? that I dread it just as much as I look forward to it. Or do I perhaps become poetic and tell her how the expectation and the dread perform a dance inside of me?

Of course, the easy way out is to listen to Melanie and simply do as she says: Take her by the hand and lead her through the streets of Copenhagen and Christiania. After *twenty years* absence! Why, I could ask her if she still remembers the brown bear we once visited on our walk through Christiania? When Amiel and I went to see if the bear was still there, we found that someone had added a part to their house on the exact spot where the bear used to be. While I was watching Amiel play with some rabbits in a cage on the other side of the dirt road, a man came out of the house. Seeing me, he came up and said it was okay that my son played with the rabbits as long as he kept the chicken wire door shut. I told him not to worry. I would keep an eye on him. And then I asked him about the bear. The guy looked at me sort of surprised. I could tell that he was pleased. Yes, of course, he knew what had happened, he said. It had been all right for some years. In fact, right until the story had come to a bad end. Once when its owner entered the cage and started to pat cute little teddy bear on its cute little teddy bear-head, the beast tore the arm off of him. And it would have torn him apart completely if his wife had not come out of the house in time to see what was going on. The wife who was also a terrible drunk reacted soberly however. Grabbing a shovel, she entered the cage and whacked the bear a big one over the head. The bear let go of its prey long enough for the wife to drag the drunk and bleeding husband out and slam the gate.

Later, the wife asked a biker friend who had a rifle to come and shoot the animal. For his favor, the biker got the skin and put it on his floor before the open fire place in the Lion House. Or that was what some people said. Others claimed that the couple had kept the incident a secret and sold the bear to the zoo in Hamburg. In the Hanseatic city, it had lived on as a celebrity right until it died of cirrhosis of the liver. As far as he was concerned, the guy told me, he thought that story a crock of shit. It was not Hamburg zoo that bought it, he said, but Humbug zoo. I nodded and said that I, too, found the story about the zoo a bit farfetched. But was it really. The world had obviously gone over the deep end. Today, there were drunken dimwits on just about every glossy cover. So why not a bear?

"Yeah, why not a bear?" the guy said.

And so on and so forth! "I come from Deeenmark!" is what the naked woman yelled when on her back in the passenger seat of the patrol car she tried to kick a hole in its roof. What am I to include and what am I to exclude? It is not only Copenhagen and Denmark that is changed since I left. I myself am not the same any more. The years that have gone by are the same that buried European communism in the oblivion that is history. When totalitarian materialism in the East broke down, materialism in the West became totalitarian. Am I to recount the change that has taken place in the land of my birth even if I am only able to do this with the aid of my present (and changed) outlook on the world and everything in it? Would it be fair to just let go the feelings and sentiments of the moment? If not I prefer to keep my mouth shut and declare Saël my love instead. In him I finally met...A MAN. What more is there to say...or do? Okay, arriving at Copenhagen airport was a shock. The silent aquarium-like atmosphere that engulfed me from all sides! The newspaper on the floor with the diagnosis visible for all:

"A study shows that we are not feeling well at all, that we suffer from sleep problems, have more headaches and take more medicine than we did twenty years ago."

The twenty years that have lapsed since I left the country...

I could also entertain Melanie with my mother's broken leg, the hospital and so on. I could explain to her how I have to take a piss and wander through the streets of Copenhagen vainly searching a public urinal; how during weekends the center of the city is transformed into a huge dump for broken glass and used condoms. But... no! I can't seem to get myself up for it. In twenty years, Deeeenmark has lost whatever feeling for human value it had before and replaced it with migraine. Today, it is *the entire country* that is throwing up. Its face is contorted, a gurgling sound like from a sewer emanates from its stinking mouth and its features are beyond recognition. It can't get no satisfaction, but it tries, and it tries, and it tries.

This, then, is as far as I have gotten. This is where I am at the moment. The instant I reached Oluf's house, he appeared from the other side in the company of his... father. Greeting me with a smile, he introduced us. Lars was the father's name. We shook hands. Like me, Lars was in his fifties. He looked grey and rather worn out.

"So you've lived out here?"

I confirmed it whereupon Lars went on: "So maybe it's not so bad after all?"

I shook my head and looked at Oluf, who was now smiling from ear to ear.

But the father had to get going, and Oluf did not have time because he was already late for an important area meeting. The two of us were standing next to one another watching Lars disappear down the path. He walked quickly with short little steps like he was afraid of falling. Oluf ran a hand through his hair, shook his head and said: "He's never been here before. And he didn't call first. I can't believe he's come. He'd sworn never to set foot in Christiania."

And still without looking at me: "He came to tell me that he was sorry for what has happened. He's very ill and wants to come back again... soon!"

Oluf was not smiling any more. He turned to me, gave me his hand and added: "You just do the same. Why don't you come out when your friend from America gets here? You can borrow my house. It won't hurt me to sleep a couple of nights with my sweetheart in town. I'd be happy to. So... see you!"

Oluf has gone the way of his father. I am sitting on his veranda watching a little bird I don't know the name of flit between the rushes. So silent and so discreet a being in the world! Every few minutes a panting jogger passes on the path that runs by the house. A neighbor is fixing a flat tire on his bike, and the sun is no longer as high in the sky as it was. I have found a piece of paper in my shirt pocket and am writing on it the only words I will send to Melanie:

"Dear Melanie. I am looking forward to seeing you in the airport on the twenty-second of September. On the twenty-sixth, we will celebrate the Freetown. Later, we will go to The Deer Park and bury Tatanka among the deer. Right where Saël once was!

At this moment, yours truly is sitting in front of a small house in between some rushes. On the path, joggers pant by with white cords coming out of their ears and in the rushes a little bird is flittering about. I will stay where I am till you come. Together with Amiel, of course! You will see and time will tell. As always, a new day will dawn. The day today. I have arrived to it and settled for good. When the sun sinks in the West, I rise in the East. Yesterday is forgotten, and tomorrow never comes. And yet only the coming is holy. Love Les."

THE END

Per Šmidl lived for two years in Wagon 537 at Christiania. Then he moved to Paris, then California and when he got back to Denmark he wrote the bestseller *Chop Suey*.

Many years as a political dissident in Prague followed after the publication in Denmark of his book *Victim of Welfare* in 1995. The book challenged the role and freedom of the individual in the welfare state.

Some of the previous publications by Per Šmidl includes the novel *Mathias Kraft*, 1999, and the essay "Ytringsfrihed", which means "Freedom of Speech", 2006.

Proof

20514678R00271